BY DELILAH S. DAWSON

The Violence

HIT

Guillotine

Hit

Bloom

Strike

THE TALES OF PELL

BLUD

(with Kevin Hearne)

Wicked as They Come

Kill the Farm Boy

Wicked as She Wants

No Country for Old Gnomes

Wicked After Midnight

The Princess Beard

Wicked Ever After

STAR WARS

Servants of the Storm

The Perfect Weapon (e-novella)

Phasma

Ladycastle

Galaxy's Edge: Black Spire

Sparrowhawk

The Skywalker Saga

Star Pig

Inquisitor: Rise of the Red Blade

FOR YOUNGER READERS

Minecraft: Mob Squad

THE SHADOW

Minecraft: Mob Squad: Never Say
Nether

(As Lila Bowen)

Wake of Vultures

Minecraft: Mob Squad: Don't Fear
the Creeper

Conspiracy of Ravens

Malice of Crows

Mine

Treason of Hawks

Camp Scare

Midnight at the Houdini

Disney Mirrorverse: Pure of Heart

IT WILL ONLY HURT
FOR A MOMENT

IT WILL ONLY HURT FOR A MOMENT

DELILAH S. DAWSON

NEW YORK

Copyright © 2024 by D. S. Dawson

All rights reserved.

Published in the United States by Del Rey, an imprint of Random House, a division of Penguin Random House LLC, New York.

DEL REY and the CIRCLE colophon are registered trademarks of Penguin Random House LLC.

LIBRARY OF CONGRESS CATALOGING-IN-PUBLICATION DATA
Names: Dawson, Delilah S., author.
Title: It will only hurt for a moment / Delilah S. Dawson.
Description: First edition. | New York: Del Rey, 2024.
Identifiers: LCCN 2024029868 (print) | LCCN 2024029869 (ebook) |
ISBN 9780593156650 (Hardback) | ISBN 9780593156667 (Ebook)
Subjects: LCGFT: Thrillers (Fiction) | Novels.
Classification: LCC PS3604.A97858 I8 2024 (print) | LCC PS3604.A97858 (ebook) |
DDC 813/.6—dc23/eng/20240705
LC record available at https://lccn.loc.gov/2024029868
LC ebook record available at https://lccn.loc.gov/2024029869

Printed in the United States of America on acid-free paper

randomhousebooks.com

2 4 6 8 9 7 5 3 1

First Edition

Book design by Elizabeth A. D. Eno

When I was in high school, I worked at a nonprofit arts center. One night, a women's watercolor class was enjoying the summer breeze through an open door, and a man appeared on the porch and exposed himself. The women, most of whom were over sixty, paused, stared at him, and laughed and laughed and laughed.

The man turned red and ran off.

I think of those women often.

IT WILL ONLY HURT
FOR A MOMENT

1

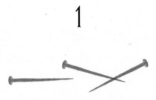

The leaves have not yet begun to turn, but the mountains hold their breath. Sarah Carpenter has been driving for three days, from Denver to north Georgia, past craggy peaks and flat cornfields, chaotic cities and verdant forests, and she still can't relax, can't stop checking her rearview mirror to see if she's being followed. The map says she's only half an hour away from her destination, and if her informational packet was accurate, she'll lose all signal soon and have to navigate solely based on the directions she scribbled off the website. Slightly terrifying, but also the point. When you're running away from someone, it's best to be utterly inaccessible.

Her phone rings from its stand on the dashboard of her crossover, startling her. It's an unknown number, an area code she doesn't recognize. She normally wouldn't answer it, but right now, she's not leaving anything to chance. If someone besides Kyle is trying to find her, she needs to know why. When she mashes the green button, she is further startled to realize that she's now on speakerphone—because yes, of course, her phone is hooked up to her car's audio system.

"Hello?" she says, over-loud and annoyed.

"Sarah?"

The voice blaring through her car's speakers is like nails on a chalkboard, and Sarah has to jerk the wheel to stay on the winding mountain highway. Gravel grinds under her tires in perfect tune with her grinding teeth.

"Yes, Carol? Is something wrong?"

"You haven't called. You should call more. Kids are supposed to take care of their mothers. Tit for tat."

If Sarah wasn't driving along a treacherous road overlooking a deep fall into a sweeping valley, she would close her eyes and pinch the bridge of her nose, where a small but persistent, familiar pang has begun to throb.

She hasn't called her mother in five years, and her mother hasn't called her. When she moved out west, it felt good, leaving Carol behind in Savannah. Sarah knows that addiction is a sickness, not a choice, but she still refuses to forgive her mother for choosing alcohol. Given the option to go to rehab and remain in her only living relative's life, Mom dove deeper into the bottle. And she doesn't even drink good wine.

Judging by the fact that she's calling and her voice is slurring, Carol has not stopped drinking—or gotten treatment for whatever sickness is nibbling at the edges of her once-sharp mind.

"Is there a problem?" Sarah asks again. "This isn't your phone number."

"Mine got turned off. Jean let me borrow hers. I always remember your number. Where are you?"

Sarah looks at the cracked blacktop ahead, winding under the summer-gold trees. She doesn't want her mother to know where she is. There's a chance she might tell Kyle, and then . . .

"What do you need, Mom?"

"I wanted to know what I should bring for Thanksgiving. Jean will drive me over to your place, but I can pick up a pie at the store, first. You always liked sweet potato."

Sarah realizes she's not breathing, top teeth sunk into her lower lip. She wants to scream at her mother, remind her what a failure she is, how horribly her mother's drunken outburst and arrest at a River Street bar messed up both of their lives, how they don't speak. She wants to tell her that she moved across the country to Denver five years ago and after hitting the BLOCK button, it was a revelation, never having to see her mom's phone number flash up on her phone a single time. She wants to tell her about Kyle.

But none of it matters. Her mother wouldn't remember it. If she was able to understand, she'd just say that the breakup was Sarah's fault for not being a more supportive girlfriend. That's another deep wound—when Dad was alive, Mom always treated him as her top priority. First Dad, then Chardonnay. Then work, volunteering at the animal shelter, church, that phone game with all the little diamonds, watching golf on TV. Sarah is always last.

"We're not doing Thanksgiving together," Sarah says. "You do it at the assisted living center."

"Their turkey is always dry," Carol complains. "I prefer a ham." There's a pause where the sound of an old woman sipping wine from a coffee mug fills Sarah's car like thunder. "Where are you?"

Nowhere. Sarah is nowhere. She's on her way to somewhere, on her way to the only thing that's felt like hope in years, but she's not going to tell her mom that. The thing about a broken brain is that all sorts of things slip through the cracks. Maybe Carol remembers Kyle's number, from when they'd just started dating. Maybe she remembers how to get on Facebook. Maybe she accidentally tells someone where Sarah is going.

It's none of her business. When she chose the bottle, she chose a life apart.

"Driving," Sarah says, as she's not a good liar.

"You should come get me," Carol whines. "I want to look at cars."

"You can't drive, Mom. They took your license. Don't you remember going to jail after you assaulted an officer?"

Carol's voice is tentative and cagey. "What? Jail? Me? Of course not. I just can't find my wallet right now. This place you put me in is full of thieves."

It's the nicest place in the area, which her mother can afford thanks to a fat inheritance from her teetotaling parents. The license is in Sarah's bag, hidden in the pages of her planner. The old woman has no excuse to be on the road. Sarah should've hidden her keys long ago, before she put Lucy Zimmerman in a coma and slapped an officer.

"Bye, Mom," Sarah says, deflated and tired.

"No! No! You listen here. I'm your mother. You— You leave me in this dump, you never call, you won't give me grandbabies. Won't even invite me over for Thanksgiving. I raised you! Gave you a good life! I did the best I could. And this is the thanks I get?"

The speech would be a lot more dramatic if Carol hadn't yet again paused to take a slurping sip.

But Sarah is done. She's made a clean break from her old life, and she might as well sever the last tendon, even if her drunk mother will forget they ever spoke.

"Mom, you were a shitty mother. You've always been a drunk. You promised you would quit, and you never did. You knocked your best friend off a barstool and broke her skull because she tried to take your keys. This is the first time we've spoken in three years, but you don't remember because in addition to the drinking, you're developing dementia. You're toxic, and we're done."

There's a gasp, and then her mother starts sobbing. Sarah blinks back her own tears, waiting breathlessly to see what her mother has to say to the truth she can only express because she's three hundred miles away and already on the run.

"That's crazy," Carol finally says. "You're crazy. None of that is true at all. You just don't want me at Thanksgiving."

"I'm hanging up now." Sarah reaches for the phone.

She's done being called crazy.

"Honey, wait. I need to tell you something."

Sarah pauses, her fingertip hovering over the red button as she struggles to stay in the lane. The line is quiet, nothing but an old woman's labored breathing. There's a rough dirt turnoff up ahead, the kind blocked off with a rusted gate that probably leads to someone's hunting land, so she pulls off the road and parks. She can't focus on staying between the lines when she's this upset. Whatever her mother says next, it'll be over soon, and Sarah can go back to pretending that Carol doesn't exist, just like she's learning to pretend that Kyle doesn't exist.

There's a terrible weight to this kind of grief, to letting go of someone who's still alive but not who they used to be, maybe not ever who you thought they were. It comes back like migrating birds, stupidly descending again and again to feed on skeletal bushes already stripped of berries. It leaves Sarah so, so tired, so emotionally barren, talking to her mother.

Maybe she'll push the button anyway.

It's not like her mother will remember.

She never does.

"What is it, Mom?"

"Don't go," her mother says in a quiet voice. "It's not safe out there. You're too little to be out on your own. They said there was a kidnapper in a red hatchback. You run right home if you see a red car. He's going to get you."

Sarah's hand falls to the shifter. Her mother's mind has wandered back to when she was nine and the whole neighborhood was in an uproar over some guy who flashed Courtney McClure on the way home from the bus stop.

"I'm safe, Mom," she says grudgingly, angry at herself for believing that her mother might actually have something new or useful to say, some groundbreaking insight on her own faults or an apology for pain caused.

"You're never safe, Sarah. There is no place safe. Not for little girls. They can always find you. They can find a way inside. A door won't save you, not if they want to get you. What you're doing . . . it's a bad idea."

A semi thunders past, shaking Sarah's car. She shivers as she watches the leaves rain down where the truck's roof scraped a low-hanging branch. The mountain is so peaceful and beautiful, the day so clear and blue with all the promise of summer mellowing into fall. The place she's going—it's safe. It's good. It's exactly what she needs. When she applied for a studio at the Tranquil Falls Artists' Retreat, she knew she had practically no chance of being chosen, considering she hadn't touched clay in five years and was relying on images from the BA she never finished. But they accepted her, and she counted down the days to her escape, and she made a clean break, and now here she is, on the brink of rediscovering her art and herself, and of course her mother has to call and say cryptic, ugly things that would throw her from her state of perfect contentment into . . . well, disarray and doubt.

That's what Carol does best.

It's like she has an uncanny way of sensing fragile moments.

And then she claims that she's the victim, because if you're the victim, you never have to change.

Sarah sometimes wonders when she stopped loving her mother.

She also wonders when her mother became impossible to love.

"I'll be fine, Mom. I always am."

"I don't think so," Carol says, her voice again wandering and frail. "You always were so headstrong. But then you made bad decisions and came crying to me, all hysterical. Always breaking a bone or busting a lip. Crazy. Crazy, foolish thing, running in the wrong direction. Causing problems. I wash my hands of it." With a peevish sigh, her mother hangs up.

"Fuck you, too," Sarah says.

Plucking her phone from its holder, she pulls up the number her mother just called her from and blocks it. She stares into the rearview mirror, checking that no cars are coming, before pulling back onto the road.

Her mother is a mess. A mean drunk. A loser.

And yet her words still hurt, don't they?

Inside every so-called adult is a scared little kid who just wants to be told they're wonderful by imperfect people they're doomed to despise.

It doesn't matter. Soon, her mother won't be able to reach her no matter whose phone she borrows. Where she's going, all the people she's avoiding will be unable to find her.

That's the whole point.

Her mother made her life hell, and then Kyle made her life hell, and then she wasn't sure what was left.

At Tranquil Falls, she's going to find out.

2

Sarah's directions lead her to a dirt road with a beautiful sign that suggests one of the visiting artists was a truly gifted woodcarver. The road rumbles through the forest under trees that kiss overhead, the first orange-dotted leaves drifting to the earth in lazy parabolas. The car windows are all the way down, the familiar scent of oak must and the first breath of fall filtering in with the crisp breeze. There's a curve and a hill, and then a valley opens up with undulating fields of dying wildflowers in a patchwork of green. When she sees what waits ahead, Sarah's eyes tear up.

It's just so beautiful.

Tranquil Falls was once a posh resort where the richest people in America came to soak in the natural beauty, bathe in the mist of the waterfall, and luxuriate in the sumptuous spa. Rockefellers, Du Ponts, Vanderbilts, and Astors stayed here and raved about it. A grand avenue leads down into the valley and up to an impressive building with two wings built into the side of the mountain. Even in a state of decay, it looks like an old hotel out of a Wes Anderson movie. Glorious goldlimned trees line the road in pairs, and Sarah thinks that this is the closest she'll ever get to feeling like she's in *The Great Gatsby*—the first part, though. Not the back half, where everything falls apart.

Although she knows she's supposed to check in at the community house by the parking lot, she continues driving, past the studios and cabins hidden in the forest, right up to the circular courtyard in front of the stately old resort. A fountain molders in the center, the cherubs missing most of their limbs and the once-creamy stone coated in dark-green streaks. This close, right where visitors would've stopped their coaches to enter, she can see evidence that the hotel is no longer the dignified queen she once was. Beyond the tall fence topped with razor wire, pieces of the façade are cracked and crumbling, and those tall front doors are lashed together with a thick, rusty chain.

All of the many, many windows are now boarded up, but the plywood is painted with ornate curtains and beautiful women in costumes right out of Jane Austen movies. A motherly figure with glasses and a gentle smile sits in profile, a book in hand. A young blond woman has her elbows on the sill, gazing out with a look of stark yearning, as if waiting for her beau to stroll up the walk. Two young girls in pigtails giggle together over an orange tabby kitten. An old woman in a bonnet and shawl stares out contemplatively, chin in her hand, as if keeping watch and wary of strangers.

Sarah loves it—loves this artistic touch. The women all look as individual as real people, with expressive emotions. She already feels at home. Satisfied that she's made the right choice restarting her life here, she circles the fountain and drives back up the promenade.

Just as the brochure and email said, the community house is impossible to miss. It's an imposing sort of place, an oversized Victorian with a turret and garrets and fanciful details, painted the same green as the surrounding pines with lavender and seafoam detailing. This grand dame served as the boardinghouse for the hotel staff with an expansive penthouse for the large family of one of the two doctors who owned the resort.

There are modern improvements, though. A big air conditioner hums around the corner, and the canted bay window out front is gorgeous stained glass with vines and butterflies. This valley was home to a lively artists' colony in the 1960s, '70s, and '80s, and all of the other cabins and outbuildings were constructed by the original founders of the colony and enhanced over the years by visiting creatives. The mountains here aren't stark and regal, like the ones back in Colorado. They're smaller, rounded, cradling the valley as their forests ripple down like a threadbare quilt dappled with green, gold, and orange. Cabins peek out enticingly from between the trees, the autumn sun flashing on a window here, a patch of roof there. The waterfall is behind the old hotel, Sarah knows, although apparently it's too dangerous to allow visitors to enter the pool as the hotel guests once did. Still, she's never been so excited about a place in her entire life.

This is the first thing she's chosen on her own, without pressure from her mother or Kyle. This is the first thing she's done for herself.

She parks in the gravel lot by the community house, leaving a few spaces between her car and the ancient, beat-up truck that's sprawled out almost diagonally. After giving her hair a quick brush and putting on some lip balm, she walks up the stairs and pauses before the front door, which looks like it might've been carved by the same person who did the sign she saw by the road. Vines and flowers curl everywhere, with pots and paintbrushes and hammers and scissors and yarn hidden among the greenery. A wooden plaque reads DECEMBER HOUSE. No dates, no further information. Sarah wonders if it's a historic landmark. When she googled Tranquil Falls while researching her next step, the only information available online came from the program's About Us page.

Pushing through the door, Sarah's first impression is of honey-gold light and incense. There's a small store like you'd see in any hotel, snacks and pain meds and feminine hygiene products, plus glass water bottles and books and homemade soap and bath salts. The reception desk facing the door is carved with what might be a scene from *Bambi*, all the forest creatures posed dramatically. Through open French doors on the left, she can see the cafeteria—and smell something fallish baking, yeast and cinnamon and apple. The door to the right is closed, but when Sarah is done looking around and gently taps the brass bell on the desk, that's the door that bursts open.

The woman who appears looks sturdy and eclectic, like she can wrestle a bear or do downward dog, as necessary. She's a young-hearted sixty, maybe, with bobbed gray hair, big earrings, bigger glasses, and a capacious purple sweater that looks hand-knit. Although she's flustered, the moment she sees Sarah, her face does a one-eighty, going from annoyed to warm and welcoming.

"Let me see your hands," she says.

"What?" Sarah is taken aback by this greeting.

The woman chuckles. "It's a game I play. I can guess who's who by looking at their hands." Instead of going behind the counter, she bustles over to Sarah in a cloud of lavender and plucks up one of her hands, turning it over. "No ink, so it can't be calligraphy. Fingertips aren't callused, so not the musician. No burns, so not the welder. No darkroom stains, so not the photographer. Although I suppose you could wear gloves." She squints as she looks Sarah up and down, making Sarah want to squirm. "Nothing knit or bespoke. That makes you either the potter or the glass artist. But I know what the glass girl looks like so that makes you . . ." She grins. "Sarah. The potter."

She releases Sarah's hand, and Sarah steps back. Between Covid and Kyle's anxiety, she hasn't been this close to someone else in quite some time. "That's me," she says.

"You're the first here, or it would be easier to pick you out of the lineup. I'm Gail. I'm the property owner and resident adviser." She gestures down at her sweater. "And an artist myself. Welcome to Tranquil Falls."

She's smiling aggressively and obviously expects some response to this, so Sarah says, "Thanks! I'm so glad to be here. I know I applied late, and I haven't been in the studio in a while—"

"Nonsense." Gail brushes a hand through the air as if wiping away Sarah's past. "We'd always rather facilitate someone returning to their passion or exploring something new than some smug little shit just out of art school who thinks they know everything, you know? This place is for rediscovering yourself. You're exactly the kind of person we're looking for."

She doesn't mention the sob story Sarah told in her application about escaping an abusive relationship, but the pity in her eyes suggests she remembers it.

"So this is December House, as I'm sure you saw," Gail says. "We have a little store here. There's a ledger, so if there's no one around, just write down your name and what you took, and we'll settle up every Sunday. George!" she calls suddenly. "George, get in here!" She looks back to Sarah. "My husband George is our handyman. He does plumbing, electrical, leaks, pests, that sort of thing."

The door swings open again, and a sleepy-eyed wizard in a bulky brown sweater appears, blinking at her like he's been napping since the place was built. He waves at Sarah, nods at Gail, and shuffles back through the door. His gray ponytail matches his gray beard, and he's wearing bunny slippers, Sarah notes. The man doesn't look like he could turn on a faucet, much less fix one.

"Now, over here," Gail says, leading Sarah toward the open double doors, "we have the café. My daughter Bridget does the cooking, and we both do cleaning. You're on your own for laundry, but we have two sets of machines in the basement around the back of the house."

The café has six rectangular tables and a small buffet, which is empty just now. To one side, a selection of teas waits, along with honey and sugar and one of those machines that heats water to scalding. Gail heads for a swinging door with an EMPLOYEES ONLY sign and opens it to show a brunette in her twenties, red-faced and dripping with sweat as she checks something in a huge oven.

"This is my Bridget," Gail says in a no-nonsense voice lacking any affection. "Bridget, this is Sarah, the potter."

Bridget looks up and shoves damp hair out of her face. Sarah wonders if she should be wearing a hairnet for this sort of thing but isn't about to ask because Bridget looks like she'd spit in someone's soup.

"Hi," Sarah says with a little wave.

Bridget gives her a death glare before refocusing on Gail. "Is that all?"

"We talked about this," Gail hisses. "Being nice to our residents is part of the job."

Bridget snorts and turns away to check the other oven. "When you pay me a living wage, you can ask me to smile."

Flustered again, Gail hooks her arm through Sarah's and guides her out of the café as if that interaction had never happened. "Breakfast is served from seven to eight, lunch from noon to one, and dinner from six to seven. You'll hear the bell ringing. If you can't make it, let us know, and we'll box up a plate for you. The food is excellent. Bridget has a degree in food science. She's just a whiz with spices."

If that spice is rage, Sarah thinks but doesn't say.

Back in the front room, the mood is calm again, the air hazy with incense. Gail reaches under the counter and holds up a key attached to a slice of wood with a bird carved into it. "You're in Cardinal Cabin," Gail tells her. "It's close enough to the pottery studio. Should have everything you need in there. Did you read all the attachments in the email?"

Sarah nods. She read everything she could about this place, like a little kid studying up on Disney World. It took approximately five minutes, as there's almost no information online, and the "attachments" Gail is referring to was a single page.

"So you know there's no WiFi, almost no cellphone signal here in the valley. If you head up the mountain, you might get a bar, depending on your carrier."

Sarah whips out her phone and checks. Sure enough, no bars, and not a single WiFi signal.

Gail nods knowingly. "It takes some getting used to." She leans down and holds up a big brick of a phone. "I've got this satellite phone for emergencies. And December House is wired, of course." She nods toward an ancient black landline phone with a curly cord. "You're welcome to make any calls you need to here. We're happy to give you privacy. If there are any long-distance bills, we'll settle that at the end of your stay. But your cabin has electricity, just no phone. Most people say it helps them find their muse."

Sarah hasn't been without a phone in twenty years, and she's a little nervous, but also a little excited. No one can reach her. There's no way to track her through social posts, no way to text her at three in the morning like Kyle was doing before she blocked his number. She feels . . . oddly free.

"Good so far?" Gail asks.

Sarah nods. "Yeah, it all sounds great."

"Good." Gail pulls out a xeroxed copy of a hand-drawn map. "You can keep this. Here we are"—she points out December House—"and here's Cardinal Cabin, right across from the pottery studio. You can see all the studios and trails here." The map shows the studios for pottery, fiber arts, painting, music, photography, printing, jewelry, and glass, as well as a forge, all inside a big oval. Around the oval, the seven cabins are set back from the road, each marked with a drawing of a different kind of bird. "We have more studios than artists, so we just keep the ones we don't need locked up." She uses a black Sharpie to put an X over the jewelry and painting buildings. "There are various walking and hiking trails around the property, well marked by color." She takes out red, blue, and orange markers and draws dots by the trailheads. "There are some old trails, too, but they're closed due to rockslides and such. They're taped off. Definitely stay off those."

"Okay."

"And here's the most important thing." Gail puts her hands on the counter and leans forward, suddenly very serious. "The old resort is off limits. *Completely* off limits. There's a fence for a reason. The doors are chained shut because it is absolutely not safe in there. The floors are all rotten, the stairs are falling down, the ceilings are collapsed in several places. If you go in there, you get kicked out of here permanently. Got it?"

"Got it," Sarah says.

"And remember—if you get hurt, it's a long ride to the hospital. If it's bad enough to need an ambulance, it won't get here in time. You don't want to risk that, do you?"

"Of course not!" Sarah says, taken aback by the fact that it sounds like a threat.

"We've just got to make sure," Gail says tiredly. "People are so accustomed to phones and living five minutes away from dependable medical care. This is practically *Little House on the Prairie*, you know? Oh, and if you see a bear, don't run away. Walk slowly away from it, backward, trying to look big."

"Are bears a problem?" Sarah asks, because that wasn't mentioned on the website.

Gail laughs like this question is hilarious and not directly based on what she just said. "Of course not! There's never been a recorded black bear attack in this county. The little guys show up and try to get in the trash, but they won't bother you. And they'll mostly be going to sleep, once the cold kicks in."

Sarah fidgets, half because this has been the most bizarre introduction of her life and half because she's been driving through the mountains for hours and has to pee. Gail nods and flaps a hand at her.

"Go on and get settled. Dinner's at six, remember. We should have everybody in by then, and we'll have a bonfire after. Bridget's making apple buckle." She slides the map across the counter, and Sarah takes it.

"Thanks," she says. "Anything else I need to know?"

Gail's face scrunches up. "I think that's it, but menopause is a real pain in the ass, you know? If anything comes up, just ask. And if I remember anything, I'll tell you. Our living quarters are through that door—our private family space, you understand—but if you ring the bell, someone is always around. Now shoo!"

Sarah takes her map and her key and heads back out to her car. Her rolling suitcases bump over the gravel path into the woods, and her arms begin to ache from tugging them over uneven stones. She passes cabins marked with a robin, a heron, a goose, a bluebird, and an owl. Well, they're called cabins, but they don't all look like cabins. One is a tree house, one resembles a castle, several look like they were just hammered together with whatever was lying around, constructions of whimsy decorated with artistry and oddly shaped, flat glass windows. There's the pottery studio, and then there's her cabin, marked with a bright-red cardinal. It's not a tree house, but there is a tree growing through the center of it, and she likes the look of the two chairs on the porch. She turns her key and opens the door, and she's hit with a wall of stench, the worst thing she's ever smelled in her life.

When she turns on the light, she sees it.

Lying on her carefully made bed is a dead possum, bloated and crawling with maggots.

She drops her bags, hurries out the door, and vomits on the path.

3

don't understand," Gail says for the hundredth time. "I was in there yesterday! I checked all the lights and outlets. I made that bed. It was clean as a whistle."

She and Sarah are standing outside with Sarah's suitcases while George, now in ancient moccasins and wearing gloves and a respirator, drags a shovel and trash bag into the cabin. Sarah has her T-shirt pulled up over her nose, but the smell seems like it will be with her forever. The possum has been dead for quite some time, obviously much longer than Gail says is possible.

"I can't sleep in there," Sarah says. "I can barely breathe out here. Is there a spare cabin?"

Gail shakes her head. "No. I mean, there is, but . . . we don't use that one. It's older. And it's not close to your studio."

"Can I at least stay there tonight? I—it—I mean." She takes a reluctant breath through her mouth. "It soaked into the mattress. I can't sleep there. I can't do it. Is there a hotel in town?"

"There's no town," Gail snaps. "I just don't understand how this happened."

From what Sarah can tell, Gail is the kind of person who plows through life like a tank and is therefore unaccustomed to things going wrong.

"Is there a spare room in December House? I know it used to house the hotel staff—"

Gail fidgets with the hem of her sweater. "No. That's strictly a personal area. We don't allow that sort of thing. I guess . . . well, just, fine. Wait here."

She leaves Sarah to watch George scrape up the possum, which does not remain in one piece. Half of it falls on the ground with a sickening splat, and Sarah has to walk farther up the path so she doesn't vomit again.

After maybe ten minutes, Gail reappears, out of breath. "Come on, then," she says irritably, as if this situation is Sarah's fault. She doesn't attempt to help with any of Sarah's bags.

Sarah follows her deeper into the forest, toward the old resort. A shape appears among the trees, wood painted the hazy purple of twilight. This cabin—well, it's more of a cottage—looks like a doll's house, with fanciful trim that suggests Hansel and Gretel would be tempted to nibble off a bit of fretwork. Much like a movie set, it's got a fake second story with painted windows similar to those at the old hotel. And like the old hotel, it was once beautiful, but now it's faded and forgotten. The downstairs windows are opaque with filth, the fabric flowers in the window boxes a uniform faded gray. Shingles have fallen off, here and there, giving it a gap-toothed feel. Every other cabin has a beautiful wooden sign with a painted bird, but this cottage only has a lighter rectangle of wood where that sign would be. Gail fumbles with the key and opens the door like she's expecting it to be horrible inside.

Much to Sarah's relief, there is no scent of rot and decay. The odor is musty and slightly damp, the air deadly still and sickly warm. There's a front sitting room, a bedroom, and a bathroom with a big clawfoot tub—no shower. The overhead light turns on fine, despite the smell of burned moths, and Gail barges in and starts testing all the other light switches and lamps.

"Everything works, thank goodness. Toilet's got a ring." The bathroom sink turns on with a sputter of brown water. Gail frowns, personally disappointed in the plumbing. "Let that run for a bit." She pulls plastic sheeting off the bed, couch, coffee table, and chairs and rolls it into a ball that looks like a portable kill room. "I'll bring over some towels and fresh bedclothes later," she says, as if in defeat. "You're going to have to excuse the dust and mess. It would've been spotless, if I'd known. Like I said—we never use this one."

Much to Sarah's surprise, the design style is . . . well, very *Mansfield Park*. There's a dinged-up writing desk with pigeonholes, the bed has four posters, the faded flowery wallpaper is flocked, even if the flocking has rubbed off with time. An elegant rocking chair waits on a rag rug by a fireplace spilling ashes, and the recently revealed sofa and chairs are worn velvet with curling wood feet shaped like lion paws. A bookshelf takes up one corner, solid wood stretching from floor to ceiling and looking as if it contains tomes spanning over a hundred years of printing. The walls are covered with paintings of flowers, oils and watercolors and acrylics, all in different styles and frames. The place is oddly charming, if neglected.

"No worries," Sarah says, because that's how she answers almost anything.

Some worries is how she actually feels.

She drags her suitcases over to the dresser and checks the drawers, but they're all empty, with old lavender sachets tucked against the wood and no remaining whispers of lavender. There are far more dead ladybugs and silverfish than she'd prefer, and she's never ached for a Dustbuster like she does now. This cottage is not what she expected, but she doesn't hate it. Anything is better than trying to live and create with the scent of death soaking into every crevice.

Gail stands at the door, holding the wad of dusty plastic sheeting. "I've got to get back to December House. The others are arriving, and we can't have Bridget greeting them. Once everyone's here, I'll come fix it up for you." She holds out the key, and Sarah takes it. There is no friendly wood-burned fob—just a plain silver ring from the hardware store.

"Thanks," Sarah says, hoping Gail will go away. She just wants to be alone now. She came here to get away, to relax, and so far, she's been plagued with problems and fussy people. Silence will be such a blessing. And as for everyone else arriving, they definitely deserve a warmer welcome than Bridget.

When Gail has finally left, Sarah gives her five minutes to truly stay gone and then props open the door and all the windows. The outside smells so much better than dust and time. She disposes of the bug carcasses and wipes out the drawers with an old sock and puts her clothes into the dresser exactly how she'd like them, marveling at the pleasure of making such choices alone, of not having to ask anyone for permission. She got so used to Kyle making all the decisions under the guise of taking care of her.

It's four in the afternoon, and Sarah doesn't know what to do with herself. She sits on the couch for a few moments, feeling the springs, then switches to a chair, which smells like a cat might've peed on it a hundred years ago. With no internet to check, no Instagram to scroll through, no TV to hum in the background, it's just her and the cottage and the forest beyond. The leaves rustle, the birds chat, and somewhere in the distance she can hear the waterfall roaring, this constant sort of numb hum, almost like a crowd whispering just out of view, a party on the other side of a door. She pulls out a book but can't concentrate. Realizing it might be quite some time before Gail returns with linens, she locks the door and heads out to visit her workspace.

Gravel paths link all the other cabins and studios, but the one to her cottage has been neglected and is mostly brown pine needles and old leaves, not that it really matters. She wanders past the other cabins, only slightly jealous, until she stands before the pottery studio. It's big and sturdy but not as whimsical as the cabins—a practical place, cement block with screened windows. The sign by the studio door shows a plate, a goblet, and a lively sculpture of a rooster.

The door is unlocked, the interior cool. When she flicks the light switch, fluorescents buzz. There are three regular wheels of different brands and also a kick wheel she will never use. Shelves hold her unopened boxes of clay and supplies—she had her purchases shipped here last week, as Kyle threw out her old tools years ago. On the other side of the room is a similar setup for handbuilding with canvas-covered tables, metal banding wheels, stools, and another shelf packed with boxes of clay.

When she pushes through the only other door, she finds a small concrete room with multiple shelves, three kilns, and their accoutrements. Nothing is brand new, but everything is a step up from what she used when she was last in the studio. The principles haven't changed, at least, and she brought her old binder with all her notes. This shouldn't be a problem. Firing hasn't changed much over the years, and she's also looking to expand her skills. As part of her application, she mentioned that she'd always wanted to try pit-firing, and her acceptance letter made it clear that Tranquil Falls would do everything it could to support her experimentation.

"Oh," someone says, and she spins to find a figure in the kiln room doorway. Panic trills up her spine—she's trapped in a small room with no windows and no other doors, and a strange man is blocking the light.

"Can I help you?" It comes out . . . not necessarily hostile but not friendly, either.

"Just checking out the studios," he says, eyes drifting from her to the kilns and back again before his mouth drops open. "Oh, sorry. Didn't mean to trap you in here. Pretty small space. Kiln rooms, right?"

He backs out of the doorframe, and she slips through and heads toward the safety of the wheels. She's shaken, but less so now that this guy has proven he's sensitive enough to recognize when he's making someone uncomfortable.

Now that she can actually see him in better light, he's annoyingly good looking in a Patagonia kind of way. He has light-brown hair to his shoulders, the top half of it pulled back like an elf from *Lord of the Rings*. He's wearing a worn white tee and cargo pants with flip-flops, and his glasses are made of wood.

"I'm Reid," he says with a small wave.

"Are you the handbuilder? I know I'm supposed to share the studio."

He shakes his head, looking a little sorry about it. "Metalwork. But I'm in the studio right next door. Apologies in advance for all the hammering."

"I'm Sarah. Potter. Not my last name. I'm a potter. Wheel, I mean." She hates how flustered she is, but she's glad he doesn't want to shake hands.

He smiles and nods. "I did a little handbuilding back in college. Would it be okay if I stopped by someday to knock off the rust? I'm thinking about doing some multimedia."

He's waiting on her to answer.

"Sure. I brought plenty of clay."

Reid frowns, looking a little guilty. "I don't want to use up your supplies. It's not like you can just pop into the shop for a new box."

"I'm fairly certain we can get deliveries out here. But believe me—I brought a lot of clay. Probably too much clay. Everyone will be sick of teacups soon." She's blabbering. Kyle used to hate it when she blabbered. "Sorry. I'm being weird."

Reid does not seem to hate it. He's grinning.

"Don't be sorry. I'm weird, too. That's how artists are supposed to be, right? But seriously, if you want to trade and try a day of hammering metal, I'd be happy to teach you. Have you been here long?"

She pulls out her phone to check the time—that's all it's good for now, anyway. "Not even two hours, but it's been an adventure. There was a dead possum in my cabin."

He grimaces. "Like, it crawled under your cabin to die, or it was just in the middle of the room with a suicide note, or what?"

"It was on my bed and kind of . . . in chunks? It looked like it had been dead a long time. Soaked into the mattress. But Gail said she set up the room just yesterday." Now that she says it out loud, it sounds insane.

"That's insane," he says, as if reading her mind. "I wonder who put it there?"

This thought has been worming its way around Sarah's mind, but she hasn't yet given it any attention at all because then it might gain some ground. Now that Reid has said it, she has to consider it, and really, there's only one person out there she knows of who wants to hurt her, and he's not supposed to know where she is.

"No idea." She shrugs it off and pushes it down. *Repress, repress, repress.* "So Gail moved me into this old cottage. It doesn't even have a sign."

"An inauspicious beginning," someone says, and they both stare at the open door to the studio, which Sarah was fairly certain Reid had shut.

"You heard that, too, right?" Reid asks.

A head pokes in from the side—a woman wearing a bizarre hat. "Good afternoon," she says with a nod. "I'm Gertrude Rose, historical costumer and fiber artist. I'd come in, but I worry the clay dust will dredge my hems." She steps into the doorway to show a plaid dress that's wider than the opening and looks like something Ma Ingalls might've sewn by hand.

"So you're really living the dream," Reid says, which is helpful, because Sarah is somewhat lost for words. She'd imagined that everyone coming here would be just like her—similar age or younger, similar circumstances. A cohort of equals. But Gertrude Rose is old enough to join AARP and is dressed like she's about to board the *Titanic.* Her hat, Sarah notices, has a bird nest on it, complete with eggs.

"The modern age leaves much to be desired." Gertrude Rose clasps her gloved hands and looks down with a martyred sigh. "I've had to seek gentility in history, and Tranquil Falls is gloriously antiquated, is it not? This place was once an oasis of repose for women of means, you know. Like us, they came here to escape their lives and find serenity in nature."

"It just looks like a hotel," Reid says. "That's not what it was?"

"I read about it online. It was more like a spa," Sarah tells him.

"A spa! Pshaw!" Gertrude Rose whips a fan out of—somewhere—and fans herself as if scandalized. "A spa is a place to have your nails or hair done. Tranquil Falls was created by cutting-edge doctors who used modern treatments to calm the spirit and invigorate the mind. They said the water here could cure diseases, ease eczema, soothe asthma. A truly beautiful and holy place. I hope you brought your bathing costumes."

Sarah and Reid share a glance.

"I brought my suit," Sarah says. "But it doesn't go down to my knees."

Reid chuckles, and Gertrude Rose gives the slightest eye roll. "I don't expect everyone to adhere to my standards, darling. I'll be in the fiber studio most days, should you wish for genteel company." With a curtsy, she sweeps away, her skirts leaving a little puff of dust in their wake.

"She didn't even ask our names," Sarah says, watching the plaid figure disappear up the trail at a fast clip.

"I don't think she cares about anything except the past."

Sarah is taken aback by such an accurate statement. Reid is smarter than he looks.

"Well, I'm going for a walk over by the fence to see if I can spot the waterfall. Want to come?" The open, friendly look he gives her suggests he'd very much like her to say yes.

And it would be great if she could, but Sarah is still gun-shy around men. Walking into the dark forest behind an abandoned building with a strange man, even one vetted by Gail and the rest of the Tranquil Falls alumni committee, simply isn't something she's capable of doing right now. As much as she'd like to see the waterfall, she's all too aware that her phone has no bars, and if she screams, the noise of the falls will drown her out.

"I have to wait for Gail to bring my linens," she says. "But have fun."

He leaves with a little wave, and Sarah unpacks her supplies and lays out her tools, remembering the sturdy curve of a rib in her palm and the stiffness of a new sponge. She took her first wheel class at fourteen because the guy she had a crush on signed up—with his girlfriend. It was awkward at first, but they quickly dropped out to dry-hump on the picnic tables behind the arts center and Sarah kept throwing. She'd hoped to fall in love with Garrett Bohannon, but she fell in love with clay instead. Judging by Garrett Bohannon's life as shown through Facebook posts, clay was the right choice. She went to Governor's Honors for art, got a scholarship to college, and was well on her way to a degree in ceramics when she met Kyle.

And now she can't remember the last time she touched clay.

That's how insidious Kyle was, how subtle. He wanted things to happen, and they just . . . did. Even if she didn't want them to. It started with him moving her studio shoes outside so she wouldn't track in dust. And then he worried her clay-crusted jeans and towels would clog the laundry lines. And then he wanted more time with her. And then her toolbox disappeared in the move.

When she brought it up, he told her it was her idea, quitting pottery.

And goddamn if she couldn't remember if that was true or not.

She shakes her head. That's over, and something new has begun.

Once she's sure Reid is well on his way, she closes the door behind her and does a full tour of the other studios. They're all clustered together in a big oval clearing, which is surrounded by a gravel road just wide enough for a truck to make deliveries as needed. The cabins around the perimeter are set back among the trees, giving each person the illusion of some privacy. Pulling the folded map out of her pocket, she realizes that her new cabin isn't on it at all.

There are signs of life from the other artists—the sound of a violin tuning, a little red wagon full of boxes parked by the photography studio—but she doesn't see anyone else. She passes the trailheads for the red, blue, and orange trails, each marked with a sign listing its mileage. The red trail goes to an ancient towering hemlock, the blue trail goes to a small waterfall, and the orange trail goes to a rock labyrinth. As she passes a firepit and completes her circuit of the big oval drive, she notices something shimmering out beyond the community house and hikes up cut-stone steps to find a human-made reflecting pool lined with white stone. Blue glass marbles sparkle under the water, and lotus leaves float, fat and green, on the surface. Herb gardens are planted around the pool, sprays of lavender and polka-dotted chamomile side by side with big butterfly bushes dropping the last of their blossoms.

This place—it's everything she hoped it would be. Wide open and thoughtful and artfully beautiful, like it was made just for her. Reaching into her pocket, she pulls out a quarter. It's warm in her hand, and she can't help thinking about how little she handles money these days. She only has change because she had to buy a bag of M&M's in a tiny one-pump gas station on the way up here so she could use the bathroom without feeling like a big-city asshole. Closing her eyes, she tosses the quarter into the pool with a gentle plop. For luck.

"You shouldn't throw quarters in there," someone says.

Sarah startles and opens her eyes to find an old-fashioned camera pointed at her. *Click.* The person holding it is a young woman, early twenties, maybe—a goth. Or a punk, or an emo. Sarah doesn't know what they call themselves these days, but the girl is in all black, her curly hair dyed an electric, violent acid green. She's wearing a black beret, too. The camera clicks, and the girl's face is revealed, her eyes heavily ringed in black, a gold stud in her nose, a bright flash against warm brown skin.

"That's not some jank old mall fountain," the girl goes on. "Shit lives in there. Flowers and frogs. A whole ecosystem. You're going to kill them."

"Sorry. I didn't know. It was just one quarter." Sarah suddenly feels like a monster, like this girl can see right through her.

The girl shakes her head and advances the film before walking away without introducing herself.

"Just because you didn't know doesn't mean you're not a killer," the girl says over her shoulder. "Ignorance isn't innocence."

As she walks into the forest, she raises her middle finger, nails painted black.

Sarah looks into the pond, hunting for the quarter, wondering if the girl is telling the truth and she's done real harm.

But no. There are plenty of quarters down there, intermingled with the glass.

"What a bitch," she murmurs under her breath.

She's beginning to think she's the only sane person here, and after what she's been through recently, that's not a comforting thought.

4

When she returns to her cottage, Sarah finds the bed nicely made with fresh linens, a stack of towels and washrags waiting on top of the toilet. Gail has also left behind a jar of potpourri that has the whole place smelling of lavender and lemons, and the bathroom finally has toilet paper, which makes the space a lot more livable. It's not as modern as her original cabin, but it smells a lot better, and it's kind of nice, being away from the main drag. At least the punk photographer won't be pointing a camera at her every time she steps outside. When she throws herself onto the creaky bed, she notices that the window looks past the trees and out on the corner of the old resort and the wild mountain beyond. There's a misty, hidden quality to the scene, a blurriness that reminds her of old impressionist paintings.

Her fingers twitch for social media, for that pleasant, slot-machine call of scrolling. Somewhere, a baby wombat is getting weighed in a mixing bowl, and a rescue kitten is having a name reveal, and a high school friend is thanking Jesus for the new Chick-fil-A milkshake flavor, and Sarah is missing it all. She tells her brain to calm down and relax; her brain tells her to find a button and click it. She stares at the water-spotted ceiling and thinks about how human beings were meant to walk five miles a day while eating fruit, to float in the ocean, to tell stories around a roaring fire, and yet we've built ourselves a magnificent cage that bores us so badly that most people would choose a mild shock over sitting patiently in an empty room, alone for more than two minutes.

She will find stillness, she tells herself firmly, because it has already found her. She will find stillness because that's why she chose this particular place. The frustration is a feature, not a bug. It's withdrawal. It's detox. It's medicine.

At six, the dinner bell rings, and Sarah waits a few minutes before locking her door and heading up to December House. She'd rather walk into the café and scope out her fellow artists than have some stiff and bumbling half-conversation on the way there. Far ahead, she can see the bell-shaped silhouette of Gertrude Rose and imagines that she might've been one of the original visitors to the resort. It's got to be hard to pee under all those skirts; does she have to loop them over the toilet like an igloo? And how did the woman ever fit in her car for the journey up here? Surely she didn't take a horse and buggy. Sarah would love the answers to all her questions about the costumer, but not if it involves asking her directly.

This time when she opens the door, she's met with an acrid, smoky smell. Whatever lovely apple treat Bridget was making earlier must've been in the oven too long. The scent does not raise the appetite, and she almost thinks about heading back to her room for a protein bar or one of the packs of chips she brought along, just in case the food was terrible.

Too late. Gail is waving her over to the buffet, where the other artists are already awkwardly jostling for food. Reid gives her a small wave and a smile, while Gertrude Rose bobs her head. She's removed a front panel of her dress; it once buttoned high up her neck, but now her freckled cleavage has been unmasked. Sarah takes a plate and gets in line. She scoops up salad, salmon patties, quinoa, and veggies but skips the charred dinner rolls, grateful that it wasn't the dessert that went down in flames. Bridget is nowhere to be seen, but angry clanks from the other side of the wooden door to the kitchen suggest she's in there and still in a bad mood.

As the last person getting food and filling her water glass from a pitcher, Sarah is worried that she's doomed herself to a sort of middle school cafeteria situation, but Gail has pushed two tables together and there's just one seat left. To her annoyance, Sarah is stuck between Reid and the aggressively rude photographer.

"Welcome to Tranquil Falls," Gail says as everyone fumbles with their forks, food halfway to their mouths. "As you all know, I'm Gail, and I've been running this program since my parents retired. We like to do a quick introduction, just so everyone knows names." Gail is at the head of the table, and she nods to the person sitting to her left. He looks like he's maybe seventeen, a tall, gangly Asian kid who's mostly elbows and Adam's apple with a crop of shaggy black hair. He drops his fork and looks like he'd prefer to crawl under the table rather than have the spotlight turned on him.

"Uh, I'm Lucas." He swallows hard and picks up his fork again.

"And what's your medium?" Gail prompts like she's his mom.

"Violin, viola, piano, banjo—"

Ah. He must've been the one Sarah heard playing earlier.

"Music," Gail finishes for him, as if this wasn't obvious. "Next?"

"Gertrude Rose. Costumer, anachronist, steampunk enthusiast, and fiber artist."

After that, they just keep going before Gail can interrupt again. It's always odd when someone who looks that artsy and free is a type-A tight-ass.

"Reid. Metalwork."

"Sarah. Pottery on the wheel."

She's immediately grateful that she's managed to get the words out without sounding like an idiot. Public speaking has never been a forte, and Kyle always said—

Well, who gives a shit about what Kyle said?

"Ingrid. Photography and darkroom."

That's everyone Sarah has met before. The next three people are new.

One is a Black woman in her sixties, thin and elegant with her white-streaked hair in a high braided bun. She's wearing a long velvet dress with a floor-length embroidered duster and big glasses that give her bug eyes, with a collection of tangled necklaces hanging heavy around her neck.

"Antoinette," she says, her voice deep and husky. "Calligraphy and inks."

The next person is a man in his sixties, white with an alcoholic's red nose and wild gray Einstein hair, a gold cross necklace, and a black T-shirt that reads DOES NOT PLAY WELL WITH OTHERS stretched over his potbelly. "Bernie. Handbuilding and sculpture." He's got that kind of smirking know-it-all vibe, and Sarah instantly dislikes him—which does not bode well, as they'll be sharing the studio.

The last person is a white woman a little older than Sarah but trying not to look it, wearing a plaid shirt, skinny jeans, and cowboy boots. Her blond hair is pulled back into the kind of high, messy bun that you can watch tutorials for fifteen times on TikTok and still have no idea how it works. She's one of those people who just looks effortless—which Sarah knows requires a lot of effort. "I'm Kim. I do stained glass," she says.

"So that's everyone." Gail sits back down. "We'll have a bonfire tonight after dinner so you can all get to know one another and enjoy some s'mores. Beer and wine for everyone except Lucas, obviously." He scrunches down in his seat and looks like he wishes he could melt directly into the floor. "After that, you're all basically on your own until the final exhibition. Come see me in the front office if you need anything. And we'll have meals together, of course, so you can find me here, too. I hope you'll all have a wonderful autumn and enjoy the natural beauty of the campus." When no one says anything, she adds, "Well, dig in!"

Sarah is hungry, and the food is unexpectedly good. The conversation, however, is balky and uncomfortable. There doesn't appear to be a take-charge extrovert among them—they are artists who purposefully sought this lonesome aerie, after all. Gail attempts an icebreaker here or there, but she can't seem to drop her air of authority; it's like trying to talk to the high school principal when he's sitting backward on his chair and using the word *tubular*. She mainly focuses on Lucas, who squirms under her scrutiny. Reid finally takes pity on the kid and starts up a conversation about Marvel movies, and Gail zeroes in on Ingrid, who gives flat, sarcastic, one-syllable answers. Sarah hates it when Ingrid's attitude is aimed at her but kind of loves it when it's aimed at someone else.

"You seemed different in your application essay," Gail says wistfully.

"Everyone is different when they want something," Ingrid replies as she pokes at her salmon cake.

With Ingrid obviously uninterested in playing nice and Reid now animatedly discussing *Star Wars* with Lucas, there's not really anyone for Sarah to talk to. Kim gives her a shy smile from across the table, but Gertrude Rose is yammering at her about how messy buns used to be done with rats made from the hair of paupers, so she can't really chat. Antoinette eats silently, carefully, staring straight ahead like she's watching a TV no one else can see. Bernie is holding court with Gail, talking about his days as a college professor. Gail softens around him, is less uptight. When she laughs, it's startlingly loud and braying. Sarah hopes every meal won't be this cumbersome.

Finally, everyone is done, and they bus their plates and scrape off their scraps.

"Going to the bonfire?" Reid asks.

Sarah nods. "Definitely. She promised s'mores."

The group walks out to the edge of the forest, where Gail's husband—Sarah has already forgotten his name but knows it starts with a *G* and is tempted to call him Gandalf—is stacking wood in the center of a circle of stones. Logs and old patio chairs are placed in a ring just far enough away to keep people from catching on fire. There's exactly one bag of marshmallows, a large off-brand chocolate bar, and an open box of graham crackers, plus a beat-up cooler full of cheap beer, tiny wine bottles, and hard seltzer. Sarah hasn't had a drink in a while—over the past year, she's had insanely bad hangovers and lots of headaches and nausea in general, it's a whole thing that she's attributed to stress—but she knows she's going to need any help the alcohol can offer if she's going to loosen up enough to make friends. It's almost like she's forgotten how. She digs up a black cherry seltzer and wipes the condensation off on her jeans.

"None for you, young sir," Gertrude Rose says, pointing a gloved finger in Lucas's face. "We know you're not of legal drinking age."

Lucas looks like he wants to run away. "I wasn't going to—I mean, I don't—"

"Oh, c'mon. He's nowhere near the cooler," Reid says, clapping the kid on the back. "And it's not like he's going to be driving."

But Gertrude Rose settles into the chair nearest the cooler like a broody hen and crosses her arms as if daring Lucas to fight her for the opportunity to drink lukewarm beer with a bunch of old people. He heads for the s'mores instead.

Sarah takes a seat across the fire, as far from Gertrude Rose as possible, and Kim points at the seat beside her with a lime seltzer. "Is anyone sitting here?" she asks.

"Nope, go ahead."

Kim settles in and sips, the fire dancing in her eyes. "This is not what I thought it would be like, you know? I guess I thought it would be people—"

"More like us?" Sarah ventures.

Kim grins. "Yeah. I guess I forget every artist isn't an Instagram mom. I thought it would look like a yoga retreat."

They watch as Lucas and Reid make s'mores using long forks left by the cooler while Bernie gives them unnecessary and unwanted pointers. Sarah is tempted to join them but still feels full after the apple buckle, and her goal is to leave the bonfire without any regrets, without saying something stupid or talking too much or accidentally insulting someone. For the past five years, every time she and Kyle went to a party or mixer with his friends or hospital colleagues, she always did something wrong . . . sometimes a lot of somethings. And Kyle always gently, kindly, seemingly benevolently told her about it once they were in the car. Eventually, he just stopped taking her along. Even if she's come to realize that he was a grade-A asshole who was just trying to erode her self-esteem in a way she couldn't quite pin down in the moment, she can't help feeling like she's walking through a minefield now in social situations. She's too loud, too flaky, too immature, doesn't know when to shut up—that's what the voice in her head tells her. The damage has left scars.

"So what brought you here?" Kim asks, her eyes on the fire.

Sarah sips her seltzer, welcomes the warmth creeping up her spine as she starts to relax for the first time in years. "I'm a few courses shy of a degree in ceramics," she says. "I dropped out of school to move across the country with my boyfriend for his residency. We—just broke up. So I thought I could get back into it, maybe get back on track here and then finish up those last credits." Her next sip is a gulp, and the bubbles make her cough and feel like an idiot, but Kim doesn't seem to notice.

"I hear that. That's a really great goal. Did you miss it? The art, I mean. Or did you, like, take classes at a local place, or have a home studio?"

Regret peals like a gong in Sarah's chest as she shakes her head. "I missed it, but I told myself I had better things to do. I mean, my boyfriend told me I did. And home studios are so messy. It's all just dirt, right? I always knew I could go back to it, that it would wait for me." She holds up the hand that isn't clutching the seltzer for dear life, opens it and closes it in front of the dancing flames. "But I missed the feel of the clay, you know? The possibility of it." She realizes she's been doing most of the talking and asks, "How about you? Why are you here? Or, I mean, what brought you here?"

Because *Why are you here?* is a pretty harsh question.

Kim scoots back, puts her boots up on the chair, and hugs her knees. "I took a class last year and really liked it. Stained glass. I mean, I've taken a lot of classes." She leans over, her head flopping toward Sarah like they're ten and at a sleepover. "A. Lot. Watercolor, enameling, polymer clay, crochet. Like I was searching for something. And then I found stained glass, and I started following stained-glass artists on Instagram and TikTok, and I realized that it could be a business. I need to make money. My husband . . ."

She looks down and sniffles.

"He's trying to take the kids. He cheated on me, and now he's trying to take the kids even though he hates them and is just going to farm them out to a nanny he can bang, but I don't have a degree and I really need the money. The essential oils just aren't enough, so I want to make these suncatchers with a little pad that holds essential oil to make everything smell nice. I can't find anyone else doing it, which means it's a good idea, right?" Sarah nods, as that's what she's expected to do. "So I figure I have the studio to myself, all that space, and I just turn into a production machine."

That sounds like some version of hell to Sarah, just churning out the same exact piece of art over and over and over, but there's no way she's going to say that. Throwing on the wheel might seem repetitive, but it's the minor variations that make each piece fascinating to her. At least Kim has a plan, and it sounds like she's willing to do the work. For all the pain Kyle has put Sarah through, she's glad there aren't any kids to fight over. She may have almost nothing—just a little nest egg her nana left her in her will—but she doesn't have to pay for a fight. As soon as this artist residency is over, the lease starts on her new rental in Athens, which is half a world away from Kyle and all her memories back in Colorado.

"So do you make mugs, bowls, that sort of thing?" Kim asks as she rubs the smoke from her eyes, trying to get back on track.

"All that. Mugs, bowls, plates, teapots, pitchers. I need to get my skills back and then figure out what I really want to concentrate on here."

Kim nods, but she's watching Reid and Lucas at the fire. "And he's a sculptor. The hot one. Isn't his studio right next to yours?" She waggles her perfect eyebrows.

Sarah blushes. "Yeah, looks like it. But I'm not—I'm just getting out of a bad relationship. I didn't come here for . . . that."

Kim shrugs. "It doesn't have to be a relationship. It can just be what it is. Things happen. I've seen *Ghost*."

She slams her boots on the ground and mimes throwing a pot and hums "Unchained Melody," and Sarah honks a laugh, a real laugh, the kind of laugh Kyle told her sounded immature and embarrassing and crazy. She hasn't laughed like that in ages, and it feels daring and free. Kim laughs, too, and Sarah's heart wrenches when she realizes how long it's been since she had female friends—since she was *allowed* to have female friends. She used to have a crew from her hometown, and she was tight with her roommates from college, but then she moved to be with Kyle and he slowly expanded until there wasn't room for anyone else in her life. He said Jill was too needy, Allie was a bad influence, Katerina was so negative. And so she drifted away from them, just so she wouldn't have to hear him complain about them.

But now, all the way across the country? She can be herself. She can make friends. She can laugh her big, stupid donkey laugh without feeling guilty. She can look at Reid, if she wants to. She can do anything. That's why she's here.

Kim leans in closer, grinning. "So I don't mean to be catty, but they're both nuts, right?" She inclines her head toward where Gertrude Rose sits beside Antoinette. The two older women are chatting animatedly. The beer looks odd in Gertrude Rose's hand, surrounded by cream-colored lace and the thick tartan fabric. Antoinette is sipping from a brass flask that winks in the firelight.

"They're artists, which means they're probably going to be eccentric. Maybe you just stop giving a shit when you hit fifty. It sounds kind of nice, actually," Sarah says, finding her tongue loosened by the seltzer. She turns the can upside down and swallows the last drops. Kim goes over to the cooler, briefly converses with Gertrude Rose and Antoinette, grabs two more cans, and returns.

"They asked me my astrology sign. Can you believe that? This place is a trip." Kim hands over one of the cans and pops her own. "I'm an Aries. Antoinette said that was obvious." With an eye roll, she clinks her can against Sarah's and drinks. "So what happened with your boyfriend?"

Sarah has never discussed this with anyone else, other than the Reddit thread she started with a throwaway account, the one that convinced her she was being massively gaslit and was living in a world full of marinara-red flags. The whole thing makes her feel like an absolute fool, that she fell for Kyle's bullshit and stayed with him for six years and even let him convince her to leave everything behind and move to Colorado with him. But she wants to talk about it—wants to squeeze out the rest of the pus, now that the wound is gaping open. Plus, it only feels fair, since Kim told her the truth about why she's here.

"It wasn't good," she starts. "We met at a coffee shop in college, when I was a junior and he was finishing med school. He love-bombed me—I'd never felt so taken care of in my whole life. Two dozen roses, concert tickets, fancy dinners. He convinced me to move to Colorado with him for his residency, and I thought it was so fun and romantic, and I'd lived in Georgia all my life. So I didn't finish my degree, I just went. I knew no one out there, and the only job I could get was as a secretary." She chews her lip, remembering how lonely it was. "I thought things were okay, but I could never tell if he was going to be sweet and loving or mean and cutting. Whenever I was sick, he was so tender, but whenever I wanted to go out or take a class or go to the gym, he was dismissive and belittling, you know? It was like walking on eggshells all the time. Then I realized I was depressed, and I told him so, and instead of trying to help me, he told me I was being melodramatic to get attention. I realized he was gaslighting me. And I wrote down everything that was bothering me and realized I was in an emotionally abusive situation. So I quit my crappy job and got out."

She doesn't mention all the strange things that happened, the way she couldn't tell what was real and what wasn't, the stomachaches and nausea Kyle ascribed to anxiety, the pills he gave her for the anxiety that didn't make her any less anxious. When she thinks about it, the shame makes her gorge rise.

She's smarter than that. Or she thought she was.

"Narcissists," she says with a shake of her head.

"Tell me about it," Kim agrees. "I married one, too. Except mine didn't really care about me at all. Not, like, as a person. He married me, got me pregnant, and then completely ignored me to chase teenagers. I was just a tick box. Pass the bar? Check. Blond trophy wife? Check. Two kids, a big house, a Porsche? Check. And when I called him on it and decided to leave, he told me it wouldn't look good at the firm and that if I didn't settle down and behave and be a good wife, he'd ruin my life." She takes a big swig of her seltzer. "And he is."

"Shit," Sarah murmurs.

For a long moment, they drink and stare into the fire. Then Kim pulls out her big purse and digs around, producing a little notepad and a couple of hotel pens. "Look, here's what we're going to do. We're going to write down what we want to leave behind in our old lives, and then we're going to throw it in the fire and release that energy into the universe. I did this at a retreat once. You down?"

It feels a little silly, but it also sounds like fun. Sarah never really got into the spiritual side of art, the kind that's in tune with the moon and tides and calls down the Muse with a capital *M,* but what she's been doing isn't working, so why the hell not? The whole reason she's here is to shed her old life like sunburned skin and start over. She already made her offering to the pool, so releasing energy into the fire isn't such a stretch.

"Let's do it," she says.

Kim tears off a sheet and hands her the pen, and Sarah puts up her knee and thinks a moment before scribbling, *I want to leave behind Kyle and everything he did to diminish me.* And under that, she adds, *I want to discover who I really am.*

She looks up as Kim finishes writing her own message and folds up the paper. She catches *that asshole* in loopy cursive and doesn't blame the other woman a bit.

"Ready?" Kim asks.

Sarah nods and stands, and they approach the fire.

"I release this into the universe," Kim says, tossing the paper to flutter into the fire. It catches and curls, going black amid the dancing flames.

"Uh, yep," Sarah agrees. She can't bring herself to say those words. It's just too cheesy. "I release it." She tosses in her paper and watches it burn until there's nothing left. It might be hokey, but it feels good, and she takes a deep breath all the way down to her belly.

"There we go," Kim says. "A fresh start. Cheers!"

They clink their cans, and then Kim has to have a s'more, so they join Reid and Lucas to share the two marshmallow-roasting sticks.

"What've you guys been talking about?" Kim asks, and Sarah is glad to be adopted by the closest thing around to an extrovert, because she's always sucked at small talk.

"TV and videogames, mostly," Reid says. "And our cabins. Although mine is more of a tree house. What about you?"

"I'm in the castle one," Kim says. "Bluebird House. It's gorgeous. The whole inside has a fairy-tale theme. It's perfect."

"Mine is like a Hobbit house," Lucas says quietly. "It's called the Goose Hut. The one with the round door?"

Kim nods. "I saw that. It looked a little stuffy."

"I kind of like stuffy," Lucas manages to say. "Our apartment back home is . . . I mean I'm grateful for it, but it's really . . . cold. Concrete and steel. This is better."

It's the most Sarah has heard him say so far, and his whole face is flushed, and then she notices that the pockets of his cargo pants contain lumps about the size and shape of tiny wine bottles. She's not going to say anything, though—what trouble can a drunk teen get into up here?

"Which cabin are you in?" Reid asks her.

"Oh, I was supposed to be in Cardinal House, but like I said, there was that dead possum in there, so Gail moved me out to—well, it doesn't have a name. It looks like the witch's cottage from Hansel and Gretel. It's old and neglected, but at least it doesn't stink."

"Candy Cottage!" Kim squeals. "That's what we'll call it. It's weird that it doesn't have a name, though."

Sarah shrugs. "I guess they just don't use it anymore. It'll be fine. I'm here for the art, not the room."

"The cabins are so far away," Lucas says, squirming a little.

Kim looks down at his pockets and smirks. "Pretty far to the out-house, huh?"

"That's why God made trees," Reid says. "Your phone has a flash-light, so just go twenty feet in and take care of business. Unless you want to run back to December House and talk to Gail."

Lucas covers his mouth as he burps. "Uh, woods are fine."

He turns on his phone's flashlight and stumbles into the nearest patch of trees. Sarah watches him go for a moment before remember-ing that it's rude to watch people on their way to piss in the forest.

"He's a good kid," Reid says. "Fucked-up family, though. He told me—"

A scream from the woods interrupts him, and he takes off running with Sarah and Kim hot on his heels.

5

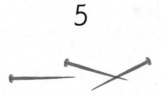

Sarah nearly trips over her boots on the uneven ground. Two drinks is a lot for her, and there is no path in this part of the woods. Kim has the forethought to turn on her phone's flashlight, and she shines it ahead of Reid as he barrels through the trees.

"Lucas!" he calls. "You good, man?"

They find the kid standing in a moonlit clearing, frozen, a wet patch on the front of his cargo pants and his phone on the ground. Reid catches hold of his shoulders, gives him a little shake.

"Lucas, what's wrong? What happened?"

Lucas's mouth drops open, but he can only point. Kim aims her phone's flashlight into the forest and lets out a shuddering gasp.

They are surrounded by eyes. Hundreds of eyes that shine when the light hits them.

The eyes belong to dolls—or the heads of dolls. Some are still attached to their bodies, creepy Victorian children made of porcelain, while others have been repurposed as the heads of twisted sculptures with animal bodies and claws that perch on branches or crouch in the dirt. Some hang from the trees like birdhouses, their mouths open and stuffed with twigs and straw. Some are seemingly hammered into the trunks of trees, like they're trying to escape from the fires of hell while screaming. That's what it feels like—being the audience to a special kind of frozen nightmare.

"They're just dolls," Reid says, although the tremor in his voice suggests he doesn't necessarily believe it.

Kim gives a low whistle. "It's a hell of an art installation. I know we're all supposed to contribute something lasting to the campus, but I can't believe this one got the green light. Fuckin' creepy."

Lucas is still stuck in place. Sarah gets that. She's a freezer, too. She always wishes she was fight or at least flight, but she just stands there, immobilized, in shock, whenever something terrible happens.

Ingrid materializes out of the darkness, mutters "Cool," and starts taking pics with her cellphone's flash.

As Kim shines her phone around, taking in every horrific grimace, Sarah notices something—a gravestone, white as bone, halfway buried in old leaves. She turns on her own phone's flashlight and kneels to dig the headstone free. Like the dolls, it's white porcelain, and a message has been stamped into the clay in a font that looks straight out of a book of Grimm's fairy tales.

THE FORGOTTEN CHILDREN OF TRANQUIL FALLS is the title. AN AS-SEMBLAGE BY JENNI LUSAK, 2015. THEY WATCH US FROM HEAVEN, JUDGING US FOR THEIR TRAGEDY. NOW YOU HAVE TO SEE THEM.

A chill runs up Sarah's spine. "Lost children?"

"I googled the shit out of this place and never saw anything about that." Kim walks up to one of the hanging heads, stares deep into its glossy eyes. "Was it like what happened in the residential schools, maybe? But this place was never a residential school." She touches the porcelain chin, making it swing lightly. "And these kids are extremely white."

"Maybe a couple of kids got lost on the mountain once?" Reid asks. "I could see that. Nobody really watched kids in the eighteen hundreds, and things were a lot wilder then. I don't see a historical date, though."

"Can we get out of here?" Lucas says, voice breaking.

Reid shakes his head, grabs Lucas's phone off the ground, and puts his arm around the kid's shoulders. "Yeah, let's get back to our cabins. I'll walk you there. Night, y'all." With a nod to Sarah and Kim, he steers Lucas back toward the gravel road, keeping him carefully away from the light of the bonfire so no one else will see what's happened to the front of his pants.

Sarah types "lost children Tranquil Falls" into the search bar on her phone before it reminds her there's no signal.

"Well, I'm done drinking for the night," Kim says. "Time to go back to my castle and dream of terrifying monster children so I can wake up and work my ass off. You coming?" She waits, and Sarah looks around the clearing one more time before joining her.

"Oh. Work. I forgot about that part," Sarah admits, because her brain does this truly unhelpful thing where she forgets about important tasks she doesn't want to do, like creating what's basically a thesis to be presented at the end of her residency. She told herself this was a problem for Future Sarah when she agreed to it in the application. She's not sure how she's going to go from not throwing a single pot in five years to suddenly producing a body of work with deep emotional resonance, but the problem must be confronted, now that she's actually here. She's not going to make a bunch of monster babies to hide in the forest, she knows that much.

She and Kim wander back down to the bonfire, toss their empty cans into the garbage bag, and wave goodbye to Gertrude Rose and Antoinette, who are still chatting amicably by the fire.

"Weren't y'all worried about the screaming?" Kim calls.

"I merely assumed someone found the dolls," Antoinette says with a smirk.

"Bad knees," Gertrude Rose adds. "I only run away from trouble, not toward it. Good night, ladies!"

As the gravel road leads Sarah and Kim under the trees, both women turn on their phone flashlights again, and Sarah realizes that this is currently the best use for the thousand-dollar supercomputer in her pocket—out here, it's just a lantern. They reach Kim's cabin first, and even in the dark, there's a lot to admire in the turret and ramparts. Sarah wishes she'd been assigned to the cheerful, fairy-tale cabin with flowering vines painted up the sides.

"See you at breakfast?" Kim asks.

"If the dolls don't get me." Sarah is only half joking. She knows they're art, she touched that cold porcelain headstone, and yet it feels as if they might come alive in the midnight silence of the mountain and crawl all over the forest, writhing, skittering, ceramic teeth clacking, hunting for fresh meat. She tries to smother that train of thought as she turns to follow the road to her far more depressing cottage. With no internet or social media to distract her, her imagination apparently feels free to run wild for the first time in years. She should welcome it, but she'd vastly prefer it stick to lighter topics. The same goes for her sense of humor.

She passes the other cabins, including Lucas's squatty little Hobbit house. Light shines from the cheerful round windows, a warm gold that leaks out into the forest and makes her want to huddle up against the glass like a flower reaching for a sunbeam. The poor kid—what a way to start a residency among adults for someone so young and obviously nervous, screaming and pissing yourself.

The walk back to her cottage feels much longer than it did on the way out, the trail dark and far less friendly than the well-used, better-kept ones. An owl hoots and she startles, looking up into the dense treetops to see if she can spot a flash of white. She's never seen an owl in the wild, and she would take it as a good omen, seeing one now. That's the sort of visual that would make the dolls seem less terrifying—as if it might balance out her evening.

Then again, she recalls reading something about owls being a harbinger of death, so maybe it's better if the owl remains purely hypothetical.

No owl reveals itself, but something rustles in the underbrush, which doesn't make her feel any better. She picks up her pace, swinging her phone's flashlight back and forth, sweeping over the path in either direction. Nothing moves, but everything seems stark and brittle, reduced to black and white—mostly black. Finally her cottage appears, a sinister shadow huddled against the darkness. *Candy Cottage, my ass.* The soft roar of the falls drowns out the night's furtive whispers as she fumbles for her key and tries to fit it into the hole while holding her phone light just so, which is harder than it looks because she's shaking.

She drops the key and squats to pick it up with the nervous swiftness of a deer scenting a predator.

Sarah has never been out in the woods alone at night.

She has never been camping, never even lain out on the back porch on a hammock to watch the stars. She'd hoped to feel at home here in the mountains of her home state, to feel as if she were one with the cosmos and part of the forest and welcome in nature. Instead, she feels like she's being watched.

This time, the trembling key slides into the lock with a crusty sort of reticence, and she turns the knob and throws herself into the cottage, slamming the door behind her and flicking on the light. Her heart ratchets down a bit, but she doesn't stop shaking. It's cold—she left the windows open to air things out, and the mountains in early fall have a chill she didn't anticipate, especially in the shade. Gail's lavender potpourri rides the still air, but underneath it slithers that scent of musty abandonment that reminds her of her grandparents' attic when she was a kid.

Sarah was terrified of her grandparents' attic.

She's breathing hard as she hurries around, closing all the windows and dragging the damask curtains shut in a puff of dust. She needs to ask Gail for a vacuum—another thing for tomorrow's to-do list. After double-checking that the door is locked, she heads to the bathroom and stares at the clawfoot tub, realizing that the romance of such an object is predicated on not having to rely on it. What she wants right now is a modern hotel shower, hot water to rinse off the oddness of the day and all the time she spent driving. What she has is a tub that looks like it's made of asbestos and water that will almost certainly begin with a dirt-brown sputter.

Oh, well. Might as well rip off that Band-Aid.

She twists the metal tap, and it squeals in protest and vomits water the color of old blood. Once the brown grunge is gone, she plugs in the stopper and tries to find the right temperature using the left and right knobs. If she'd known she would have a tub like this, she would've brought Epsom salts and bath bombs that would probably stain the ancient tub outrageous neon colors that would give Gail an aneurysm, but all she has is a squirt of shampoo to provide enough bubbles that she'll feel less like a bowl of human soup. She puts one of the Beetlejuice-green towels on the Beetlejuice-green bathmat Gail has helpfully provided and chuckles at how they look as out of place here as she feels.

Carefully chosen towels would be black to go with the black-and-white-checked tiles and once-white walls of the bathroom, but these towels are Skittle green, acid green, Neitherworld-Waiting-Room green. A comforter selected for this bed would be damask or flowers or paisley, maybe, but instead it's the same puffy white duvet you'd find in any nice hotel in America. It's not bad; it just doesn't fit. This place—it's very particular, and it's clear that Gail doesn't have anything chosen to go here.

Sarah looks around as steam clouds the windows.

What's so wrong with this cottage, that they would let it sit empty when they could have one more artist in residence?

She shakes her head. After the murder dolls, maybe she doesn't want to know.

Maybe they always leave one empty, just in case.

She wishes the bathroom windows had curtains, but at least the steam provides some privacy as she takes off her clothes and steps into the half-full tub. The water is deliciously hot, just bubbly enough, and the scent of coconut is a welcome change from dust and lavender. She picks up her phone and opens her reading app. She's halfway into a psychological thriller, something grisly and addictive. Sarah buys these e-books on a discount site and devours them like popcorn. Something about terrible things happening to women is comforting to her, probably because she's a woman to whom terrible things have happened and it's reassuring to know she's not alone.

The seltzer fizzes in her blood, the water softens her skin, and the book takes her somewhere else, somewhere with snow and a watcher outside and a woman with a hidden past. She keeps reading until the water is cool and she reaches The End, then gets out and dries off in the frosty air and puts on her favorite pajamas, the cozy ones Kyle hated. Although she hunts around, she can't find a thermostat—or air vents. Does this cottage seriously not have heating? That's going to be a problem, especially as fall turns to winter.

When she gets ready to settle into the big bed, she realizes that the outlets are so ancient they can't even accommodate a polarized plug. Thank goodness her phone charger doesn't need one, or she'd be in serious trouble. She plugs it in, gratified to see the battery light turn green, then crawls into bed.

Now comes the difficult part.

The world is silent around her but for the muffled roar of the falls and the soft susurrus of the trees outside. She has never before had to fall asleep like this, with a backdrop of blank nothing. She used to go to sleep to music, and then, with Kyle, he always turned on the TV and set the sleep timer so they would fall asleep to the noise and laughter of his favorite shows, almost like happy families and supportive friends were ushering them into their dreams. And, yeah, she could play music on her phone, but . . . well, isn't this why she came all the way out here?

To find a new way of doing things?

She came to the mountains to unplug, de-stress, and shake off the constant noise and business of her life. She came here for the silence. Why then is the silence so aggressive and sinister? Why does it feel like it's plucking at her mind, whispering secrets she can't decode? As she lies there, looking for stories in the water stains on the blank white ceiling, her mind runs a thousand miles a minute, playing back old embarrassments and pangs, flashing the image of the porcelain dolls in the forest, forcing recollections of painful moments with Kyle, moments in which she felt small and broken and hopeless.

"What the hell, brain?" she mutters, rolling onto her side.

She picks up her phone and selects a Jónsi album from her downloads. If she's going to listen to something meaningless, it's going to be on her own terms, and because it's beautiful and in a language she can't understand. The music merges with the whistling wind, the pounding falls, the whispering trees, the calling of hypothetical birds. She falls asleep certain someone is saying something she can't quite hear.

6

Sarah sleeps deeply and remembers no dreams, which is a nice change from all the nightmares she's had while waiting for the right time to leave Kyle. Her phone alarm wakes her for breakfast, and she's stunned at how refreshed she feels, even after two drinks. Over the past year, she began to wonder if she was allergic to alcohol, or if she was in gut dysbiosis, or having hormone issues. When she and Kyle shared a bottle of wine, she was often absolutely wrecked the next morning while he was always fresh as a daisy. But today, she has no hangover, no headache, no raw, scraped-out stomach—this place really is magical.

She struggles with what to wear, how to present herself. She's a resident artist in the mountains of north Georgia, surrounded by yet more artists. She has no one here she needs to impress, no boss or co-workers, no one with control over her future. There is no Kyle to frown and stick out his lower lip should she guess incorrectly at the clothing and makeup required to make a good impression. And yet . . . she is rediscovering herself here, and she wants to be liked and respected as herself. But that doesn't mean she needs to put on a full face of makeup and curl her hair.

She settles for comfy but cute; minimal but, she hopes, respectable. She's a potter, after all, and her actual job here involves getting splattered with clay. Black leggings, a tee and hoodie, plus her tall shearling boots should cover it. She brushes out her hair, puts on eyeliner and mascara but no foundation or lipstick. Maybe one day she'll mature into the sort of complicated, eccentric style Antoinette and Gertrude Rose exude, but today is not that day.

The breakfast bell rings, and she locks the door and sets out. The day is bright and crisp, the forest brilliantly alive all around her. Sunlight spears through the trees as leaves crunch merrily underfoot. Her cottage looks charming and homey to her now, by daylight, and she thinks perhaps it's more fun than the plainer cabins. As she passes by one of the tree houses, Gertrude Rose pops out the door and hurries to join her. There's really no way to avoid the older woman, who's now wearing a more *Sense and Sensibility* dress, filmy white with a green satin sash, her hair done in girlish curls that look more than a little ridiculous. Sarah can't help noticing that she is wearing incongruously modern hiking boots underneath her floor-length skirts.

Gertrude Rose matches Sarah's pace, then grabs her arm so they're walking side by side, attached at the elbow. Sarah wants to jerk away and gain some space, but she's well aware that she doesn't want to have any enemies here. They'll be together for three months, and everyone knows exactly where she lives and works, and she's still so burned from everything that happened with Kyle that there's no way she's going to risk angering someone, or even vaguely annoying them. She'll just swallow down her feelings. She's good at that.

"Such a delightful morning, don't you think?" Gertrude Rose has a genteel British accent today. "I'm in absolute raptures over the sun rising on the mountain. Simply too splendid for words, is it not?"

"It's really pretty," Sarah says, knowing how unenthusiastic she sounds by comparison but unwilling to venture into *pip pip cheerio* territory.

"Pretty, hm." Gertrude Rose clucks. "We must work on your vocabulary and elocution. You are an artist, are you not? Is the world not your canvas, is language not your palette?"

"I'm not really awake before coffee" is all Sarah can say to that.

Gertrude Rose harrumphs. As in, she literally says, "Harrumph." Sarah has never heard anyone say that in her entire life. They walk the rest of the way in uncomfortable silence, arms linked, Gertrude Rose towing Sarah along.

They're the last ones in to breakfast, but there's still plenty of food with no sign that anything got burned today, thank goodness. When Gertrude Rose finally releases her, Sarah makes a break for the coffeepot and adds plenty of sugar and creamer to her mug. She's a coffee snob back home—well, Kyle was—but nothing has ever tasted better than doing things her own way. Once she has bacon, toast, dry scrambled eggs, and a bowl of fruit, she joins Kim, Reid, and Lucas at one of the tables. Gertrude Rose and Antoinette sit together with Gail, Bernie hunkers down by himself with a Dan Brown book, and Ingrid rushes in, fills her travel mug with black coffee, grabs a muffin, and leaves.

"So how was your night?" Kim asks Lucas. "Were you able to sleep at all?"

He clears his throat and stares down at the food mounded on his plate. "Yeah. I mean, it was freaky—the doll thing—but once I knew what it was, I was fine. I just put on a playlist and went to sleep. Did you guys hear the owl?"

Kim shakes her head. "Once I take my Ambien, I am out. Boom. Nothing."

Reid shakes his head, too. "Nope. I use a white-noise machine."

"I heard it," Sarah says. "I like it."

Lucas nods. "It's not that I don't like it. More like . . . it's so random. It doesn't follow a pattern. Music is supposed to follow a pattern, you know? So it trips me up."

After breakfast, they head out to the studios. It's chummy, walking down the gravel road with the people who feel like her friends. They separate, each heading for a different building. When Sarah opens the door to the pottery studio, she's surprised to find half the available space already a huge mess. There are canvas tarps on the floor, big coils of wire, chunks of plywood, and rolling stands, plus all sorts of junk piled on the handbuilding tables.

Oh. Right.

Bernie.

He must've started working yesterday after she left.

At least he's confined his mess to one side of the room, although the visual chaos is not ideal for Sarah's frame of mind. She likes a tidy studio, everything in its place.

She's not going to get that.

Ah, well. She can't change it. She wanted to escape Kyle's fastidiousness, and that means she has to be open to other people's clutter.

Tying on her crisp new apron, she's flooded with memories. Her first clay class, the first time she managed to throw anything functional, the first time she threw a complete matching set of dishes, the day she decided to move to Colorado and leave her program behind, telling herself it would always wait for her. Her last apron was dark-blue denim, crusted with white clay, abandoned on her shelf in the college wheel studio. This apron is black canvas with split legs and big pockets—a splurge to help her reenter a world where she no longer feels like she belongs. She ties her hair back with a bandanna and opens a box of clay, pulling out a twenty-five-pound bag and hunting around for the crusty old scale she spotted yesterday; it has already ended up on Bernie's side amid his jumble of junk.

This part of the process is so satisfying. Sarah loves the meditative state she enters while cutting and weighing the clay and patting it into uniform gray balls full of hope. It feels welcome and right in her hands, her skin soaking it up like lotion after a long time of feeling dehydrated. Soon her palms are grayish white and powdery, and a neat row of six matching clay balls sits waiting on a board. She goes over to the wheels, inspects them, turns each one on and steps on the pedal to see how it sounds and feels. Once, she would've known all the right brands and models, but now she's only heard of one of these manufacturers, so she goes with that one. As she pulls over her stool and puts her clay and tools and water bucket in position, she realizes she's forgotten to trim her fingernails.

"Oh, hell," she mutters.

She tosses a piece of plastic loosely over her clay and hurries back to her cabin, where she trims her nails down to the skin. She generally keeps them relatively short, but she throws better this way. When she gets back to the studio, the door is open, and Steely Dan is blaring. She's only been gone ten minutes, but the entire vibe of the studio has changed. Sarah would like to be the kind of person who didn't take this as a terrible sign, but her heart sinks.

Inside, she finds Bernie rooting through the pink Caboodle she's using as her toolbox.

"Do you need something?" she asks stiffly.

He looks up and smiles like a grandfather about to teach something to a toddler.

"Looking for a wire loop. You got one?"

Sarah goes to her tidy table, where her cleaned loop waits by the bag of clay. She holds it out, and he takes it, swinging it around like a lasso.

"Thanks. My process is a little all over the place." He carries the loop over to his side of the room and starts cutting into a bag of clay. "You good with the tunes?" he shouts. He grins the way men do when they know they've already won the fight.

"I actually work better when it's quiet," she shouts back. "Or maybe with classical playing softly in the background."

He snorts. "Then I guess you're going to have to learn to be flexible. My muse doesn't alight unless there's magic in the air." He keeps working—and doesn't turn down the music.

With a sigh he doesn't register, Sarah heads back to her cottage for her headphones. When she returns, Bernie is singing along at the top of his lungs as he rolls out slabs, oblivious to her.

She sits down on her stool and struggles to draw in a deep breath.

This feeling—like her chest is caving in—is a familiar one. Disappointment. Being made to feel small. A hope dashed. She'd dreamed of a quiet, tidy studio, sunlight streaming in the windows, a little Satie playing in the background as she gently, in her own way, reconnected with her old passion. At no point did she have any clue she would be sharing space with a loud, messy, clueless, overbearing old guy who has no sense of studio etiquette.

"Oops."

She looks up from where she sits at her wheel, and Bernie has just spilled a Yeti mug of coffee all over the floor.

"Can you get me some paper towels?" he asks before turning back to his work.

Sarah starts to stand, but then—no. No way. She did not drive across the country with her entire life in the back of her SUV just to be the idiot housekeeper for a sexagenarian boor. She did not leave Kyle just to fall right back into a position of servitude.

Instead, she puts on her headphones, cranks up her own music, plops her phone in her apron pocket, and slaps a ball of clay in the center of her wheel. Her hands remember how to hold the sponge, how to brace and center the clay. It comes back to her so easily, like riding a bike or kneading bread. She cones up and down until she's certain the clay is centered, then opens a hole and begins to pull up the sides. The clay is the center of her world, her focus, the—

Bernie appears in front of her, squats down with his hands on the rim of her wheel so she has to look in his face.

"I asked if you have any paper towels?" he shouts.

"No!" she shouts back.

"Do you know where they are?"

"I'm kind of busy here."

And then the absolute asshole has the audacity to unplug her wheel. She's so startled that her hands jerk against the clay, collapsing the side and making the half-formed pot fold up and smash with a splatter. Sarah looks up at Bernie with rage in her eyes.

"That was a real dick move," she says, heart yammering in her chest.

He blinks slow, like a reptile, and pulls the headphones off her head. "Yeah, well, I don't particularly like your attitude."

"I assure you the feeling is mutual."

Bernie stands and points at his T-shirt.

DOES NOT PLAY WELL WITH OTHERS

"You just ruined the first pot I've thrown in forever because you can't be bothered to open some cabinets," Sarah says, astonished at herself. She hasn't spoken to anyone like this in—years, if ever. First her parents and then her teachers and then Kyle urged her to be good, be quiet, be ladylike, be the bigger person, just get along. But there is no one here with any power over her, except maybe Gail, and surely Gail would take her side, just now.

"Looks like you ruined it because you couldn't be polite," Bernie observes. "Now can you help me look for some paper towels?"

Sarah stands. "Absolutely not. You spilled your coffee, you clean it up. When do you expect to be out of the studio today?"

The look he gives her is cold and hateful. "If you don't like the way I do things, maybe you're the one who should leave."

"I'm not going anywhere. I'm trying to set up a schedule so we can avoid each other."

Bernie looks at the big schoolroom clock on the wall. "If you want to be that way, fine. I'll take morning to lunch, you can have lunch to dinner."

The look she gives him is equally cold and hateful. "Fine. Don't touch my shit."

Stepping around him, she puts her remaining clay balls back in the bag and twists it shut, then swiftly cleans her wheel, tossing the ruined pot into a waiting slurry bin. She washes her hands, hangs up her apron, and snatches her wire loop from his rat's nest of a workspace. All the while, he just watches her, arms crossed, sneering.

"I taught girls like you," he says. "Think you know everything and the world should just bow down to you. They always washed out.

Didn't have what it takes. I don't care what your generation says—snowflakes don't survive. You might as well leave now."

Holding her toolbox, she stops at the door, knowing full well her cheeks are red and her anger is about to take the form of tears. "This is an art studio, not the army. And I knew guys like you in college—pushy blowhards who bullied everyone else around because most people were too polite to push back. Their art was always derivative and empty."

Before he can respond, she turns and marches out.

"And Steely Dan sucks!" she throws over her shoulder.

She's made an enemy, but she's not sure that she cares.

7

With her hopes of enjoying a quiet studio—at an artist residency—dashed, Sarah heads up to December House. Not to complain to Gail, because that's not the best way to start her time here. But because she has another project she'd like to get started.

When she rings the brass bell, it takes a few minutes before Gail appears looking frazzled. "Tough day?" Sarah asks.

"Personal issues," Gail says, glancing back toward the door she's just passed through. "What do you need?"

"A shovel, if you have one. I said in my application that I'd like to build a pit kiln, and since I can't throw right now, I figured I could start digging the hole."

Gail's head jerks up. "Why can't you work?"

Sarah realizes her mistake too late but can't really take it back, so she tells the easiest part of the truth. "Bernie and I have very different processes, so we've worked out a daily schedule to share the studio. It's all his until noon."

"You two can't work together?" Gail asks. "We've had people share the studio just fine before."

"I just . . . Bernie is really loud and messy, and that doesn't work for me. Hence the schedule. I didn't come here to complain, though. I just thought I might start digging, if you could suggest a good place and let me borrow a shovel."

"Are you asking me to talk to him?" Gail asks, completely unaware of how uncomfortable this conversation is.

Sarah wants to shrivel up and sink into the earth . . . but she's also done taking the fall when she's not in the wrong. "No, please. He'll just say it's all my fault because that's what guys like that do. I mean, you saw his shirt, right? Does not play well with others. Like he's actually proud of it?"

Gail's lips twitch like she thinks Sarah is probably the problem. "Okay, if you think you guys can work it out. I didn't anticipate any trouble. But sure, you can borrow a shovel. The best place for that sort of thing would be up on the hill to the right of the old hotel, where there aren't any trees and it's just weeds. Nothing out there to catch fire, and you can't really see it from the road."

It's one of the sites Sarah had considered and will suit her fine. It'll be nice to have some distance from the studios, and hopefully the Steely Dan won't carry over the pounding of the waterfall.

Gail leads her outside and around to the back of the house, where she rolls up an old garage door to reveal a riding lawn mower and other yard tools, some brand new and others ancient and brown and rusted. She produces a new shovel with a square blade, which Sarah takes with thanks.

"Am I okay to keep this for a while?" Sarah asks.

"We shouldn't need it. That's not the one George used for the possum, by the way. We have a different shovel for that sort of thing."

As they walk back around, Sarah remembers that she has something she wanted to ask Gail when no one else was around.

"We found *The Forgotten Children*. Is there a story behind it?"

"The what?" Gail asks, more flustered than before.

"The art installation in the forest. All the creepy dolls. The plaque called it *The Forgotten Children of Tranquil Falls*. I just wanted to know if it was part of the history of the old hotel or what."

Gail shakes her head. "Oh no no no. Just an art project. Jenni was a creative one. A little odd in the head, but we get those. As you've probably seen. But harmless. It's not based on anything that happened here."

"So, what was the inspiration?" Sarah pushes.

They're back at the front door now, and Gail stops in front of it, arms crossed and brow drawn down. "Who knows? It's art, not the Declaration of Independence. I wasn't the director back then, so I never read the Artist's Statement. In those days, my mother refused to use a computer, so it was all paper copies, and the records got lost all the time." Gail goes inside, and Sarah follows.

"So you weren't the director, but you were here?"

Gail sighs as if this is deeply annoying to answer and Sarah should take the hint. "My mother was the director, and I was the chef. She was getting old and let people do whatever they wanted to, didn't say no to anything or anyone. Things got a bit out of hand. We were more careful after I took over."

"Careful about what?"

Gail pins her with a look that suggests she's in trouble. "Careful about just letting anyone put a bunch of scary dolls in the middle of the forest for no good reason. These days, we have a process for vetting everyone's final project, which you agreed to in the application." She cocks her head, smirking. "Really spooked you, didn't it?"

"It spooked all of us," Sarah admits.

"Yes, well, art exists to make you feel, so the art has done its work. Do you need anything else?"

Even if she has loads of questions, Sarah is aware that this is a dismissal. Armed with her shovel—and conscious of how weird it is to hold a shovel inside a building—Sarah thanks Gail and leaves, which is a relief for them both. Even though Gail insisted that there was nothing to the artwork, she certainly acted rattled. Much to her frustration, Sarah is left with yet more mysteries. What's the story behind the dolls? How did the artist find that information if no one else's internet search mentioned it? And, if the artwork is the product of a troubled mind and doesn't have a greater point outside of its lurid shock value, why hasn't Gail taken it down?

These are questions for another time. Sarah is just learning how to be herself again, out of Kyle's oppressive shadow, and she has been pushed to her limits already. It's not even nine in the morning, and she's exhausted from trying to interact with people who seem impossible to deal with. She recalls, from her college days, that artists are often stubborn, intractable, and socially awkward, but she'd forgotten exactly to what degree. She's glad to have something to do. Digging large holes is easier than peopling.

It's a pretty hike out to the spot Gail recommended. The hill rises off the right wing of the old resort in a bare patch where neither trees nor bushes grow. The falls' roar drowns out all sound, almost like the ringing in your ears after a loud concert, and Sarah walks around until she finds a spot that just feels right and uses the shovel to mark out a shallow rectangle, maybe three feet by five feet. When they used a pit kiln in college, it had already been dug, but it was about this size, and she wants to make sure she has plenty of room for some plates, which take up a lot of real estate.

If she throws ten pieces a day—if Bernie will *let* her throw ten pieces a day—she should have something bisque-fired and ready to pit-fire by next week. She's not going to dig the whole pit right now— it would just fill up with rain by then, probably. But she needs to make sure she's found a good site that's not too rocky or rooty. When she was a girl, she had to help her dad plant bushes, and there was nothing worse than trying to hack through thick pine roots or getting a hole mostly dug and finding what had to be a boulder at the bottom.

She takes a moment to look around and drink in the beauty of the mountains. The hotel rises, dignified and grandiose despite its years, and behind it, rocky crags are covered in thick hemlock trees, the waterfall pouring foamy white down a zagging course of wet gray stone.

Sarah tries to imagine what it must've been like here when the resort was in full swing, the many windows twinkling with gaslights. She can envision couples strolling arm in arm, ladies in delicate, bell-shaped dresses and men in top hats and breeches. She can almost hear the horses whinnying as they trotted up the grand promenade to deposit their wealthy owners into the hands of a tuxedoed concierge.

And here she is now, 150 years too late, digging a hole she plans to set on fire.

She likes that odd juxtaposition. This place was built for rich people, but she has almost nothing, after Kyle. People dressed to the nines vied to spend time here, but she's in what amounts to pajamas, clothes that would've scandalized the original Tranquil Falls clientele.

Maybe that's what she'll focus on for her project—odd juxtapositions.

Dainty porcelain teacups and saucers fired to an ashy black in roughly dug pits.

Craggy, barklike planters painted with violets and roses.

A series of figures in grand dresses from another era, decorated with logos and patterns and visuals straight out of the twenty-first century.

The idea is just a seed now, but she's warming to it. She can see the possibilities webbing out, the tendrils poking up toward the sun.

Tranquil Falls. Even the name suggests a study in opposites.

Can falling ever be tranquil, when most falling objects break?

Choosing a spot in the very center of her proposed pit kiln, she slams down the shovel blade, then steps on it to dig deeper. The ground is hard and compacted, probably contains its own share of clay, but she didn't feel the juddering clank of a rock or the thudding deadness of a root. The first spadeful of dirt is heavy, Georgia red clay mud. Satisfied, she pats it right back down, then tests a corner of the rectangle the same way. Again, just heavy soil with a few small rocks, nothing to suggest she'll have any trouble digging out the full rectangle. The second corner is fine, too. But when she goes for the third corner, the shovel blade cracks into something that's definitely not dirt. When she lifts out the square of clay and scrapes the dirt away, she finds an old wood board.

Sarah is not the kind of person who could stop digging at this point. Maybe she's found a rubbish heap from the resort, or maybe it's an old wagon. The history of this place calls to her, and she scrapes and digs until she finds a corner. The wood is soggy like old cardboard, the rusted nail she sees askew. As she reaches down to brush the dirt off with her hand, the nail wiggles out, and she holds it up to the light, marveling.

It's not a modern nail, with a round, flat head and round shaft. It's rectangular and tapers and looks rough and humble, more real some-how than anything she would find in a yellow box at the hardware store. Such a cool artifact from a different time. She pockets it, plan-ning to take it back to her cottage and wash it off.

With the nail gone, she pries up the corner of the box. The smell that assaults her brings immediate thoughts of the possum she found on her bed. When she shines her phone's flashlight inside, she sees a mass of yellow hair—

And what can only be a skull.

8

This time when she rings the brass bell, Sarah is the one who is flustered. Gail arrives already annoyed by the second interruption, but when she sees Sarah's face, she can immediately tell that this isn't another polite request for a garden implement.

"What's wrong?" she asks.

"Coffin," Sarah manages. "Corpse."

Gail cocks her head. "Are you sure? Over the years, folks have left behind a lot of junk that might—"

"There's a smell."

That, at least, is something Gail can't allow. Sarah leads her out to the hill, where her neatly planned rectangle has become an absolute mess. She had to uncover the entire thing, just to be sure. Gail squats down and waddles into place, and Sarah helps her lift the corner, and this time, the whole top peels back to reveal the very old body of a woman. Her long, blond hair is a tangled wreck, her face turned to the side with a few wisps of dry, leathery brown skin clinging here and there. She's wearing the tattered remnants of a long, white dress over wet-looking brown bones.

Gail shoots upright and stumbles back. "Oh, lord, you weren't kidding. Smells like death—"

"Because it is," Sarah finishes weakly.

"Maybe we should just rebury it, let sleeping dogs lie—"

"No, Gail," Sarah says with more firmness that she generally possesses. "That's . . . desecration. She deserves respect. She was someone's family."

Gail gives Sarah an appraising look before gazing off in the direction of the old resort. "Fine."

They head back to December House, where Gail calls the local sheriff to report an unmarked grave.

"Very old. Uh-huh. Yes, I'm sure it's not a Native American," Gail says peevishly.

"She," Sarah reminds her.

Gail rolls her eyes. "Yeah, I'm sure. *She* has blond hair."

After a few more minutes, Gail hangs up and sighs in resignation. "They want us to protect the gravesite and leave it alone. Someone will be out this afternoon."

"To do what?"

"Hell if I know. I'm just glad it's not my job."

"So this has never happened before?"

Gail looks aghast at this thought. "Of course not! Do I look like someone who digs up corpses for fun? I've lived here my entire life and we've never found anything like this."

It's bothering Sarah, on more than one level. "Is there any way that might be a graveyard? And the stones or markers or whatever were just lost to time?"

"Oh, no," Gail says, deeply affronted. "Like I keep telling you: This was a posh resort. A spa. No one died here, much less got buried here. That's like asking if there's a graveyard at Disney World."

Which sounds great, but it doesn't explain the presence of the coffin. And Sarah is fairly certain that somewhere under the carefully painted cheer of the happiest place on earth, bones of a certain age could be found with a little digging. Still, Gail looks more irritable than ever, and Sarah doesn't want to get on her bad side. "Want me to go cover her up?" she asks.

Gail flaps a hand at her. "Absolutely not. You go back to the studio, or pick some other place to start your kiln. I'm sure this has been quite the morning for you. I'll let you know if they find out anything else. I'm sure they'll just cart her away to a real cemetery." She bustles off through the door, shouting, "George! Get out of your dang pajamas and come help me!," and Sarah knows she should go back to her cottage and wait until lunch, but . . .

The poor woman.

She feels this overwhelming pity for the woman in the coffin. With hair that blond and long, she must've been young. Maybe it was someone visiting on doctor's orders and she succumbed to her disease anyway. People died so easily back then, it seems. Before the body is carted away by people who will just view her as work or a curiosity, Sarah has to see her again. She has to say goodbye.

Knowing Gail will take a while to get George moving, Sarah hurries back out to the hill. It would feel more poetic if there were wildflowers waving or trees bending over the grave, but instead the dirt is cut with the roughness of a stab wound, the box rising like a splinter. The top is still off, lying in the grass where Gail left it. There's a ribbon at the girl's chest, moldering green, and light lace at the sleeves and hem of her dress. The bones of her hands are delicate, knotted into fists over her stomach.

"Goodbye, whoever you were," Sarah says. "I'm so sorry I disturbed you."

She's about to leave, but something is holding her here. The mountains are silent but for the pounding of the falls, a light breeze seeming to tug her closer. She looks again at the corpse, at the elegant bones of her face, the wild nest of her hair, the curled fingers. There's something there, tangled with the slender fingerbones, clutched in the long-still hands—

Another old rectangular nail.

And then Sarah looks at the top of the box, recently turned over.

It is stained brown and covered in gouges, deep scratches. Some are from the nail, it seems, the deeper lines. But there are lighter lines, too, set close together.

Like an animal, scratching to get out.

A fingernail is embedded in the wood.

This woman was buried alive.

9

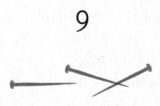

Sarah doesn't tell anyone what she's seen. She takes a pic of the horrifically scarred wood with her phone and wishes she could hold this woman's hand, wishes there was some way to really, truly apologize to her because, long ago, something so terrible happened and no one knew. She glances nervously at December House, knowing Gail and George will be here any moment, and replaces the top of the coffin so that the scratches aren't showing. Uncertain what to do or, really, how to be a person when faced with such tragedy, she walks back to her cottage. Even if she could throw, which she can't because Bernie is taking up all the air in the studio and they made a deal, she's aware that any pots she made right now would be wobbly little wrecks because she herself is a wobbly little wreck.

Her hands shake as she unlocks her front door, and she kicks off her boots and falls into bed. The puffy white duvet cradles her, and she rolls onto her side. Unwelcome thoughts creep in.

What was it like, being buried alive?

At what point did the woman finally give up?

Why was she there in the first place?

Sarah rolls onto her back, her hands mimicking the position of the corpse. It was as if the poor woman scrabbled and fought and scratched, and then finally just sighed and accepted her fate, turning her face away and neatly folding her hands over her stomach.

But—she was buried in a coffin. She didn't crawl away to die like a dog under the porch—other people took care of her, put her there. And yet she was in a nightgown, or maybe some kind of chemise. It didn't look like a formal dress—it was filmy, plain. She was barefoot—Sarah remembers that much. So someone went to the trouble of putting the woman in a coffin, but didn't bother dressing her in her nicest clothes and shoes.

And they didn't check to see if she was truly dead.

Nothing about this situation aligns with what Sarah knows of wealthy people in the 1800s, which she's guessing is when the body must be from, according to the coffin, weirdly rectangular nails, and clothing.

The adrenaline has drained out of her system, and she feels both tired and full of nervous energy. Time passes strangely as she just lies there on her back, her thoughts swirling around a dead woman. When the lunch bell rings, it's a relief. She snaps out of her catatonic state and checks the mirror before heading to the cafeteria. Although she hasn't actually cried, her eyes are wet, and she touches up her mascara and brushes her hair.

Judging by the lively energy of the other artists, no one else knows about what happened this morning, and Sarah isn't the kind of person who's going to tell them. She doesn't want to scare anyone, and she also feels like the dead woman deserves some modicum of privacy. Soon—if not already—strangers will be pulling her out of the ground, inspecting her, probably undressing her, touching her with gloved hands and an impersonal air of business. She doesn't need Gertrude Rose postulating on her lack of hygiene or Bernie suggesting she probably died of the lady crazies.

Sarah fills her plate with salad and ham roll-ups and joins Kim at one of the tables. Kim prattles on about her morning in the studio, cutting glass into hundreds of identical pieces while listening to a self-help podcast for boss babes. Reid joins them, sweat in his hair, the sleeves of his Henley rolled up to show muscular forearms flecked with black ash. Shyly, Lucas sits down next to Reid and, like Sarah, is happy enough to let the more talkative people take the spotlight. Sarah moves her food around her plate, not really hungry, but aware that if she doesn't eat now, she'll be ravenous by dinner. She can still taste the thick stink of the corpse in the back of her throat. The world is muted around her; her body feels thick and slow.

After tossing her picked-apart meal in the trash, she grabs her toolbox from her cottage and heads to the studio, worried that Bernie has decided she's a pushover and will be there despite their agreement. At lunch, he snuck in to grab a to-go plate and disappeared with an apple in his mouth like a barbecued pig.

When Sarah pushes open the studio door, she's immediately relieved that there is no 1970s rock blaring. She finds the remains of Bernie's lunch on one of the handbuilding tables and thinks about throwing it away—but no. She's not his housewife, not the bangmaid to his dime-store Picasso. He's building something out of slabs, supported with wadded-up newspapers and thick wire. So far, it looks like a mermaid. Sarah would bet good money that it will be a disappointingly sexy one.

At least his mess is confined to his side of the studio. The wheel side is untouched, her five remaining balls of clay swaddled in plastic and waiting. She plugs in her wheel, turns on a favorite playlist, and gets to work.

The thing about throwing pots on the wheel is that if your head isn't centered, your pots won't be, either. Long ago, Sarah learned how to get under her own anxiety, to find the current beneath the waves. She's a little rusty, but she knows that place is inside her still, the calm in the storm. The clay feels so welcoming in her hands, and she hasn't forgotten the steps of this dance. Up and down, up and down, flat, hole, widen, pull up. She knows her first few pots are a little bottom-heavy, but as her favorite professor used to say, that's not a throwing problem, it's a trimming problem.

Later on, she'll choose a shape and replicate it to make a set, but for today, she's just playing, making friends with the clay, rediscovering how to shape curves with her fingertips and her wooden rib. She makes a mug, a vase, a bowl, a plate, and a goblet, smoothing each vessel before cutting it off the wheel with her wire loop and placing the finished forms on a board to dry. With no pieces to trim or glaze, it's a short day at the studio, but she is satisfied with what she's accomplished. As long as Bernie isn't in the vicinity, she can still throw. Hopefully he'll keep his side of the bargain and stay out of her way. People like him suck all the art out of the air, and she's not willing to cede this little bubble she's claimed for herself.

Leaving her pieces loosely tucked under a piece of plastic, she cleans her wheel and her tools and hangs up her apron on a hook. As she moves around the room, something prods her thigh, and she remembers: the nail from the coffin. Taking it out of her pocket, she cleans it under the sink, marveling at the sturdiness of it, the homely but noble shape of it. She's going to incorporate it into her work somehow, find some way to make impressions or marks in the clay. If she had the studio all to herself, she would leave it out on a windowsill in honor of the girl in the coffin . . . but knowing Bernie, she doesn't want to explain her stupid little lady voodoo or have him swipe it to use as a bottle opener. Instead, she slips it into the pocket of her apron, a secret and hidden token in this space that's only half hers.

She feels good as she leaves the studio, with that delicious, languid fatigue she always gets after working with clay, almost like she's had a hand massage. She feels satisfied. Part of her had wondered if she'd lost her magic, if she would arrive here and discover that the clay just wouldn't center anymore, if every piece would end up in the slurry bin, waiting to be recycled into something useful by someone who better deserves to be here. She secretly worried that this was one more thing Kyle had stolen from her, one more gift squandered as he slowly consumed her life in small, delicate, unnoticeable bites.

But no—perhaps he denied her the chance to express herself creatively for a few years, but it seems silly now, to think that just being around an asshole could drain away her powers completely and permanently.

By dinner, she's more awake, more herself again, and when Kim asks if anyone knows what the police cars were doing here earlier, Sarah is glad to tell her what she knows. Everyone goes quiet to listen to her tell the story of finding the corpse—until Gail grouchily breaks in with, "Let's not get dramatic here. It's a historic site. There are bound to be a few mysteries."

"Do we need to worry?" Gertrude Rose asks, a hand pressed to her bosom.

"Of course not," Gail snaps. "This property has been continuously occupied for nearly a hundred and fifty years without a lick of trouble. This is just an interesting historical discovery. The DNR lady said she was from the eighteen hundreds, and she probably died of natural causes."

From the natural cause of suffocating underground, Sarah thinks but does not say, because Gail is glaring daggers at her right now as if daring her to stir up more trouble. Sarah can't help but be aware of the fact that she doesn't have a place to live until this residency is over, and if she upsets Gail too many times, Gail has the power to kick her out. She doesn't want to waste her nest egg on a long-term hotel, so she has to play nice. And anyway, why should it really matter how someone died centuries ago? It's not like there's a murderer on the loose today.

"That's so crazy that you found her," Kim says, eyes shining like she's listening to a murder podcast. "Like, out of all this land, you picked that one exact spot. I bet you're great at Battleship."

Sarah focuses on her pudding because that line of thought makes her feel uncomfortable. "Gail pointed it out to me. I mean, if we both thought it was a nice spot to dig a big rectangular hole, I guess that just means that someone else thought so, too. It's a bare area, not much chance of tree roots or rocks. It just makes sense."

"Great minds think alike," Kim says with a knowing nod.

But Sarah isn't so sure she wants to think about whoever buried that coffin, because they buried it with a living person inside of it.

That night, as she snuggles into bed, she feels a new ache in her neck, squeezing down her spine. She hasn't thrown in years, and her body isn't as spry as it was in college. She's got a lot more tension, these days. She lies on her back and plays a downloaded yoga nidra meditation on her phone, willing her body to go limp and slip into the right frame of mind for restful sleep. Big toe, second toe, third toe, fourth toe, pinkie toe. Ball of the foot, sole of the foot, heel, back of the heel. Bit by bit, she allows her body to relax, and she drifts off before the meditation reaches her aching back, much less her head and heart.

10

This is a dream.

The valley falls open before her like the pages of a book she hasn't yet read. Trees line the drive, as stately as guards at full salute. It's spring, and their leaves are light green and dancing. She looks up, dappled sunlight flashing in her eyes. She likes it, the way it burns and blinds her for a moment. When she closes her eyes, she sees lightning against the black, little explosions like the bubbles in her first sip of champagne.

She is excited. She's been counting down the days, waiting for this very moment.

Waiting for today.

In the way of dreams, she's now standing on the front steps of the old hotel, but it's not old at all—it looks like a movie set, the colors thick and vibrant. Everything is freshly painted, gleaming white. A man in a crisp gray suit holds open one of the tall doors, bowing her through. The lobby is too grand to take in all at once. The floors sparkle, white and streaky green squares of stone creating an elegant chessboard with polished wood columns sprouting like carved trees. The ceiling is pressed tin, bright as a new dime. Real live parlor palms spread in the big windows, giving something like privacy to little sitting corners with plush velvet sofas. A parrot sits on a perch, calling hello and bobbing its green head.

"Ah, here are the newlyweds!" the smiling man at the front desk says.

A hand squeezes hers. "Go on, darling. I'll be in the smoking room while you settle," a pleasantly rumbling man's voice says.

There's a key in her hand, heavy brass attached to a metal tag. Number 312. She runs a fingernail over the carved number, enjoys the feel of the thick, shiny metal in her palm. She is walking down a hallway, her boots sinking into the soft carpets. The wallpaper is the color of perfectly clear water in a white ewer, and there are many doors, identical oiled wood. She finds her door and the lock gives a satisfying click as the key turns.

Her room is simple but elegant. The brass bed is bigger than her usual one, and she is struck by the thought that she's never slept in someone else's bed before, and surely other people have lain here in various states of undress. The idea is curious, maybe a little exciting.

The window is open to let in the birdsong and fresh mountain air. Her trunks will be up soon, and she's been given an itinerary to take advantage of the resort's Change of Air prescription, created by a revolutionary doctor from faraway California. She is anxious to begin her life as a wife and feels very adult, taking part in the program here. She looks at her hands, and they're young and soft and unlined, the tightly fitted butter-yellow sleeves all but cutting into her wrists.

Her mind seems to diverge; is this wrong?

She hurries to the dressing table, looks in the mirror.

Ocean-blue eyes, milk-pale skin, rosebud lips, cornsilk hair in a chignon studded with baby's breath.

This is—

Is not—

Her face?

Her eyes shuttle back and forth, trying to stitch together two truths.

"Who are you?" Sarah says with the girl's mouth.

And then . . .

Nothing.

11

The room is dark, and Sarah's covers have fallen off the bed. She's freezing—that's what's woken her up. She clicks on her phone to check the time—after three—and uses the screen's light to remake the bed.

The dream lingers like a drop of sugar on her tongue. It was so real, so clear. Usually, her dreams are in black and white, and it's like she's sitting in the audience of a small movie theater, watching things happen to herself. Unlike other people, she doesn't have control, can't choose what to say or just decide to take off flying. She can only watch from a removed position.

This dream was different. She felt things. Noticed details. Smelled the lilies on the entry table of the hotel. Felt someone else's feelings like echoes in her chest.

And isn't it true that numbers don't stick in dreams? She's certain she's read that somewhere. Yet she can still see every detail of that key and its tag, feel the stamped metal under someone else's fingertip: 312. The number didn't change, not on the tag and not on its matching door.

Since she knew there was no WiFi at Tranquil Falls, Sarah made sure to load a few favorite movies and shows onto her tablet in case of emergency. She'd hoped to return to the land of excellent sleep hygiene while she was here and set herself up for good habits once she began her new life, but that could wait for another night, when she's not so aggressively awake and distracted. Pulling out the tablet, she queues up a favorite episode of one of the baking shows Kyle made fun of her for watching, hoping it will lull her into comfortable boredom and thence, sleep.

It takes several episodes before it works. Her mind holds on to the dream like a dog chewing on a beloved toy. She felt such hope, such trust. There was an innocence to it.

She hasn't felt that innocent in years.

Her phone wakes her at the usual time, although sleep tries to pull her back under. She bathes in the big tub, wishing it was a shower. Her hair feels greasy, and she has to wash her face in the sink, the water annoyingly running down her arms and into her shirt. This place isn't as convenient as what she'd been promised. At least it's not like the room from her dream, which she now realizes didn't have the extra door that would signal a private bathroom.

When she opens the cottage door to leave, she stumbles back with a gasp.

There's a snake on the porch—

No. A dead snake.

A kingsnake, the poor thing.

Harmless. Helpful.

And it's been nearly chopped in half with something not quite sharp enough to cut through the spine. This was no natural death, no dropped meal of a night bird. A human did this.

Someone put it here on purpose.

Are they trying to scare her?

Was it the same person who left the possum in her original cabin?

She steps over the snake and looks all around, as deeply as the forest will allow. The trees go on endlessly, the national forest stretching up to Tennessee. Anyone could be hiding out here, in the wild woods around the valley.

Would Kyle—?

No.

No. He hates the great outdoors, hates sand and dirt and the possibility of rain that even the best weather app can't predict.

And he can't find her. There's no way he could find her.

With a heavy sigh, she finds a stick and uses it to carry the snake around the side of the house, leaving it curled in the leaf litter. Maybe some animal will get a good meal. The poor little thing. Sarah likes snakes, and it strikes her that whoever is trying to scare her doesn't know her very well.

As she walks up to the café, mist writhes around the campus, swathing the old resort in a private cloud like a silver fox stole sitting proudly on a dowager's rounded shoulders. There's a chill in the air, but the birds are a riot of noise as they chatter and sing about the changing season. Breakfast is normal, although everyone is still talking about the body in the coffin. Sarah is distracted; the snake sits unpleasantly in her mind, and the dream is caught in her teeth. What she really needs is time in the studio, but according to her agreement with Bernie, she won't get that until after lunch. He sits alone, wolfing down bacon biscuit sandwiches as he reads a newspaper, snapping each page open and folding it more carefully than she would expect, judging by his workspace. How she envies Kim, with a studio all to herself.

When everyone else heads out to work, Sarah lingers by December House. She has to do something, and it's a beautiful day, so she heads out to where she remembers seeing the blue trail. The trailhead is easy enough to find, surrounded with stained-glass wind chimes in various shades of blue. They sparkle in the light, sharp as knives, and make a musical clink when she brushes one with her fingers.

Maybe she should've brought a map, but Gail said the trails were easy and well marked, each one a loop. It's nice, walking outside on a brisk but sunny day. The trees sway overhead, sun dappling the path ahead as the mist burns away. Every fifty feet or so, someone has helpfully painted a blue rectangle on a tree. Birds sing and scold from overhead, and each corner or rise brings something delightful. A quartet of old pines are fitted with little fairy doors and windows and door-mats made of glazed clay. One has two pairs of red galoshes, another has window boxes full of carnivorous plants. She sees something gold winking in a patch of moss and finds a handmade bird nest with three gilded eggs. The indigo bridge over the burbling creek looks like some-thing out of a Monet painting, and the rainbow-hued birdhouses hanging here and there have been accepted as homes to bluebirds that complain of her interruption as she walks past.

This is exactly what she'd hoped to find here. Not dolls and corpses but moments of mercy and magic. She begins to imagine an art instal-lation, delicate teacups swaying in the branches of a plum tree, catch-ing the pink blossoms every spring and making rainwater baths for sparrows all summer.

As she walks alongside the creek, the rushing water gets louder. This must be the trail that leads to the small waterfall—not the big one behind the old resort, but still something impressive enough to make a trail worthwhile. The path leads her through a grove of moun-tain laurel and then she's facing a beautiful pool surrounded by a low rock wall. The wall has been built with a wide top, almost like a bench, and she's drawn to sit there and peel off her boots and socks. The water is frigid, her feet turning to ice the moment her skin is submerged, but she likes it. It makes her feel alive, causes nerves to thrum up and down her body in a way they haven't for years. As she's learning, life with Kyle made her numb. She lost all connection to her own physi-cality. A book she read called this dissociation, but she doesn't like that term. It makes it sound like she floated up out of her body to bob along the ceiling like a balloon.

It wasn't like that. It was more like closing a door so she would feel things less, would hurt less.

It worked.

But now the door is opening again. She has allowed herself to feel anger, and now she will try to remember how to feel joy.

One comes more easily than the other.

The anger was there all along.

"They used to come here as part of their cure," someone says.

Sarah startles and jerks to standing, her body ready to run, but it's just Ingrid. The goth photographer stares at her from halfway up a tree, her old-timey camera hanging by a green velvet strap around her neck. As the panic drains away, Sarah realizes that now the ankles of her jeans are soaking wet and freezing.

"You just about gave me a heart attack," she mutters, sitting back down. "Someone needs to bell you, like a cat."

"Just what I need as a woman in America. Less freedom."

Sarah shakes her head and closes her eyes, trying to regain her chill, but it's impossible with Ingrid's cold gaze shining down. The girl is, as ever, in all black, torn leggings with black shorts and a frayed black sweater over a black turtleneck. Black boots, black half gloves, black beanie. It must be impossible for her to find anything in her closet.

"Stretch your legs out again," Ingrid commands.

With a sigh, Sarah follows directions.

Then she jerks her feet back in.

Is she that conditioned from Kyle that she just does what anyone randomly tells her to?

Ingrid sighs forcefully and hops down from the tree. Sarah can't really predict what she's going to do, which makes her uncomfortable. She just can't get a read on Ingrid.

"They thought cold water would calm agitated minds and treat depression," Ingrid says. "Hydrotherapy. Sometimes they put people in tubs, and other times they wrapped them in sheets. Sometimes they just sprayed them. The doctors probably encouraged people to sit in this pool. You can still see the stones they put in, like a couch."

When Sarah looks, sure enough, there are flat stones arranged near the waterfall where the water gets deeper, a place to sit and a surface to lean back against.

"How'd you know that?"

Ingrid snorts. "Google."

"I googled it, too, but I didn't find anything about that."

"Then you don't know the right things to google. I'm an expert in hidden archaic shit with a minor in antiquated cures for crazy."

"Why?"

"Because I'm wondering if they're any better than today's cures. From what I can tell, nothing has ever worked. We shouldn't have swung down from the trees, much less crawled out of the ocean."

Sarah rolls her jeans up higher, plants her feet in the soft mud so she can squish it between her toes. "That's a dark way of looking at it."

"Dark is how I look at everything." And a beat later, "So you're in the doctor's house. What's it like?"

Ingrid sits down on a rock and crosses her legs. She does not stick her feet in the pool; her outfit is way too complicated for that sort of whimsy.

"What do you mean, doctor's house?"

"I can't believe you don't know any of this," Ingrid begins, finally showing some excitement. "Okay, so you know this place used to be a resort for rich people or whatever, right?" Sarah nods; she knew that much. "Well, it was run by two doctors, Henry Calloway and Warren December. December, like December House, see? They built it together as a resort and as a way to try out their"—she makes quotation marks with her fingers—"revolutionary cures."

"Cures?" The word tastes odd on Sarah's tongue. "I thought it was more like rich women going to a spa."

Ingrid shrugs. "A little of column A, a little of column B. They didn't come here to swan around. They came here to follow a specific regimen. They called it a Change of Air."

That phrase pings off Sarah's memory, but she doesn't know why.

"They arrived and were given loose dresses and soft shoes. They were fed specific diets at specific times. They had schedules of treatments to follow, even if the treatment was like, sit in the nice waterfall pool for an hour. They came here to feel better."

Sarah snorts. "I can relate."

"Midlife crisis?" Ingrid asks.

A sharp look. "Jesus, how old do you think I am?"

"Old enough to look like you need a reboot."

This is perhaps too close to home. Sarah wishes she could poke a paper clip into a secret slot and do a hard reset, wiping the last six years out of her memory, return everything to default settings, but this is the best she can do.

"I'm like five years older than you," she says.

"Feels like more." Ingrid holds the old camera up to her eye and looks around. Finding nothing worth snapping, she plucks a leaf off a nearby tree and tosses it in the water, but no matter which direction she turns her camera, she apparently can't discover an angle that pleases her.

"So what's your body of work?" Sarah asks. "For the exit show."

Ingrid looks up, judging her. "I'm going to get into the old resort and take pictures of whatever I find."

That takes Sarah by surprise. "The one thing we're not allowed to do," she muses.

"Yeah, well, art comes from risk and discomfort. Although I'll admit that hearing Gail shriek is not my kind of discomfort. She seems tragically uptight for a hippie artist, don't you think?"

"God, she really does." Sarah snatches a stone out of the pool, and when she washes off the mud, realizes it's an old glass marble. "Are you really going to sneak into the resort?"

Ingrid nods and snaps a pic of the marble in Sarah's hand. "That's the plan. I've scoped it, but so far, it looks tighter than a turtle's butt. There's only one gate in the fence, and it's got a huge lock and a thick chain. Barbed wire all around the top. Still, there's got to be a way in."

"Isn't it condemned, though? Dangerous? What if you, I don't know. Fall through a hole in the ground?"

There's that I'm Young and Invincible and Know Everything look, suggesting Sarah is an idiot.

"I've been in condemned buildings before. Urbex. That's kind of my thing. I applied here with shots from the zoo and forest, though. I didn't want the selection committee to know what I was going to do. That's part of the fun. And you're one to talk. That cottage they put you in is original to the property and is probably chock-full of lead and asbestos."

She stands and slips the camera strap back over her head. When she holds the camera up to her face, Sarah notices the pebbled leather and shiny metal. This camera probably uses real film.

"Don't look at me," Ingrid says in that same bossy but disdainful tone.

"I'm looking at your camera."

"It's a Leica. Best they ever made. Now look at the waterfall. Think about the corpse. About how she once sat here, probably, in this same pool, watching the same waterfall, feet in the same water."

This time, Sarah doesn't resist. Ingrid has struck a chord.

The corpse—the girl—she likely did sit here, or over on the bench. She came to Tranquil Falls because she was looking for something, some magic cure, or at least a sense of calm or fulfillment, or maybe a break from her real life. Whoever she was, whatever her story might've been, she was missing a piece of herself, too.

Snap.

"Got it," Ingrid says, smug.

Without another word, she turns and walks into the forest, following the path back toward the main campus. Sarah dislikes her less now, but that doesn't mean she likes her. The belling metaphor was accurate; Ingrid is indeed like a cat, the wild kind that mostly hisses but will occasionally creep near with a creaky purr. Sarah hopes that the girl dislikes her less, too, because if Ingrid manages to get inside the old resort, she wants to see those photos. Wants to see the place where the girl in the coffin once walked. The dead girl is a puzzle, and Sarah feels called to give her the attention she's been denied for a hundred years or more. She found the body, and now it feels as if she owes a debt.

But what was it Ingrid said—that Sarah's cottage was original to the resort, like December House? It makes sense, considering it's nearest to the main building and looks completely different in style and form than the other, more obviously artist-built cabins. The wallpaper is like nothing you can buy these days, the furniture ancient. When she gets back, she'll have to look around, see if there are any remnants left behind by the doctor who used to live there.

Now that her mind is turning, she starts to wonder if her cottage really does have two stories. Maybe someone walled off the upper story, which might mean that there are still all sorts of interesting things up there. While Ingrid focuses on breaking into the resort—which seems like a very bad idea to Sarah—maybe she'll take a closer look around her cottage to see if there's a way upstairs.

Perhaps she came here to discover herself, but what she's discovered so far is her drive to solve puzzles. She'd almost forgotten that, around Kyle. He told her puzzles were a waste of time, that she was always looking for reasons and answers and patterns when in reality life was messy and chance was lumpy. He told her that it was nonsensical and crazy, always looking for answers that aren't there.

There's something here, though—she can feel it.

This place is a puzzle that wants to be solved.

12

That afternoon, Sarah focuses on throwing vases. Fat-bellied vases and skinny vases and amphoras and triple bubbles and whatever shapes her fingers find. She chokes their necks until they can each hold just a stem or two, a single rose or perhaps a spray of wildflowers. She likes the idea of repetition on a theme, and it's a challenge to make them all utterly different and yet similar enough to work as a set. When she's done, ten vases are lined up on her shelf. Yesterday's pots are still wet, so she loosens their plastic to help them dry and harden.

There's no sign of Bernie, thank goodness. Well, there are signs he's been here—an apple core, a beer can, that stupid boombox surrounded by a stack of cassettes. His mermaid sculpture is indeed busty, her hair as big as the girl in a Def Leppard video. He's begun another one, this version on her back with her tail in the air, and Sarah is already bored. How did he get past the selection committee, when his work is so eye-rollingly sexist and derivative? What was his Artist's Statement, "Yay, boobs!"? Why should she have to share the studio with a slob who thinks an army of horny mermaids is making a statement?

She cleans her station and hangs up her apron before heading back outside. Curious about the other buildings, she peers into the window of Reid's studio. Fortunately, his back is to her, straining as he reaches into a fire with big tongs and pulls out a piece of metal. He's sweating, wearing safety goggles and big gloves and boots, wailing at his anvil with a hammer. His studio is full of big machines she can't name, dozens of tools hung neatly on pegs. It's tidy but dim beyond the reach of the fire, almost primal, with just a leather messenger bag and a notebook on the table beside his coffee mug.

Next she moves on to Antoinette's calligraphy studio—the printing studio. At first, she's worried Antoinette will notice her watching, but the older woman's sole focus is on her work. The studio is all white inside, bright and clean. There are shelves and presses around the walls and tables down the middle, and Antoinette sits at a light box in the center of the room, carefully drawing lines with a pencil and ruler. Her paper is in neat stacks, her pens in a handmade cup, her inks nestled in a beautiful wooden box. Sarah is envious of how it must feel to work in this space—everything where it belongs, bright lights, the gentle burble of jazz.

Everyone else, it seems, has their studio set up to their own liking even though they've only been here for one day. Resentment pings in her heart, that Bernie's culture has already smothered her own in the studio. Entropy and cruelty win again. She tromps off.

When she looks in the next window, the music studio is a little different from the other all-white spaces, with thick burgundy carpet and walls covered in gray foam. Sarah is as fascinated by the egg chair and record player as she is by the variety of instruments set up around the edges of the room—guitars on stands, cases for stringed instruments, and a gleaming black piano. Lucas is in the egg chair, tucked up like a spider and smiling with big headphones over his ears. *Good for him,* she thinks. The poor kid deserves a cozy sanctuary.

Next door, the stained-glass studio is a one-woman factory, with color-coded piles of iridescent cut glass and perfect lines of half-finished suncatchers marching down the tables. Kim is wearing

AirPods and moves from station to station like a nervous bee trying to hit all the flowers. Sarah wonders how she got into the program, because Gail doesn't seem like the kind of person who would respect industry over art, but she admires Kim's drive to succeed and her willingness to spend that much time doing the same work over and over to win back her family. Maybe Gail does, too.

By contrast, Gertrude Rose's studio has a comfortable sort of chaos, an overstuffed room filled with sewing mannequins and looms and spinning wheels and stacked bolts of fabric and boxes of notions. The costumer is muttering to herself, her teeth clenched around several pins as she sticks them into the rich damask hanging off a dummy's waist. Looking up, she sees Sarah watching and smirks, giving her a bow as if to suggest that Sarah should be honored to catch her at her work.

Beside the fiber studio, Sarah finds a rabbit hutch, surprised to see two enormous white rabbits with long, puffy hair. She sticks her fingers through the wire mesh, and one rabbit hops over to nibble at her in a curious manner. Is Gertrude Rose going to shave the rabbits to make yarn, she wonders, and did she bring them herself? If she asks Gertrude Rose, she will be here for hours, so she bids the rabbits farewell and continues on to her current home, ignoring the photography studio completely. With a couple of hours before dinner, she's got time and light to really look around her cottage closely in a way she hasn't bothered to before.

The wallpaper is old and well stuck, but she runs her fingertips over the walls and around the corners, looking for a seam or the telltale bump of a door or bricks or something to denote a cover-up or possibly a "Cask of Amontillado" situation. She can't find anything, not in the main room or the bathroom. She wonders for a moment why there's no kitchen or even a little kitchenette, but then it occurs to her—whoever lived here wouldn't have needed to cook. They could've taken their meals up at the resort, where someone else did all the work. If Ingrid is indeed correct, it makes sense that a doctor would choose to build his home here, just a little removed from the hotel and his—well, *patients* is really the only word that serves. But he would most likely need his own office at home, a place with a desk and files.

Not until her third perambulation does it occur to her that there's a very obvious place where a door might be easily hidden: behind the bookcase. It appears to be handmade of solid wood, but it's not a built-in; it's pushed up in a corner, flush to the wall. The baseboard has been cut away to accommodate it, which feels like a clue. But before she unloads a ton of old books, she's going to make sure she's right.

Sarah steps outside, realizing that she's never walked around this cottage, not any farther than it took to deposit the dead snake out of sight. Why would she? There's one door, and it's not like there's a secret Jacuzzi out back. As she walks around the corner, feet sinking into the leaf litter, she's surprised to find a knee-high black metal fence leaning crookedly, outlining a rectangular plot. Cold trills down her neck, bunching her shoulders.

This can only be a grave—maybe a family cemetery.

There are no headstones or statuary, and the ground is covered in years and years of leaves and pine straw. Gingerly, she steps over the fence, careful not to touch it, as it looks like the slightest breath of air could knock it over. There must be some kind of memorial—or else, why the fence? She once did gravestone rubbings in a middle school art class and remembers that sometimes there were plaques at the foot of graves from this period of time. When she gently probes around the logical place for such a thing, she feels something firm under her shoe. Rubbing away the years of neglect, she finds a tarnished brass plaque.

ELIZABETH CALLOWAY, it reads, 1861 TO 1898.

Nothing else. No *beloved wife* or *cherished daughter* or even a sculpture of flowers or the winged memento mori skulls that were so popular back then.

"Elizabeth," she murmurs. "What happened to you?" She wonders if this woman went by Liz or Beth or Bettie. And how did she die? It seems odd that the wife of a prominent doctor would pass away so young, at only thirty-seven, but there have always been so many ways to die. Tuberculosis was big back then and the reason so many people went to the mountains for fresh air. Even the most skilled doctor couldn't cure that. Cancer, dysentery, being crushed by a horse.

The fenced-in plot is the right size for two graves, and yet there isn't a plaque on the other side. Maybe space was left for the doctor, but he never joined his wife? So many mysteries.

With a nod of sorrowful respect, Sarah steps back out of the bounds of the fence and returns her attention to the cottage. There are windows around the second story, all boarded up . . . but one around back still has a few shards of glass clinging to the frame, which suggests that these were once real windows and not just set dressing. A thrill zips through her; now she just has to find a way upstairs.

She squints at the corner where the bookcase is, and she's fairly certain the outer dimensions of the cottage don't match up with the inner dimensions. Hurrying inside, she begins pulling the books off their shelves and stacking them lovingly, carefully, across the room. Some of the books, she sees now, are ancient, and when she opens an old leather Kipling, it is indeed from the 1890s.

Dust fills the air, and she turns on a playlist so there will be something to listen to besides the thump of books. She'll have to show them to Ingrid, she thinks; they'd look great in black-and-white photos. Does Gail even know what's in here? There are probably very valuable tomes hidden among the old copies of *National Geographic* and science-fiction paperbacks from the 1960s.

When the huge bookshelf is finally denuded, she takes a deep breath, sips from her water bottle, and considers the many ways this could all go wrong. Maybe the bookshelf is actually attached to the wall and all this work has been in vain and she is, as Kyle often suggested, crazy. Maybe she'll start to pull on it and it'll fall apart like Ikea furniture, leaving her with a huge mess and another reason for Gail to consider sending her away.

It doesn't matter. She's in it now. She has to know.

She grabs the side of the bookshelf and pulls, but it's heavier than expected—not at all like Ikea furniture, actually. This wood is sturdy and hardy, hand-hewn and hand-joined. She has to brace herself and heave with her shoulder to make it budge at all while keeping it from toppling over completely.

The shelf is maybe two inches away from the wall now, and when she looks behind it, there it is: the open doorway. The framing has been removed so that the bookshelf can sit flush against the wall, leaving only a roughly sawn hole in the old boards, its interior a deep velvet black. She pulls the shelf out a little farther and can now see that the wallpaper behind the shelf is gloriously colorful, the delicate flowers picked out in butter yellow and blush and lavender, a far cry from the muted tones that now read as a uniform gold. The rush of satisfaction at solving this riddle bubbles in her blood, and she uses that energy to wedge the bookshelf away from the wall until there's enough room for her to just barely squeeze into the hole that was once a door. Before she's fully through that pitch-black void in the wall, she remembers her phone. Music off, flashlight on, she passes into the unknown.

The light reveals exactly what she'd expected: stairs.

They immediately turn left, then continue upward. She shines her light all around. The black board steps are still shiny with old paint, slightly worn in the center, the dull wood grain showing through. Sarah feels a sense of heaviness, or gravitas, almost like she should be carrying a candelabra or lantern instead of an iPhone. The walls are whitewashed, pebbly, and cold to the touch. Each step creaks underfoot as she tests its strength, and the space smells like an old man's held breath. When she reaches the top of the staircase, she's met with an open doorway. It's freezing up here, motes of dust dancing in her phone's light as she steps into history.

She is in a small hallway. Not a drop of daylight shines in through the boarded-up windows. There is dark, and then there is a darker dark, the sort of dark that is almost solid. Only the bright-white light of her phone makes it bearable to be here. She steps up to the first room and finds an office. There's a wall of wooden bookshelves, a worktable, and a desk with a chair. A terrifying form on the table turns out to be an old ceramic model of the human head, but the skull beside it is truly a skull, and, she's certain, a real one. A rag rug nearly trips her as she steps up to touch a ledger spread out on the worn wood desk.

There are so many books and papers and files that she could spend hours investigating the tiny space, but for now, she wants to know what else is up here. The room is cramped and dark and still, and she can't help feeling like she's being watched, like someone is very close nearby and holding their breath so she won't feel a breeze on her neck. She spins, but of course there's no one there. There would be no way to mask the sound of feet creeping up those creaky, croaky steps.

She knows, at an intellectual level, that it's perfectly safe. No one is here, and no one has been here for many years. If someone did approach, she would hear it, thanks to the utter absence of sound. The floors seem solid, the structural integrity of the cottage intact. And yet, at an animal level, every cell in her body is screaming danger, urging her to run down the stairs and burn the entire cottage down.

Silly animal body, she thinks to herself. *Silly cells.*

This is fine.

There is no danger.

Back in the hall, she goes to the next open door, the middle room. This one features opulent wallpaper with big, blowsy roses and a bed made up with a pretty mauve coverlet and ivory pillows. She can't believe no animals have wriggled into this secret upstairs to chew paper and burrow in the soft blankets, but everything appears untouched, as if someone just boarded up the windows and walked away one day, leaving everything perfectly preserved. In addition to the bed, there's a small armoire and a vanity with a mirror and ewer. A hairbrush rests on the table, and Sarah picks it up and holds it directly under her flashlight. Long, dark hairs cling to the ancient bristles, glistening in the artificial light.

There's a creak behind her, and she drops the brush with a clatter and spins, pointing her phone's flashlight back toward the door.

There's no one there.

Because no one *could* be there.

It's simply not possible.

Feeling foolish, all the hairs on her arms standing up, she squats to pick up the brush and then carefully replaces it on the vanity, right where she found it. She hurries out of the room without opening any of the vanity drawers or the doors of the armoire. The air is too cold, too still, as if this moment were captured in an icy shard of glass.

It's warmer in the hall, somehow, and she moves to the last door, the only door that's closed. There's no lock on it, at least, and it pushes open silently, as if someone has taken great care to oil the hinges. She shines her light around the room and takes a shuddering breath, almost a gasp.

This—it was a nursery.

Not the sort of rambling nursery from Fanny Price's neglected youth at Mansfield Park, but a little cubicle the size of a walk-in closet with barely enough room for a tall, spindly wooden crib, a narrow dresser, and a rocking chair. The wallpaper is striped in yellow and cream, and a few oiled wooden toys sit atop the dresser—a rattle, a ball, a horse. They look untouched, as if someone painted them just yesterday and listed them in an Etsy shop.

Sarah stands over the crib, gazing down at the carefully folded afghan within. She can't stop herself from reaching out to touch the soft wool, half expecting it to turn to dust under her fingertips. It doesn't. Things used to be made to last. Like the toys, the blanket looks like it was never used.

More curious than ever, she opens the top drawer of the dresser. There's a dish of big diaper pins, several stacks of linen. The next drawer has long, white gowns. She pulls out the top one, marveling at the perfect embroidery around the neck and the tiny buttons. Amazing that babies were once dressed so formally, so fussily.

When she holds the tiny dress up to her nose, it smells like cedar and bleach. There's not a single mark or stain on it.

Nothing here, it seems, ever served its purpose.

Sarah holds the tiny dress to her chest as sadness washes over her like a wave from far away that has traveled an eternity just to lap at her heart. Something happened to either the baby or the mother or both. Whatever happened, it wasn't good. Lovingly planned nurseries full of beautiful, handmade clothes and toys don't just get hidden away behind closed doors for no reason. The dresses should be stained, the rattle riddled with the marks of perfect tiny teeth. A tear slips out as she carefully, carefully refolds the gown and puts it right back where it's been for more than a hundred years.

Now she can't help thinking back to the small, homely cemetery out back. Elizabeth is there, dead earlier than she should've been. There's no grave marker on the other side of what's clearly a two-grave plot. Is her child buried there? Or did Elizabeth die giving birth?

All the answers fill her to the brim with pain, squeezing her throat shut with sorrow for these forgotten lives locked up long ago.

"I'm so sorry," she says to the empty room.

The house seems to sigh in response.

And then—a knock.

She startles, but this is no haunting. Someone downstairs is knocking on her door.

13

Closing the nursery door behind her, softly, gently, as if an infant slept soundly within, Sarah hurries down the dark hall and into the twisting stairwell. The steps are too tall for modern feet, and she nearly trips and falls but catches herself on the wall. The knocking grows louder as she gets closer, and when she squeaks out of the hole in the wall and past the bookshelf, she can hear Reid calling, "Sarah, you in there? You missed the dinner bell."

Sure enough, time has passed, and evening has fallen with uncanny speed. While she was up there in the frozen dark, the world outside kept on spinning, and now her stomach grumbles in sudden resentment. When she opens the door, Reid is standing there with a plate covered with foil, a glass of ice water, and a crooked smile.

"I figured you just got caught up in the studio," he says. His brows scrunch down. "Why are you covered in cobwebs?"

Oh.

She didn't think about what she might look like after exploring the second floor. She must be a complete mess. She checks the time on her phone and grimaces. It felt like twenty minutes, but it was more than two hours. How did that happen? It can't be right.

Reid is still holding out the plate, and his arm is probably getting tired, and his smile is growing uncertain, so she takes it and heads for the couch, pulling the coffee table closer.

"I was exploring. Any chance you brought silverware?"

He pulls a napkin-wrapped packet from his back pocket and places it on the table, along with the water. "Want some company?"

Not really, not right now.

Not as she grapples with what she's just seen and how time has strangely, unnaturally slipped away and how she can't stop thinking about that empty crib. Not when she's skittish around handsome men after what happened with Kyle.

"Sure."

Okay, fine.

Now.

It feels like the right answer, and just because he's a man doesn't mean he's interested in her.

Then again, he's the one who brought her a plate, not chummy Kim or stern but motherly Gail or bossy Gertrude Rose.

She takes off the foil to find roast chicken and veg with a light salad on the side, topped with a few strawberries. He took care when he put this together for her—or someone did. It feels awkward, eating when he isn't, but at least he's sitting in a chair off to the side rather than just staring directly at her. Like they were on a date or something.

"So did you have a good day in the studio?" she asks, hoping to distract him while she chews. It doesn't appear that he's noticed the mess she's made yet. His back is to the bookshelf corner, at least.

He nods and leans back, testing the old chair and finding it sound. It does look like it might collapse at any moment, but so far everything in this cottage has proven to be made with a level of care and sturdiness that is rare these days. "Good enough. I came out here to try working big for once. I have a studio in my garage back home, but the neighbors complain about the hammering and smoke. My wife wanted to be in one of those real tight-knit neighborhoods, but those folks do not like any noise besides their own leaf blowers."

She glances at his ring finger. There is no ring. No tan.

He sees her looking.

She stuffs more food in her mouth, her cheeks going red.

"She died," he says simply, running a hand through his hair, which seems to be a nervous habit. "Car accident. Last year. Stupid fuckin' drunk driver went straight through a red light. She'd gone out to pick up Thai food because she hated all the extra fees the delivery services add on."

"I'm sorry."

"I know. Me, too. Thanks." A pause. "I never really know what to say to that. It doesn't get any easier, you know?"

"I don't know. I can't imagine."

And she can't. She can't imagine losing someone she loves because she's never loved someone that it would hurt to lose.

She thought she loved Kyle, but when she realized she didn't, a lot of things made so much more sense.

"I should probably move away, get a fresh start, but it feels almost . . . like I'd be a traitor, you know? She loved that house. Got herself a saw and did all this reno stuff. It's beautiful. But every time I think about giving away one of the fluffy blankets she tossed over a couch or chair, I pick it up and smell her perfume and realize I'll probably die there, never having changed a thing."

Sarah swallows the mouthful of food she's been chewing and chewing. This is . . . a lot of information from a stranger. He burps lightly into his fist, and she notes he's a little flushed.

"Are you drunk?" she asks gently.

Reid looks away and stands, pacing as he talks. "Maybe. Probably. I'm sorry. I didn't mean to come here and barf my baggage on you. It was just . . . I was just going to bring the food. But there's something about you. You listen. It's like you're waiting for something, and it's okay to fill that space."

She loads a perfect bite onto her fork. When she decided to come here, she told herself she would be more honest with people. Swallowing down her thoughts and feelings to avoid ridicule was something that happened around Kyle, and she grew to hate how she would just let herself be silenced. She grew to crave his love and attention, and thus fit herself into the cramped box he built for her.

She won't do that anymore.

It doesn't matter if Reid is handsome and interesting and, well, here.

She's just going to say what she feels.

"People have taken advantage of that fact in the past," she says carefully. "I've gotten too accustomed to waiting my turn. In my last relationship, I got the message that what I had to say didn't matter, so I got good at being quiet. But I don't mind listening when it's something real. It sounds like you needed to say what you said."

"Okay if I sit back down?"

She nods and takes the bite waiting on her fork. It was nice of him, to bring the real silverware.

"I don't want to monopolize the conversation for sure. I'll admit I haven't really talked to anyone about it except my therapist. But, well, Kim brought a bottle of wine to dinner, one of those double-sized ones, and it went down real easy. I would've brought you a glass, but Gertrude Rose and Antoinette got their hands on it."

Sarah smiles. "I can imagine. I don't think either of those two gives a single thought to anyone else."

"Nope. Well, Gertrude Rose thinks a lot about how to keep Lucas from drinking. I can't imagine giving that much of a shit about someone else's kid when they can't even drive and there are no other kids to party with. What's he gonna do, TP somebody? They'd just call it art."

As she composes her next bite, Sarah asks, "Got any kids?"

Pain flashes across Reid's face like he's just received a nasty shock. "No. We were going to. It was in the works."

Sarah flinches, too. Whether that means his wife was already pregnant or they were trying, it's still sad. She wanted to have kids back in

Colorado, but Kyle kept putting it off, saying they could get married and start a family when he hit this milestone or that milestone, always moving the goalposts just a little further away. Even though she's young, she's always wanted to have babies; her clock is ticking, and she's had a pillow over it since the last time Kyle snapped at her. The muffled noise is as regular and faithful as her heartbeat.

He looks up, trying to hold himself together. "You got kids?"

She shakes her head. "Wanted them. Still do. But now I'm glad I didn't have kids with him. My ex. He was . . ."

A narcissist? A gaslighting jerk? An emotionally abusive asshole? A monster?

"He wouldn't have been a good father."

He lets her get a few bites down before he asks, "Why? If you don't mind my asking. You get to the age where you want to be a father, and you had a shitty father, and you wonder what it takes to makes a good one, you know?"

This is an interesting question. She hasn't spoken about Kyle to anyone other than Reddit—and Kim, briefly, at the bonfire—mostly because he cut her off from all her friends and discouraged her from making new ones and told her that therapists are vultures and psychology is a lie. It's hard to describe, actually; in the moment, he didn't seem awful, but in the aftermath, he did, and she worries that if she tries to explain it to someone who doesn't have time for six years of backstory, she'll just sound melodramatic.

"He's an anesthesiologist. You know how surgeons are egotistical? He's like that. The kind of guy who expected dinner on the table without ever actually asking for it, then gave backhanded compliments about the food, then, when I started tearing up, denied he'd done anything remotely cruel and called me a drama queen. It doesn't sound that terrible when I say it out loud, but . . . it added up. He's the kind of guy who bought me a treadmill for Christmas when I'd asked for a stand mixer, if that makes any sense."

Reid makes the exact face a cat makes when it smells something terrible. "Oh, no, I hate that kind of guy. But . . ." He pauses. "How'd you end up with someone like that?"

Because you seem smart, he doesn't say, but she hears it in the silence.

Sarah pushes her plate away and leans back. Something about this place makes it easier to open up. They're tucked away in the mountains, away from everything, away from cameras everywhere and phones listening in and social media and prying eyes. They're in an ancient cottage that time has forgotten, the door closed, and no one within a five-minute walk.

"Because I should've seen it coming, right?" She snorts a laugh and shakes her head. "See, guys like him don't start out like that. They're predators. They're wolves that spend a lot of time fashioning well-fit tuxedos out of sheep's wool." As she was preparing to escape him, she read a lot of books on the topic, found new words for things she thought she alone had experienced.

"We met in college. I was a poor art student, and he came in like a hurricane. Fancy dinners and dozens of red roses that made my roommates swoon. He gave me a diamond necklace on my birthday when my friends' boyfriends were giving them homemade coupon books for massages and car washes. They call it love-bombing, and it works. I felt like a princess. He was older, so mature and refined, and when he looked at me, it felt like I was in a spotlight. When he moved out west for his residency, I went with him. It was like I couldn't breathe without him. I thought it would be an adventure. But once we were out there, thousands of miles away from my friends and family . . ." She looks down.

This part feels so shameful.

"It was like Dr. Jekyll and Mr. Hyde. Everything I did was wrong. I was letting myself go, I wasn't fitting in with his work friends, I couldn't find a job worthy of his wife. God, he even complained about how I did the laundry. I got to where I'd do anything for a kind word. And even so, sometimes it wouldn't come. My self-esteem did a nosedive."

And then she holds her head up high, feels her jaw clench with determination, like she's a pot that's been waiting forever to boil over. "So I left. And I came here. I was going to get a degree in ceramics, but I never finished it. Up until yesterday I hadn't touched clay in five goddamn years."

Reid reaches over, gently, and puts his hand over hers where it rests on the old burgundy velvet. His hand is rough and warm, so different from Kyle's smooth ones.

"Good for you," Reid says. "Goddamn good for you."

She turns her head a little, and their eyes lock. The light in her cottage isn't great, but his irises are some brand of shifting hazel behind his glasses. His hair is down, a strand of it falling over his forehead. He moves in, a question, and she startles and pulls her hand away, breaking the fragile connection.

"Sorry," he says quickly. "I didn't mean—"

"No, it's okay." She's a little breathless. "It's me. I'm a mess."

A chuckle. "Sounds like we've got that in common." He runs a hand through his hair, shakes it out like a dog shedding water, like he's trying to do a reset. "I guess broken people shouldn't try to kiss broken people they've just met when they're a little tipsy, huh?"

"I don't know about should, but some people just need a little time to figure things out." It comes out softly, an apology. Not quite a no. Not quite a yes.

"I should probably go." The poor man is flustered, probably hasn't leaned in for a kiss since his wife was still around. He stands and does a double take when he notices the stacks of books. "Okay . . . so you weren't lying about exploring."

It's not a question, but it is, and now she's flustered, too.

"You can tell from the outside that there are two stories. I wanted to know what was up there," she says.

"Does Gail know? Did you ask her?"

Sarah wants to crawl out of her skin; this is too private for Gail. What's up there—she wouldn't understand it. Why did she let Reid in the door?

"I don't know what Gail knows, and I don't really want to ask her. When she walked me out here, she clearly didn't like the idea, and it made her snappy and weird. This cottage—they don't use it regularly, like the others. I think it was either put me in here or let me stay in December House, and she's very territorial about her space. So she just gave in and brought me towels." She stands and walks over to one of the many piles of books. "I'll put it all back. I'm not trying to steal antiques or anything. I just . . . I mean, if you were living someplace with secret rooms, wouldn't you want to know?"

Reid walks over to the bookshelf, puts a hand on it, and peers into the gaping doorframe beyond. "Yeah, I'd want to know. I'm not saying I blame you. You're just getting the lay of the land." When he looks back, his eyes sparkle with mischief. "So what did you find?"

Now that the question is out there, Sarah is forced to confront the fact that she feels . . . protective of what's upstairs. It isn't some public building where kids go to spray-paint their initials and smoke up; it's a personal, intimate family space that has been allowed to enjoy its privacy for over a hundred years. The nursery especially feels sacred, and the thought of anyone, even Reid, picking up that baby blanket or one of the wooden toys makes her want to bare her teeth and growl.

"An office and some bedrooms," she says blithely, as if it were a lot less interesting than it actually is. "I left everything just like I found it. There's a grave out back, too. I think maybe that's why they don't use this cottage—it's not meant for that. It was a private home."

Reid turns on his phone's flashlight and turns sideways to sidle past the bookshelf, and Sarah hurries over and puts a hand on his shoulder. "I don't know if you should do that. The floors aren't always so sturdy up there."

It's a lie. Those wood boards feel like they could hold up an elephant. But she doesn't know how to explain it in a way that makes sense, that wouldn't make Reid think she's crazy or the drama queen that Kyle always told her she was.

The ghost of a dead mother won't like you sounds totally nuts, and yet that's how she feels, like the cottage has gone silent, crouched and ready to pounce, a lioness sensing something dangerous near her den. Although the doctor's study is one-third of the upstairs, the overall feeling is not masculine. The doctor, whoever he was, likely died somewhere else. His energy isn't here.

Everything upstairs feels female and wounded, and Sarah empathizes with that, even if the thought feels silly and impossible and a little unhinged.

Reid edges back out, looking disappointed. "I always wanted to see a place like that, you know? Urban spelunking. Old asylums, that sort of thing. But I've never done it."

"There's nothing that interesting, really," she says. "An old bed, a desk. You're not missing anything." She touches her hair. "Lots of cobwebs."

He grins. "I'm not worried about cobwebs, and I'm sure the boards are fine. These old places are built to last. I've gotta see this." Before she can stop him, he squeezes behind the bookcase and disappears.

Sarah freezes as his big boots ring on the wood stairs. Panic rises. This feels wrong. He shouldn't be up there. She didn't invite him. He doesn't . . . he isn't . . .

She just feels like he'll be brash and loud and not show respect to the quiet sanctuary, to the sad testament of lives unlived, to a mother's love torn away too soon. She flicks on her phone's flashlight and sucks in a breath to follow him, and that's when she hears him scream.

14

"Reid, what happened?" Sarah calls, sidling past the bookshelf. She smacks into his chest on the first stair, and he drops his phone to catch her by the shoulders.

"A bat flew right in my face," he says.

She can't see him, but he sounds shaken.

"Mind if we get out of here?"

She backs out of the space and, from right outside the bookshelf, shines her flashlight around to help him find his phone. As he squeezes back into the light, he's dusting himself off, slapping his hair and shoulders. There are so many cobwebs he looks like he's wearing a wedding veil. Sarah doesn't remember it being that bad, but he's a foot taller than her, so maybe things are worse closer to the ceiling.

"Didn't even get all the way up the stairs," he says sadly. "I know most bats don't have rabies, but I'm not going to risk it." He looks down at her, concerned. "You should probably put the bookshelf back. You were right. It's not safe."

Relief cracks in her chest. "Yeah, good call. Want to help me?"

He gallantly pushes the bookcase back into place and halfheartedly places a few books on a convenient shelf, but he's jittery now and obviously doesn't plan on sticking around.

That's fine.

Because Sarah is lying. She doesn't think it's unsafe, and she definitely plans on going back up there. But he doesn't need to know that. Reid is probably a good guy looking out for another human being, but she's in no mood to do what someone else says, just now. He is not her husband, not her boss. And he didn't feel what she felt, upstairs.

For a moment they just stand there. It's awkward. The momentum of the night has been stopped three times now, and Sarah doesn't know how to get it rolling again, or even if she wants it to. If she's honest with herself, she wants to be alone to take a bath and go to sleep and not feel like someone is invading her personal space.

Because that's what it felt like, when he charged upstairs.

An invasion.

An unwelcome intrusion.

"Thanks for the food." She looks back to her half-eaten dinner on the coffee table. "I really appreciate it."

"No problem," he says, back on solid ground. "See you at breakfast?"

"I'll be there."

In another world, he might lean forward to peck her on the cheek, but he's still covered with cobwebs and looks like he wants to hurry home to bathe in fire.

"Night."

"Night."

And then he's out the door, and she's locking it behind him and sighing.

When she's certain he's gone, she walks back to the bookcase, puts a hand on the cold wood. She'll go up there tomorrow, maybe look through the doctor's files or the lady's vanity, but not tonight. Even though pitch-black is pitch-black, there's still a major difference between exploring a hidden attic in the daytime and exploring it at night. It doesn't make sense, but she feels it in her bones.

Instead, she picks up an old novel off the floor, the leather cracked and the pages the color of polished ivory. As she finishes her dinner, she reads the tiny print, marveling at how different books used to be, cramped and thick and slow, the prose as sticky and dense as oatmeal. After she's dredged up the last of the salad, she tosses her scraps around the corner outside, washes the plate and silverware in the bathroom sink, and puts them by the front door so she'll remember to take them back up to December House tomorrow. It's almost like camping, but with a lot more moth-eaten velvet.

Sarah is still unaccustomed to not having TV or a computer or social media to occupy her time, and she's now filled with an annoying, nervous sort of energy. She wants to pace, to move, anything but be trapped in this little cottage with a secret world sitting silent overhead. She looks at her phone. It's just past eight. Even though she and Bernie agreed that he had the studio before lunch and she had it after, they didn't make arrangements for the evening.

Maybe it's deliciously empty.

Sarah pulls on her shoes and jacket and lights up her regular flashlight. The forest is quiet but always, always rustling. She doesn't feel unsafe as she hurries up the neglected trail, but she does move quickly, as if the darkness is an unsavory character she must pass on the sidewalk, glancing away so she won't be noticed. Much to her disappointment, the light is on in the clay studio, some godawful 1970s song about banging a teenager blaring out the open door.

She peeks in, first. Bernie is on his side of the room, legs spread defiantly as he carves away at one of his mermaids. When she notices her toolbox sitting open nearby, rage sings in her blood. She got so comfortable earlier that she must've left it behind. Then she sees her ribbon tool in his hand, her needle tool behind his hairy old man ear.

The absolute goddamn nerve of this derivative dinosaur!

She steps in the room, turns off the grating music with the push of a button.

Bernie spins toward the door, the ribbon tool clutched in his fist like a knife and his lips already drawn back in a snarl.

"We made a deal, little girl," he booms. "This is my house."

"You said you got mornings and I got afternoons."

"I get night, too."

"That wasn't part of the deal."

His chin goes up as he shrugs. "If you wanted more, you should've asked."

"Yeah, I didn't really stop to do the math until I thought about how pleasant it would be to actually be able to use my own goddamn studio instead of being bullied around."

She's legitimately startled to hear the words come out of her own mouth, to hear the fury in her tone; it's like some portal has opened up inside her, like things that were once held back are finally allowed to roam free. Maybe it's because she doesn't like this man or respect him, maybe it's because she knows he can't hurt her, or . . .

Or can he?

Her bravado lurches away as he marches across the room, stopping close enough that his spit flies in her face when he speaks. "If you didn't like the terms, you shouldn't have agreed to them. People your age make agreements and then think you can just go back on 'em, like your word doesn't count for anything."

Up close, his body odor and bad breath are powerful, and she steps back for a lot of reasons. "Not demanding evening time in my own studio isn't going back on my word, you asshole. You're just trying to take something that doesn't belong to you and then pretending like it was an accident when you got caught."

"Okay, then. Let's play nice." He pantomimes a curtsy, smirking. "I'll take Monday, Wednesday, Friday, and Sunday nights. You take—"

"That still leaves you with one more day than me," she growls.

He shrugs. "Age before beauty."

She bristles, her hands in fists. "I won this residency, just like you did. I don't see why you should get more studio time just because you think you're—"

What? What does he think he is?

He takes her pause as a weak spot.

"Because I think I have a right, is that what you were going to say?

I do have a right. Because I was here first and I claimed it, fair and square. If you're too weak to take what you want, that's your problem, not mine."

Sarah shakes her head. "This is stupid. I did not come here to argue with a bully."

"And I didn't come here to have my studio time interrupted by a whiny crybaby. If you don't like it, maybe you should leave."

She pushes past him and gathers up her toolbox, throwing in all the tools lying around his work area; they all have her initials Sharpied on them in stark black. This close, she's forced to look at his latest mermaid.

It looks a lot like her.

Well, her if she had significantly larger breasts and had her head thrown back in ecstasy.

"Is this supposed to be me?"

Bernie snorts. "You wish."

Standing before him, eyes burning with hate, she says, "Don't touch my tools again."

He grins the grin of a middle school bully who knows he can't get caught. "I found 'em lying around. No one was using them. Didn't anyone ever teach you how to share?"

"Apparently someone taught you how to steal."

At that, his face wrinkles up like a bulldog taking a shit. "It's only stealing if you don't plan to give it back. I'm borrowing."

"You're done borrowing." She holds the open toolbox toward him.

Staring directly into her eyes, projecting every bit of disgust and superiority he can, he pulls the needle tool out from behind his ear and drops it in the box, along with the ribbon tool in his hand.

She snaps the toolbox shut and turns to leave.

"Anybody ever tell you you'd be a lot prettier if you smiled?" he calls.

"Anybody ever tell you you'd be a lot less horrible if you shut your mouth?" she calls back.

As she walks out the door, back stiff, she hears him mutter, "Crazy bitch."

And then the music is back, blaring its creepy pedophilia into the quiet night.

Sarah stops.

She turns around.

She isn't done.

"I get four nights a week," she shouts over Ted Nugent's rancid yowling.

"If you want it that bad, come and take it," he shouts back, his shadow blocking the open door. "Nobody is stopping you. Go sit your perky little ass down and make all the pissy little teapots you want. You're the one with the problem, snowflake, not me."

And she hates it, but he's right. He can't stop her—not physically. She could go back right now—at any time really—sit down, throw whatever she wanted to.

Except she can't, because he makes the studio so uncomfortable, so hostile, that she knows damn well she wouldn't be able to accomplish anything other than raising her blood pressure and adding more perfectly good clay to the slurry bin.

"You're a real asshole, you know that?" she shouts. "I'm telling Gail about this."

"Good luck with that, princess," he shoots back. "Me and Gail go way back. You think you can go up against me and get your way, believe me: You're gonna lose."

She flicks him off and leaves, so bubbling with rage that she's sweating inside her coat. How dare this man—well, he didn't really threaten her, did he? It's not that he seems dangerous, even. He's just rude and arrogant and thinks he's more important than anyone else. A lot of the same qualities she hated in Kyle, actually, but instead of Kyle's quiet hauteur, Bernie goes for in-your-face aggression.

Crack.

Something explodes on the ground at her feet, and she jumps and screeches and drops her toolbox. She's looking in every direction, searching for some danger, unsure if she should run, and if so, to where. Nothing feels safe, the night is dark and sinister, and—

There, in the open studio door, is Bernie, looking smug, arms crossed.

She looks down and sees shards of leather-hard clay, perfectly smooth.

One of her mugs.

The bastard lobbed one of her recently thrown mugs at her.

"Oops!" he shouts over the music, which is somehow even louder now.

"Throwing things at me is considered a threat," she shouts, loud enough that birds take flight from the nearby trees.

She hopes someone else hears it.

She wishes there were a witness.

But wait—there is. Sort of.

She snaps a quick photo with her phone, then starts recording a video.

"I didn't throw anything," Bernie says, smiling smugly at her phone. "Looks like you dropped it. You might want to be more careful in the future, little girl."

He dusts his hands off, gives her the finger, and slams the door.

She snatches up her fallen toolbox and hurries home to her cottage, heart pounding, hands shaking, feet numb, mind going a mile a minute like a horse that can't be caught.

He may say that wasn't a threat, but they both know it was.

15

t takes a long time before Sarah can calm her nerves enough to even think about sleeping. She's out in the woods by herself with no phone, no protector, no weapon. There's an angry man out there who knows where she is, who knows that she's scared.

Who clearly wants her to leave.

Maybe Bernie will throw a pot at her door at midnight. Maybe he'll throw a rock through her window. Maybe he'll crush every pot she's made so far, claim a shelf collapsed. She can't predict what a man like that will do next, but she knows she can't keep sharing a studio with him, even if there was a schedule that she agreed was something close to fair.

Tomorrow morning, she's going to talk to Gail. She did not come here just to quake in the presence of another asshole who thinks he can rule by fear. She'll tell Gail what Bernie did and said, show her the pic and the video, tell her that she doesn't feel safe around him. She'll ask if one of the other empty studios might be used as a makeshift wheel studio while she's here. Yes, it's nice to have all the equipment she needs, but she can make do with a wheel, a sink, and a table—and the painting studio is right next door and available. She could throw whenever she wanted to, trim as needed, then walk her pots to the studio when she's ready to fire them at a time when Bernie isn't around. She could even ask Gail to accompany her so she wouldn't have to be alone with him.

Even if Bernie is telling the truth and he and Gail are friends, surely another female artist will understand. There's not a woman alive who hasn't dealt with this kind of asshole, whether in the studio or out in the world at large, a swaggering jerk who makes her feel powerless, who threatens without directly threatening. Great art can't be created with shaking hands.

She practices her speech out loud, trying to get the words just right. She doesn't want to sound like a Karen, doesn't want to behave in a way that could be called hysterical or melodramatic. Those are the words Kyle used, and they weren't true, and she knows that hearing them spoken out loud would just make her shrink into herself, a snail instinctually withdrawing into a familiar shell when pelted with yet more salt.

"I've tried to be civil, but I can't share the studio with Bernie," she says, willing her voice not to shake or get too high. "He's resistant to compromise, and he makes the space so hostile that I'm unable to work. He's already ruined two of my pieces and was utterly unrepentant. His music is vulgar and demeaning to women, bordering on pedophilic. He's sexist and behaves in a threatening manner. It's just not going to work out. With your permission, could I use one of the empty studios if I promise to take full responsibility for its cleanliness and to return everything that I take from the pottery studio at the end of the residency?"

Yes. That sounds good.

Demanding but reasonable. Firm but calm. Honest but not over-emotional.

God, she wishes she could send it as an email.

She hates that she has to take these things into consideration. Bernie certainly doesn't go to such lengths to make himself palatable. He has likely never given a single moment's conscious thought to how he makes people feel or how his words or intonation or gestures might be construed as anything other than perfectly acceptable. What a heaven that must be, to forever remain utterly ignorant of what an absolute ass you are—and to usually get your way.

Content that she has a plan in place, Sarah finally falls asleep. Her dreams continue to be murky things, like wandering in the smoky dark, unsure of time or place, lost but always searching. She has flashes of the familiar, of her hand on the baby blanket or catching on the wall as she nearly tumbled down the stairs, interspersed with flashes of the unknown and the surreal—of a door opening in the darkness, a splash of red on a rug, a chamber lined with cold white tile in every direction, steam wreathing the floor like fog. For a moment, she hovers in the pottery studio, her skin as cold as ice, watching Bernie work on the mermaid that looks like her, sculpting a knife planted between the bulbous breasts as he grins like a little boy with his hand in the cookie jar who knows he will never, ever be punished.

When her alarm rings, she wakes up muddle-headed, her eyelashes gluey and her mouth tasting of dirt. She rinses with mouthwash before taking a quick bath in the old tub and getting ready to head out for breakfast. She spends more time than usual getting her hair and makeup right and selecting an outfit that looks put-together. Again, because she knows perfectly well by now that anything even slightly off can and will be used against her in the court of a man's anger.

The sky is heavy and pendulous with thick gray clouds as she walks up to December House. They recommended she pack an umbrella, but of course she forgot. The rain will likely hold off, and maybe there's an umbrella she can borrow—or buy, since there's that little store. She puts all her energy into being cheerful and friendly as she fills her plate and makes her coffee. Reid and Kim are sitting together, and Reid smiles at her, half hope and half apology. Kim looks hungover and slightly resentful, but like she's used to it.

"Where were you last night?" she asks.

Sarah's eyes flick to Reid's, and she smiles, grateful that he apparently hasn't told everyone what she's been up to. "I just got caught up in work," she says, which is true.

"I was going to bring you a plate, but someone beat me to it . . ." Kim trails off, rolling her eyes before grimacing and putting a hand to her head.

"Yeah, that was really nice. I was starving, even if I didn't realize it." The moment the words are out of her mouth, she understands that they sound like they have a double meaning, and she hurries to add, "The food here is so great, right?"

Kim glances at the kitchen. "Yeah, as long as Bridget isn't cussing and throwing things. She burned the dessert last night, and she and Gail had a shouting match. It was embarrassing."

"What were they fighting about?"

Kim has a mouth full of eggs and toast, so Reid says, "From what we could hear, Bridget came home because her restaurant failed and she was seriously in debt, and she thought they would just give her a cabin and let her live here for free, but instead they drew up some sort of contract that requires her to work and then live with them in December House. Gail wants to train her to take over, says it's her duty. And it sounds like Bridget hates it here."

"Whoa. That's a lot of information from a shouting match."

Kim looks at the kitchen. "Well, it's a very thin door, and they were really loud. Sounded like Bridget threw the pan full of whatever dessert got burned against the wall. Gail was shook."

Uh-oh. That doesn't bode well for Sarah. If Gail is already upset, she's unlikely to find an ally, especially if Gail and Bernie have the prior relationship he's suggested.

"Speaking of Gail, is she here?" she asks.

Kim and Reid look around, but of course Gail isn't here, or Sarah wouldn't have asked, because she's not a complete idiot.

"No idea," Kim says. "I haven't seen her since she stormed off last night."

Sarah's smile ratchets down a notch as her dreams of handily solving her problem today fly out the window. She hates having to wait for the right moment to move forward. She wants this done, wants the giddy freedom of unlocking the door to some other empty studio and making it her own.

The one comfort of the morning is that Bernie doesn't come in, as he usually does, to grab his breakfast to go and fill up his gigantic Yeti mug with coffee. Sarah is constantly on alert for his presence; every time the door opens, her head jerks toward it. At one point, Gertrude Rose notices from the next table over and frowns and says, "You're jumpy as a long-tailed cat in a room full of rocking chairs, Sarah darling. Is there something we need to know?"

"Just looking for Gail," she mutters.

Gertrude Rose shrugs, her shoulders extra big today, thanks to giant poofs on her dress sleeves. "Haven't seen her, but that's why there's a brass bell in the main room."

Sarah considers it but doesn't want to risk a public scene if Gail is already feeling emotional or defensive. "Good point," she says, hoping it's neutral enough to stop the conversation completely.

Reid is mostly quiet, but she catches him watching her, notices a few gentle smiles, which she returns shyly. Last night was odd, but she does like him. This feeling of light flirtation is a new thing, and the butterflies in her tummy are a pleasant surprise, something she hasn't felt in years. Maybe if she can solve the studio issue, she'll have more energy to expend on daydreaming about what it might be like to kiss Reid. She holds herself so carefully, as if her heart is just as tight as all the other muscles and bones protecting it. Kyle hurt her, a slow and insidious kind of hurt, a sneaky hurt, and she is still raw from it, and it will take time for her to remember how to let herself be vulnerable again.

When she's done eating, she steels herself to go down to the studio. She knows Bernie will be there, but she wants to rescue all the pots she's made so far and take them to her cottage for safekeeping as they dry. After last night, she doesn't trust Bernie not to destroy everything she creates. She can fit everything on one board, in and out before he can get too riled up, hopefully. It will have to do, until she can talk to Gail.

Reid follows her to the trash station and holds the door open for her on the way out. "Mind if I walk with you?" he asks.

"Not at all." Sarah looks up at the darkening sky. "Did you bring an umbrella? Because I forgot mine."

"I brought two, a big one and a little one. You're welcome to borrow one."

She grins at him. "Thanks. I used to always forget something when I traveled. One time when I was a kid, I managed to forget to pack a bathing suit to go to the beach. We had to go to one of those awful, overpriced shops, and I ended up paying like fifty dollars for a brown bikini. It fell apart after a week."

"So you like to travel?"

The question hits her hard, falling like a heavy weight and obliterating her smile. It's a normal getting-to-know-you question, absolutely nothing unusual about it, and yet it only serves to remind her of what she's lost. "I used to. Kyle wouldn't let me, but before that, I loved it."

"I don't want to be rude, but this guy sounds like a real dick."

"He was a real dick." She breathes out forcefully as if expelling the last of her old relationship, then sucks in a new breath full of oxygen that feels new and cleansing and entirely free of Kyle. "But I think once I'm on my feet again, I'm going to book a cruise. I can't figure out if I want to go somewhere warm or somewhere cold with whales, but I've always wanted to do a cruise."

Reid chuckles. "Me, too. I like the idea of . . . a closed set piece. You're trapped on a ship. You can't feel bad about not cleaning the garage or finishing that project. Your only job is to have fun and eat yourself sick."

"That's the dream. Gluttony and whales."

They're almost to the pottery studio, but Reid isn't breaking off to head for the metal shop. "Have you started any work?" he asks.

"A row of matching vases and some basic vessels. Just knocking the rust off."

"I'll show you mine if you'll show me yours." He grimaces. "Art. I meant art. That was weird. Sorry. But I'd like to see what you've got so far, if you don't mind."

It's nice—Kyle never wanted to see her art, especially not in the early stages. "I don't mind. But I hope you're okay with loud cock rock and being yelled at by an angry old man."

Reid stops. "He yells at you?"

Sarah has also stopped and is annoyed with herself for being so flippant. She doesn't want Reid to think she's high-maintenance, and yet . . . well, she's not going to lie. She doesn't feel any need to protect Bernie's assholery.

"Oh, yeah. Yells at me, steals my tools, breaks my pots. It's like sharing a studio with a giant toddler who needs a nap and some deodorant." She says it blithely, as if it doesn't matter, but she can see the effect it has on Reid, see his jaw go rigid and his big, rough hands tighten into fists.

"Let's go see what he's got to say to me, then."

The clay studio door is open, but there's no music playing this morning. This is both a relief, because Sarah absolutely hates Bernie's music, and also a slight frustration, because she wants someone else to know exactly how terrible the whole situation is. Being subjected to music she hates at a high volume makes her feel like a panicked animal, and she assumes that anyone else trying to make their own art would have some sympathy upon being ear-slapped by the word *poontang* at two hundred decibels before their breakfast has even settled.

She moves in front of Reid so Bernie won't think that she's sending in her white knight first. As glad as she is that Reid is here, that she has a witness, she wants it universally understood that she can handle her own business and is not scared of her atrocious studio-mate.

When she steps into the open doorway, she's immediately struck by the wrongness of it. It's too cold in here, too still, too quiet, entirely lacking the frenetic, messy, angry energy Bernie generally brings to the space and leaves tainting the air like the scent of a cheap cigar. She looks down and realizes why.

The bluish fluorescent lights shine down on Bernie.

He's on his back, eyes staring at the ceiling, mouth open, his face a grotesquely mottled purple.

Bernie is very, very dead.

16

S arah doesn't scream, because she's not a screamer. Her hands go over her mouth as she backs out of the doorway, skittering away from the second corpse she's seen this week. Fourth, if you count animals.

"What's wrong?" Reid asks, but she can only shake her head. She can barely make her eyes blink. They're stubbornly refusing to close, as if something terrible is waiting to happen in that tiny sliver of darkness.

Reid hurries to the door and stands there, stunned.

"When did you see him last?" he asks, and she wonders if he watches a lot of *CSI* and listens to murder podcasts, because he should be freaking out a lot more than he is, not asking sensible questions like a hardened detective.

"Last night," she says, breathless and creaky. "After you brought me dinner. I was going to try to get some work done. He yelled and threw one of my mugs at me. I'm surprised no one else heard it." She points to where the shards still sit in the gravel.

Reid shakes his head and puts his arm around her shoulders, pulling her close in a gesture that's less prospective suitor and more emotional support dog. "We need to go tell Gail. Do you want me to take you to your cottage, or my cabin, or do you want to come with me? Or maybe go wait with Kim? I know you're pretty shaken. God, who wouldn't be?"

She's trembling, and even turned away, she can't stop seeing Bernie lying there, like when too-bright light leaves an imprint on her eyelids. She can't help imagining the unbearably heavy silence that followed the click when his last cassette tape ended.

"I'll go with you," she says. "Just . . . maybe close the door."

She wonders if this happened last night, if the studio door has been open all this time. Bernie looks like he's been there awhile, his skin a pasty gray, almost purple where it touches the floor. She's eternally grateful that some hungry forest creature didn't come in here and maul him—maul the body. She doesn't like—didn't like—Bernie, but no one deserves . . . that.

Reid leads her up the road toward December House. They pass the glass studio, where Kim is blasting Taylor Swift. Sarah likes Kim, but she hopes they're not spotted as they walk by; she doesn't want to have to explain the situation multiple times, and she's fairly certain Kim would be morbidly, garishly fascinated in a way that currently repulses her. The pop music fades, the air taken over with slow, steady scales played on a violin. It almost sounds like Lucas is . . . unsure and a little wobbly? Is he drunk, or has he gone so long without playing that he's rusty? When he introduced himself on the first night, he confidently named multiple instruments as his specialty, and that's a ridiculous thing to lie about. It's not like Gail would let him stick around if he came here under false pretenses. Sarah hopes he's okay, because something sounds off.

They finally reach December House, and Reid opens the door, holding it as Sarah passes within. It feels blessedly safe and normal. If crystals and water bottles and cloth maxipads are for sale alongside granola bars and Cheetos, things can't be too dire.

Gail, as usual, is nowhere to be found. Reid rings the bell, one solid ding, then hits it a few times for good measure.

No one comes.

He hits the bell again—again and again and again.

"Hello?" he calls. "We have an emergency!"

Finally there is noise beyond the door, but when it opens, they're faced with Sleepy Gandalf, or whatever Gail's husband's name is. He blinks at them like a half-dead owl.

"George, there's been an accident," Reid says. "Bernie is dead."

Such simple words for such a complex state of affairs.

George blinks a few more times as if hoping reality will change like a TV switching stations, but when Reid doesn't follow that up with a cheery *Ha, ha, good prank!* the old man sighs heavily.

"She's out with the people digging up the coffin," George finally says. "Good timing, I guess, if there's another body."

This may be the darkest thing Sarah has ever heard another human mutter, and she can't tell if George is joking or just so dry and practical that he hasn't stopped to consider what a borderline sociopathic thing this is to say.

"Come on."

He tromps out the door in his pajama pants and Crocs and oversized green sweater, and Sarah and Reid share a look of befuddlement and follow him. Once they're behind the house and up the ridge, Sarah can see the ruckus over by the area where she first started digging. She expected a hearse, but instead there's a work van, plain white. The back doors are open, and three figures hover around.

"Body's so old the coroner didn't want it," George says, answering the question Sarah would like to ask if she wasn't in shock. "Local historians came to check it out. Heard the guy call it a neat find."

"Her," Sarah murmurs. "She's not an it."

"Her," George repeats with the tired carelessness of a man who has to placate people often and no longer takes it personally.

Over by the hole, a man in his fifties and a girl in her late teens or early twenties are lifting the coffin out of the ground with ropes.

There's a big pile of dirt where they've uncovered it completely, and Sarah is eager to see what it looks like when revealed in its entirety.

It's just an old wooden box, she realizes as they get closer, nothing decorative or special about it. No carvings, no woodburning, no polish, nothing to indicate that anyone ever cared about the poor soul within. The top is back on, at least, not nailed down but placed loosely. Gail stands nearby, frowning. Sarah wonders if it's because she's worried about the property's reputation or because it's just one of many annoyances throughout her day, if she would offer the same frown to an empty box of cereal or a sock left outside the hamper. Thus far, she seems annoyed most of the time.

And then she spots Sarah and Reid.

"Oh, no," she barks, flapping her hands. "Shoo, you two. This is not the sort of thing that requires nosy nellies."

"There's an emergency," George wheezes.

"Oh?" Gail narrows her eyes at the three of them like they're naughty children.

"It's Bernie," Reid says. "We found him in the studio."

"So?" Gail asks.

"He's dead." Sarah's voice is tiny, but as she's the one who found him, it feels like she's the one who should say it out loud.

Gail rolls her eyes and crosses her arms. "Probably just drunk, the old skunk. Or stayed up too late working. He always does that. Pushes himself too hard and then crashes."

"So you guys are friends," Sarah says before she can stop herself.

Gail gives her a sharp look. "What's that supposed to mean?"

"He was yelling at me last night, and he said you two went way back, and that he didn't have to share the studio with me because . . ." She trails off, wags her head. "It doesn't matter. He's not drunk or sleeping. He's dead. In the pottery studio."

"Very dead," Reid says, backing her up.

The older guy and the young woman heave the coffin into the back of their work van and slide it all the way in. The man dusts his hands off and joins them, the young woman trailing behind him. This guy looks like a cross between a mountain man and a scholar, wearing a vest with a pocket square over a plaid shirt with a knife on his belt and sturdy, well-worn boots, all in shades of brown and what Sarah suspects is butternut. The young woman is wearing a college sweatshirt and holey jeans, her hair up in a loose bun and her white Keds stained the red of Georgia clay.

"I take it the more recent decedent isn't an antique?" the man asks with a southern accent.

"He's sixty-eight," George answers. "Well, was."

Gail looks lost, her eyes focused on something far away and darting around like she's doing math in her head and it isn't matching up.

"Was the cause of death obvious?" the man asks.

"No blood, no marks," Reid says. "A heart attack or aneurysm, maybe?"

The man shakes his head. "Well, let's go see him and make sure there's nothing we can do. And perhaps, George, you might go phone the sheriff?"

George sighs like this is a big ask and lumbers back toward the house at the speed of an ancient basset hound. Gail doesn't make a move, so the man—the historian—looks up at the hotel and squeaks like a little kid gazing at a Christmas catalog full of things he'll never have.

"You sure I can't just go take a quick peek?" he asks Gail. "No cameras. Just poke my head in the lobby?"

That certainly gets her attention. "Absolutely not. The floor's all rotted away. So let's not lose track of what's important, just now," she responds, her mouth in a hard line.

The historian shrugs good-naturedly and leads the way back to the studios at a sprightly pace, like he's academically delighted by the possibility of more death. The girl follows him, and then Gail wakes up and hurries to join them. Sarah pauses by the van doors, looking down at the plain wood top of the coffin. From this side, the bloody scratch marks aren't visible. She hopes the historian will do honor to this woman, to her suffering. She hopes he will treat her tenderly, touch her bones with delicacy, show her the kindness she deserves after all these years.

"So that's the corpse you found, huh?" Reid asks.

"Yes," Sarah says softly.

"What did it look like—the body?"

"Show some respect," she says with an unexpected burst of indignation.

"Is it disrespectful to ask?"

Sarah isn't sure how to put her feelings into words; her brain is still roiling with thoughts of Bernie. Bernie last night, shouting. Bernie throwing the mug at her and flicking her off. Bernie now, all the wrong color, too still, his T-shirt straining over his belly, purple tingeing the backs of his ears.

Did this girl look like that when she died? Did her skin go white, mottled purple where she was trapped in this coffin, lavender shoulder blades like fairy wings, the nape of her neck the mauve of a rose? Did this girl die with her eyes open, staring stubbornly up at the sky she couldn't see, or did she close her eyes and dream of the sun?

Reid is looking at Sarah like she's acting very strange, and maybe she is, but this is a hill she will die on.

It is a hill the girl died *in*.

"She died a violent death."

Because being buried alive is a very specific kind of violence.

"How do you know?" he asks.

"Let's catch up." When she starts walking toward the swiftly disappearing historian, Reid has to follow or seem like a creep.

They make a strange group, striding across the mountain. The historian—Louis, as he introduces himself during the walk; his daughter Ann, who attends the local college; Gail in her lime-green sweater and multilayered paper beads; and behind them all Reid sticking close by Sarah's side as if worried she's going to faint. Louis stops when the studios and cabins are in view.

"Wait, where's the body again?" he asks.

"Pottery studio," Reid supplies.

Gail takes the lead, and soon they all crowd around the closed door.

Somewhere in the back of Sarah's mind, she's hoping that it was all a prank to make her look stupid, that Bernie is going to pop upright and laugh at her, call her a hysterical bimbo, tell everyone the story about how he fooled a tender little stupid snowflake crazy girl.

But that doesn't happen because when Gail opens the door, Bernie is still very dead.

"Oh, my God," Gail moans. "I thought—but—maybe he's—"

The historian, kneeling by Bernie's side, grasping the man's wrist, shakes his head.

"Looks like a heart attack," Ann says. Louis moves away, and she darts around the body with a businesslike precision, checking Bernie's eyes and opening his mouth and lifting his arm to inspect it from every angle.

"She's a nursing student," Louis explains, pride clear in his voice.

"Yeah, so notice the sallow skin, the lividity, the slack jaw," Ann says.

Sarah feels bad for thinking of her as "the girl" at first, because she is clearly a woman, but it's odd how the mind divides women into these two staunch categories. Even at twenty-six she still sees herself as a girl and wonders if she will ever feel like a woman. She sees the woman in the coffin as a girl, too. Maybe it's the long hair or the white gown, but there was something so innocent and youthful about her.

"No wounds, no signs of a struggle. Did he have any preexisting conditions?" Ann looks from person to person, but no one seems to know.

"He drank too much," Gail finally says, almost guiltily. "Didn't eat right, didn't drink enough water, didn't get exercise, lived on coffee, smoked cigars and a lot of weed, barely slept."

Sarah notes the familiarity, the sadness. Gail knew Bernie, more than she knows anyone else here. A tiny fire of rage blooms in Sarah's chest as she wonders if perhaps he wasn't chosen for this residency because of his art but because of his relationship with Gail, which means that if things had been fair, she would've had the studio all to herself to begin with.

If things had been fair, she wouldn't have been terrorized by this man.

She wouldn't have had to stand there in the door to what should have been *her* studio, staring at her first dead body.

Well, her first fresh one.

George appears in the doorway, raises caterpillar-like white eyebrows at the sight within. "Sheriff's on the way," he says, then, a beat later, with the same matter-of-fact tone, "Well, that's it for Bernie, then."

Great, Sarah thinks. *George knew him, too.*

"Wait, what's this?"

The young woman who's been examining Bernie has his whitish-gray fist in both of hers, uncurling his stiff fingers. She pulls something out of his grip and holds it pinched between two fingers.

It's small, dark, metal.

It's familiar.

It's the nail Sarah put in her apron pocket.

The nail from the dead girl's coffin.

17

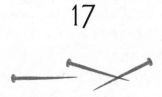

"Τ hat looks familiar," the historian says. He takes the nail, holding it up to the light, turning it this way and that. The part of Sarah that binges true-crime media grimaces at how many fingerprints everyone is leaving behind. Then again, this isn't a murder. This isn't a crime scene.

Is it?

"Eighteen hundreds, I'd say," he murmurs. "They call it a cut nail. Notice the tapered rectangular shaft. This was probably made right before they switched to the more modern wire nails with a round shaft. In line with what you would've seen around the original hotel, back in the day, as cut nails were still seen as superior."

Sarah shrugs in relief that he didn't immediately identify the nail as missing from the coffin outside. Then again, who knows? Maybe this land is covered in a blanket of such nails, fallen from boards and wagons and the pockets of carpenters. People have been building here for two hundred years, after all. There are surely thousands of replicas of this nail holding together Sarah's cottage. Just because it was in Bernie's hand and it's in the studio doesn't necessarily mean it's the one she took. She'd love to check her apron pocket, but she doesn't want to be associated in any way with Bernie's death, which means she won't be acting weird and suspicious just now.

Nevertheless, a tiny voice in the back of her skull whispers that it's good Bernie is gone. That's what the old man gets for touching her things, for disrespecting her belongings.

For disrespecting her.

Reid must notice the hanging of her head and the collapse of her shoulders, as he appears by her side, wrapping an arm around her. "This is a lot to take in," he says quietly. "Want to get some fresh air?"

Sarah nods, and he guides her outside.

He probably thinks she is merely a sensitive woman, distraught in the presence of death. He can't begin to fathom the maelstrom of different emotions running rampant in her blood.

Yes, she is shocked by this grisly scene.

Yes, she is again reminded of the dead girl in the coffin.

But yes, she is still furious about last night, about the rudeness and presumption of her every interaction with the dead man. Judging by his age and his pleasure in exerting his power over her, she understands that this was the story of his life, that no one ever stopped him or demanded a change in his behavior. He was never forced to face consequences or even question his right to live life exactly as he wished. This man, now a corpse, spent nearly seventy years running roughshod over women like an elephant stomping a mouse in the mud.

And yes, she isn't sorry that he won't be around to torment her anymore.

Does that . . . make her a bad person?

It doesn't matter. Dead is dead.

"A heart attack," Reid says once they're outside. "At least he died doing what he loved."

The morning is still gray, the clouds hanging even heavier, pendulous with rain, threatening to burst. Antoinette's jazz wars with Taylor Swift's *1989,* the other artists innocently pursuing their creativity in their own studios, blissfully unaware of the gruesome scene just a few yards away. Birds twitter their apprehension, trees shift uneasily like nervous feet outside an operating room. Sarah feels as if she's always waiting for something to happen.

But it's like she told Reid—hasn't she been that way for years?

Waiting for the other shoe to finally drop, waiting for Kyle to finally break down and hit her instead of just using words to make her feel small, waiting for some definitive moment that would draw a firm line in the sand between what she will and will not live with? And now that she's here, isn't she waiting for some lightning strike of creativity, for some message from the heavens directing her in how to begin rebuilding her life? She has always hoped to be one of those artists who is body-slammed by the muse, who is driven to create as if whipped by some otherworldly force, a galloping horse pulling a wagon full of future masterpieces. Something is brewing inside her, the ground buckling over a seed fighting for the sun. But it's not yet ready to crack that shell. She is tension, she is bursting with possibility, she is anxious to hear the starting bell.

She looks up at the clouds, wishing she could see beyond them, like when an airplane breaks through and emerges in clear blue sky.

As if the heavens can sense her need, lightning shakes the air, and rain bursts forth with the pregnant power of a feather pillow torn open with a knife. They're immediately drenched, and Reid darts under the eaves of the studio, but Sarah stands there and stares into nothing, trying to interpret this message from beyond. She wishes she were alone, that she could look up, arms open, and scream into the void, that she could lie down on her back in a field of clover and feel the earth reaching for her, soaking her, the grave anxious to stake its claim as she laughed and laughed and laughed.

What do you want of me? she aches to ask this place.

But she can't, she won't.

Reid is watching from a few feet away, Gail and the historian and the nurse just inside the building. Such odd behavior would not bode well for her under such scrutiny. To howl into the sky is to suggest madness, and madwomen rarely get to do as they please. Again, she needs this place, needs this interim of art and quiet to gather herself until her new home is ready.

There's an irony, she thinks, in an artist fearing being perceived as mad.

"Come on," Reid calls over the building storm. "It's not safe out here."

Sarah walks to where her broken mug is melting into the gravel road. She picks it up, her hands smearing elephant gray with the mud. Carefully she carries the pieces inside the studio—*her* studio—past the dead body, and places them on one of her empty canvas tables. The mug was already impossible to fix, but now it's melted and twisted, a lump of ruined shards.

Even as it is, even as itself, it's art.

There's a thing called kintsugi, where fragile areas are mended with gold to highlight their imperfections, their cracks and broken points. This sad little mug is beyond such remedies. Maybe, Sarah thinks, she is, too. But that doesn't mean it isn't art, that there isn't beauty in saving the unfixable.

"Sheriff'll be on the way," Gail tells her, gruff voice and red eyes permanently betraying any thought that she didn't know and care for Bernie. "He might want a statement, but he won't want anybody in here while his boys investigate. You two had better find somewhere else to canoodle."

"We're not canoodling," Sarah says coldly.

"Can't you see she's in shock?" Reid asks, and if Sarah's statement was cold, Reid's is positively Antarctic.

"Then take her up to December House for a cup of tea." Gail raises her chin, begging either of them to argue. "That way, the sheriff will know where to find you."

Reid looks like he has more to say, but Sarah nods and heads for the door, wet boots squeaking on the polished concrete. She had nothing to do with what happened, and she doesn't want to be here any longer, not with Bernie lying on the ground, unmoving. She pauses at the open door, looking out at the pouring rain.

"Should've brought that umbrella," Reid murmurs. "We can stop at my cabin. You ready?"

She nods, and he sprints out into the weather. After a few beats she follows. There's no escaping it. They can't stay here, and everything else is absolute chaos. She shivers under the eaves by his front door as he reaches in and pulls out a black umbrella, holding it over her and crowding near. She wonders if under other circumstances he would have invited her into his cabin, but they're already on the move toward December House, under orders, jogging in step together, breathing heavily in the intimate atmosphere created by two people sharing the same patch of sanity in a tiny world surrounded by a maelstrom of chaos. Neither speaks; it's hard to hear over the rain. Lightning strikes, and they put on speed, their minds one when it comes to outrunning a storm. Finally they burst through the doors of the café, panting and drenched.

Reid closes the umbrella and leans it against the wall, shaking out his hair. His tee and jeans are plastered down, his flannel hanging limp. She watches as he wrings it out, the tee pulled up high enough to show that he works out and doesn't manscape. She hasn't moved, and she's becoming aware of how awkward that is. She is frozen, thawing in slow motion.

"Tea," Reid says decisively. "What's your poison?"

For no reason she can name, the word makes her flinch.

"What do they have?"

Reid walks to a wooden box, lifts the top to show her the color-coded paper packets lined up inside. "Chamomile, maybe?"

She hears water dripping from her hair to the wood floor and is suddenly aware of how terrible she must look. "That would be great," she says. "Can you get it started for me?"

Reid nods and plucks an insulated tumbler from the shelf, and Sarah heads to the bathroom. When the light turns on, the fan kicks in like a jet engine, and she's forced to confront herself in the mirror. She looks like a ghost, like some lost creature with raccoon eyes and drowned hair. She dabs at the running mascara and eyeliner with a piece of tissue, coils her hair up into a bun with one of the rubber bands she keeps around her wrist. That's really all she can do, other than try to look less cold and pale and shocked, which is a tall order just now.

Back in the cafeteria, Reid sits at a table by a window, two steaming tumblers waiting. Sarah longs to wrap her hands around that warmth, but then she notices a figure curled up in the window seat in the farthest corner of the room.

Lucas.

He's tucked into a ball, long legs pulled up and head against his knees, rain-slick black hair dripping on the wood floor. He looks like Sarah feels: shaken to the core.

"Hey, Lucas. You okay?" she asks softly, standing nearby but not uncomfortably close.

He looks up, his dark-brown eyes wide and wet.

"I saw a dead body," he whispers.

Reid is with them now, and Sarah is glad, because she knows nothing about helping a kid get through something like that. She can't even help herself get through it.

"In the studio?" Reid asks softly.

Confusion blooms on Lucas's face. "What studio?"

Sarah and Reid exchange a puzzled glance.

"Never mind. What did you see?"

Lucas sighs heavily, his head falling forward against his knees. "Ingrid took pictures of the girl in the coffin. Like, a lot of pictures. Really detailed. Up close. She showed them to me." He points at the door to the main part of December House. "She went in the private area, you know. We were out here, and then Bridget came out of the kitchen and said she had to run to the store, and Ingrid waited until she was gone and just . . . went for it. I told her we weren't supposed to do that, and she laughed. She said things were only forbidden if you got caught."

Sarah is relieved and then furious, a roller coaster of feelings she can barely keep up with. She wants to charge through that door and find Ingrid, but she's not willing to get caught breaking Gail's laws.

Maybe Ingrid doesn't fear repercussions, but Sarah has nowhere else to go.

"Is she still in there?" she asks.

Lucas shakes his head. "She was in there for maybe fifteen minutes, then left in a hurry. She looked happy. And she's kind of scarier when she's happy."

She's so glad Lucas didn't see Bernie, but the next time she sees Ingrid, Sarah is going to wring her neck for not only disrespecting a corpse but also showing the corpse's pictures to a kid who's too young to absorb something like that. Ingrid probably thinks it's cool or funny, some weird goth thing. She's probably so wrapped up in making edgy art that she's forgotten the shared humanity of a girl who died long ago and was just left to molder. And poor Lucas. He's likely never seen anything like this before.

"She died a long time ago," Reid says, his voice gentle. "She died peacefully. There's nothing to be scared of."

He's wrong. Sarah knows he's wrong.

People who died peacefully don't leave their fingernails lodged in the wood of their coffins. But she's not going to say that.

"I've never seen a dead person before," Lucas murmurs, rocking back and forth a little.

Was she ever this sensitive? Sarah wonders. Or did growing up with someone like her mom cause her to build up a thick skin, a walking callus to protect her from the darkness of the world? A child who has grabbed the steering wheel from her drunk mother on the way home from getting a Happy Meal just to keep the car on the road is not the sort of person who goes catatonic at the first sign of stress. This is not to say Sarah is one of those people who wishes the younger generations were tougher, who thinks they deserve to be run through some invisible gauntlet so their trauma is equal to hers. If she could, she would wrap this boy in Bubble Wrap, sit him gently in front of a piano, place his fingers tenderly on the keys, and help him remember that the flip side of death is living and art and passion and beauty. It doesn't pay to dwell on the dark side too long—she knows that much.

"I heard you practicing scales earlier," she says, hoping to get Lucas thinking about something else. "Are you a composer, too?"

Lucas uncurls like a wary hedgehog. "I am. I dabble. I mainly came here to get a feel for my instruments again." His feet hit the floor in his soaked black Chucks and he holds out his hands. His right hand looks different from his left, smaller and thinner, and as he turns them in the light, she notices scars.

"Broke it really bad mountain biking," he explains. "Had to have surgery. My mom's been pushing me to jump right back into playing. It hurts, and I fumble a lot more than I ever have before. The tendons and joints are still pretty sore. I had to get out of the house so she'd stop crying outside the door while I tried to play." A small grin tugs at his lips. "This place seemed perfect. She doesn't know I'm here. I had to call the cops and tell them I was leaving of my own volition so she wouldn't nag them into a manhunt."

"What happens afterward?" Sarah asks, because that's her big question for herself, too.

"I start college next spring. Full scholarship. If Mom doesn't let me come back home, I'll just couch-surf until then."

Oh, to be young and able to sleep on some random, beer-stinking couch! And to have friends to offer said couch! It's only been five years since Sarah was in college, but it feels like ten, maybe twenty. Kyle wanted her to be a little housewife, and so he molded her into the perfect shape. He wanted her to be an adult, and so she shed every habit and word choice and outfit that made her seem immature. She still remembers when he taught her about red wine, told her it was a classier drink than any cocktail. She hated it, but she learned to tolerate it. He took her out for her birthday once, and she longed for a French 75, but he bought an expensive bottle of Cabernet instead. As it glugged into her glass, drier than dusty velvet, she wondered if this was how the next forty years would go by: slightly disappointed, feeling utterly displaced and misunderstood, like a little girl wearing her mother's heels.

She has not had red wine since she left him.

She likely never will again.

"I think our tea is ready," Reid says. "You need a cup, Lucas?"

Lucas shakes his head. "Nah. I'm cool. I have Gatorade and Red Bull in my cabin. I think I'm okay now. It was just..." He shivers before standing. "It threw me for a loop. I'm not into all that morbid stuff. My mom's super religious, you know? Seems wrong, taking a bunch of pictures. Like paparazzi or something, except the girl can't even hide."

"Or punch the photographer," Reid adds, trying to lighten the atmosphere.

It works. Lucas chuckles. "Yeah, right? If somebody punched Ingrid, I bet she'd put on her pointiest rings and punch them back."

He waves as he leaves, and Sarah and Reid head back to their table. She takes the lid off her tea, tosses the tea bag, and makes sure it's not going to scald her. Reid has added a little too much honey, but honestly, she probably needs it.

"Poor kid," Reid says, echoing her thoughts. "Ingrid should know better."

"I'm sure she knows better," Sarah replies. "I just doubt she cares."

He sips his tea and stares out the window. "Shock value. She probably got excited when she heard there was a coffin." He looks up, disturbed. "I hope she didn't take pictures of Bernie. The door was already open..."

"But he always works with the door open," Sarah says, scowling into her tea steam. "Because otherwise, we wouldn't all be forced to listen to his offensive music." She winces. "I'm still talking about him like he's alive. Sorry."

Reid leans back, swirls the tea around in his cup. "No worries. I mean... it's hard to make the abrupt U-turn from alive to dead like this. We barely even knew the guy, and suddenly he's just gone. It's not like you're supposed to just feel terribly sad and pretend like he was a saint." He glares out into the rain. "I wish I'd known he was being a dick to you. When I'm working, I've got on headphones and I'm blaring prog rock and hitting things with hammers. I don't hear a thing other than what's in my own little world."

"You couldn't have done anything. He wasn't the kind of man who thought well of women, I don't think. It was . . . an impersonal sort of abuse." She sips her tea, glad for something to do with her hands, grateful for the hot liquid scorching a path down her throat. She knows something of the personal sort of abuse. This wasn't great, but it was preferable.

"You hungry?" Reid asks.

Sarah shrugs. "Yeah, but it's not like there's food. Not until lunch. I guess Bridget hasn't started yet."

"Well, Bridget ain't here." Reid hops up, grinning at her. "You're my lookout. You see anybody coming, you talk real loud and distract them for me."

He heads for the door to the kitchen, and Sarah glances at the door that leads to the family area. Residents aren't supposed to go in the kitchen, and she already feels like she's in enough trouble, even though nothing that's happened has been her fault. She found a dead possum, she found a coffin, she found a corpse. Gail is probably starting to see her as the local enfant terrible even though it's all been bad luck.

Very bad luck.

But Reid has no such worries and has already slipped into the kitchen.

After an interminable amount of time, he reappears with two apples and several of the small pastries that were on the breakfast bar this morning. They eat like kids who've just found their parents' post-Halloween candy stash, wolfing the food down while glancing from the door to each other and grinning. The apple is small and mealy and the little croissant and Danish are stale, but the food immediately makes Sarah feel better. She belatedly remembers that they just could've grabbed some snacks from the shop and left their names behind on the tally sheet, but apparently that didn't cross Reid's mind.

With the sugar in her system, she's less shaky. The world doesn't feel as cold and dark, and she takes great joy in the fact that she hasn't had a single stomachache since she came here. For the past year or so, she's had digestive issues that she couldn't quite explain, sometimes waking up in the early morning dizzy and heaving, only to puke up her guts and fall back asleep. The next day, she would feel raw and jittery and scraped out, and Kyle always took great care of her and encouraged her to stay in bed and take it easy with Gatorade and toast. One time it was so bad she burst all the little capillaries around her eyes like a red-masked raccoon. She had blood tests done at Kyle's hospital, kept a perfect food diary to look for problem foods, saw a GP and then a gastroenterologist, got scoped up both ends. No one could find any rhyme or reason behind it.

At least Kyle was nice to her when she was sick.

Maybe that's because he's an anesthesiologist who did his residency at a busy hospital and is just better with his patients than with his girlfriend. He knows how to treat patients, always gets great reviews. The person he swore he loved, when not sick and when having her own opinions and feelings, however . . .

Well, that's why she's here.

The rain has slowed down, the lightning tap-dancing farther and farther away. Pastry crumbs and apple cores sit on the table, the tea nothing but honey-thick dregs.

"What now?" Sarah says.

"Gail asked us to wait for the sheriff," Reid reminds her.

But Sarah didn't come here to do Gail's bidding. Gail has already failed her. "That's going to take hours." She stands and heads for the door, picking up the umbrella. "Let's go talk to Ingrid."

18

Neither of them knows which cabin is Ingrid's, but they don't have any trouble finding her. The photography studio has a sign like all the rest, a smaller building of the usual white-painted cement block with closed blinds. Sarah pauses at the door, unsure whether to knock or not, but Reid just twists the knob and barges right in.

"Knock, knock," he calls belatedly and without a trace of apology.

Sarah is surprised to see that the lights are on, as she remembers something about needing darkness for old-fashioned cameras, but then she notices the closed door marked DARKROOM. Out here it's just a perfectly normal room full of equipment she's completely unfamiliar with. Big machines, metal cabinets, lots of tables. A black bag is slung over a chair, Ingrid's Leica sitting on the table, a cup of tea gone cold beside it. Sarah knocks on the darkroom door before Reid barrels in and ruins something. Maybe she doesn't agree with Ingrid's morals and methods, but that doesn't mean she wants to destroy her art.

"What?" an annoyed voice calls.

"It's Sarah."

Not an answer, but Ingrid can come outside if she'd like to know more. And if she doesn't come outside, Sarah will annoy her until she has no choice. Even if she's not an assertive person, she can come to terms with politely and passive-aggressively knocking Morrissey songs on the door for hours until Ingrid breaks.

The door bursts open, and Ingrid stands there defiantly, green hair pulled back, tense and glaring as if ready for a fight. "I said, what?"

"We heard you took pictures of the coffin," Reid begins. Sarah admires the elegant simplicity of his bluntness.

"Yes, and?"

"And you showed them to the kid."

Ingrid huffs a sigh and throws her hands up. "Yes, and?"

"Maybe that wasn't the best idea," Sarah breaks in, softer than Reid could ever be. "He's shaken. It really messed him up."

"Is that all?" Ingrid rolls her eyes and cracks her neck. "This is an artists' colony, not a nursery. Art is supposed to make you feel things. Sometimes what you feel is fear or discomfort. That's the whole point."

"But maybe there's a difference between going to see an exhibit of *Portrait of Ross in LA* and giving an already traumatized teenager nightmares."

Ingrid raises an eyebrow. "Why do you care? He's almost an adult, and you're not his mom."

"No, she's not," Reid breaks in, his voice even despite his annoyance. "But his mom is a jerk, and he's all alone, and he doesn't need to be in panic mode right now. He came here to heal. Just seems like an asshole move to set him back."

Ingrid tips her head, considering it. "Okay. How about this? Next time I have gruesome photos of a corpse, I won't show him."

"Maybe just don't antagonize him at all," Sarah says, barely making it a statement and not a question because she doesn't do well with confrontation.

"Okay, are we done?"

Ingrid's fingers tap along her sides, one-two-three-four-five over and over again. She's wearing baggy black jeans and a slouchy black sweater that's more hole than yarn. She glances back over her shoulder to the darkroom door, then meets Sarah's eyes and raises her eyebrows.

"I guess so," Sarah says.

"Did the pictures come out?" Reid asks, one hand on the table.

A frown. "They're not done yet. Hence my burning desire to return to the darkroom before something gets ruined. If you don't mind?"

She turns back to the darkroom door, but Sarah says, "Wait."

Ingrid doesn't turn around, her hand on the knob.

"What did you find in December House?"

A pause.

"Stuff." Ingrid flicks them off and slips inside, but not before throwing Sarah a meaningful glance over her shoulder.

When the door is shut, Reid sighs. "I didn't know I'd be playing babysitter here."

"Yeah, and I didn't know I'd be emotionally abused by another artist, but this place is just full of surprises." Sarah looks at Ingrid's backpack, wondering if the photos of the dead girl are in there. If she showed them to Lucas, then there must be at least a few that have already been printed, and it stands to reason they wouldn't all be in the darkroom. But she's not about to go through someone else's belongings—that's the sort of thing that could get her thrown out, plus she knows all too well what it feels like to lose one's privacy.

Back outside, Reid takes up the umbrella, and they stand there in the rain. Not the pouring, pounding rain, but not a reasonable drizzle, either. The kind of functional, hardworking, tenacious rain that ruins groceries, makes anxious dogs pee by the door, and requires fifty dollars' worth of ponchos to salvage a family trip to Epcot.

"What now?" Reid asks.

Sarah is about to suggest he show her his studio, since there's not much else to do, but Gail appears under a flowery umbrella, looking pissed.

"I told you two to wait up at the café," she shouts over the downpour. "Sheriff's been looking for you."

"We've only been gone ten minutes—" Sarah starts.

But Reid speaks over her, saying, "Well, we're here now. Where do they want us?"

"Café! Now!" Gail shakes her head at them like a disappointed mother and Sarah begins to see why Bridget is so angry all the time.

They walk shoulder to shoulder under Reid's umbrella, back up the road to December House. Sarah's boots squelch in the drenched gravel. There are two big black police SUVs in the parking lot, hulking menacingly.

Once they're in the door, the rain is muted, and it feels like taking off earmuffs and finally being able to hear again. Two cops are at the counter staring into the tea box with a look of shared disappointment.

"You guys want coffee?" Reid asks, walking up with that bluff swagger that Sarah can't imagine having.

"If you got it," the older man says. He's in his late forties, probably, and built like a piece of candy corn, but he appears intelligent and good-natured.

"Hell yeah," adds the younger man, who looks fresh out of police academy and like he watched a lot of *Dukes of Hazzard* as a kid.

Reid uses Gail's French press to make a pot of coffee, then makes more tea for Sarah and himself while the cops wait for their coffee to brew, standing over the glass carafe with the absolute focus of dogs at a rabbit burrow. Sarah isn't sure what to do, so she and Reid just stand there, dipping their tea bags, waiting for the police to take some kind of control of the situation. Clanks and curses from the kitchen suggest Bridget is back in there and hating life, as usual.

Finally the sheriff must decide that the coffee has steeped enough, as he pours out a hefty mug for himself and leaves the dregs for the younger officer. As he saunters toward them, he sips the brackish liquid and hisses at the heat. He inclines his head toward a table in the middling distance, showing his bald spot.

Sarah and Reid sit side by side, and the sheriff sits across from them. He's a big man, and his knee jostles the table as he pulls a pen and a little notebook out of his shirt pocket. The younger officer dolls up his coffee with sugar and cream and takes a seat by the door, his back to everyone else like he's keeping watch while listening in.

"So first of all, I'm Sheriff Harley, and I'm sorry y'all had to see that earlier today," the sheriff starts. "Is it true that you two found the body?"

Reid looks to Sarah. "I did, I guess," she says. "I was the first one through the door."

The sheriff writes that down, holding his notebook up so they can't see what he's writing. "Tell me what you saw."

Sarah takes a shaky breath. "We share a studio. Bernie and I. Or we did. Share it. I was going in there to—" She can't remember exactly. But why should she need a reason to go to her own studio?

"You were going to show me your work," Reid supplies.

"Let the lady talk, son," the sheriff says, and Reid bristles slightly, but not enough to cause offense.

"I was just going to my studio with Reid. After breakfast. Bernie always got his breakfast to go and went to the studio to work. We had an arrangement. He had it until lunch and I had it until dinner. So I guess it wasn't my time, but—I mean—"

"What did you see, honey?"

She doesn't like it when anyone other than a Waffle House waitress or a phlebotomist calls her honey, but now is not the time to prevaricate.

"So I went in the door first, and—well, usually he has music blaring. Steely Dan, Ted Nugent, the Eagles, that sort of stuff."

The sheriff nods in approval but doesn't write that down.

"So there was no music. And he always worked with the door open, so it was open. But when I walked in, there he was, on the ground. Same as when you got here."

The sheriff nods and scribbles, and Sarah wonders if his handwriting is as bad as the frantic movements suggest.

"When was the last time you saw him alive?"

Sarah frowns and looks away. This part is going to be difficult. "Last night. We had a—an altercation. He didn't like me. He shouted at me—called me names—and threw one of my mugs at me. It's in my studio, what's left of it, if you want to see it. I recorded the last thing he said to me on my phone. I had realized the arrangement he'd insisted on only gave me five hours in the studio, whereas he assumed he had the whole rest of the day, and I wanted to negotiate." She huffs a sigh. "He wasn't nice about it."

The sheriff leans in, brow furrowed in worry. "So he threatened you? You recorded it?"

Reid's hand lands on her knee, a reminder that for all his supposed kindness, the sheriff might not be kind.

"There was no actual threat," Sarah says carefully. "He seemed like the kind of guy who was accustomed to intimidating women to get his way but who knew better than to make overt threats. He used my tools even though I asked him not to, called me names, got in my space, taunted me. Made me feel unsafe in my own studio."

"You two had a contentious relationship." It's not a question.

Reid squeezes her knee, a warning.

But Sarah isn't going to lie. If anyone heard their fights, he'll find out soon enough.

"Bernie was an asshole," she says simply. "A bully and an asshole. I left the studio last night, he threw a mug at me and showed me both of his middle fingers, and I went back to my cottage."

"Can anyone prove that?"

Sarah looks around the cafeteria. "I just caught the last bit with my phone. I wish I'd started recording sooner. Maybe there's more if Gail has cameras or something, but I didn't see anyone else on my way back."

"You see any of that?" The sheriff turns to Reid.

Looking rueful, Reid says, "Nope. Wish I had. I would've had some very particular things to say, if he was throwing things at women."

The sheriff's pen scratches in his notebook for a moment. "I'm going to need you to send me that file, honey. Now, did he say anything about pain in his chest or arm, feeling light-headed or out of breath?"

She shakes her head. "No. But he didn't talk to me about things like that. He seemed like the kind of guy who never wanted to appear weak."

"Did he look odd—pale or pained or like maybe panting for breath?"

"Not that I noticed."

"But . . . I mean, he always looked a little unhealthy, you know?" Reid says. "Red nose, didn't look like he took good care of himself. I've seen him smoking cigars. If you're saying it was a heart attack, I don't think anybody would be surprised. Angry, out-of-shape alcoholic who smokes and yells at girls for kicks? That guy wasn't going to be running marathons and watching his cholesterol." He cocks his head. "So are you saying it was a heart attack?"

The sheriff looks at him like Reid has been sneaking looks in his notebook. "I didn't say that, no."

"But you asked if he was in pain, light-headed, or out of breath, which are the main signs of a heart attack, and there wasn't any blood or signs of a struggle, so it certainly would make sense. Like the nurse already said. Probably got all riled up hollering at Sarah and his heart just gave out."

Sarah feels a rush of appreciation for Reid, because she knows guys like the sheriff, and if she'd put two and two together like that, he probably would've called her a witch.

"Coroner will decide the cause of death," Sheriff Harley says, a little snippy. "Either of y'all know anything about the object found in Mr. Johnson's hand? A historical nail of some sort?"

Luckily, the sheriff is looking at Reid when he asks, as Sarah feels her body jump, just a little.

"Nope," Reid says. "I just know this place was originally built up in the eighteen hundreds, so there's probably plenty of 'em around here. I bet if you brought out a metal detector, it would go crazy."

Unsatisfied with that answer, Sheriff Harley turns to Sarah. "Ma'am?"

She doesn't feel like a ma'am. She doesn't feel like a miss, either.

She isn't sure what word would satisfy her, but she knows she hates ma'am. It makes her feel like she's old and in trouble.

"It's the kind of thing I could see him picking up," she says, side-stepping the question. "Something old and sharp and rusty."

"Are you saying it was a weapon?" he asks, voice a little high.

Sarah's jaw drops open. "An old nail? I mean, no? Not unless somebody hadn't had their tetanus shot. The clay studio is full of weapons, if that's what you're asking. Needle tools and clay wires and knives and poisonous chemicals. Pretty much every art medium has something dangerous about it. A nail is just a nail."

"But when you're holding a hammer, everything looks like a nail," the sheriff says, squinting like this is a very clever thing to say.

"Was . . . was there a hammer in the room?" she asks, confused.

"Should I go back and look for a hammer, Ms. Carpenter?"

The room goes quiet enough that they're forced to listen to Bridget cursing at the goddamn fucking succotash. Sarah is caught off guard, that he knows her last name without asking, but then she remembers that Gail obviously has all this information and would freely provide it to law enforcement.

"I don't think so, sir," she finally says, because clearly he's going to hold them hostage until she answers.

Harley nods like he's won. "Well, look. This case seems pretty cut and dried, but we'll know more after the coroner's investigation. Y'all stick around the property in case we have any more questions. You're here a bit longer, right?"

"Five more weeks," Reid supplies. "We just got here."

The sheriff looks out the window at the wet green hills undulating under the gray clouds and shakes his head. "One week, and you already had two stiffs turn up. That's a hell of a record."

He takes photos of their IDs and gets their phone numbers, not that their numbers will be particularly useful up here, and asks Sarah to show him the video. She does, and she can feel Reid fuming beside her like a geyser about to erupt. The sheriff has her type in his email address, but of course the file won't send.

"Wish you'd recorded more. That little snippet's not real helpful, I reckon, but don't delete it. We might need it one day." He nods decisively, then puts away his notebook and stands.

"You-all have a good day, now."

"Am I allowed to use my studio again?" Sarah asks.

The sheriff sharpens right back up. "Why are you so anxious to get back in there?"

She shrugs, arms out, feeling exhausted. "I came here to make art. I just want to make art."

He whistles, one low note. "Dead body still on the floor and the little lady wants back in. Be careful, Ms. Carpenter. Talking like that makes you sound guilty."

"Of what? Coexisting with an abusive old man who made bad choices and had a very predictable heart attack?" Reid says, his face going ruddy. "You know that sounds crazy, right?"

The sheriff doesn't rise to it, just runs his thumb over his gun like it's a fidget cube. "Never understood artists myself. Reckon I never will. As long as there's yellow tape on that door, you'd best stay out of there. Gooch, you ready?"

"Yes, sir," the younger officer says, chair screeching as he stands.

The sheriff saunters to the door and holds it open. Glad for any excuse to get out of his orbit, Sarah hurries outside, muttering her thanks. Reid is right behind her and just manages to get the umbrella over her head before she's exposed to the steady rain. They walk back toward the cabins, and only then does Sarah feel herself shaking.

"That guy was a dick," Reid says simply.

Sarah chuckles ruefully. "He really was. But why am I not surprised?"

"It was a heart attack. You don't have to be a doctor to see that. This county is so sleepy this is probably the most exciting thing that's happened in years."

As they walk past the studios, they see the coroner's van backed right up to the pottery studio door, two people in rain slickers fussing as they load something in the back.

"You still want to see my studio?" Reid asks.

Sarah shivers, feeling like a drowned rat. "Some other day. A sunny day when I haven't found any corpses. I need a nap."

"Good call," he says. "Let me walk you to your door."

When they get to the cottage, he stops and turns to her as they huddle under the umbrella. "I'm going to leave this with you," he says. "I've got another one in my cabin."

"But then you'll get drenched."

"Oh, no!" he trills. "I'll never be dry again!"

She grins. "I don't plan on leaving this room for a while."

"But there's dinner."

"But if I skip it, you'll just bring it to me again."

His face lights up, and she belatedly realizes she's flirting.

"I can do that. I can bring mine, too, and we can eat together, if you like."

She lights up, too, answering like a firefly's flash. "That would be nice. I don't want to answer Kim's questions today."

Reid grimaces. "Me neither. Not for all the wine in the world."

They stand there like teenagers, almost kissing, before she turns to her door and steps inside.

She's just not ready yet.

"See you later, then."

"See you."

He winks at her, drops the umbrella on her doorstep, and runs off into the forest.

"Keep it!" he shouts in his wake, and she laughs and folds it up so it won't blow away. He's a good man, she thinks, and she doesn't know what she's going to do about that yet.

Only when she turns around does she realize that something is wrong.

Her lights are on, and her door is unlocked.

That's not the way she left it.

19

S arah snatches up the umbrella, holding it like a bat.

"Hello?" she calls into the empty cottage.

She scans the room, noting that the bookshelf is still pressed almost where it belongs, the books splayed around it in their towering stacks. Then she notices that the door to the bathroom is closed, light shining underneath it. Umbrella clutched in shaking hands, she creeps toward that old black door, each step creaking on the ancient boards of the floor.

"Who's there?" she barks, hard and loud.

The door opens, and she winds back the umbrella like she remembers from that one awful spring the school made her play softball, and—

"Hi."

Ingrid steps out of the bathroom accompanied by the sound of a flushing toilet. Only then does Sarah notice the black bag slung on her sofa. She exhales, sagging, and tosses the umbrella back outside and shuts the door before Reid turns around and notices that something is wrong.

"Did you break into my cottage?" she asks.

Ingrid shrugs. "What, like it's hard?"

"I don't care about how easy it is, it's a crime."

"I guess. But it's not technically your cottage, not even on paper. You were supposed to be in Cardinal Cabin." When Sarah's jaw drops open, Ingrid adds, "I looked through Gail's paperwork today. She just leaves it out on the desk for anyone to find." And when Sarah shakes her head in disgust, the girl adds, "I get bored." Like that's any kind of explanation.

"Why are you here, Ingrid?"

Ingrid waves at her bag. "I thought you wanted to see the photos. I only showed Lucas a couple, but there are more. And I thought you'd want to know about what I found in December House."

She opens her backpack and pulls out a sheaf of papers, fanning them out on the coffee table. Sarah knows what's coming—she's seen it, has it seared into her brain—and yet somehow the corpse has become art. Rendered in shades of black and white, the stark subject is no longer one big picture but a series of intimate vignettes that hold more beauty and fascination than fright.

She picks one up with reverence, fingertips light, holding it by the edges so she won't mar it with smudges. Here is an eye socket with a translucent, mummified eyelid, the lines somehow soft and feminine despite the coldness of bone. Here are fingers interlaced around a nail, their shadows suggesting the patience of death. Here is corn-silk hair, catching sunbeams this girl never lived to see, the glistening waves falling over the fabric of her gown.

"You do care," Sarah says softly.

"Of course I do. Art can be worship." And then, as if she can't leave that statement to stand on its own, Ingrid adds, "Or protest. Or fury. Or satire. But here, it's . . . fellow feeling, maybe."

"That's why you didn't want Reid to see."

Ingrid reaches into her bag, pulls out another image. Sarah takes it from her, and it's like being punched in the gut.

It's the top of the coffin, grooved with scratches, the fingernail in sharp relief.

The word SANE is roughly, blindly scored into the wood.

Sarah didn't notice it before, but the camera's lens has revealed it in sharp relief.

"I didn't think he would understand," Ingrid says.

Sarah takes her time with the images, almost as if she's sidling up to an angry animal she can't quite look in the eye. When she stood over the grave, her brain was unhelpfully shouting *corpse!* And *dead!* And *bones!* But taken in thoughtful pieces through Ingrid's careful cropping, she can better accept the totality of the whole. Before holding them in her hands, she was furious with Ingrid, assuming the photographer had exploited a tragedy for her own amusement. Now she understands that for all her bravado and bluntness, Ingrid has a tender heart buried under those black clothes, beating bravely even though it's wounded. Ingrid, too, looked at the girl in the coffin and saw what was there: someone who didn't want to die, someone whose vitality was either overlooked or ignored, who was put in the ground when she should've been standing in the flowers, breathing deep under blue skies.

"They're beautiful," Sarah says.

"I know," Ingrid replies with the sort of unquestioning confidence that Sarah has never felt a single day in her life.

"Why did you bring them here?"

Ingrid blinks at her, slowly, with both eyes.

"You tell me."

When Sarah doesn't respond, Ingrid nods her head toward the photographs.

Is it a test? Is she missing something?

Feeling slightly suspicious, Sarah picks up the photos and pivots toward the nearest lamp. All the light here is warm, and she squints down at each image in turn, hunting for something, unsure what it is she seeks. Ingrid watches her, fidgeting with the silver rings on her thumbs.

Finding nothing and feeling a twist of pique, Sarah goes through the photos again. There must be something she's missing, or else Ingrid wouldn't be here, watching, waiting, demanding something of her. She doesn't want to fall short of what's expected—and she's deeply curious about whatever it is that Ingrid wants her to see. Her eyes greedily follow the curve of an orbital bone, the tendrils of papery skin stretched over a cheek, the silver flash of blond hair in shades of gray. She checks the hands again, stares at the nail, imagines how the fingertips must've looked like raw meat for decades.

"Tell me what I'm looking for," she murmurs.

"No."

Increasingly frustrated, she fans out the photos on the table. "At least tell me which photo."

"No."

Fearing she's about to fail this test, or whatever it is, she runs her palm over the photos as if she were drawing a card from a magician's fanned deck. Why not? If the secret isn't obvious, she's as likely to find what she's looking for randomly as she is specifically. Thunder rumbles, and her hand freezes. She reaches for the closest photo and holds it under the light, letting her eyes refocus as she searches for something out of the ordinary.

"Warmer," Ingrid says.

The image is one she'd overlooked before because her eye, like anyone's, is drawn to contrast, the play of light and shadow. This image shows folds of fabric, the hem of the girl's soft white gown. White on white, gray on gray, rippling like wind on sand.

Crack!

The rain pounds, the thunder building.

It's just an image of a sleeve.

And yet . . .

She traces a line with a finger.

It's hard to see, she might be imagining it, but . . . A single line of thread in what she thought was the hem has loops and whorls that don't belong in the even stitching of a garment sewn by well-trained human hands.

With dawning horror, she asks, "Does that say . . . HELP ME?"

Instead of answering, Ingrid hands her another image. This one is the dress's hem, edged in lace. Again, the stitching isn't uniform.

I'M NOT MAD, it says.

She looks up at Ingrid, completely stunned.

"How many of these are there?"

Ingrid pokes around and hands her several more photographs. Upon closer inspection, she finds the words IT HURTS and HE SAID HE LOVED ME and OBEY. And then, in all capital letters, I AM SANE.

"There might be more," Ingrid says, "but I didn't have a ton of time and I also didn't want to touch her. Seemed rude."

Sarah places the photos back down before she damages one, which would feel like blasphemy, even if they're just prints that could be easily re-created from negatives. The pieces of a puzzle are slotting together in her mind, but the image is still so incomplete.

"So she was buried alive, and some time before that, she secretly stitched words into her dress," she says.

"And she wasn't buried in consecrated ground, or even a cemetery. She was just out there in the middle of nowhere. No headstone, no plaque. Even the one behind your cottage has a plaque."

Sarah's head jerks up. "You know about that?"

Ingrid gives a one-shouldered shrug. "I'm very interested in death. But since the plaque was uncovered, I'm guessing you found it first."

Sarah lines up all the photos in two rows along the coffee table. "So what do we do? Do we tell Gail?"

A snort. "Tell her what? Hey, fussy old bird, that dead girl you're so anxious to get rid of died under mysterious fuckin' circumstances. Get out the time machine and tell 1893 that something naughty is afoot!"

"Okay, fair point. But shouldn't we tell someone? Louis?" When Ingrid looks at her blankly, she adds, "The historian guy who was here when we found the other corpse?"

Ingrid's black-rimmed eyes go wide. "There's another dead body, and you didn't tell me?"

"Tell you what? Hey, angry Gen Z Wednesday Addams, there's another corpse you might want to secretly photograph?"

At that, Ingrid finally breaks character, cackling until her eyes are watering. "Okay, fair point. But—please explain."

So in the spirit of sharing, Sarah tells her what happened to Bernie. She doesn't leave out their previous arguments because, well, Ingrid seems like she, of all people, would understand. And she does understand, muttering things like *pig, dillweed,* and *fuckin' misogynist dinosaur* under her breath at the appropriate beats of the story. When Sarah gets to the part about finding his body today, Ingrid goes very still except for her fingers, which are constantly moving, her fingertips tapping or her rings spinning.

"No cause of death?"

"It just looked like a heart attack. He was old and in bad health. Maybe yelling at me got him agitated, but he was perfectly functional last night when he was flipping me off and throwing my own mug at me."

"I wish I could've shot him," Ingrid says sadly, before shaking her head vigorously. "Not like, *shot* shot, but with my camera. After he was dead. That would've made a really interesting juxtaposition. Long-dead young woman, newly dead old man who hated women."

Sarah shivers. The storm is building when it should be dying down, and she's had to deal with entirely too much mortality salience today.

"Anything else weird about his death?" Ingrid asks, eyes alight.

"Well . . ." Sarah trails off, unsure whether or not to reveal the odd detail, but if Gail and Reid know, it's probably not going to stay secret for long. "They found a nail in his hand. It looked like one of the ones from the coffin. Like the one she's holding." She does not mention that she took one of the nails from the coffin. That fact just seems too private, and she hasn't yet been able to check and see if it's still in the pocket of her apron.

"Oh, that's not too weird. They're all over the place." Ingrid reaches into her bag and holds out her hand, and Sarah is stunned to see yet another of the old rectangular nails.

"Where'd you find that?"

Ingrid smiles a sly, secretive smile. "Behind the old hotel. It had fallen out of a railing in the garden, I guess, just outside the fence. They're neat, right? They just feel good in your hand. Heavy." She tosses it up lightly and catches it, and Sarah can imagine how it must feel, warm from her skin.

Unlike the one Bernie held, which by now is much colder, probably zipped up in an evidence bag.

"I thought we weren't supposed to go near the hotel," Sarah says carefully.

Ingrid rolls her head back, as if this conversation is so boring she has to stretch to keep from going permanently stiff. "I told you, the whole reason I came here is to get inside that building. I haven't found a way in yet. But I mean . . . *near* is a relative word. Where does the forest end, where do the grounds begin? What if I want to go see the waterfall? And even if I did start looking for a way through the fence, who's going to know? There aren't any cameras." She taps her temple. "I checked. And Gail's too busy running around like a chicken with its head cut off and a stick up its butt. Especially since you manage to keep finding corpses."

Sarah isn't sure what to say to that. She's painfully aware of the bad luck surrounding her and is indignant that any of it might seem to be her fault, and yet she can't deny it. She doesn't appreciate how amused Ingrid is by the situation, and she's eager to change the subject.

"Speaking of things you're not supposed to do, what did you find in December House?"

"I'll tell you if you tell me what's behind Bookshelf Number One."

They both look at the books in teetering stacks on Sarah's floor by the recently denuded bookcase. So much for that secret.

"Family rooms," she admits. "A study, a bedroom, a baby nursery. It's all very . . . sad." When Ingrid's eyebrows go up excitedly, she adds, "Not now. God, you're horny for depressing shit."

Sarah is surprised when Ingrid cackles and mutters, "Guilty. I'll get up there one day. Maybe when you're somewhere else."

"No! Do not break into my cottage again!"

Ingrid doesn't agree. She sticks out her tongue and pulls out the newest iPhone in a glitter case. "Speaking of breaking in, here's what I found in December House." She scrolls through photos at just the right speed to be enticing but not enlightening. "Let's see. The downstairs looks like it was renovated in the 1980s by old hippies who went to a thrift store, but the upstairs is creepy as hell and hasn't been touched since the 1880s. I guess they all sleep in tall poster beds like weirdos. The turret door has an industrial-strength lock on it, and even I can't break in. There are old oil paintings everywhere. One had a plaque that said DR. WARREN DECEMBER, so I guess it's the doctor himself. Freaky dude with tiny little dark sunglasses like Dracula. And I looked through Gail's desk. Bernie wasn't even supposed to be here. He usually stays in Cardinal Cabin and was pissed there was another potter."

"No wonder he hated me," Sarah murmurs. "It wasn't even my fault! I followed all the rules to earn my spot here, and it sounds like he's the one who didn't belong."

"Well, he's gone now, so you don't have to worry about him anymore." Ingrid leans in, weirdly giddy for someone wearing that much black. "Unless he decides to haunt the pottery studio. Just imagine. Led Zeppelin at all hours, your tools disappearing, the scent of cigar smoke and BO as a phantom paw swipes at your chest . . ."

A chill runs up Sarah's back. "Please, no. This place is haunted enough."

Ingrid's toothy smile is not comforting. "I agree. So let's go get proof. Want to come with?"

"To where?"

"The hotel garden, obviously. Around back, you can kind of see in the windows. And there's some gronky old furniture lying around, like I guess somebody tossed it out and Gail didn't want to have to haul it away. Or maybe she doesn't know. She seems like an out-of-sight, out-of-mind kind of person."

"I don't want to get in trouble . . ." Sarah trails off rather than letting the word *again* end that sentence.

"What trouble? Two gal pals at an artist residency, going for an inspirational hike in the woods. That's totally innocent. Just . . . I don't know, collect some feathers and shit to decorate your pots. Bring a bucket and scoop up some clay from the waterfall. You're an artist—be creative about it."

Sarah chuckles despite herself. When Ingrid isn't being awful, she's at least interesting. And lively. And Sarah does want to see the hotel—or at least its garden. With all of the front-facing windows boarded up, she just assumed all the windows were blocked, but if the back is open, she wants to see what's within.

An ice-cold shard trickles down her neck, images from that one, too-real dream pecking at her consciousness. She can't remember the whole thing—just flashes, the trees overhead and the number on the room plaque and the flowers painted on the ewer. But she has to know if what she saw in the dream took place at the resort.

And she has to see where the dead girl once walked, and where the doctor practiced, and where nails like the one from the coffin might be found.

"Okay," she says. "But we can't get in trouble."

Ingrid waggles her eyebrows. "Oh, I never get in trouble. I'm a photographer. Media always gets a free pass. I'll be here tomorrow at dawn, as long as it's not raining." She looks Sarah up and down. "Do you have anything black?"

Now it's Sarah's turn to smile. "Of course. I'm an artist."

Ingrid gathers up the photos, stacks them neatly, and zips them into a gallon ziplock bag before arranging her backpack's zipper so it won't leak. Without any sort of goodbye, she heads outside and picks up Reid's umbrella, opening it as she strides into the drizzle.

"That's not yours!" Sarah calls after her.

"It is now," the girl calls over her shoulder as she walks away.

"It belongs to Reid."

"So come get it if you want it."

Ingrid turns around, twenty feet away in the rain, looking like a goth Mary Poppins and grinning the grin of someone who often gets away with things. But Sarah is done being stomped all over, sick of people assuming she'll just roll over and take any abuse they wish to dole out. She charges out into the storm and snatches the umbrella out of Ingrid's hand. Ingrid is laughing, the rain slicking her acid-green hair down into her eyes. Sarah closes the umbrella and smacks the younger woman with it, just a light tap to the hip.

"I didn't think you'd do that!" Ingrid shouts, turning to leave.

"Me neither," Sarah shouts back.

When she slips inside, now soaked to the bone and beyond ready for a hot bath in the old clawfoot tub, she finds that Ingrid has left a photo jammed into the corner of the mirror over the sink. It's another shot of the white gown, the edge of a hem.

The stitched script reads HE'S A LIAR.

20

This is a dream.

She lies on her back in bed under the blankets, waiting in a close darkness lit only by a candle. A storm rages outside, echoed by the tight fist of dread in her belly. She is uncertain, a little scared, a little excited. The door opens and closes, and she shivers, eyes wide.

A shadowy form says, "Darling, are you ready?"

"I think so," she says, barely a whisper.

"Show yourself to me."

Her fingers play along the edge of the blanket. "I—I'm a bit nervous."

He looms over her as he sighs in disappointment. "I was told you would understand your wifely duties," he says in a stern voice, and she loses her grip on the covers as strong hands pull them away.

Time skips, in the way of dreams. Her legs are cold, her chemise pulled up over her back, and she's on her stomach. Everything is pitch-dark now, and a man breathes heavily in her ear, breath reeking of rot and tobacco and sherry. She can feel him inside her, heedless of her discomfort and pain and fear, but she can't protest, can't make a sound. Someone might hear, might ask him awkward questions, and he is most cruel when he is embarrassed. She gasps as something rips inside her, tearing her in half. It feels like she's falling, like she's spinning, and then she's floating on the ceiling looking down as a man covers her, rutting roughly as a dolphin defiling an otter's corpse.

"This is what you were made for," he says. "God made you this way, a perfect gift, built to receive and to bear fruit."

And then she's in her own body again, in Sarah's body, and Kyle's lips are against her ear as he thrusts and mutters, "You won't even remember this, will you?" in her ear, and the scent of hospital soap chokes her.

The world spins again and she's on the floor of the hotel room in someone else's body, the rug rough under her palms, throwing up into the painted bowl, the ewer sitting nearby with a rag beside. There is blood on her chemise, a hot, wet burning in her most secret places.

"Not one for tenderness, your new husband?" says a middle-aged woman, sitting on the ground, dabbing her forehead with a wet cloth. The woman's belly is hugely swollen with child under her gown, and her face is exhausted and full of pity. "Some men don't know how to be soft and sweet. They're simply not made that way. I can bring you one of the doctor's patent medicines, a salve that will make it easier. Does your husband know you will need time to recover?"

She shakes her head. "I can't tell him—I couldn't—"

A tutting sigh. "I'll tell my Henry to mention it one night in the smoking room," the older woman says. "Man-to-man."

"Oh please, do not!" she cries. "He won't take that well, as a gentleman."

The woman shifts restlessly around her belly. "Well then. Best just use the salve before you go to bed, just in case. He'll be kinder when you are with child. He'll leave you alone."

She closes her eyes as her gorge rises, and then Kyle is there dabbing her forehead.

"Poor baby," he says. "What did you eat this time?"

"Nothing strange." She feels guilty saying it, as if she should know what she did wrong. "Just the usual things."

"This always happens to you. You're just so very sensitive, aren't you? Maybe you—"

She hates it when he talks this way, and she's glad when the spout of vomit interrupts him as she heaves into the toilet.

There's a loud crack somewhere, splitting the world in two. Splitting her in two.

She is lying on the floor, cold and wet. She isn't sure who she is, which body she's inhabiting.

"Ready to try again?" a man says from somewhere overhead.

She doesn't know which man it is.

It doesn't really matter.

It means the same thing.

21

The next morning, Sarah is waiting by the door at dawn, dressed in black leggings, black boots, a black jacket, and a black cap, her hair braided and coiled in a tight bun at her nape. She woke up nauseated and shaky from dreams she couldn't quite remember, so she ate a protein bar and drank a glass of cold, metallic-tasting water from her bathroom tap, hoping like hell the pipes aren't actually made of lead.

Ingrid appears in black skinny jeans, black Docs, and an oversized black hoodie. She's got her backpack over one shoulder and her Leica around her neck.

"You ready?" she asks.

"Let's do it," Sarah says, realizing instantly how silly it sounds.

Last night's storm has fled, leaving every inch of the forest glittering with rain. A fresh layer of bright leaves and fallen branches coats the ground, knocked down by what must've been high winds. Sarah is glad she slept through it—and also surprised. Storms have always made her uneasy.

Ingrid leads her back into the woods behind her cottage, walking like she knows exactly where she's going. Her Docs sink into the wet pine needles, squelching. Mist hovers among the trees, clinging to the stern trunks like a child to a mother's skirts. They don't immediately hurry up to the resort, though—Ingrid heads up the mountain a little, winding among the hemlocks, giving it space and approaching from behind, as if sneaking up on it.

"Well, hello," Ingrid says, delighted.

A huge tree has fallen on the tall fence that surrounds the old hotel, so big and heavy that the stern metal has folded down underneath it like crumpled aluminum foil. Raindrops twinkle on the razor wire, which looks a lot sharper from the ground. Ingrid climbs up onto the tree trunk and walks across it with the grace of a gymnast, hopping down on the other side of the gleaming wire.

"Should we be doing this?" Sarah asks.

"Everything happens for a reason," Ingrid assures her. "The hotel wants us here."

"That seems like a convenient thing to say when it serves your purposes."

"Well, if it doesn't like it, then I'm sure it can drop a chandelier on my head. Otherwise, I feel perfectly welcome. Are you coming or not?"

Sarah glances all around, expecting Gail to pop out from behind a tree and send her back home. Gail, of course, fails to appear, and Sarah has no choice but to follow Ingrid over the fence. She may not be as brazen and confident, but she, too, feels a certain . . . pull. A welcoming, almost.

Seen this close up, the old building is more intriguing than ever. The stones don't have that purposefully chaotic uniformity of walls these days, where a manufacturer cuts four different shapes and it's up to the builder to make it look as haphazard as natural rocks pried from the earth. The stones here are all different shapes, different sizes, slightly different shades of gray, the mortar chipping away charmingly between them. The windows that have been covered up with plywood around back don't have the same beautiful paintings that grace the front. The wood here is stained black and green, runny as a grieving girl's mascara.

They round the corner, and Sarah's attention is drawn to the waterfall. It plunges down the side of the mountain behind the hotel, a misty column of fury cutting a firm swath through the rich green conifers. Its noise reminds her of a TV turned to the gray channel, to the feeling of staying over at her grandmother's house as a toddler and waiting for *Sesame Street* to start on her ancient cube of a wood-paneled Zenith. The sound is blurry, numbing, unending, whispering. She can't tell if she's waiting for it to stop or for something else to begin, but it's unnerving.

"That noise," Ingrid grumbles. "It's white noise until you're close to it, and then it becomes intolerable. You can't get away from it. I can't believe people used to pay for the privilege of having it shoved in their earholes."

"People can get used to anything," Sarah says, but she doesn't disagree.

The back garden is paved with walking paths, the big stones uneven with moss and weeds grown up between them. Sarah has to focus on where she places each foot so she won't turn an ankle on rain-slick rock. They pass eroded statues of nymphs, decorative walls, and another fountain filled with black-green algae. The remains of what appear to be lounge chairs molder in a perfect row under the eaves, preserved from the elements. An elegant wooden railing crumbles like candy canes in the rain. The ground floor is almost entirely windows back here—or it once was. It's mostly plywood now.

"See? They're everywhere." Ingrid smoothly squats and stands, holding her palm out flat. The chunk of wood nestled there features one of the rectangular nails, wriggling out like an angry grub. With one yank, Ingrid extracts it and holds up her prize for inspection. "You want it?"

Sarah does not want it.

She doesn't want any more proof that she's done things she shouldn't.

She doesn't want to hold the same kind of nail Bernie was clutching when he died.

And yet.

To leave it here, to abandon it, almost seems . . . rude.

Like rejecting a gift.

She holds out her hand, and Ingrid drops the nail. It's rusty, smearing burgundy across her palm like an old bloodstain. She shoves it in her pocket, the adult's version of saving the earthworms after a downpour.

"Here's where we go in," Ingrid says, pointing to a pair of French doors, which are chained securely shut. Their glass has been papered over on the inside with butcher paper that's peeling down like a bad sunburn.

"Do you have the key?" Sarah asks.

Ingrid grins and picks up a loose paver. "Sure. Let's call it that." Before Sarah can protest, Ingrid bashes in the bottom panes of glass, and the wood framing is so far gone it crumples inward like gingerbread. Using her steel-toed boot, Ingrid kicks out the remaining shards and dusts all the sharp bits off to the side. She reaches into her backpack and pulls out a raggedy towel, which she folds and places over the shattered glass.

"So you've done this before," Sarah says, unsurprised.

"Like I said, urbex forever." Ingrid pulls out a small flashlight, sticks it in her teeth, slides her backpack inside the hotel, and crawls in on her belly. When Sarah doesn't immediately follow, the girl's hand appears, beckoning with one finger. Sarah begins to understand how Alice felt watching the White Rabbit disappear down the rabbit hole. With a sigh, she falls to her knees, pushes her own backpack in, and ducks her head into the building.

The first thing she notices is the smell. Old, mildewy, like minerals with a faint overlay of rot. Anything could be in here, she thinks— dead bodies, dead animals, live animals, murderers. When she was growing up, her mother both forced her to stay home alone too early and also delighted in telling her grisly stories about the serial killers, pedophiles, kidnappers, and burglars who were lying in wait to snatch her, so she's spent most of her life assuming that she'll one day find a guy in a ski mask who wants to do her harm hiding somewhere in her home.

The second thing she notices is the silence. The rumble of the waterfall is muted, and otherwise there's not a single sound in the entire building. It's like putting in earplugs. Ingrid isn't far away, her flashlight swinging around as she takes stock. Shit. Maybe Sarah should've brought her own big camping flashlight instead of relying on her phone's flashlight. Oh, well; too late now. At least the hotel doesn't seem too dark inside. Satisfied that it's relatively safe since Ingrid hasn't screamed or belly-flopped out of the door, Sarah pushes her body in through the hole, contorting to avoid the broken glass, and stands.

Once her eyes adjust, the world separates into figure and ground, thanks to the light shining through and around the old butcher paper, and her heart nearly stops in her chest. This place—she knows this place. It all comes back to her in a rush. She knows this green-and-white diamond chessboard floor, these carved wooden columns in the shape of palm trees, these little nooks with elegant couches and chairs, now just ghostly shapes covered in dusty sheets the color of an old man's teeth. The plants and the parrot are gone, but this is clearly the lobby from her dream.

"Oh, my God," she mutters as she walks to a nearby couch and pulls back the sheet to reveal the exact shade of mauve velvet she expected.

"Wild, right?" Ingrid says, pausing to snap a photo of the empty bird cage. "Ancient as fuck."

But Ingrid has of course misinterpreted Sarah's shock. The other woman thinks she's just in awe of the crumbling beauty, the aging grace of what's been left behind, the Miss Havisham of it all. She can't possibly know that Sarah's brain is flashing two realities, one over the other like an optometrist testing prescriptions, one or two, two or one, the overlay of the dream falling down over the dingy reality.

"We need to find a map," Ingrid says, excited. "I want to go straight to the so-called spa. What about you?"

"I . . . I'd like to see the rooms." Sarah walks to the reception desk, a grand and gleaming thing of wood and tarnished brass. Behind it is a checkerboard of cubbies, each cubby marked with a numbered brass plaque. The cubbies are just wide and deep enough to hold an envelope, although they are all currently empty of correspondence. A brass key hangs in each one, and perhaps this seemed quotidian for the time, but Sarah is repulsed by the idea of reaching her entire forearm into that dusty darkness. She finds the cubby for 312, closes one eye as if she's looking down the barrel of a gun. There is the key. She wiggles her fingers like she's preparing to reach down a dog's throat to retrieve some piece of contraband, half expecting the cubby to close around her fist with teeth just as sharp.

She steps closer, shines her phone's flashlight inside. The dust is thick and untouched, the key waiting. There are no spiders, no cobwebs, nothing to make her think anything bad should happen, and yet . . . she doesn't want to do it.

Ingrid approaches the desk. "See a map? A pamphlet? How did they even print that kind of shit back then?"

Before Ingrid can get close enough to see the sweat trickling down her temples despite the chill, Sarah reaches into the cubby and pulls out the key with its stamped metal tag. It's cold and smooth and heavy in her hand, and she slides it into her pocket. Unaware of this intense personal drama, Ingrid rifles through the desk, opening and shutting drawers. Sarah brushes some papers away and finds an old ledger, dark green and covered in powdery mold. She opens it carefully, the rich, damp smell of the ancient paper somehow both horrid and compelling.

The pages within are the color of weak tea, heavy and thick. Line after line is filled with elegant script, names and dates and room numbers, the pen's marks graceful and stark. It's hard to read, almost another language. She turns to the last page and finds blank lines, turns back and back until she finds the final entries.

"Do you know when the resort closed?" she asks Ingrid.

Ingrid looks up from a drawer and does that slow blink that implies Sarah is an idiot. "Just look at the last date in that ledger."

"Okay, but do you know *why* it closed?"

With a shrug, Ingrid returns to her raccoon-like scavenging. "From what I could find, no one knows. They didn't, like, take out an ad or anything. Which means it was probably something embarrassing. Foreclosure, probably."

Sarah looks at the final check-in date: July 15, 1898. Mr. and Mrs. Joseph Laurent. Room 338.

There's no checkout date listed for the Laurents, and as Sarah scrolls back, there are fifty-seven guests without a checkout date. These people—they were here when the resort closed, and whatever happened was startling enough that no one bothered to check them out. Odd, that their keys are in the cubbies, because every cubby has its key, but perhaps there were multiple keys. Some hooks do have more than one key, she notices upon further inspection.

Next she runs a finger up the ledger, looking for the occupant of room 312.

There it is. Her finger stops, lands on the paper as if pinning a butterfly down.

Mr. and Mrs. Bertram Engle.

Of course the woman's name isn't there. Back then, she was merely an extension of her husband.

"Okay, no convenient hotel maps," Ingrid mutters. "The eighteen hundreds were dumb."

She's made a cringeworthy mess, and Sarah wishes she had the time and confidence to put everything back in Ingrid's wake. It just feels . . . disrespectful, disturbing this place, not that she even knows where everything goes.

"Left or right or up the grand staircase?" Ingrid asks.

Identical halls wait at either end of the lobby. The staircase, while grand, is also falling down. Sarah can imagine what it would feel like if her foot sank into that spongy old carpet and fell right through an ancient board. The staircase just feels wrong. From where they stand, there is no real difference in the identical hallways. She looks both ways, remembers the dream.

"Left."

Ingrid nods. "Left it is." She swings her flashlight in that direction and starts walking. Sarah follows.

All the hallway's windows are covered in plywood—this is the front of the resort, and if she were to peek through a crack, she would gaze out upon the artists' retreat, maybe catch a few of the artists walking up the gravel path to grab an early coffee or start working. The first door they find on the left is a ballroom, and Ingrid nudges the door open with a squeal and shines her flashlight around a huge, grand space perfectly preserved by time. The waxed wood floor still gleams in places, the dainty chairs and tables are stacked up around the striped walls. A slightly raised dais at the far end of the room still has chairs and music stands set up, an elegant fence around the outside as if to keep the musicians from running wild like spirited ponies. Ingrid heads for a closed wooden door, and Sarah follows, hating the sound of their wet boots squeaking on the floor. Their very presence feels like an affront.

Beyond the door, they find the kitchens, and everything here has been left in utter disarray, with pots and ladles spilled on the floor and plates still stacked as if waiting to serve the crowd. It almost looks like whatever ended the hotel struck in the middle of some grand cotillion. Sarah marvels at the ovens, the piles of wood, the cauldrons, the army of pots. To think: People stood here, in this room, fires roaring, no refrigerators, no KitchenAid mixers, and worked themselves to the bone while just feet away, far richer people danced and dined while clad in clothes that cost a kitchen maid's yearly salary. There's a back door that must open up to the grounds, but someone has recently applied a heavy-duty lock.

"Do you think Reid has a saw?" Ingrid asks, eyes alight. "If we cut off this lock, it'll be much easier to get inside next time."

Sarah shrugs, mostly certain this isn't a place she'll want to explore again. She feels like a child sneaking into a forbidden room, and every moment she waits for a fist to close around the back of her shirt, to be caught by Gail or, or . . .

It makes no sense, but it's as if something dangerous is sleeping here, and she doesn't want it to wake up and find her.

They retrace their steps out to the hall and continue. There's a meeting room, a library that has sadly fallen victim to a leak, a parlor done up in lavender that looks like it was designed for a ladies' party. All interesting, all worthy of hours of study, but Ingrid is hellbent on finding something medical and Sarah secretly wants to find room 312 and see if it matches her dream. At the end of the hall, they find a pretty solarium, the most ruined room so far, thanks to the broken glass ceiling overhead. It's open to the elements now, the wood floor so swampy that even Ingrid won't step inside. She does, however, peer at a hole in the floor with interest.

"That's not ground," she says, wiggling her fingers greedily. "It's open air. There's something down there."

"I mean, there's obviously a basement where servants did laundry," Sarah reminds her.

"But look. What's down there—it's white, not rock. It's part of the hotel."

Sarah can see it, a little, but the floor isn't firm enough to allow them to get any closer.

"We've got to get down there." Ingrid spins around and pushes open the wooden door labeled STAIRS. It's a landing, with wooden steps going both up and down.

"Let's try upstairs first," Sarah says. "The guests wouldn't want to go into the basement for a spa experience, right? Didn't doctors back then tell their patients to get sunlight and air? Like, the treatment was called a Change of Air."

"But that room is all white, and I think I saw a bathtub. Come on." Ingrid starts downward, but Sarah is done with following a whimsical goblin around.

"I'm going upstairs." Without waiting to hear Ingrid's thoughts, she tests the stairs and finds them sturdy and dry. The carpet is dusty and the only light is her phone, but she'd rather go up in darkness than down, and Ingrid can follow her or descend into hell by herself.

There are gaslights on the walls, intricate wainscoting, shiny wallpaper. The staircase turns several times before the next landing. As soon as she reaches it, she hears Ingrid thundering up behind her, muttering.

"A hotel is a hotel," she grouses. "Rooms are rooms. They're all pretty much the same. Beds, dressers. The basement is where it's at."

"We can go there next," Sarah says, prim as a schoolmarm. "Now hush."

Ingrid stops on her stair.

"No."

She turns around and heads back downstairs, leaving Sarah alone. The space is suddenly darker, the air more still, and she feels that ancient prey animal's trill of fear.

She is no longer with the herd. She's on her own.

The staircase seems to constrict around her, hurrying her upward to the possibility of windows and light and airflow.

She reaches the top of the stairwell and emerges in a pitch-dark hallway. So much for her dreams of sunlight, of windows with gold limning the cracks around the plywood. Whoever shut this place up, shut it up tight. The hairs in her ears twitch as if there's some sound she can't quite hear, and she shines her phone up and down the hall in both directions, remembering what it felt like the first time she watched *The Blair Witch Project*.

"Creepy as fuck," she murmurs to herself.

In this moment, oddly, she misses Ingrid. She knows this place is empty, that there are no monsters hiding here, that there is nothing here that could possibly wish her harm.

And yet . . . it feels as if some great, sleeping beast is gently waking, stretching its claws, nostrils flaring.

But . . .

No. This is a sad old building, not a beast, and buildings have neither feelings nor claws.

Sarah focuses her light on the nearest door plaque. She guessed the correct hall, at least. There's 327. Then 326. Across the hall is 325. Some old memory bubbles up and turns in her heart, something about *The Shining*, but that's just a book and a movie and Stephen King isn't always right, and Sarah doesn't care because she's caught the scent and is counting down the plaques: 315, 314, 313 . . .

The hallway seems endless, door after door going on forever in the darkness. There are no little tables, no photographs, none of the touches of hotel décor she's come to expect to break up the monotony among repetitive patterns that makes the human brain so uncomfortable.

Finally, there it is: 312.

Sarah reaches into her pocket and withdraws the key. It's heavy and warm like a recently dead mouse, and she shines her phone light on it and says, "Okay, Alice, let's see what the Red Queen has in store."

The key gleams in the stark beam of light as Sarah inserts it in the lock. She feels the tumblers align as it turns with a meaty clunk. The doorknob is oddly cold under her hand. The door swings open with a desperate, whining creak.

And everything goes dark.

22

Firm hands grasp her shoulders and pull her up to sitting, and she blinks until the world comes into focus. Her head is throbbing, her cheek stinging. She puts a trembling hand up to touch it, worries a molar with her tongue.

"Look what you made me do, you silly little fool," a man says, his voice fond and almost chiding.

The room materializes around her. The bedclothes are askew, a lamp glowing orange on the vanity beside a bouquet of lilacs that perfume the still air. She looks down to find the neck of her chemise torn. She looks up, and her body jerks when she sees the man's face, sees the raw beast pacing behind his guileless blue eyes.

"Why—why, you hit me!" she says, but it's not Sarah saying it. It's someone else, the same someone else from the last time she was in this room. Her long blond hair is in a braid over one shoulder, tied with a brown velvet ribbon with the velvet all rubbed away.

"What was I to do? You clawed at me, you little minx!" the man says, holding up his hairy forearm to show four red lines. He's wearing a ridiculous nightshirt, almost like a long poet's blouse, his hairy legs striking her as absurd and grotesque.

The other woman, the woman she's sharing space with, this body she's in—she's shocked and horrified. She has not, Sarah begins to understand, seen a naked man before, not even a man's hairy feet.

"I was sleeping, and you—"

"And I came in to claim my husbandly rights." His voice is stern, teaching. He's older than she is, maybe even twice as old, probably weighs twice as much. She's a small woman, this one, barely out of her teens. Just a girl.

"You didn't even knock," she admits with a look of betrayal. "No sweet words or—or fond touches. Mother told me that I was to be accommodating, but I thought . . . it might be different between us. All those promises you made during our carriage rides . . ."

"I was told you were a tractable girl," he continues, as if he hasn't heard her at all. He kneels and pulls her close, cradling her, and she feels his—his man-parts!—pop up against her haunch. "That you understood the expectations a gentleman would have."

"I . . . wasn't told much. Just that I was to lie still and accept it. But I'm still recovering from . . . from . . ."

"Oh, that wasn't such a trouble. Just took you a bit to get broken in."

"It's . . . it hurts . . ." She blushes, her face gone hot, to speak of such things.

His parts stir and pulse against her, not at all derailed by her pain. Possibly even excited about it.

"You just need to relax. That's your problem. It won't hurt if you just stop fighting it. Now, let's get you back in bed."

He stands and helps her up. She's unsteady on her feet, still half asleep, her body on high alert. The ancient sleeping animal of her heart tells her she was attacked, and even if he's acting soft and mannerly now, she replays what just happened.

She was sleeping in her room after a lovely day of croquet and a trip to the baths, her limbs tired and heavy and soft. And then she woke to a heavy weight on her body, pressing her down into the crackling mattress as a hand fought its way up her skirts. In the dark, she saw nothing, only felt the assault, and she fought back like a trapped rabbit, screeching and kicking and clawing away the hand pressing ever upward. She's still sore from his last claiming, and her half-dreaming body could only defend itself. The weight lifted, and she was pulled out of bed, and that's when the strike came, jerking her head to the side and sending her directly to the hard, wooden floor.

He . . . he hit her.

Her husband hit her.

Mother had not prepared her for such a possibility.

Her father was always gentle and kind, if stern. He'd never raised his voice, never so much as swatted one of his hounds when it pressed too close for tidbits.

Why, she didn't even know men could hit women . . . until now.

"Go on," he commands. "On your back. Pull up your shift for me, that's a good girl."

She swallows hard. When he urged her to return to bed, she thought he understood her, that she requires tenderness and care and rest. But he understands something quite different. And she now understands what else his hands can do.

She nods and crawls into bed as if she is being punished. She wishes she had used the salve that Elizabeth brought her, but she thought he would chivalrously allow her at least one night alone. On her back, head nestled in the soft down pillow, braid uncomfortable under her spine, she reaches for the hem of her chemise and begins to pull it up with shaking hands. Shame floods her, that he is seeing such parts of her, such private parts that she's been taught to keep covered from her earliest days.

But this is her duty, this is why she exists. To marry well and run a household and provide heirs. And she does long for a child, a chubby little laughing baby to push in a pram in the sunshine. And, if Elizabeth is right, he might leave her alone for a while, if she was big and swollen. How lovely that might be.

Sarah squirms within this body, this memory, this dream, as if trying to escape what is coming.

This is not *her* duty, not why she exists.

No father, both gentle and stern, sold her like chattel to the highest bidder.

Perhaps this girl feels it is her duty to lift her gown, but Sarah feels no such compunction. She tries to push the shift back down, but it's like fighting the flow of a river, like fighting the tide. She can't budge it.

The hem creeps up. The man looms over her, smiling smugly, benignly, almost fatherly, the scant light turning his graying stubble into a sinister shadow.

"That's a good girl," he repeats, as if she is a well-behaved dog.

Her hands stop at mid-thigh, trembling. She thought this would happen under the covers, not exposed to the world, not inspected like some peculiar insect in a museum.

"Perhaps we could lie under the blanket?" she asks, voice tremulous.

The big hands push her own aside and tug the shift up to her waist. "No. Let me see you. A man deserves his due."

She is bare, cold, the stark air of a spring night rippling over shy, aching flesh, bringing up goosebumps. His hand lands on the inside of her thigh, squeezing it like he's testing a fruit for ripeness. It edges up, his wide, flat thumb caressing roughly as it inches up toward her . . . her . . . surely he isn't going to?

But he does, shoving the thumb hard into her and making her gasp and whimper.

"Dry as a bone," he says, disappointed. "Well, we'll have to fix that, won't we?" The thumb rubs brutally, crushing what feels something like a flower, and she tries to wriggle away. His other hand comes down on her shoulder, holding her firmly in place. "Settle, girl," he says, as if she is one of his prized horses. "It will only hurt for a moment."

And then he covers her, and there's a wrenching, searing pain, and she floats up to the ceiling again like a little ghost. Her back bumps against the cold white plaster as she watches his back heaving like a pig giving birth. Her husband, the distinguished banker, pumping away like a savage barnyard beast, and underneath him is another woman, a woman with her hair up in an odd hairstyle, her eyes surprised, leaking tears.

Sarah looks up past the man to the blond girl on the ceiling. Their eyes meet with a jolt, like lightning arcing between them, a tether binding them in this crude, impersonal prison, both of them inside it and outside of it at once.

She blinks, and then she's the one floating on the ceiling—of the guest bedroom of her house in Colorado. The man pumping away below her isn't the banker in his nightshirt with his muttonchops and curly auburn hair; now it is Kyle, naked and sweating.

"You think you know everything," Kyle mutters. "You dumb bitch."

There below him, below her, is her own body laid bare, still and rubbery, awkward, her own face, her eyes wide open, their pupils blown so big and round that there is almost no iris left, just gaping, empty pools of black.

"You, too?" the girl whispers, and then everything goes dark.

23

"What the literal fuck?"

Sarah opens her eyes and is briefly blinded by Ingrid's flashlight shining down from overhead, a dusty pair of Docs nearly touching her nose.

What the literal fuck indeed.

"What happened to you?" Ingrid asks.

Sarah is lying on her stomach, half in room 312, her legs out in the hall. Her phone is on the ground just out of reach inside, the flashlight pointing a beam right at the ceiling. She looks at that white circle on the ancient plaster and imagines a girl in a long white gown floating there as if underwater, looking down.

She was just there. They were just here. It was . . .

It must've been another weird dream. This place is getting to her, worming its way into the raw, fresh meat of her creative mind. Her muse has been dormant for so long that it's latched onto the dead girl in the coffin and is spinning stories out of the air. She sees here what she wants to see, makes little narratives in her head like she always has.

But why does the dream make sense, when dreams never make sense? Why does it follow a story as if leading her deep into the dark forest, following a trail of rain-wet gumdrops?

She pushes herself up. "I hit my head."

Didn't she? It aches. The pain radiates out from her cheek, her jaw. She sends her tongue around to probe the teeth on that side.

"How the fuck can you hit your head alone in a hotel? Jesus, you must be the clumsiest motherfucker since Bella Swan."

Ingrid doesn't offer a hand or bend down to make sure she doesn't have a concussion; true to form, the girl stands over her, shaking her head and staring down in embarrassment. Sarah snatches up her phone and stands. The faintest waft of lilac filters past her nose.

She slowly runs her flashlight around the entire chamber. It's exactly as Sarah saw it in her dream—vision? Hallucination? The earlier one and today's—without the people or the vase of lavender blooms. Even the coverlet is the same, the painted flowers on the ewer identical. She walks to the ancient dresser and pulls out the top drawer. She finds an ivory brush-and-comb set, a tin box of what were once pastilles, and some handkerchiefs. With trembling hands, Sarah pulls out a hankie and unfolds it. The letters E. E. are stitched into the soft white fabric, surrounded by little flowers. Each of the hankies has the same initials and different embroidery, doves or trees or fruit, all in softly faded pastels.

In the bigger drawer on the left, she finds a sewing kit, everything neatly snugged in right where it goes in rainbow order. The white thread, she notices, is missing. She glances at Ingrid, wondering if she's noticed, too.

"Boring," Ingrid says, which means she either didn't notice or didn't make the connection.

Sarah slides open the drawer on the right and finds a gentleman's things—a comb, mustache wax, cologne, yet more handkerchiefs plainly embroidered with B. E. and no fancifully stitched plants or creatures. There are cuff links and old coins in a small porcelain dish and . . .

Two rings, one a dainty gold band and the other a bigger, manlier band. They match. Yet they are not with their owners.

"Curiouser and curiouser," Ingrid says. "Why would they leave their stuff behind? If you were in a hotel and left, you wouldn't leave all this shit here."

Sarah wonders this as well, so she shines her phone light at the nearby armoire. When she opens it, she half expects to find a doorway to another world, but it's just old clothes. On one side are three gentleman's suits, stiff and smelling slightly of antediluvian BO. On the other side are several dresses, including a heavy satin ballgown with delicate embroidery and puffed sleeves. Ingrid reaches in and pulls this one out on its old-fashioned hanger, holding it up to her body.

"Damn, girlfriend was teeny," she says.

Seeing the ivory satin in Ingrid's hands fills Sarah with a strange, possessive rage. "Put it back," she all but growls.

Ingrid gives her a look that suggests she's gone entirely bonkers. "Okay, Cujo, take it down a notch." She hangs the dress back up, carelessly stuffing the train into the armoire.

"These things deserve respect." Sarah takes a deep breath of cedar and mothballs from some hidden sachet in the old chifforobe. "You can't just touch things that aren't yours."

"If the owner wants to come back and fight me, I'm ready."

Sarah shivers. She doesn't want to meet the owners of anything that remains in this hotel.

She isn't sure what it is she's looking for, but there's not much left to find. Maybe if there were a happy, healthy, comfortable source of light and Ingrid didn't bring the energy of an annoyed wasp, she'd do a more thorough search, like someone in an escape room who knows that clues are hidden somewhere. But as it is, the darkness creeps close, and there is some repulsive force here that makes her want to back out and quietly shut the door. When she heads that way, thankfully, Ingrid follows.

"Okay, I went on your errand," Ingrid says. "Now come on mine."

Ingrid leads her down the hall with the flashlight, and Sarah shines her phone light around, half hoping some strange sign or portent will appear . . . and half dreading it. There's something about a peculiar stillness in a long-empty space, as if the ghosts have grown too accustomed to silence and don't wish to be reminded of the life that's passed by. Sarah wants to let these ghosts rest, wants to sneak out before her presence has been noticed. She walks carefully, her boots making no sound on the carpet. Ingrid walks more heavily—the girl moves through the world as if she's never known fear. Or maybe she's just one of the rare ones who somehow escaped childhood unscathed, who's never been followed by a catcaller on the street or cornered by a friend's big brother in the basement.

No. No one acts that tough unless they have to.

Whatever Ingrid has been through has made her bolder. All the black clothes, the cursing, the anger—it's a cat puffing up its fur to look bigger. Not that Sarah blames her. She, too, is puffier than she once was.

Ingrid disappears into the stairwell, and Sarah follows her down. The twisting space feels smaller, like it's constricting, like it's trying to trap them, and Sarah nearly steps on Ingrid's boot in her hurry to get to a more open area. They pass the first stairwell and continue down toward the cellar. Ingrid's confidence balances out Sarah's fear. She's already been down here, so it must be safe.

Well, safe-ish.

"So did you find anything?" Sarah asks.

Ingrid chuckles in the dark. "Yeah, you could say that."

The stairwell ends, and Ingrid pushes a heavy wooden door open to reveal a hallway very different from the one upstairs. There is no carpet, no wallpaper, no elegant brass plaques. The walls were once white but are now dingy and weeping with mold. The floor is white tile, the grout gone black between the smooth rectangles. White doors march down the hall, their numbers painted in stark black. These are the 100s. Each door has a small glass window, but the glass is cloudy, the rooms beyond pitch-black.

Sarah steps out onto the tile and immediately regrets the echoes of her footsteps.

"What's in the rooms?" she asks.

"Didn't find the keys yet." Ingrid sets out down the hall, shining her flashlight ahead, although it isn't strong enough to reach whatever lies at the end of the tunnel.

Anything could be down there, Sarah thinks.

Anything.

And then they come to wide double doors, and Ingrid pushes them open easily. They're light and swing in both directions, and Sarah immediately realizes they are exactly the sort of doors that she's seen in hospitals. The room within is, much to her surprise, an operating theater. There's a table in the center of the room surrounded by benches on wooden risers. Gaslights gather dust, hanging down from the ceiling, and Sarah wonders how anyone could learn anything in such a dark space, why even the most competent doctor would perform a complicated surgery way down here in the basement without the benefits of electricity.

Her heart sinks as the answer becomes obvious: *to keep it hidden.*

Ingrid gestures to her with the flashlight and opens a beautiful wooden case to reveal rows upon rows of surgical instruments. Elegant little drawers hold tiny bottles, and Ingrid presents two of them for Sarah's inspection: SULFURIC ETHER and CHLOROFORM.

"I was right. They did operations down here."

She replaces the bottles and pulls out a slender drawer brimming with sharpened scalpels and various hooks and clamps. Sarah shivers, imagining what sort of havoc these instruments must've wrought, long ago, before surgery was really well understood. One of the blades still holds rusty stains. Sarah's feet take a step back without really consulting with her head.

Ingrid drops her backpack on the ground, the noise loud enough to make Sarah jump. She hands her flashlight to Sarah and pulls the Leica out of the bag. "You aim the lights while I take photos." It isn't a question.

Something about the whole process feels . . . dirty. Although Sarah recognized the empathy and respect in Ingrid's photos of the dead girl's dress, there is something tawdry about shining a phone light at the restraint dangling from the table.

As if sensing Sarah's reticence, Ingrid snaps her head around to glare at her, eyes burning. "People need to know," she says. "They say this was a fancy hotel, a resort, but resorts don't come with chains. This is some real Nellie Bly shit. Elizabeth Packard would be furious."

As Sarah holds both lights as directed, Ingrid snaps pictures of the instruments, the restraints, the benches made for the rumps of the well-dressed white men who would've come to watch patients drugged and held down, their ribs spread open like the cracked covers of books. Again and again, Ingrid changes out her film and snaps some more. She swaps the Leica for a newer camera, mirrorless and expensive looking. Sarah's arms begin to ache. As she watches how Ingrid carefully sets up each image and moves the flashlights in Sarah's hands to best illuminate them, she begins to see that the other woman worships truth. She isn't using clever Instagram tricks, isn't arranging the instruments into a more pleasing display. She is merely documenting exactly what's there, exactly as it's been left behind.

Sarah's shame over vulgarity is replaced by a shared sense of righteous indignation.

Finally Ingrid is satisfied, and she tucks her camera back in the bag and holds out her hand for the flashlight. Sarah hands it over and gently nudges all the drawers of the chest closed. Such things, she thinks, should not be left bare to the world, those blades gleaming to themselves in the darkness.

Ingrid heads outside into the hallway and huffs a breath; the air is colder down here, almost frigid. "I want to find the hydrotherapy room. They had to have one, right? They all did, back then."

Sarah doesn't know much about the topic, but she figures that *hydro* means "water" and that the resort sprang into existence for the waterfall's supposed healing properties, so it makes sense that water would form an important part of whatever treatments happened here. She pulls out her granola bar and chews as quietly as she can, trying to work out what she's heard about this place in comparison to what she's seeing.

The operating theater doesn't quite go with the idea of the upper

IT WILL ONLY HURT FOR A MOMENT

class paying high prices for healthful vacations, but then again, the property is twenty miles from the nearest hospital by modern standards, which would've been hours and hours from any medical facility when the resort was serving customers. She knows there were doctors on hand, especially since she's currently living in Dr. Calloway's old home, so it makes sense that he would've needed a place to perform surgeries other than the front desk in the lobby. If someone at the resort had an accident or an infected appendix, it naturally follows that it would be best to handle that here rather than putting them on a horse and pointing them toward the nearest town.

On the other hand, the basement is noticeably less posh and more . . . yes, fine, it looks like an asylum. And the operating room seems like the kind of place where someone might be held down against their will and experimented on. Then again, maybe all operating tables had restraints, back before they really knew everything about anesthesia.

This is not Sarah's area of expertise. She watched *Ratched* and *American Horror Story* and has read some thrillers about asylums, and that is the sum total of her personal knowledge on the matter.

Still, when you want someone to feel relaxed and pampered and well taken care of, you don't generally paint everything white, lock all the doors, and leave chains dangling off tables.

"Okay, it's not hydrotherapy, but I'll take it," Ingrid says, pushing open the next swinging door, labeled DENTISTRY.

Sarah's teeth clack together as she swings her phone light around to reveal basically the worst nightmare of her childhood: an ancient, rusting dental chair. Another chest of instruments waits nearby. This room is wetter than the last, the walls a constellation of black mold with brown stains dripping down the corners.

"We must be near the waterfall," Ingrid says. "But I've got to catch a couple snaps. Light?"

Sarah obediently holds up her phone's light, and Ingrid hands her the flashlight and pulls out her Leica. They move around the room, focusing in and stepping back, catching the shine on pliers and scalpels, shining the light on a single hair caught in an old screw. It's almost better, working as an assistant; instead of listening for sounds, feeling the weight of the building overhead, recalling that she is doing something illegal that she's explicitly promised not to do, Sarah simply focuses on the work in front of her. Ingrid, on the other hand, is slipping into frustration. She was calm at first, but now she's growing twitchy and restless, for some reason. She doesn't have as much focus, has only taken one roll of film and a few snaps with her modern mirrorless camera.

"Let's try lucky door number three," she says.

Sarah follows her back out into the endless hallway and realizes they've reached another lobby, or something like it. There's a reception desk and, behind it, a big wooden door with a familiar name on the plaque.

DR. WARREN DECEMBER, it reads, and Sarah is confused.

"Only Dr. December," she murmurs. "But what about Dr. Calloway?"

Ingrid holds up her phone and takes a quick pic of the plaque. "Maybe Calloway ran the upstairs and December was in charge down here. Heaven and hell. Happy customers and hidden inmates."

Without further preamble, she turns the doorknob, but the wood must've expanded with moisture and time. It won't budge. She puts her shoulder against it and shoves, but it refuses to open.

"Is that how it is, Dr. December?" Ingrid says. She steps back and kicks the door open hard enough to make it bounce off the wall within.

Sarah's heart nearly leaps out of her throat. That noise—so loud— like a gun—echoing down the hallway and back, must be the loudest sound here in over a century. Her shoulders rise up, and she feels that age-old sensation of a prey animal that knows it's done something stupid to alert the nearest predator.

Ingrid, on the other hand, clearly gives no shits.

"Now, this is what I'm talking about!" she crows.

This is the Platonic ideal of an office. Wooden bookshelves, a desk so big it must've been built within, piles and piles of paper. Ingrid goes into scavenger mode and starts digging through the drawers, muttering, "Keys, keys, c'mon." When she gets to a side drawer, she cocks her head. "Dude had a lot of sunglasses. Like, a lot."

Sarah goes around to look, because everything they've seen so far is somewhat expected. There in the drawer are six pairs of glasses with lenses so dark that when she holds a pair in front of her eyes, she can barely see anything.

Now . . . it's starting to make sense.

"I had a teacher like that once," she says softly, because she's fairly certain she will never raise her voice in this graveyard of a place. "Mr. Granville. He had horrible migraines, and the sun was a big trigger. He wore sunglasses all the time, kept the blinds shut."

"December is probably the guy who decided to build a medical ward in the basement," Ingrid finishes for her. "So he could do his best work without a major ouchie."

As Ingrid continues tossing the desk, Sarah goes to the bookshelf and runs her phone light along the leather spines. Sure enough, she finds a section on neurology, migraine, vasodilation, nerve storms, and trepanation.

"Bingo," she says. "He was totally a migraine guy."

"So he builds a treatment center that works for him, not necessarily for the patients. Probably figured what's good for the goose is good for the gander."

"Or what's good for the gander is good for literally every bird ever."

Ingrid snorts. "Sounds like the kind of guy who'd be in charge. Yes!" She holds up a ring of keys, dozens and dozens of them jangling. "Now let's go see what's in the rooms."

But Sarah pauses a moment. There's something about this office, something she needs to do here, something she needs to find. She shines her phone light all around again, hoping for some ping on her memory, but nothing comes.

"Let's go," Ingrid says at the door.

Sarah's fingertips rest on the edge of the huge wood desk. There's something—

Ingrid's flashlight flickers, the light going a shade dimmer, and that's all it takes. Sarah joins her, and they head for the nearest locked door. Its number is 115.

"You brought batteries, right?" Sarah asks.

"For the flashlight? No. I bought it just for this trip. It's fresh as a daisy."

"Then why is it flickering?"

Ingrid sighs dramatically. "For ambience. Now hold it for me while I find the key."

She hands the flashlight over, and now Sarah again has a light in each hand. She shines them both down on Ingrid's key ring, watching her flick through the keys, clank clank clank. They're numbered, but the numbers are tiny.

"One fifteen. Come on. No whammies," Ingrid mutters. "Aha!"

She holds up the key, which looks like every other key except for that tiny little number. The flashlight flickers warningly as she shoves the key in the lock. It sticks as she turns it, and she has to force it a little.

"Come on, come on," she urges.

Sarah hears a noise, somewhere down the hall. Something shuffling, some animal, probably, but jerky and confused. She suddenly wants very, very much to be on the other side of that door. She wants to be anywhere but in this open hall.

Click goes the key.

"Hello?" a voice echoes from across the years.

24

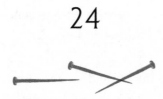

ngrid's flashlight turns off and she grabs Sarah's phone, snuffing its light. Sarah hears her pulling the key from the lock, trying to keep the entire ring of ancient metal from jangling like a klaxon. They're in complete darkness now.

Sarah's heart is pounding so loud that she's certain it's echoing up and down the hallway with each jerky thump. When she heard that voice, she hoped it was just her overactive imagination, but Ingrid's response means it's very real.

"Hello? Is somebody down there?"

Silently she sighs in partial relief.

It's not a ghost, not some monster—it's the old wizard. Gail's husband, whatever his name is. And it sounds like he's coming down the stairs. Her heart doesn't let up a bit as she realizes that if he finds them here, she'll get kicked out, and she has absolutely nowhere else to go.

Ingrid grabs her arm and pulls her away, back toward the lobby and office. They're tiptoeing in their boots, running as quietly as possible, keeping close to the wall. Ingrid must have her hand on it to guide them as they hurry blindly down the hall. She yanks Sarah into the open office doorway and flicks on her flashlight, throwing the wrecked room into stark relief. She points the beam at the massive desk, and Sarah immediately understands. They scurry around and crawl underneath it. Ingrid turns off her flashlight, and Sarah is overwhelmed with darkness, with silence, with the ancient, moldering scent of slowly rotting paper and leather and wood.

"Hello?"

Footsteps shuffle to the office door and stop.

Sarah can hear the old man's phlegmy sigh, his rattling cough. It sounds like the end of things, for her and eventually for him.

She goes completely still as a flashlight beam jitters over the back wall, glinting off the gold titles on the books, shaking to the rhythm of an old man's hand. The light disappears and the footsteps shuffle off. Sarah leans forward, but Ingrid's arm blocks her, making her jerk back.

"Give him time to leave," Ingrid whispers. "That's, like, Urbex 101. He's gotta go past us, then double back, then decide there's nothing here, then leave. If we go now, he'll be behind us on the way out."

Sarah takes a deep breath and tries to center herself. She remembers a yoga instructor once telling her that she could find a breath in even the smallest space, that she could center herself in the moment and take three deep breaths and feel her heart rate go right down.

Bullshit.

It's all fine when you're lying on the Roomba'd floor of a posh yoga studio, enveloped in essential oil mist with a professional recording of Sanskrit chants playing softly in the background. But when you're sitting under the desk of some sort of vampiric mad scientist from the eighteen hundreds waiting to see if your entire life is about to implode for the second time in a year, there just isn't enough fucking space, not even for a single breath.

"Are you panting? Are you about to have a panic attack? Don't you fucking dare," Ingrid whispers angrily, as if this could possibly stop someone from having a panic attack. "He's going to find us, and—Fuck. Hold on."

Quietly, slowly, Ingrid unzips her backpack and roots around in it. Sarah hears the rattle of pills in a bottle, then the top opening, then the tiny, chipping sound of a pill being split in half, a sound that carries a peculiar weight when you're trapped in an abandoned asylum.

"Hold out your hand and take this." Ingrid's hand paws at her, but Sarah doesn't reach for the pill.

"What is it?"

"Lorazepam. It stops panic attacks."

"But what—"

"It's not a big deal. Not Drugs with a capital *D*. I have a prescription for anxiety. I'm taking the other half. So take it and let it dissolve under your tongue before you freak out and ruin everything for us both."

Sarah's hands and feet are going cold, and she's shaking, and she has the strong, animal instinct to stand up and start pacing, which she absolutely cannot do. Her heart is fluttering uncomfortably, and she wonders if this is a heart attack, because she's never had a panic attack, but she's not panicking, she's dying—

She flails around for Ingrid's hand, takes the sliver of a pill, and slips it under her tongue where it dissolves like bad-tasting sugar.

"Okay, good. Now listen. Do exactly what I say." Sarah nods, although Ingrid can't see it, but maybe she can hear it, because she goes on. "This is what my therapist taught me. Breathe in for four counts—one, two, three, four. Now hold it for seven counts. One, two, three, four, five, six, seven. Now breathe out for eight counts—one, two, three, four, five, six, seven, eight. Now in for four . . ."

Sarah closes her eyes—not that it makes a difference—and focuses on Ingrid's angry, husky whisper. Somehow the darkness behind her eyelids is friendlier than searching the darkness that's actually around her. It's hard to hold her breath for so long, even harder to stretch her exhale, but she falls into the familiar rhythm of it, syncs herself up with Ingrid until there is no noise in the entire world other than two scared women inhaling and exhaling through their noses.

Gradually, Sarah stops shaking, and the world goes from being a terrifying, spinning pandemonium to a small, dark space filled with someone else's patchouli and rose perfume. The old man's footsteps shuffle past, but the breathing continues. It's hypnotic now, a lifeline, a knotted rope that she's not going to release until she's certain she's been dragged out of the pit. She realizes Ingrid is holding her hand, and she wonders who reached for whom and how long that's been happening and how to let go without drawing attention to it.

Ingrid solves the problem by letting go and saying, "Should be safe now. Let's get out of here."

When Ingrid is out from under the desk, Sarah unfurls her crossed legs and stands. Her feet are asleep and cold, but her head feels swimmy and calm and pleasant. She doesn't mind being underground at a creepy medical facility now; she just wishes there were real lights. Ingrid turns on the flashlight and keeps it pointed at the ground until she's listened carefully for several moments. Sarah doesn't hear anything, and Ingrid is apparently satisfied, as she heads out into the hall. All the way upstairs, they are utterly silent, and the cramped, twisting stairwell feels like an old friend, now that it leads back to the surface. Ingrid pauses before stepping out into the upstairs hallway, and the tiny seam of light outlining each window is so welcome and beautiful and pure that Sarah could weep from joy.

Jesus, what was in that pill?

It only occurs to her in this moment that Ingrid is a liar and it could've been anything. She feels as calm as a cow being led to slaughter, but she's aware of it, and there's something agreeable and familiar about it. It brings that same level of surrender she gets before a surgery or an airplane flight, that stupidly serene acceptance of what's to come.

As they cross the lobby, Ingrid pulls the big ring of keys out of her pocket and stashes it in the drawer of an ornamental side table.

"Don't wanna get caught with those on me," she whispers.

Sarah nods, just grateful to be back aboveground, in a room with enough light that they don't really need the flashlight anymore. Ingrid slithers under the French door, and Sarah stops to look around one last time.

This place—it was so beautiful once. She can see it in the bones of what remains, in the elegant curves of the sofas and the wide chandeliers and the perfection of the stone floors. Such promise, such hope. A little flash rises in her mind, a dream barely remembered, a young woman driving up to the resort for the first time as if seeing the gates of heaven opening before her. Sarah wants to save that feeling like a dragonfly in amber, wants to put it on a shelf so she can pull it out and examine it whenever she needs a little lift.

What's down in the basement is so far from that fond dream.

She shivers a little as she wiggles out through the hole in the door, feeling as if she's overstayed her welcome.

Outside, the clouds have lifted, the sun the exact color of a lemon drop before the sugar's been sucked off.

"If we hurry, we can catch breakfast," Ingrid says. "Oh, shit. Cobwebs."

Without asking, she brushes off the back of Sarah's hoodie and swats at her hair.

"Now do me."

Sarah, too, bats at the cobwebs and dust that only shine all the brighter against their all-black ensembles. She knows she looks like shit, but she can stop in at her cabin and tidy up.

"So did you have fun?" Ingrid asks, walking back along the same route that brought them to the old resort.

Sarah follows her up the log and over the fence, considering her answer because whatever Ingrid gave her makes her feel like she actually has enough time to think, for once, instead of rushing through to avoid boring people or looking weird. "I don't know about fun. It was interesting, but that doesn't really balance out the heart attack. I don't think I'll go back."

"Oh, I will. Now that the fence is down and I've got my own set of keys, I'm gonna explore every inch of that place. Anytime you want to join, just let me know."

They tromp along, and Sarah considers it, what it would take to get her to crawl through that door again with broken glass crunching under her knees. She wanted to see if the lobby matched her dream, and it did, but that only made her feel more unsettled. Because . . .

Why?

Why did she dream of this place as it once was?

And why do her dreams follow this one girl as if she were reading a book, chapter by chapter? And why does she only remember those dreams in haunting, infuriating flashes?

The human mind can make a story out of anything. The human mind can name a beetle Horatio and then kill the beetle and have a tiny little beetle funeral for it and then think about the beetle fifty years later with fondness and one noble tear. And it would appear that Sarah's mind has latched onto the girl from the coffin and is making up its own narrative. She probably saw a picture from the old resort somewhere and then her monkey mind filled in the blanks to amuse itself, and now she's force-feeding herself a story because . . . well, that's what she's looking for, isn't it?

Her own story.

It's like her time with Kyle snatched her out of her own life and forced her into Kyle's world for six years, into the exact mold Kyle had made for her, and now she's been spat back out again to pick up the pieces and forge ahead. She isn't sure what she really wants yet, doesn't know how to put those pieces back together to make a whole person. She's that borrowed puzzle that's been on the shelf so long that there's no telling if there are enough pieces left to make a real picture anymore.

If she can make up a story for a stranger, maybe she can make up a story for herself.

Although . . . it kinda sucks that the story her brain has concocted for the imaginary girl involves domestic abuse and what today would be considered rape and what the 1800s called A Slight Annoyance For Mr. Engle, Who Deserves A Willing And Obedient Wife.

They're back at her cottage now, and Ingrid waves a curt goodbye and tromps onward as if they haven't recently been uncomfortably contorted into four square feet of space, entwined together like Cirque du Soleil artists while having dueling panic attacks. Sarah unlocks the door and heads directly for the bathroom, where she runs damage control on her dusty hair. She switches out her black hoodie and puts on an old T-shirt that's a little more appropriate for a day in the clay studio, because that's where she's going to be. With Bernie finally gone, no one can keep her from doing what she came here to do, what she should've been doing all along. Hair cobweb-free and bunned up, black boots traded for her favorite throwing moccasins, she reaches for her phone to check the time, and—

Shit.

Ingrid has her phone.

In between the terror and the pill, she didn't even think of it until now.

The moment she realizes it's gone, she feels utterly lost. Even if it's basically a brick up here in the mountains, she's still come to think of it as an extension of her body, as something she's tied to. Without her phone, she feels like she's missing out on something vital, some call that might make it through the lack of signal or an important email or—

No justification is required. It's her phone. She wants it back.

She hurries to the café for breakfast and makes a beeline for Ingrid, who's alone in the corner with her back to the wall, flicking through the photos on her modern camera.

"Hey, have you seen my phone?" Sarah asks, because she may be desperate and she may be a little stupid from that pill but she's not stupid enough to say anything incriminating with Kim right there at the next table, listening in like a vulture draped in mala beads.

Ingrid flashes her a warning look as she digs through her various pockets. "Sorry, no."

Sarah cocks her head. "Could you look a little harder? Check your bag? It's important."

Ingrid blinks several times, making direct eye contact as she methodically and melodramatically checks her hoodie pockets, jean pockets, and the front pocket of her backpack. "Guess you must've dropped it somewhere."

"I guess I'll have to go look then."

"I guess you will."

For a long moment, they fence with their eyes, and then Sarah realizes that she will never, ever be able to intimidate Ingrid no matter how severely she glares. She huffs a sigh and gathers her breakfast and coffee, which she takes to the studio just like Bernie used to. In her current state, she's too chaotic and out of it to be under Kim's scrutiny, and she doesn't want to embarrass herself in front of Reid. She gives them a little wave as she heads out and notes that Antoinette and Gertrude Rose are nowhere to be found, which is unusual.

It's also unusual to find the door to the pottery studio closed, but it's proving to be an unusual sort of day. At least the caution tape is gone. Coffee mug in her armpit and clutching her breakfast platter so it won't spill, she opens the door and turns on the light.

Until this moment, she didn't consider the fact that there might still be a body within.

There's not, but . . .

Something is very, very wrong.

Again.

25

ernie is gone, but all of his work has been destroyed.

His overly sexualized mermaids lie in pieces, strewn over his tables and tarp. In some places, they've been crushed to leather and dust, as if someone pushed them over and danced in the rubble.

Sarah is shocked . . . and disgusted.

Maybe she didn't like Bernie, and maybe she hated his art, but she respects his right to make it and not have it destroyed.

She sets her breakfast on the nearest table, snatches up a pastry and her coffee, and marches right back up to the community house, chewing and gulping to fortify herself along the way.

"Hey, are you okay?" Reid asks as he opens the door for her on his way out with Kim.

"Yeah, I mean no, I mean . . . have you seen Gail this morning?"

"She popped in to refill the coffee and then went back to the main office, I thought." He looks closely at her, worried. "What's wrong?"

She shakes her head. "I just need to find Gail."

Kim stares at her like she's an absolute lunatic as she ducks under Reid's arm and through the door, headed for the front office. Gail isn't there, of course, because Gail is never where Sarah needs her to be. She pings the little brass bell multiple times, but no one appears, not even the sleepy wizard. Frustrated now, and feeling like she's somehow done something wrong, she bangs on the door to Gail's private residence, but even that doesn't raise a response.

As a last resort, she finally pushes through the EMPLOYEES ONLY door to the kitchen. Bridget is at the industrial dishwasher, blasting dishes with a sprayer and looking like it's the last thing in the entire world she wants to do.

"Employees only," she growls, glaring at Sarah like a dog protecting its shitty kibble.

"It's kind of an emergency. Is your mom around?"

"She's already dealing with an emergency. Something up at the old hotel. She and Dad are both up there. What's your problem? Is someone hurt? Is something on fire?"

"No, it's—"

"Then it doesn't matter. I'll tell Gail to find you when she's done. Which one are you?"

"I'm Sarah."

Bridget snorts and rolls her eyes. "I'm not going to remember that. What's your medium?"

"Clay."

At that, Bridget finally looks at her like she's a person and not just a stain that won't wash out. "So you're the one who found Bernie?"

In the excitement of the morning, Sarah had almost forgotten that part—that there was a corpse in her studio yesterday and she was the one lucky enough to discover it.

"Yeah."

"That guy was trash. He's been creeping on me since I hit puberty."

Bridget doesn't stop blasting the dishes, but something about her seems just slightly more open.

"So he was friends with your mom?" Sarah asks.

Bridget nods. "He helped build some of the cabins, back in the day. They all wore jorts and no shirts and had long hair and drank beer while they built shit. They used to say they hammered all day and got hammered all night. He was always trying to get me to sit in his lap." She shudders. "Is that your problem? Was he creeping on you? Mom told me the coroner already took him away."

"It's his artwork." Sarah picks up a dropped fork, puts it in the sink. "He'd been working on these sculptures, these mermaids. They were fine yesterday, but I just opened up the studio and they're all smashed."

Bridget's smirk is unrepentant. "Good. Every sculpture he ever did had huge boobs or a giant penis. It was embarrassing. He thought it was transgressive. I told him he was using that word wrong and it was actually just unoriginal and overdone. And then he told me there were better things to do with my pretty mouth. So, yeah. No big loss."

"I just . . . I thought Gail should know."

"You don't want to get in trouble for it, you mean," Bridget says, accurately summing up the situation. "Don't worry. They'll probably blame me. I begged Mom not to let him come back, but I guess he got kicked out by some woman who finally came to her senses and he needed a place to crash and just showed up and asked for a cabin, which of course he got. I'll tell her you were here. I'd be working on my alibi, though, if I were you. She liked him, for some odd reason." She goes back to spraying the dishes and glowers. "Now get out of the kitchen. There really is a legal reason you can't be back here, and I'm not in the mood to get yelled at again."

"Okay. Thanks." Sarah gives a weak wave as she heads back out to the café.

She has an alibi—sort of. She and Ingrid were together doing something explicitly against the rules, but if they discuss it beforehand they can just tell Gail they were hanging out in her cottage or going for a hike or something, that they were together and therefore couldn't possibly have been causing problems in the old hotel. Except—

Shit. What if Gail and George find her phone?

Ingrid must've dropped it, which means it's just sitting in the old doctor's office somewhere, obviously out of place. It's locked and the lock screen isn't a selfie of her or anything that obvious, but all they really have to do is ask everyone present to hold up their phone and Sarah would be sent packing immediately.

She has to get back inside the hotel and find that phone before someone else does. Which means she's got to find Ingrid and get her to come along, because there's no way she wants to be in there alone. She doesn't particularly want to be there with company, either. If the whole place burned down right this moment, she would be just fine with that, even if it meant having to use what little money she has for a new phone.

The cafeteria is empty, and of course Ingrid is long gone. It would've been so easy if she was here, and nothing here is easy.

If Sarah hadn't had the lorazepam, or whatever it was, she would be a lot more upset than she is . . . but as it is, she's still extremely upset.

She quick-walks out to the photography studio, but Ingrid isn't in there.

A strange sound makes her shoulders hunch up around her ears, and she walks to the music studio. It's piano music, something old and sprightly that makes her think of Fourth of July picnics in a park with marching bands and gazebos and fireworks. It doesn't sound at all like the sort of thing Lucas would play, and she sidles up to the window to peek in. There he is at the piano, hunched over, tension in every line of his wiry arms and long, elegant fingers. His hair falls over his face, but he's playing like he's learning the song under a strict master, his fingers mashing the keys harder than they need to as he feels his way along the melody. The song draws to a close, and his body moves in a wave as he draws a big breath, straightens momentarily, and then folds back over the keyboard. He shakes his hands briefly—they look reddish, the knuckles angry—and dives right back into the song with the energy of a runaway horse. On the ground is a violin or viola, tossed carelessly aside, the hair snapped away from the bow lying nearby.

Is Lucas angry? she wonders. The last time she saw him, he was upset about Ingrid's pictures of the dead girl, but now he seems fully consumed by this strange, repetitive, mesmerizing, maddening song, playing it with a simmering sort of rage. She knows that most teen boys are angry in general, and that Lucas has plenty of reasons to be angry at circumstance and especially at his mother, so it doesn't strike her as terribly unusual, just odd. An angry teen boy should be playing "Smells Like Teen Spirit" or death metal, not this weird old carousel song. Thus far, he's seemed sensitive, quiet, and shy, but decently normal. Maybe he's practicing this particular song for a performance or something he needs to get just right, but it feels . . . uncomfortable. Makes her want to plug her ears and screw up her face and turn away.

To each their own, she supposes.

Lucas is an artist, and his business is his business. She leaves him there and heads to the next studio, glancing in the window to see what Antoinette is up to. Of all the people here, she knows the least about the older woman, only that she's often in cahoots with Gertrude Rose and that she appears to silently judge everyone through those big round glasses, her mouth pursed in what looks like distaste and one eyebrow raised in judgment.

Antoinette is perched at the center table again, leaning over the illuminated box, carefully dipping her pen in a round bowl of black ink. Her face is close to the page, her every movement thoughtful and tight. An artist at work—exactly as expected.

That is, until Sarah notices that the floor is absolutely covered in calligraphed pages. Letters march across the center of each creamy white sheet of paper, tightly packed together and dominated by diagonal slashes and flourishes. From where she stands, Sarah can't make out any words, but the writing looks unfamiliar and off, a strange font from another time. As she watches, Antoinette holds up the piece of paper she's been working on, shakes her head in dismay, and throws it over her shoulder. It swoops to the ground in elegant arcs to lie on the layers that fell before it. Sarah thinks she can see the word OBEY.

Antoinette's head whips around suddenly, and Sarah stumbles back at the power in that piercing gaze. She's flooded with panic and something like shame, because peeping in at working artists is considered rude. When Antoinette beckons with one curling finger, Sarah has no choice but to go inside.

"What's up?" she says with more cheer than she feels.

"You look guilty," Antoinette says, twisting her back until it cracks.

"I know it's rude to stare. I'm sorry. I was just curious about your studio. I don't know anything about calligraphy." It's not a lie, but still, something about it feels dishonest. Sarah does feel guilty, but not about staring.

Antoinette focuses on her light box and puts a new sheet of paper on top, right over another paper with crosshatched lines to guide her hand. She dips her frilly glass pen in the dish of ink and looks down as she makes firm strokes. "The earliest calligraphy was done in ancient China during the Shang dynasty, we think. They carved auspicious tidings into animal bones—scapulae—and then baked them to make them last. It took nearly two thousand years before the Western world caught up and honored the gods—or god, in this case—with the famous illuminated manuscripts I seek to replicate."

Sarah looks down as she speaks, sees that each piece of paper has one word on it.

OBEY. WHITE. HURT. LIES. FLOWERS. PROMISE. SANE.

"Is this for your final project?" she asks, her voice much higher than it should be.

"Did you ever read about the Delphic Oracle?" Antoinette inspects her page, blows on it, and then lets it drop to the floor. DECEMBER, it says.

"I think I read about it in school."

An aristocratic sniff of dismay. "The procedure for consulting the priestess was complex, but in short, she drew her inspiration from the vapors that rose up from underground. Her poetic answers were gifts from the gods. Artists are like that, I've always believed." Antoinette looks up, meets Sarah's eyes through her huge glasses. "But you have to have the TV turned to the right station. This place?" She chuckles, a pleasant sound with a sinister edge. "It's like that big dish antenna out west. This valley . . . it's a cup."

"Okay . . ."

Antoinette takes another piece of paper, writes the word HADES.

"So the question is this: Are you open to receive messages from the vapors, and what will you do with what you learn?"

Sarah swallows hard; her brain hasn't really powered down from this morning, and Antoinette is acting just as strangely as everyone else.

"I had this idea," she starts shyly. "Juxtapositions. Like the resort and the retreat. Old and new, hard and soft—"

Antoinette shakes her head like she's disappointed. "Look deeper. Listen better. Separate signal from noise. There's a story. Go find it." She flaps a hand at Sarah and selects a new piece of paper, placing it on her light box. Sarah can tell that she's been dismissed. She mutters her goodbye and hurries out of the studio, careful not to step on any of Antoinette's work. It may appear as if Antoinette is tossing each page on the ground like trash but Sarah isn't willing to test the calligrapher's patience further. That's what she gets for being nosy.

Not that it stops her from checking out Gertrude Rose's studio. If she's going to have one person annoyed with her for peeking in a window, she might as well have two. Gertrude Rose is the kind of person who's eventually going to get involved, anyway, and it's not like she's immune to expressing curiosity about the other workspaces herself.

The fiber studio is set back in the woods with the rabbit hutch off to the side. Remembering how nice it was to pet the fluffy white rabbit, Sarah goes to the hutch and murmurs to the snowy forms nestled together in a corner.

"You guys awake?" she asks, wishing she'd brought a carrot, or some little tidbit from the buffet.

She puts her fingers through the cage like she did last time, and one of the rabbits turns toward her—and lunges. She whips her fingers away just in time, and the rabbit's face slams into the metal wire. As she watches, it bashes its head into the wire mesh again and again like a windup toy that can't stop going. She backs away hurriedly, not wanting the animal to hurt itself further on her behalf. It was sweet last time, but maybe it's hungry or sleepy or angry today. Maybe they're not meant to be pets and are only used for fiber and don't get a lot of affection, hence the aggressive reaction.

She has to get away from the rabbit, so she dares a glance in the fiber studio window. It's just as chaotic as last time she peeped within, maybe even more so. Swatches of fabric hang off the dressing dummies, pinned without the careful elegance she would expect from such a talented costumer. Bolts of cloth have been taken down from their neat stacks and unspooled, button boxes spilled across tables as if someone has been searching frantically for something they've lost. Gertrude Rose is knitting in a rocking chair in a formal black gown with a high neck, and the flash of her metal needles captures Sarah's attention.

She steps closer to the window, certain Gertrude Rose can't see her, as she's angled away and intent on her work. It's a scarf, but . . .

It's long.

Really, weirdly long.

Longer than a *Doctor Who* scarf.

As wide as a hand and tightly knit in a rainbow of colors, the garment winds all over the room like a lazing python.

It must be some statement piece, the sort of art that was never meant to be worn but was instead inspired by some woman from history who died in a scarf factory fire, or maybe it has a different color for every suffragette. It has to mean something, and Sarah will most likely find out at the final exhibit when they all display the work they've created over the six-week residency.

Sarah doesn't know much about knitting, but it seems like an awful lot of work for the few days they've been here. Has Gertrude Rose . . . been sleeping? Or maybe she started the scarf back home?

Sure, she could ask Gertrude Rose now, just walk in and say the words and hear the answer. But she would rather read a self-important, bombastic paragraph of an Artist's Statement at some point in the future than have to stand in that disorganized room and listen to Gertrude Rose give a lecture on whatever it is that has motivated her to knit a scarf that could stretch to the moon and back.

All these people, Sarah thinks, are crazy.

But isn't that what art is? The unique and personal expression of how a person sees the world in a way no one else can?

Maybe someone walking by her studio in a few days will think the same thing about her when she's thrown an army of identical teacups.

At least when she looks in at Kim's studio, she sees exactly what she was told to expect: piles of glass, neatly cut and sorted, assembly-line-style, the suncatchers all a little further along than they were yesterday. Kim is a woman on a mission, and her mission is to make a shit ton of succulent window catchers, and even if that sounds boring as hell to Sarah, she's not going to look down on a woman trying to claw her way to financial freedom.

All along, she's heard hammering, but it's more of a background noise, like the waterfall. She's been putting off going to see Reid because honestly, that pill Ingrid gave her made her all loose and sort of stupid and she doesn't know if she trusts herself around him just now. Maybe she'll tell him all about her morning of trespassing, or maybe she'll jump his bones. She isn't entirely sure. It depends on what his forearms look like while he's hammering, which is why she suspects it may be a little of column A, a little of column B.

Following the sound of metal on metal, she finds Reid in an outdoor workshop under a rough tin roof, something like an old airport hangar. His white T-shirt is spackled to his chest, his biceps in stark relief as he hammers a piece of cherry-hot metal. He's wearing work boots, beat-to-shit jeans, eye protection, and heavy leather gloves, and Sarah simply observes from afar, remembering what it was like to see Kyle at work. He was tightly wound, fussy, careful, frowning. Anesthesia is such a precise science, and the stakes so high, that he always looked like he was taking a really difficult test while constipated.

Now that she has some distance, she realizes that she hated how he tucked in his scrub top and slicked his hair back and always wore truly hideous gray sneakers. Sure, there's not a lot of variance in a required hospital uniform, but . . . well, watching Reid work is like watching a god form the planets. There's fire, smoke, sweat, skin, the hiss of water. It's elemental, primal. His forearms do in fact look good enough to make her stupid.

He's wearing earbuds, but maybe he senses her watching, as he looks up, sees her, and smiles.

"Want to hit stuff?" he shouts, taking out an earbud and hefting his hammer.

She smiles and shakes her head. "Maybe later. Just wanted to say hi. I've got pots to make."

She waves, and he waves and goes back to hammering, and she is mercifully released from the spell of a man who knows what to do with his hands.

Back in her studio, she finds her breakfast cold and drawing flies. She pecks at her remaining pastries before portioning out a bag of clay and wedging the balls to get out all the air pockets. It's meditative and pleasant, and she always enjoys this part of her work, preparing the space and materials and dreaming of what she'll make, especially now that she's alone here.

But when she sits down, she can't get the clay centered, and her attempt to throw a simple teacup ends up collapsing into a mess. She beats on it with her fist a few times for good measure before tossing it in the slurry bin.

She can't concentrate. When she looks up, she sees Bernie's smashed work and knows she'll have to answer for it soon. When she looks down, she remembers that she doesn't have her phone. If she's not centered, she can't center, period. She doesn't know if it's the day's emotions or, again, that stupid pill she stupidly swallowed in the stupid dark, but she's fairly certain she's not going to create anything worthwhile.

There's nothing for it.

She's got to go back and get her phone, and she might as well do it before someone else finds it and ruins everything.

26

Sarah is back in her black hoodie, this time equipped with her own huge, stupid flashlight. She didn't bring a bag or anything; she's going to get in and get out. Her only goal is to find her phone.

She's standing just outside the door of her cottage, putting her hair up in a bun, when she sees Gail and George walking down the gravel road, arguing about something—or, more accurately, Gail arguing and George just absorbing it like an ancient sea sponge. Again, she questions that goddamn pill—she had completely forgotten about the witch and the wizard and was just going to march right up to the hotel while they were apparently still there looking for signs of a break-in. Luckily, they're headed in the opposite direction, back toward December House. If they'd found her phone, they would surely be walking toward her. Even if Sarah is a little chemically off her game, she should be able to sneak into the hotel, head downstairs, grab her phone, and leave with no trouble.

The hotel seems bigger, now that she's alone, more imposing. She slips on the log going over the fence, almost falls. The stained, cracked statues in the garden glare at her with blank black eyes, and something splashes furtively in the algae-filled fountain. An old urn, oddly, holds countless cigarette butts, as if someone has been sitting on the low stone wall for years, staring at the resort and trying to die just a little faster. It's creepy enough without ever stepping foot in that abandoned relic, and for just a single, clear moment she wonders: What is it about the human heart that loves a place forsaken? She goes directly to the hole Ingrid kicked in the old French door and notes that the towel is gone. But did Ingrid take it with her, or did Gail and George grab it? They left so quickly this morning that she doesn't remember. She pulls the sleeves of her hoodie down over her hands as she crawls inside, glass crunching under the soft fabric, and dusts her hands off when she stands in the lobby once more.

She can almost see how it used to be, see the parrots and lamps and lively guests reading newspapers on stiff horsehair couches. She shakes her head—this is no time to get lost in daydreams of a history that was a lot less romantic than PBS miniseries suggest.

Flashlight on, she marches purposefully down the hall and through the door to the stairwell. She doesn't slow down long enough to con-sider how much she hates this twisting passage, the sponginess of the carpet like a blanket of moss, like something dead and softly rotting. She doesn't let herself consider the sounds that might've once echoed down the long, white hallway, the squeak of an old wheelchair or the clank of a chain pulled taut. With her flashlight pointed directly ahead, the shadows crowd greedily around her, cloaking her legs from the knees down and threatening to engulf her. She follows the single beam of light directly to room 115, where her phone lies on the ground, halfway under the door.

The door, which is ajar . . . and shouldn't be.

They didn't open this door.

And she's fairly certain Gail and George would have no need to open it, and no way *to* open it. The key, after all, is on the ring Ingrid hid in the drawer upstairs.

Isn't it?

Sarah picks up her phone and turns it on, glad that it doesn't appear damaged. The screen protector is really doing its job. When she shines her flashlight on the door, there's the key, innocently stuck in the lock. She pulls it out and slips it in her front pocket. Once her phone is securely in her back pocket, she turns to go.

But . . .

Well, she wanted to see inside one of the rooms down here, didn't she?

Ingrid or no, she's curious, and she's here, and she can spare thirty seconds to see what's inside.

No harm can come from opening a door just a little more.

The metal knob is cold under her hand, and the door creaks as she pulls it toward her. This strikes her as odd, as most doors open into the room, but then she notices that the hinges are on the outside. She moves into the open space, holding her breath.

As she shines her light around, she's surprised at how unsurprising it is. There are no torture instruments, no chains. The walls are white-washed, the floor plain, cold stone. A narrow bed is pushed into the back corner, barely a cot, with a chamber pot underneath it. Instead of an armoire and vanity, there are nails in the wall, familiar nails with rectangular heads, four of them, placed so that someone might hang up a dress, a hat, a bag. Her eye is drawn to a wooden crate beside a plain wood chair. She takes a step forward—

And stops.

If that door shuts behind her, there is no way out.

This door, after all, locks from the outside.

She may have the key, but there's no keyhole on this side.

She is here alone, and no one knows she is here.

She slips off a boot and wedges it into the door, testing it from the safety of the hallway. The only possible way she could get locked inside is if someone purposefully moved her boot. And there is no one who could do that, no wind, no earthquake, no furtive rat.

With the boot in the door, she is safe.

Satisfied, she crosses the room, which is barely eight feet long and six feet wide, and shines her flashlight into the crate. Inside are a brush, a handkerchief, and a small sewing kit.

The hairs rise up the back of her neck as she notes that the only thread is white, and it is nearly gone. The needles appear to be missing.

When she inspects the handkerchief, she's unsurprised to find the initials E. E. surrounded by tiny white petunias.

This feels too intimate, and the full weight of her precarious position slams down around her. She is in a cell. Not a room, but a cell. She is in a cell in an asylum. If the pieces of the puzzle fit together the way she thinks they do, a well-to-do guest of the hotel above somehow ended up down here, locked in a small white room, where she was left with nothing to do but embroider cryptic phrases into the hems of her clothes.

Sarah's foot, clad only in its sock, is freezing on the rough old stones and . . . wet, like she's stepped in a frigid puddle. The feeling is invasive and horrific and slimy, and Sarah tucks the handkerchief in her pocket and lunges out of the room before the door can swing closed on her, entrapping her in what increasingly feels like a tomb. She puts on her boot and leaves the door ajar, exactly as she found it, touches the phone in her pocket for reassurance, and jogs back to the stairwell. As she runs upstairs, her flashlight's beam bouncing off stark white walls, it feels like she's being chased, like someone is looming right over her shoulder, following her close enough to almost step on her heels.

The scant light upstairs is welcome, but the sense of paranoia doesn't let up. She's going to get caught, but she doesn't know by whom, nor why the concept makes her blood run cold. She hurries down the hall and wiggles out through the hole in the door, barely breathing until she's standing in the courtyard, out of reach of whatever threat seemed to dog her throughout the hotel and the—yes, yes, it has to be an asylum—hidden below in the cellar.

Ingrid's pill has worn off; the pleasant stuffiness is gone, and the world is sharp again. As she hustles back to her cabin, she can't stop breathing heavily, can't stop her hands from shaking. The Tranquil

Falls literature states that the old hotel was a posh spa for the wealthy, but wealthy people would not knowingly choose to be locked inside tiny, simple, uncomfortable, sunless closets in the basement. They would not have come way out here into the mountains for surgeries performed underground in chains. Even if her mind is creating a narrative of this girl, this woman, Mrs. Bertram Engle, the mysterious E. E., the pieces are fitting together far too well.

But why would someone who was excited to stay here for her honeymoon end up locked in a cell?

If Sarah had the internet, she could search the name, search for more information on the purported cures, look up the bona fides of the doctors who ran the resort. But there is no internet here, and in order to access the internet, she'd have to drive around the mountain until she had enough signal to do even the simplest search, and then she'd have to answer Gail's questions about why her car was missing.

As time goes on, she just might have to do that.

The curiosity will drive her mad.

Back in her cabin, she changes for the third time today, back into her studio clothes, and again brushes the cobwebs out of her hair. Remembering the key in her front pocket, she takes it out and inspects it by the light of day. Old, brass, heavy, not special in any way, a rougher thing than the slender, more elegant key to room 312 in the posh upstairs. She tucks them both into her bag, way down on the bottom where no one would ever look.

The bell rings for lunch, and she can't believe how much has happened in one morning. She heads up the road, taking the remains of her breakfast with her. The other artists emerge from their studios looking almost zombie-like as they crunch up the gravel. Sarah hangs back; she doesn't want to talk to Antoinette or Gertrude Rose or Lucas. She sees Kim waiting in the door of the stained-glass studio, her eyes all but burning a hole in the sculpture studio. As soon as Reid emerges, Kim closes her door and makes a beeline for him. Sarah would get judgy if she hadn't been kind of doing the same thing. It's funny, how the human heart works. Ten people out in the middle of nowhere, artists meant to be focusing entirely on their work, and still two broken women look at the one available man and think, *Maybe he's the one.*

Ingrid doesn't show at lunch, which is just as well, as Sarah is furious with her for leaving her phone behind in the hotel and then acting like it was no big deal. She sits with Reid and Kim and Lucas, and Kim hovers protectively over Reid like a Yorkie guarding its dinner. Kim wants to hike up to the waterfall behind the resort after breakfast the next morning, and everyone is invited although the look she gives Sarah suggests that she should invent other plans.

"That sounds fun," she says instead, because she wants to, and because it's not like they're best friends who call dibs.

Kim smiles as she glares daggers. "Great. It's a date."

Sarah expects Lucas to come along, but he's distracted, his eyes glassy and his fingers tapping on the wood table like he's still practicing that same raucous song.

Reid nudges him with his shoulder. "Lucas. Want to come see the waterfall tomorrow after breakfast?"

Lucas shakes his head. "Nah. I'm working on something."

"New song?"

"Old song. But it has to be perfect."

"I thought you were here to get back in shape, not drive yourself crazy."

Lucas's eyes slide away. "I'll know when it's good enough."

Reid shrugs good-naturedly. "You do you."

When Sarah stands to put up her trash, Reid stands, too. He holds the door for her as she leaves, and Kim quickly cleans up to join them.

"I've done a little handbuilding before, but never throwing on a wheel," Reid says. "Is it hard for beginners?"

"Super hard," Kim breaks in, bouncing between them as they walk. "Wheel is nearly impossible. Stained glass is so much easier. I mean, it takes a lot of skill, but I can teach you how to make a little suncatcher in a couple of hours."

"I'd still like to try clay, if you don't mind?" He looks around Kim to

Sarah, making it clear who he's actually talking to. "Kim, see you at dinner?"

Kim sighs and peels off toward the stained-glass studio. "See you then," she says, throwing Sarah a glare that says See You Next Tuesday.

Sarah would gloat, but she doesn't feel like this is a competition. She's just escaped a disastrous relationship, and she did not come here on the prowl. She likes Reid, and she likes his sinewy forearms and gentle eyes and wild hair, but she's not about to get in a catfight over him.

Well, especially not if he's choosing her of his own volition.

"Wheel is challenging, but not as bad as she made it sound. It's just messy."

He grins and swipes at a black charcoal stain on his wrist. "I don't mind messy."

It's still a surprise to open her studio door and find silence and stillness instead of an ornery old jerk and his obnoxious music. Reid looks at the mess on the tables and floor, the dry clay cracked into chunks and powder as if thrown with great force.

"Revenge?" he asks, one eyebrow raised.

She flinches. "Not by me. I found it this way."

"Want help tidying up?"

Yes, but also . . .

"Probably ought to leave it as is. I tried to tell Gail today, but she wasn't in. I feel like she needs to see it for herself."

He nods and goes to a canvas-covered table, putting his hands on it and leaning forward with a smile. "So what do we do first? If I'm not cutting into your studio time."

Sarah pulls the tape off a new box of clay and pulls out a fresh bag. She thunks it on the table in front of him and brings out her toolbox, which she can just leave in the studio now that Bernie is gone. "First I cut it into manageable chunks, wedge them to get the air bubbles out, and then I can show you how to throw a simple pot. You have to see the whole demonstration before you try anything or it won't make any sense."

He nods, and his eyes follow her as she goes through the comforting routine of preparing the clay. It's odd, but also nice. Kyle never visited her in the studio, never asked about her work at all. He missed her last student show, had to study for an exam that night. And he preferred drinking his coffee out of smooth, uniform, factory-made mugs, claimed he didn't like the feel of bumpy glaze against his lips.

Funny, how in hindsight he was absolutely horrible, but taken in small doses, washed over in infatuation and familiarity, she built up a sort of immunity, almost a blindness to the worst parts of him.

"So what are you doing now?" Reid asks her.

Feet braced, she rocks the heel of her palm into the ball of clay, almost like kneading bread dough. "Wedging. It gets any air bubbles out. If you get an air bubble, you can't keep the piece centered, and it will eventually collapse. These newer clay companies say you don't have to wedge their clay, that it arrives ready to throw, but that feels incomplete and risky, you know?"

He nods. "I still wash prewashed salad, so I get that."

Sarah pats the clay into a tidy ball and takes it to the bench she's positioned by her wheel. She fetches a bucket of water and a towel and her apron and sets out her tools like she likes them. She normally throws bigger than this, but she knows this is the ideal size for learning; she taught a few summer classes for kids when she was younger. She sits, knees spread around the wheel, and explains the process as she works. Reid watches, and she likes that he seems genuinely interested; he might be flirting with her, but he's not *just* flirting with her.

It is odd, though, being watched. She is aware of every move she makes, of her legs spread wide, a towel draped over them, her fingers encircling the clay. She feels his eyes, the focused attention of the artist and of the man. It doesn't matter; her body knows how to throw, and narrating every move takes her mind off his level gaze. Her center is back, for now.

After a few short moments, she uses her wire to cut a basic pot off the wheel. After placing it on a board, she cleans the mess off the wheel and holds out her towel.

"Think you can do it?"

He selects a ball of clay from the table and considers it. "I guess we'll see."

He sits and spreads the towel over his lap before slapping the clay down in the center of the wheel. As he watched her, now she watches him. She does feel a pull toward him, not only a chemistry, but a level of respect as an artist and as a person. He's thoughtful, kind, generous with his time with Lucas, almost like a mentor. He works on his feelings and expresses them and wants to be a better man. He hasn't said or done anything so far that she would consider a red flag—

Well, except when he barged upstairs in her cottage when she was doing her best to dissuade him. He ignored her signals and her words then, and even if it was with a certain excited innocence, it felt like he crossed a boundary. She was so furious with him in the moment, filled with rage that he would desecrate such a sacred space where he had no right to be, no right at all—

She shakes her head.

A curious man wanted to go up some stairs.

It was nothing more than that.

"What now?" he says, face alight with interest.

"Grab the sponge to wet your clay," she narrates. He does, and it's way too much water because newbies always throw too wet. "Now start the wheel—a little faster. Not that fast!" Water flings across his lap, and they both laugh. "Gotta find just the right speed."

It strikes her in this moment that so many of the terms and movements around pottery can be sexual, and she blushes. Not that he notices, because he's entirely focused on the clay.

"So remember, you're pushing into the clay with the heels of your hands, firmly, to get it centered . . ."

He dutifully leans forward, presses the clay in just the right place—

And jerks back, barking, "Oh, fuck!"

Blood pours down his hands, mixes with the mud and water, flinging out as the wheel keeps spinning, spinning. Reid stands and stumbles away, staring down at his palms and hissing through his teeth as bright red ribbons drip onto the floor.

"What happened?" Sarah asks, heart pounding, not knowing what's under all that blood or how it possibly could've occurred.

"I don't know," he manages. He hurries to the sink and turns on the faucet, running both of his hands under the water and making the various grunting, hissing animal noises a man makes when he's in a lot of pain and wants to seem tough while also wanting pity. "I think there's something in the clay."

Sarah steps on the pedal to stop the wheel, and the blood-wet mound of clay slowly stops spinning. As soon as it's no longer moving, it's clear what has happened.

The clay isn't smooth, as it should be.

It's riddled with shards of stained glass.

27

eid's hands are wrapped in paper towels, the blood seeping through and mixing with water to create a horrifying but almost pretty tie-dye effect. They stand together over the canvas-wrapped table where Sarah wedged the clay, staring down at the lump she's carefully cut off the wheel. She's pulled out seven shards of stained glass, all in the iridescent pastel colors Kim favors. Along with them is another rectangular cut nail.

"How did this happen?" Reid asks. "Like, I get how Kim could go all Single White Female because she's so clingy it makes me uncomfortable, but I watched you pull out a new bag of clay and put your full body weight into kneading it. There's no way all this stuff could've been in there while you were doing that. There's just no way."

"And after it was wedged, it went straight to the wheel. In plain sight."

She takes up her needle tool and uses it to dissect the last two balls of clay, but neither of them contains anything more offensive than an air bubble she missed. She prods the bag the clay came from, but it looks entirely unblemished.

"I don't understand," she says.

He looks around the studio. "Me, neither. Maybe Bernie hid it in there to mess with you?"

"I don't think he had the kind of intelligence or patience it would take to remove the tape from a box and reseal it without tearing it apart, much less make a deconstructed bag of clay look untouched. And that still doesn't explain how I wedged that particular ball by hand without a single cut. And the nail—what's with that?" She swallows hard, hating how she somehow keeps being the center of attention here for things outside of her control. "Let me get out the first-aid kit and clean you up. You've had your tetanus shot, right?"

"I'm a metalsmith. I always stay on top of my tetanus shot."

She noted the red tackle box her first day here but couldn't imagine needing it. Sure, it's always possible that someone might jab themselves with a needle tool or scrape their skin with a serrated metal rib, but pottery is not a particularly dangerous medium. When she flips open the top of the box, she finds Bactine spray, bandages, gauze—all the usual supplies. She reaches for one of Reid's hands, turning it over gently to look at the palm. The cuts are seeping with blood, but it's not just one or two little lacerations. His skin looks like raw meat that's been torn to shreds, and she takes a shuddering breath as she considers what this will do to his own work, which involves clutching heavy tools tightly around fire. Holding his hand over the sink, she sprays it with Bactine and rubs antibacterial ointment over almost the entire palm, then wraps it with gauze and secures it with tape. He tries really, really hard to pretend it isn't agonizing.

"You seem to know what you're doing," Reid says, his voice fond and rumbly, like they're eating brunch and not tending to impossible wounds.

"My ex-boyfriend is an anesthesiologist," she says. "And he assured me I have absolutely no idea what I'm doing when it comes to medical care."

It slips out only because she's focusing on his other hand, and she feels a blush rise. She doesn't want to put this on him, doesn't want to pour out all her troubles and let him see how cracked a vessel she really is.

"Well, sometimes it's more about caring and gentleness than it is about understanding germ theory. I just appreciate it, is all I'm saying."

She releases his hand and reaches for his other one, unwrapping the bloodied paper towels like the world's worst birthday present. This hand isn't quite as bad, but she goes through the same motions. She can feel the tension in his muscles, can tell that he would like to cuss and wince and wrench his hand away but is fighting it to impress her.

"Do you think you need stitches?" she asks before applying the gauze.

He looks down and slowly makes a fist, grunting as he releases it. "Maybe. Shit. I don't want to leave. Even if I can't keep working, this place . . . it just feels good, you know? Slow. Easy. No rushing around, no going to the store, no leaky dishwasher. Maybe I can take up some other artistic medium that is one hundred percent guaranteed safe. Maybe Gertrude Rose can teach me how to crochet."

Sarah snorts. "Yeah, locked in a studio with Gertrude Rose telling you you're doing something wrong. Sounds like heaven." She takes up the gauze and wraps his hand, because whether or not he needs actual medical care, he needs more blood on the inside than on the outside. "So . . ." She trails off. Is she ready to actually talk to someone about the weird shit that's been happening here?

"So?" he asks with a gentle smile.

"Have you ever peeked in on anyone else's studio?"

A chuckle. "Just yours, but it was mostly occupied by an old guy in jean shorts who had some messed-up ideas about mermaid nipples."

"But not Gertrude Rose or Antoinette or Lucas?"

"No. Why?"

She's done with his hands, and he holds them up and makes fists, testing for pain. As she puts the first-aid supplies back in the toolbox, her back turned to him, she says, "They're all . . . acting strange. Lucas was playing this one crazy song on the piano, all hunched over like a gargoyle. An old song, Moulin Rouge–style. Again and again. And

Gertrude Rose is knitting a scarf that's like a mile long. And Antoinette . . . well, she caught me watching her and then started telling me bizarre calligraphy facts about carved bone and claiming this valley is a big antenna for the muse. And her work—she's doing one word per page and throwing it on the floor. Just . . . odd."

His hand touches her arm before he sucks in a breath and removes it, instead shifting to mimic her posture, leaning his back against the table, his hip against hers.

"Artists are weird. I've never met a working artist who wasn't, you know? The process is weird, and the downtime is weird, and the exhaustion after hard work is weird. All of those behaviors sound reasonable for creative people actively creating. But I'll check in on Lucas. I'm worried about that kid."

"I wasn't, but I am now. Why would a teenage boy be playing carousel music over and over again, right when he can finally play whatever he wants? Where's the Nirvana of it all?"

"Maybe some people are into carousel music," he says, teasing. "Maybe he likes that big oom-pah-pah sound."

"Yes! That's what it sounded like. But crazed."

"At least he doesn't have a tuba."

Sarah snorts. She likes Reid. Probably more than she should. But in her defense, he's likable. And nice to look at. And nice.

And he's also the first decent guy she's been alone with in six years, and she probably shouldn't fall headfirst into a rebound right now. She's completely out of shape for it. She has to find herself before she can let someone else discover her. And she needs to find herself in a time and place where she isn't constantly questioning everything that's happening, a place where she isn't digging up dead bodies and finding dead bodies and marching into the bowels of lunatic asylums and having strange dreams that feel all too real.

And . . . well, she has to ask herself . . . why would he be into her?

He barely knows her. They've had a couple of conversations, shared several meals. Sure, she's got a little crush, and maybe he does, too, but she's been with Kyle so long that she's forgotten what's good about her, what another person might look at her and see. Kyle systematically tore her down until even she couldn't remember why he was with her, outside of pity. She's not fierce like Ingrid or outgoing like Kim, she's pretty but not jaw-dropping. And she's more than a little messed up right now. If someone fell for her, would it be the old her, or the new her, or some strange in-between liminal version of her?

Then again, this is not the eighteen hundreds. She doesn't have to promise to love someone forever to have a little fun with them. Tranquil Falls is a temporary place, a vacation from life, an experience, and shouldn't experiences be stretched to their limits, milked for all that they're worth? She came here to feel, and indulging in an artistic friends-with-benefits arrangement could only help to stoke the fires of creation.

She decides in that moment that if he tries to kiss her again, she'll let him.

And after that kiss, she'll make sure he understands that she wants to keep it casual.

Needs to keep it casual.

She is now leery of cages made of promises.

"Where are you?" he asks, head cocked.

How long has he been watching her? How long has she stared off into space, suggesting she might need to be watched?

"Knock knock!"

Their heads whip around to find Gail standing in the open door looking disappointed, like she's just caught them being naughty despite the fact that they're two independent adults casually leaning against a table.

"Oh, hey, Gail," Reid starts. "We were just talking about—"

"Okay, what happened here?" Ignoring him, Gail walks over to the mess that was once Bernie's art. With a grunt, she awkwardly bends down to pick up a chunk of mermaid tail. She stands, wincing, and pins Sarah with a measuring stare. Gail has clearly been crying. "Did you do this?"

Sarah takes a deep breath. She's getting sick of explaining herself when she's done nothing wrong. "No. I found it when I opened the studio this morning. I asked Bridget to tell you."

"So who did it?"

"How would I know? I was in my cabin, sleeping."

Gail places the mermaid chunk carefully on a table, her lips a flat line that curves down at the corners like a marionette's. "Do you know, we've never had this many problems? A coffin, a—the—the passing of a student. Someone broke into the old hotel. And now this. This is *art*. Bernie's art. It's disrespectful. Everyone here should know better."

The way she's looking at Sarah suggests that it's Sarah's fault—all of it.

And on one hand, it's infuriating.

But on the other hand, Sarah has been at the center of every crisis Gail has named, whether or not Gail can prove it.

"Maybe you should put up cameras," Sarah suggests, because honestly, it would make her feel a lot better. If someone really is up to no good, it seems to be centering on this studio and on her, which is . . . worrisome. And Gail doesn't even know about the most recent incident. But . . .

"Wait. Reid, what's wrong with your hands?" Gail asks. "Did you have an accident?"

Reid holds up his palms, blood already seeping through the gauze, red blooms polka-dotting the white. "Weirdest thing. Sarah was teaching me how to throw, and there was glass in the clay. And a weird old nail." He moves over to reveal the pile of glass and pokes around in it to show Gail.

She just stares. At the glass. At Reid's hands. At Sarah.

"That looks like Kim's glass," Gail says carefully.

"We noticed that, too," he goes on. "Funny thing is, I watched Sarah open a new box of clay, pull out a fresh new bag, and knead it for five minutes, and she never got cut."

Gail shakes her head like impossible information causes her pain. "That doesn't make any sense."

His eyebrows rise. "We know. Maybe Sarah's right. You should put up cameras. She might be in danger."

Gail rolls her eyes and carefully scoops up the glass and nail. She goes to the paper towel holder and pulls out several sheets, bundling up the glass and storing it in the pocket of her purple linen overalls. "We don't have money for cameras. And part of what makes this place work is privacy. People come here to get away from the world, not have their every move watched. I don't have time to sit around in front of a bank of TVs anyway."

"These days you can just have it go directly to your computer and check it as needed," Reid says.

"With what WiFi?"

Reid's eyebrows rise. "Good point, I guess."

"We've never had problems before," Gail repeats sternly, as if saying so will make the problems stop. "In fifty years, not a single problem."

Which seems like a good segue into something Sarah really wants to know. "What about the old hotel?" she asks. "Do you know why it closed? There wasn't much information on it online."

The older woman takes a step back, cagey. "Old things close. This place was a fad, and the fad ran its course. Guess they finally realized mountain water couldn't cure everything."

"I think I read somewhere that they did weird experiments—"

"They didn't." Gail's voice is sharp as she glares at Sarah over her pink plastic glasses on their rainbow chain. "It was a resort hotel and clinic run by the most celebrated doctors in the country. Everything they did here was humane and based on cutting-edge science."

It's odd, how Gail has her dander up over a basic question of history, and Sarah wonders if she's just trying to protect the land, but then . . .

"Gail, what's your maiden name?"

"Wheeler," Gail snaps. "Why?"

"Just curious. I know you've been here a long time, so I wondered if your family originally owned the hotel or something."

Gail nods; this is a subject she likes, apparently, when she gets to soak up the reflected glory instead of getting defensive. "I grew up in December House. My parents started the artists' colony. I was raised here." She smiles fondly. "And I met George here." The smile disappears. "And Bernie. So you can see why I'm concerned about what's been going on. I won't let anything bad happen to this place."

She stares intensely into Sarah's eyes like Sarah is going to suddenly admit to digging up a corpse on purpose, and Sarah stares back because she most certainly did no such thing, and then Reid interrupts them with a hiss as he holds up his right hand, showing that blood has completely soaked the gauze.

"I think I need stitches," he says, defeated. "Where's the best place to go?"

Gail turns her attention to him, and Sarah nearly sags in relief to be out from under her scrutiny.

"Come on. I'll take you to the urgent care. It's about a thirty-minute drive."

"I can just use my GPS—" he starts.

"Don't be stupid. You don't know the area, your GPS won't get a signal until you hit the highway, and you can't drive with both hands wrapped up and bleeding. So let's go." She points at Sarah. "And you stay out of trouble."

"Want me to come along?" Sarah asks Reid, ignoring Gail's command.

"Nah. Stay here and work. Just check the clay first. If someone's been messing with it . . ." His eyes flicker toward the stained-glass studio, and Sarah knows exactly what he means. If stained glass was in the clay, then maybe the stained-glass artist put it there to mess with the potter.

"Okay. Be careful out there. Get the good drugs."

He snorts. "For stitches, I'm lucky if they'll give me an ibuprofen."

For a second, Sarah thinks he's going to kiss her on the cheek, but he just waves with his bloody hand and follows Gail outside.

With nothing left to do, Sarah paces for a moment. Her hands automatically go to her apron's pockets, where her fingers find the old cut nail. So it wasn't the same one Bernie was holding, or the same one in Reid's clay. This is the one she pulled from the coffin, and it hasn't moved from where she left it. Her fingers trace the old metal, her thumb meditatively rubbing the point, which is too dull to do any harm. It feels good, this nail. Sturdy. Real. She puts it back in her apron pocket and pats it like a lucky rabbit's foot.

The studio is her own, finally, she realizes; this place is her place. She is filled with energy, with anxious potential that needs to go somewhere, that needs to . . . create? She turns on her music, opens a new box of clay, pulls out a new bag, checks it for signs of tampering, wedges it oh so carefully, and starts throwing.

Nothing bad happens. There is no glass. With her music on and no one bothering her, she taps into flow and lets chance and whimsy shape her vessels. There's a fierce joy in it, and the world falls away as she rediscovers what was once her great passion. Time passes strangely, reducing Sarah's reality to nothing but wet hands, a spinning wheel, the smooth sweep of a wire at completion. She read once that women used to go into trances while spinning fiber into yarn, that the repetitive, circular work of women's hands, the work that fed and clothed the world, the work that had to be done every day, morning to night, season to season, could also drive women mad. She remembers reading a short story in high school—"The Yellow Wallpaper," by Charlotte Perkins Gilman—in which the smudge of a woman's shoulder marred the walls when she was trapped in her room with nothing to do but walk in circles, compelled into furious motion because she had been denied any other outlet for her nervous energy.

The clay on Sarah's wheel goes around and around in circles, pushed and pulled by her design, just as the woman in the room goes around and around in circles, trapped behind a closed door, pushed and pulled by someone else's design . . .

The thought is fleeting, a vision of circles and cycles, beginnings and endings, smudges and hems, and then there are no thoughts, just work.

She doesn't look up until the dinner bell rings. She went through the entire box of clay. She is surprised to realize that, in her stupor, she's made the same shape again and again.

Twelve perfect little replicas of the chamber pot she found in room 312.

28

Dinnertime is almost over, and Sarah is waiting for Reid and Gail to return from urgent care. She made sure to fix a plate for him because she knows Bridget will soon emerge to start angrily whisking away the leftover food. Gail can fend for her own damn self. Even if Sarah didn't personally have anything to do with the glass in the clay, it still happened in her studio, and she feels partially responsible for the man she'd just decided to kiss. The least she can do is make sure he gets fed.

Ingrid and Lucas ate dinner with her, and they both seemed a little out of it. Everyone does, really. A little unfocused. Maybe they're just tired from arting too much. That's how Sarah feels—deliciously drained and a little stupid. She doesn't really understand her series of tiny, unusable chamber pots, but that's how art works sometimes—it shows up, and the artist is left to make sense of it. The pots are lined up neatly under plastic, and when they're leather-hard, she'll add elegant little handles. She usually uses high-fire glazes, but this series calls for something more playful—graffiti-style, maybe. The whole point of a chamber pot, after all, is to pee in it, and these little replicas are far too small to serve their lone purpose. If she wasn't so worried about digging up another corpse, they'd be perfect for her original plan to do a pit-firing.

Kim sat with Gertrude Rose and Antoinette, butting into their conversation until they'd polished off her bottle of wine and left. She seems determined to avoid Sarah now, and Sarah wonders if it's just because Kim sees them as antagonists in the pursuit of Reid or if Kim maybe did have something to do with the glass and is trying to avoid getting caught. It's a shame; on her first night here Sarah thought they might actually be friends.

Sarah is the last one left now, sitting by the plate of food, and Bridget busts out of the kitchen and starts her nightly cleanup.

"Want help with that?" Sarah asks, but Bridget just shakes her head angrily as she pulls the food out of the buffet and carries it into the kitchen. She's got earbuds in, and the loud, tinny echo of whatever she's listening to goes with her general attitude of messy fury.

But Sarah was taught to never let someone clean up the kitchen alone, and she needs something to do besides stare at the door, so she picks up the vat of soggy green beans and carries it into the kitchen, placing it on the prep table by the corn Bridget is covering with industrial plastic wrap.

"You're not allowed back here," Bridget says, pulling out her earbuds.

"Who's going to turn me in for carrying green beans?" Sarah shoots back. "Everyone else is gone, your mom is at the urgent care with Reid, and your dad is a drowsy wizard."

Bridget actually breaks character and laughs, shaking her head. "Okay, that's very true. I guess you can help if that's what you need to do. Just dump the beans in the trash."

"The trash?"

A shrug. "Corn can become corn muffins. Green beans can't become shit."

And that gets a chuckle out of Sarah. Much to her surprise, Bridget reaches into the huge fridge and hands her a hard seltzer. They clink cans and drink for a moment, and Sarah welcomes the warmth that unspools in her belly, her body relaxing just enough for her to realize she's been holding herself tight as a fist. It's still a marvel to her, to be able to drink here without getting sick. Kyle made her so nervous, made her constantly question her every decision—what to wear, what to say, if it was even worth speaking or if she was being immature or melodramatic. Her stomach was always in knots, her shoulders tight, her body so tense she couldn't take a full breath. She pulled a muscle smothering a sneeze, once. She was more anxious than she knew.

In between sips, they bring in the rest of the food, and Bridget tells Sarah what to do with it. It's kind of interesting, seeing what happens on this side of the door. When everything is put up, Bridget pulls out tubs of flour and sugar and a packet of yeast.

"Not much left to do, if you want to go," she says. "Just gonna get the cinnamon roll dough prepped."

"I've never made cinnamon rolls. Is it hard?"

Bridget peeks out the door before coming back. "Not really, but it's a pain in the ass. I wouldn't make them myself, except for Christmas or something, but my mom still sets the menus. Not like I have any-thing else to do here, you know?" It comes out dripping with resent-ment, and she shakes her head as she measures out warm water from the sink, tests it on her arm, and pours it in a big bowl, along with the packet of yeast.

Emboldened by the drink—and the fact that Bridget isn't yelling at her or throwing things—Sarah asks, "So you really hate it here, huh?"

Bridget shoots her a suspicious glance as she pours in sugar. "Yes."

"Why? I mean . . . it's beautiful. It seems like a great place to grow up."

Bridget snorts, measuring out the flour. "Yeah, I guess it does seem that way, from the outside. But it's . . . I mean, you only see the pretty façade. Not the dark underbelly."

Sarah waits, hoping for more, not wanting to break whatever spell is making Bridget almost friendly.

"I mean, I was pretty young when I found—" Bridget's eyes shoot to the door, and she shakes her head again as she dumps in the flour. "Imagine being an only child here, a girl, and having a new crop of hard-drinking, horny art guys from the free-love era showing up every season and telling you you're cute and asking you to model for them."

"Shit."

"Yeah. Bernie wasn't the worst of them, even. So the fact that I'm stuck here, even without any old goats, sucks. I had a life out there. I could still have one, if my mother would just—" She puts the bowl on an electric mixer with a dough hook and stares into the dough like she wishes it was someone's guts being twisted around. "Doesn't matter. My job is just to make the cinnamon rolls."

"I heard you used to own a restaurant . . ." Sarah starts.

Bridget's face hardens, then goes slack with sorrow. "I did. That was my dream. Did you know that thirty percent of restaurants can't survive their first year? I thought I could beat the statistic. I was wrong. Turns out nobody in a crappy little north Georgia town actually wants fine dining." She pounds the rest of her seltzer and tosses the can in the trash. There's no recycling in the mountains, apparently.

"So why don't you work in a different restaurant? I passed so many wineries on the way here. They must have nice restaurants. It just seems like . . . you don't like what you're doing."

Bridget finally looks her in the eyes with a familiar desperation that Sarah recognizes all too well—the look of someone who is trapped. "I can't leave. She gave me a loan. My beloved mother, who said culinary school was a waste of time, gave me everything I needed to start my very own dream restaurant. She's loaded, for Chrissakes! But because she's Gail, it wasn't a gift. It was very official. There were terms. I had to sign and initial wherever she pointed. If I couldn't pay back the loan, I had to come back here and fulfill my duty. Cook, and then take over, just like she did. And if I misbehave—" A harsh chuckle as she pulls another seltzer from the fridge. "Well, there are repercussions for that, too."

"She certainly seems obsessed with misbehavior."

Bridget holds up her seltzer in acknowledgment. "Makes you wonder what she's up to, doesn't it? Makes you wonder what she's hiding out here, away from the world."

Sarah goes very still. "Well . . . what is she hiding?"

It's like a wall comes down behind Bridget's eyes.

Ah, yes.

There's the irrational hatred, the usual Bridget.

"It doesn't matter. You signed your papers, too." Bridget puts in her earbuds, ending the conversation.

Sarah throws away her seltzer can, says, "Thank you," and heads back out into the café, wishing she could've kept Bridget talking just a little longer. If there were three more Bernies hanging around, she could understand the ongoing anger, but Bernie is gone and he'll never be back, and Reid is not like that at all. Maybe being the chef and maid isn't the best job on earth, but it's not difficult and this place is idyllic and there's got to be plenty of free time. Sarah can't stand her mother, but if her mom lived in a sprawling resort in the mountains and Sarah could live there rent-free, she'd probably find a way to get along. There's something to be said for not having to worry about every little thing in life and being able to make art somewhere pretty.

Sarah feels free here, but it's clear that Bridget is committed to misery.

Oh, well. This is not Sarah's hill to die on. If Bridget wants to be angry then Bridget will be angry. At least there will be cinnamon rolls in the morning, provided Bridget doesn't burn them to spite her. Or Gail. Or whoever she's mad at.

As she's closing the café door behind her, the paper plate going soggy and drooping over her hand, headlights rumble up the road. She waits as Reid and Gail get out of the car. Gail shoots her a sharp look and ducks into the community house without a word, but Reid stops and jerks his chin at the plate.

"That for me?"

"Yeah. I figured if I didn't save it, they'd starve you. Bridget is especially pissed tonight."

"Then I guess I'd better eat at my cabin."

He starts walking, and she falls in step. "So how'd it go?"

When he holds his unwrapped hands up, the moonlight shows black lines crisscrossing them like Frankenstein's monster. "Twenty-three stitches. They'd never seen anything like it. Mostly skin, a little muscle. I got lucky. Didn't hit any tendons or nick any bone."

Sarah shudders at the thought. "Jesus."

"So . . . I can't use the forge. I can barely hold a pencil. I think . . ." He tries to make a fist and winces. "I might need to go home."

The lift Sarah felt at seeing him bottoms out like a plane hitting turbulence. "But . . . there are other media! You could paint or . . ."

He sighs.

"It's all with your hands, isn't it?" she says. "Art is all about hands."

"I guess some people learn to use their mouth or their feet, but I don't want it that badly right now," he says, trying to keep the tone light. "The forge is not a good place for open mouths."

The thought of open mouths makes her realize that things will change with him gone. Even if she told herself again and again that she was in no place to be in a relationship, she always looked forward to seeing him. But was it him, who he really is as a person, or was it the tummy swoops—the hope of it all? The possibility? The dreaming? The crushing? The flirting? The big Maybe? It's been so long since she had a big Maybe, and it looks like her big Maybe is going away and becoming a Probably Not.

"Well, that sucks," she says plainly.

"Yeah, it does."

It's dark out, the sky alive with stars, and Sarah feels something shift in her heart. She was going to ask for his number, ask where he lives. Instead she remains silent.

Sometimes you want something, and sometimes you just want the wanting.

They reach his cabin, and he fumbles with the key. His fingers don't want to uncurl, and she can't imagine what it must feel like, those stitches pulling as he tries to do something as simple as turn a key. She almost offers to do it for him, but she can tell that he's the kind of man who would find that emasculating, or at least depressing. He finally gets it, and she steps inside the cabin and places his plate on the coffee table.

"You want company?" she asks.

A look of pain crosses his face. "I'd like to say yes, but I don't think I'm fit for it. I just want to eat and take a sleeping pill and fall unconscious, you know?"

"Makes sense."

For an awkward beat, she just stands there, and maybe before today, he would've taken a step toward her, brushed her hair out of her eyes or rubbed her upper arm. But this time he keeps his distance. This thing between them—he can feel it dying, too.

"Thanks for saving me dinner."

"I guess we're even now."

There's a finality in the air as she realizes that just as she's decided it can't work right now, so has he. Whether that's because he got hurt in her world or because things are just too weird, it doesn't matter. The tingles have fallen down dead, a murmuration massacred in one afternoon.

She walks to the door and smiles sadly. "Hope you feel better."

"Yeah, me, too." He sits down and takes the napkin off his plate. "Would you mind closing the door behind you?"

She nods, knows she can't speak or her voice will sound strangled. She's lost something, and whether or not she wanted it, it's gone. There's something painful there.

The door clicks shut behind her, and she walks to her cabin alone, sweeping the gravel drive with her phone flashlight. It does not escape her that she's been through a month's worth of experiences and emotions in one day. When she woke up this morning, she'd never been inside an abandoned asylum, never seen a man's hands savagely torn open by seven pieces of glass spinning on a wheel.

Her thoughts are scattered, worrisome, troubled. She unlocks her cottage and relocks it behind her and goes through the rituals she created long ago to manage her chaotic mind. Kyle suggested she had ADHD, that she was flighty and ridiculous and disorganized, but she now thinks that he wanted someone who was the complete opposite of that and couldn't figure out how to fit her into his Procrustean bed. He told her once that his ultimate fantasy was for her to be totally submissive in bed, and she admitted that she couldn't do that, that it made her want to toss her head like a wild horse and run away. Maybe that's why he tried so hard to mold her—because she was so determined to break that mold.

Maybe Reid wouldn't need a mold at all.

Now she'll never know.

Such a strange sadness, when a door closes before you're ready.

And yet . . . she's not walking back over there, asking for his email.

He's not walking over here, asking for hers.

Sometimes, it is what it is.

She brushes her teeth and puts up her hair and moisturizes her hands, which always get dried out when she's in the studio. She thinks about the bookshelf and the fallen books and the passage to the secret upstairs, wonders if there are any medical records up there that might shed some light on what she saw today in the hotel basement, but she's just too tired to care right now. Both offices have sat silent and alone for more than a century; they can keep for a night.

She turns on her side, eyes watering as she stares at the silky wallpaper, missing Netflix. But when she opens her eyes again, she smells lilacs, and she knows that something is extremely wrong.

29

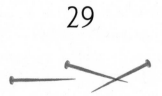

This is a dream.

It's nighttime, and something woke her.

The door—it's creaking open.

Her entire body goes rigid, every cell intricately aware. She feels the need to run away, to pump her arms and legs, to disappear over some impossible horizon.

Instead, she is trapped, and so her body does the next best thing: It freezes.

The door shuts softly, the click of the lock sharp in the nighttime silence. It's funny, how he plays at tenderness, gentle and quiet as he steps across the room, his bulk taking up far too much space.

"Are you awake, little dove?" he whispers.

He is completely unaware, this man, her husband, that women always wake when danger is near. That they are always listening, always watching, that they can sense how the air changes when they are targeted. Like those of wild creatures, their eyes pierce the darkness, taking in every detail of the approaching enemy. If only, like wild creatures, they had ready claws.

He does not understand women.

He does not need to.

You don't need to understand a porcelain cup to shatter it completely.

She is on her side, turned away to the wall, knees drawn up protectively, and he sits on the corner of the bed, runs a hand up her leg under the blanket. "Darling, you have duties to perform."

Duties.

Like she's a—a scullery maid, or a stable boy.

Like she ever agreed to—this.

Like she could quit and walk away if she wanted to.

Like she has any choice.

The heavy palm rubs circles on her haunch like he's currycombing a jumpy mare. His touches are like that—as if the tricks he's learned for calming horses will help her, too, to be amenable.

She feigns sleep, puts careful attention into making her breathing seem deep and heavy. The hand travels over her rump, into the curve under her ribs, and she can't help but flinch away. These are not parts she wants to have touched, and she can't make her body agree to it no matter what her mother and her husband say is good and right.

"Ticklish, eh?" His fingers dig into her side, and she convulses and whimpers. It is not a laugh, but knowing him, he'll mistake it for one. "That's it. Uncurl for me, little pillbug."

She curls tighter around her center, shoulders hunched up. "Please, no," she whispers.

The hand stills on her shoulder. A long moment passes. In a voice she's never heard before, a voice dreadful and terrible and incredulous and almost pitying, he says, "Darling, it is not a wife's prerogative to tell her husband no. You swore an oath under God to obey me."

She shudders, curling her arms around her head, trying to disappear. "It hurt, last time," she says. "There was blood again."

She's hard and tight as a cannonball under the covers, and his hand probes clumsily around at her middle, digs painfully until he clasps her breast, molding it with his fingers like he's greedily weighing a bag of coins. "Every part of you is mine, darling. You have been given to me. There is always blood, the first time, sometimes the second. You don't need to worry. I shall be quick."

"No."

She is surprised to hear her own voice, tremulous as it is.

An annoyed sigh. "Now look. I have been terribly patient with you. I brought you here for your honeymoon, and it is not cheap. You have tasted the finest foods, enjoyed the waters, had your every need met. And now you must meet *my* needs. That is how a marriage works, sweetness."

"No."

It's a little louder this time.

His fingers pinch her so hard, as if proving he can do whatever he likes. She is certain she'll have a bruise.

"No is not an option."

"No."

"Emily!" His voice is a harsh, sharp rebuke. He releases her breast and stands, looming over her like God himself clad in a stark white nightshirt. "You will stop this ridiculous, childish behavior immediately!"

"No."

He grabs her wrist and yanks, dragging her halfway out of bed so that she must catch herself on her feet or risk falling. Once she's sitting on the edge of the bed, he wrenches her up to standing. He's ever so much bigger than she; her nose barely comes up to his armpits. He reminds her of the bear in a storybook the governess read her as a child, a great monster that swallowed bad children up in one unrepentant gulp.

"You're hurting me, Bertram!" she cries, trying to pull her arm away.

But he doesn't let go. He grabs her shoulders with both hands, pinning her in place. She struggles to escape his grip, but that only makes him clutch her all the tighter.

"Emily Engle, you will submit to me," he growls.

"No!"

This time, it's a feral, rebellious yelp. She kicks out at his shins, and he hisses in pain as her toenails connect. When he pushes her away, she twists and falls halfway on the bed, barely stopping her knees from hitting the floor. A big hand comes down on her shoulder, pinning her there. It reminds her of being very young and told to kneel at her bedside and say her prayers, but she knows that no prayer will save her now. She's been praying all week, and nothing has improved. She can't enjoy the balmy, healthful days here because she dreads the terror of the nights. Hard fingers grind into the tender skin between her shoulder and neck, and she squirms like a butterfly as the pin enters its abdomen.

"Your father said you were biddable. Well behaved."

"I am!" she cries, sucking in a breath as the tears fall. "This is not— no one ever told me—"

"Biddable means you do what you're told whether you like it or not. It is not for you to decide."

He kneels behind her, wraps an arm around her chest, pulling her close to the immense, hairy heat of him.

"I am a good man. You will grow to love me," he says, his voice somehow both certain and begging.

His hand finds her calf, shimmies up under the hem of her chemise.

With her free arm, she feels around under the bed, knowing what she'll find. As he struggles to both hold her tight and give himself enough room to undress her, she picks up the empty chamber pot and slams it over her shoulder, smashing it against his head.

"You bitch!" he shouts, pulling away to stand.

The coolness that rushes in is exhilarating, and she stands, too, edging around him, aiming for the door, for escape, for anything but this.

He stumbles to the dressing table, struggles to see what little the mirror will reveal in the light of a single candle. "You've cut me, Emily!"

As he focuses on his own pain, she opens the door and runs down the hall, darting down the grand staircase to the main level. The lanterns are lit, the world bathed in warm orange. Downstairs, the lobby is silent, the parrots hidden under cloth drapes and murmuring softly like sleepy children. She runs to the front desk, only realizing she's in her nightclothes when the sleepy clerk gawps at her.

"Help," she says simply.

"Is there a problem, Mrs. Engle?"

"I—"

She doesn't have the words to describe to a strange man exactly what her problem is. None of these words are polite ones.

"Stop her!"

They both look to the man striding purposefully across the lobby in his nightshirt, blood dripping down his face from a wound on the side of his head. This is her handsome husband, the well-bred banker, the man who wooed her and made her promises of a beautiful future and gallantly won her hand. He wasn't her only suitor, and she chose him because he was gentle with his horses and kind to his sisters and jovial with his servants. Because he was understanding and sensitive—or so she thought. Now he is looking at her like he wishes he could incinerate her on the spot.

"Stop her, Mr. Engle?"

"She attacked me!"

"She—she did what, sir?"

Bertram puts a hand to his face and draws it away, his entire palm coated in blood. He holds it out to the clerk as if his very presence in nightclothes isn't evidence enough that something very unusual is occurring.

"She did this! Call the doctors. I want her restrained."

The clerk looks from Emily to her husband, uncertain.

Emily shakes her head. "He attacked me, and I fought back," she explains, knowing very well that her voice is high-pitched and desperate. "He was hurting me."

"Think, boy, about who pays the bills. Who tips the help. Who will complain to the proprietors," Bertram says, drawing on the mantle of a successful and powerful businessman despite the fact that he's barelegged and barefoot in public, drenched in blood and shards of chamber pot.

The clerk licks his lips and nods, then looks down at whatever is behind his desk. Emily doesn't know what could possibly be there, but she knows in full certainty that it will be her undoing. She takes a gasping breath, spins, and bolts for the front door. She'd rather run away into the forest by herself than find out what's behind the clerk's desk.

It's only a few steps away, but when she tugs on the handle, the door doesn't budge. Ah! There's a lock. She fumbles for it, but in that moment of confusion, strong hands grab her around the middle and her husband hefts her off the ground. Her feet dangle, and she kicks out, thrashing with her whole body, growling and hissing.

Footsteps pound down the hall, and two men appear in odd uniforms she hasn't seen before, all white. One of them is holding a sinister contraption, almost like a rope loop on the end of a long stick. The other has something behind his back. They move to flank Bertram, arms out to block her escape.

"Where's the doctor?" the clerk asks.

"On his way," one of the men replies. He focuses on Emily, gives her a dumb smile that wouldn't even fool an infant. "Let's calm down now, missus. No good comes of fighting. Be a good girl."

A new figure appears from the hall, a thin bald man in a satin dressing gown with darkly shaded pince-nez and the cutting look of a hawk.

"What seems to be the problem?"

Bertram pivots to face the new man, holding Emily against his chest. She's gone still, now that she knows she's blocked in by men who seem quite familiar with this sort of thing. She throws a longing glance at the door, and Bertram wrenches her back into place.

"Mrs. Engle is hysterical," he says calmly. "She attacked me, unprovoked."

"We'll have to see to that wound, sir," the man says soothingly. He turns his attention to Emily, tucking his pince-nez into the pocket of his gown and giving her a thorough, probing look from her mussed braid to her bare feet, now dangling limply. "Madam, I am Dr. Warren

December. Tell me, do you have a family history of nervous problems? Hysteria, melancholia, fever of the spirit?"

"Where is Dr. Calloway? He is my doctor," she says, chin held high.

Dr. December's smile is pitying. "Our dear Dr. Calloway has had a family emergency, but I'm his partner, and I'm eager to help you."

"My husband hurt me," she says, ignoring the embarrassing question of her family history and drawing forth every bit of pride she's earned as her father's daughter. "It is natural to fight back when one is attacked in one's own bed."

The doctor shakes his head sadly. "On the contrary, it is *unnatural* when a woman lashes out in such a way, especially against your beloved husband and protector, who only wants the best for you. You are sick, my dear, and we must help you to be better, yes?"

"I'm not sick." She blinks, confused by this thought. "I am fine."

"People who are fine do not strike their husbands." The doctor sounds so infinitely disappointed in her. "People who are fine do not resort to violence. This is a very grave issue, but I feel certain we can help you. Aren't you fortunate, that your illness surfaced here, where we are experimenting with state-of-the-art medical techniques?" He claps his hands once, delighted now, and gestures to the men waiting on either side.

"Restrain her, please, with care. Mrs. Engle is a valued guest, after all, and she needs our help."

The man holding the stick with the loop on the end sidles toward her, angling the loop for her head. Bertram—her husband—pulls her tight against him, his lips harsh against the fine shell of her ear.

"It's for your own good, little dove," he whispers soothingly. "I pray they can help you overcome whatever demon inspired these hysterics. When you are willing, I will welcome you back to our marriage bed."

He squeezes her and drops her, and the loop comes down over her head and tightens around her throat. She grabs the rope and tries to pull away, but that only makes it pinch down harder into her skin. "Please," she gurgles, falling to her knees as the rope pulls her down onto the soft, rich carpet.

"Now, now," the doctor in the dressing gown says, voice gentle. He takes something from the man not wielding the stick and holds it behind his back as he approaches her. She is losing the ability to breathe, her body slumping downward. "Do hold still, Mrs. Engle. It will only hurt for a moment, my dear."

She feels a little pinch in her neck, and Dr. December holds up a metallic syringe. He hooks a finger under her chin, tips her head up so that she must look into his face. There is an excitement in his pale, watery eyes that she does not like.

"You must trust us, Mrs. Engle," he says, and the world swims around him, a whirlpool dragging her over a cliff and into some sort of blurry, dreamy, welcome abyss. "We will make you better."

When she next opens her eyes, she's in a white room, arms and legs strapped to the narrow bed.

And she starts screaming.

30

er voice is shredding, her eyes focused on the white ceiling, lit only by the gaslamp trapped within a metal cage upon the wall. Everything is cast in mysterious dancing shadows. It is somehow both then and now. There is no water stain, no scent of age and mildew. The only odor is something antiseptic and sweet, and the door opens abruptly.

"Quiet," says a man in a uniform, but she can't be quiet.

She can't stop screaming.

If she screams loud enough, long enough, she'll wake up.

That's how dreams work.

This dream . . . is a nightmare.

"I said quiet!" the man barks, storming toward her.

But she will not.

She's said no too many times.

She's starting to get a taste for it.

She does not like being in this strange, small room. She does not like the leather restraints holding her down.

But she likes it better than what Bertram did to her on the first night of her honeymoon, and so she will take this instead and she will scream as much as she wants to scream.

"Won't shut up?" another man says, appearing in the doorway.

"You know how it is when they're new."

"I'll get the bromides."

Somewhere else, another scream starts up, an answering scream, and she screams all the harder. There must be other people down here, other people like her. They call to one another like wild wolves in a children's storybook. *I'm here,* they say. *I'm here, and they can't make me be quiet.*

And then the man brings in another syringe, and she thrashes and throws her head back and forth like a mad horse, but he plants the needle in her buttock and she is beyond scandalized and ashamed and then she's falling into that blurry crevasse again, falling down down down into nothingness.

She opens her eyes, and there is darkness, and she gives an experimental shake and finds that she is unrestrained. Her hand fumbles to the side of the bed and produces a phone. The phone tells her it is after midnight, and she shines the phone's flashlight around the room to confirm that she is Sarah and she is wearing her favorite pajamas with sloths on them and there are no restraints and she is not in the all-white room.

She is not Emily, *she is not.* She is Sarah.

Her throat hurts, and she gets up and drinks metallic water directly from the bathroom tap. When she used to have nightmares, back in Colorado, she would scream and scream until Kyle woke her up. In real life, she was never actually screaming—it was more like breathy little groans and twitching—but Kyle was always kind and understanding. Her suffering brought out his best qualities. That's what was so very odd about him—he was never violent, never angry. Everything he did was subtle and quiet and carefully thought out. There was never anything she could put her finger on or say out loud. But when she was hurting or sick or scared or needy, he was there. Almost like he liked her better that way.

With the bathroom light on, she inspects herself, regaining understanding of her body. The dream was so vivid, so real. She *was* the girl—the woman—in mind and body. She was Emily. She felt what Emily felt and saw what Emily saw and knew what Emily knew. Everything Emily did made perfect sense. She wanted more than anything to protect Emily—to protect herself. And now her throat hurts as if she, too, has been screaming, and when she looks down at her feet, one of her big toenails is chipped. Maybe she really was thrashing in her sleep, after all.

But something is bothering her, some subtle sound barely heard over the pounding of the waterfall. It's screaming—but not a person. Something wild and weird and mad, because no human throat could make that sound. She walks to the front window and looks outside, but it's nothing as convenient as a deer being mauled by a bear in a patch of moonlight or two raccoons angrily fucking. Whatever it is, it's out of view of her cottage window, and there's no way in the world that she's setting foot outside in the forest when something is clearly in the process of being mercilessly murdered. She turns on the outside light and double-checks that the door is locked, then paces before it, unnerved.

She's fully awake now, her body ready to run despite the fact that the only real threat was in a dream, a dream of something that happened to someone across acres of time, if at all. The bizarre thing is that there was something so familiar about whatever drug they injected Emily with, that swoopy, heady sensation of falling off a cliff into a velvety dark hole. It nibbles at the edge of her memory. Maybe it's a little like taking Nyquil, or laughing gas before having a cavity filled?

But no. This memory is something deeper than that, and she's thinking so hard it's giving her a headache.

Sarah sits on the edge of the bed, considering her choices. It's the middle of the night, and she's out here alone in a cottage without WiFi, internet, or TV. She could read a book, but she's almost certain that she's too distracted to absorb anything, much less fall into the story. The screaming outside has stopped, but she doesn't want to investigate it, nor does she want to go to the clay studio alone when no one else is awake or around.

She picks up her flashlight and walks to the bookshelf, shoving it away from the wall to expose the brightly colored wallpaper surrounding the ruined doorway. Flashlight on, she heads up the stairs, the wood cold under her bare feet. Maybe it was scary a few days ago, but a lot has happened since then. It's almost friendly now, just another part of the house.

It's not as scary as the white room, that much is certain.

Stepping into the office, she puts her phone on the desk, flashlight pointing up, and sweeps her actual flashlight over the desk to the ledger she noticed the first time she was up here. The green canvas cover is dry under her fingertips, and she turns to the front and struggles to read the doctor's spidery, old-fashioned script.

It's a record of guests and the treatments they received, but there is no mention of injections, restraints, or long sticks with nooses at the end like those of the dog catcher in an old cartoon. Just nice, normal things, like hydrotherapy, massage, baths, lists of medicines with ridiculous names like Dr. Bateman's Pectoral Drops and Londonderry Lithia. His notes to the right of each entry are almost all positive and hopeful.

Shows marked improvement in pallor.

Nervous habits have all but disappeared.

Patient reports a reduction in piles.

She turns to the back of the book and looks for Emily Engle, unsurprised to find that exact name right where she would expect it, matched with the check-in date from the hotel ledger. Emily took the waters and was given medicines for a nervous disposition, labeled "Fever of the Spirit." The last entry for her says merely, "Transferred to the care of Dr. Warren December for marital troubles and hysterics."

And then nothing. There are a few dozen more entries after Emily's name, and then the ledger is blank. Sarah pages through the rest of the book, finding nothing. No explanations, no notes, just blank pages meant to be filled.

Whatever closed down the hotel, she thinks, must've happened in the weeks after Emily was sent downstairs. And it would appear it happened quite suddenly, as everything both in this house and in the hotel was left almost untouched. No boxes or crates, no estate sale. This place is a time capsule, sealed and abandoned, lonely and forgotten.

There is no more information on Emily, no more handwritten ledgers. The books on the shelves are the sort of thing an erudite man would surround himself with, and she can imagine a benevolent, bespectacled doctor pleasantly making his notes, so certain that his wealthy patients were reaping the benefits of his cures.

Except . . .

Well, if Emily was sent downstairs, she couldn't possibly be the only one.

Sarah opens the ledger to Emily's name again, runs a finger down the right-hand column of those who checked in after her.

There.

Seven more entries with the same phrase as applied to Emily Engle.

Transferred to the care of Dr. Warren December.

Another woman, Miss Theresa Montgomery, age 17, for moral weakness and sinful behavior.

And then Mrs. Dorothea Payne, 26, for melancholia after childbirth.

And then Miss Nicolette Vincent, age 32, "friend" of a guest to remain unnamed, for "being in an inconvenient way," which Sarah reads as a mistress inconveniently impregnated.

Now that she knows what she's looking for, they shout at her from the page. Whenever she sees the name of Dr. Warren December mentioned, she finds a woman sent downstairs for depression, rebellion, masturbation, hysteria, violence, insanity, even, to her horror, a twelve-year old girl for the seemingly simple act of defying her father.

Sarah swallows around the lump in her throat, her entire body gone cold.

These women . . . so many women.

They were wealthy or entangled with the wealthy, and they were sent downstairs into the small, white rooms not necessarily for insanity, but for going against society's requirements of the fairer sex. If what she saw in her dream was true for Emily Engle, if fighting off a rapist was enough to get a wealthy woman locked away, then it stands to reason that most of these women were innocent of any real crime and probably not even mentally ill, beyond several instances of postpartum depression that the doctors of the day likely didn't know how to handle.

"You poor things," she murmurs to the book, her voice loud in the empty cottage.

She's suddenly aware that she's in a pitch-black room in the middle of the night, and she tucks the book under her arm and heads back downstairs. She has the answers she wanted, and she'll be able to make connections with more savvy after some sleep and with daylight shining through the windows.

When she crawls into bed, she can feel the ledger's presence on the bedside table. At first it felt sinister, but now . . . there's a tenderness in her heart for all the women within who have been reduced to a few elegant lines in a dusty book. To Dr. Calloway, they were patients beyond his skills, sent to a trusted colleague to get the help they so desperately needed—or perhaps he understood exactly what he was doing and knew his powerful male guests were paying him to make the transfer of care whenever a female became troublesome. Sarah may never know if Dr. Calloway built the hotel to help people or to make even more money by getting rid of them.

The only thing Sarah knows for sure is that these were women just like her, women who were under the power of the wrong men in the wrong lives, and when they proved too vexing to keep, they were instead imprisoned.

SANE.

That was the word scratched crudely in the top of the coffin with a cut nail.

Emily's last proclamation to the world—that no matter what the ledgers suggested, she was sane.

Whether or not Sarah's mind is merely making up a story for the girl in the coffin, these women were once very real, and she is the only witness to what they suffered.

Sarah has to find Ingrid and convince her to go back into the old hotel, not that it will be very difficult. Ingrid wants to find the medical equipment, and Sarah wants to find the ledger of Dr. Warren December.

She wants to know, exactly, what he did to cure them.

On the way to breakfast the next morning, Sarah hears crying and follows the sound to find Gertrude Rose sobbing in front of her studio. Or, more accurately, in front of the rabbit hutch. Gertrude Rose looks, to the outside eye, eccentric as always in her filmy white dress, but her distress is very real.

"What's wrong?" Sarah asks, although something pings the back of her mind, some animal warning thumping a foot in the soft grass of her heart.

"The rabbits," Gertrude Rose sobs, turning to show her white gloves soaked with blood. "Something horrible has happened to the rabbits."

31

"The poor darlings are dead!" Gertrude Rose wails.

Sarah steps closer to the hutch and immediately steps right on back. The two white angora rabbits look like they've been put through a paper shredder. Snowy-white hair drifts about the cage, the rabbits' soft bodies flopped at unnatural angles, their ears torn off and their eyes gouged out. Sticky burgundy blood splashes the metal wire, the hutch door left wide open.

Sarah notes with a frisson of unease that the looped wire of the hutch door closes by hooking over yet another old cut nail with a rectangular head.

"The screaming last night," Sarah says, remembering. "They were screaming."

Gertrude Rose looks at her sharply. "You heard screaming?"

"I heard a sound ... around midnight. Like an animal being attacked."

"And you didn't check on them?"

Sarah gives her an odd look. "No, when I'm in a cottage out in the middle of the forest alone at midnight and hear animals screaming, I do not go outside to look at someone else's caged rabbits. I assumed it was some kind of carnivore doing what carnivores do. And carnivores shouldn't be able to get into cages, so I didn't even think about your rabbits."

"They're not mine—weren't mine," Gertrude Rose says with a sniffle. "They belonged to Tranquil Falls. I was taking care of them, of course, but they're for the program. Poor things. Gail said their names were Henry and Warren, after the men who founded the hotel."

She reaches toward the wire of the hutch like a dowager theatrically bidding adieu to the *Titanic* as the lifeboat rows her away.

"What do you think did it?" Sarah asks.

"Who, you mean."

Sarah is confused by that. "Who?"

Gertrude Rose takes a shuddering breath, bosom heaving. "No animal does this. Animals kill to eat, not for amusement. Even a coyote would take some meat. Mark my words: A person did this."

Sarah looks around the clearing like she might find a rabbit-hating axe-murderer hiding behind a tree. "No one here would do this."

Gertrude Rose fans herself with a fan she has produced from her gown. "Strange things are afoot. Corpses everywhere. This place is cursed."

"Are you going to leave?"

Finally, Gertrude Rose drops the affectation and looks at Sarah like she's an idiot. "Hell, no. I'm committed to finishing what I came here to do."

She strips off her bloodied gloves, shoves them in her reticule, and sighs deeply. "George will clean them up, don't you think? Come along, let's go tell Gail, and she'll set it to rights."

She links her arm through Sarah's and begins to tow the younger woman up toward the community house. Sarah generally doesn't like being this close to other people, especially someone as bossy and commanding as Gertrude Rose, but this appears to be the older woman's way of getting people to do what she wants. She jogs to keep up, noting that Gertrude Rose moves like a boat cutting through ice, a prow pushing aggressively into the world, ready to crush whatever gets in her way. How nice it must be, Sarah thinks, to know exactly who you are and exactly what you're doing, even if what you're doing seems completely nutballs insane to the rest of the world.

"What are you working on?" she asks, remembering the bizarrely endless scarf she saw pooled on the floor of Gertrude Rose's studio.

"It's a secret," Gertrude Rose says. "All will be revealed at the final show."

Whenever Sarah thinks about the final show, worry trills up her spine. She came here ready to work, ready to dive back into pottery, but so far she's been held up again and again by increasingly bizarre happenings. With Bernie dead and Reid leaving, nothing should now stand in her way. She has to figure out what to do with the army of tiny chamber pots she's made and then build the rest of her body of work around it. She's still toying with the idea of dainty teacups and saucers, which would contrast nicely. One for eating, one for the opposite. Perhaps she'll paint elaborate flowers on the chamber pots and use plain, simple glazes for the teacups, reversing their assumed design styles.

Yes, that's it exactly. Today she'll find the design of her teacup and begin replicating it.

They arrive at December House and Gertrude Rose theatrically throws the door open and sighs when there's no one in the immediate vicinity to appreciate the drama of her gesture. She tows Sarah into the café and doesn't release her until they're both standing in front of Gail, who's fighting, as usual, with the French press.

"The rabbits are dead," Gertrude Rose says loudly as if announcing to a full complement of servants that the lord of their house has passed beyond.

That gets Gail's attention. She puts down the French press and asks, "Are you sure? What happened?"

"They've been torn asunder!" Gertrude Rose begins. "Cruelly, hatefully mutilated. Sarah says she heard screaming last night but didn't bother to investigate."

Gail looks at Sarah like a teacher identifying the problem child standing by the broken window.

"Look, I don't go into the forest alone at midnight when I hear an animal screaming," Sarah says, again, hoping Gail is at least reasonable about such things.

"Good. Gertrude Rose, you didn't hear anything?"

Gertrude Rose shakes her head. "Medical cannabis and earplugs. I was utterly insensate."

"Did anybody hear screaming last night?" Gail shouts, loud enough to make everyone in the café stop talking—not that there are many of them left, with Bernie gone and Reid missing. Lucas isn't there, either, so it's just Ingrid, Kim, and Antoinette, scattered as far as possible from one another.

"No, but you have my attention," Ingrid says with a smirk.

"The rabbits by the fiber studio were apparently killed last night, and I need to know what happened." Gail puts her hands on her hips and stares at them each in turn.

"Oh, my God." Kim's jaw is dropped, her voice louder than it needs to be. "That's so horrible!"

"I'm going to go check it out." Ingrid stands and slings her bag over her shoulder. Sarah is fairly certain she'll be taking as many photos as she can before someone shows up and points out how macabre it is.

Kim stands and follows her, exactly the sort of person who slows down to really get a good look at a car accident, and Antoinette goes to Gertrude Rose to ask if she's okay, which is all the permission Gertrude Rose needs to be even more melodramatic than usual.

"You didn't see anything else?" Gail asks Sarah as Gertrude Rose happily caterwauls.

"I didn't see anything," Sarah corrects. "I heard screaming, assumed it was an animal, and went back to sleep."

The way Gail is rubbing her temples she doesn't quite believe it. "Two artists gone and the rabbits killed," she mutters. "This place is falling apart."

Sarah has no response to that; she's just a visiting artist, and everything bad that's happened to her has been very much against her will. She came here to throw pots and fire them, not dig up coffins and wake to dying rabbits.

Except—wait.

"Did Reid already leave?"

"This morning. Said he doesn't like long goodbyes." Gail flaps a hand at the parking lot. "Left a lot of his supplies here, too. Which, okay, he can't carry them right now. But what am I supposed to do about it?"

A response is apparently not required; Gail shrugs and pushes into the kitchen, freeing Sarah to fix her breakfast. Gertrude Rose and Antoinette leave, and then she's alone in the cafeteria, a far cry from the busy community she felt the first few days here. She's more disappointed than she expected to be at Reid's exit, which makes her feel a little cowardly. Why would he just run off like that, without saying anything? Sarah would've been happy to help him carry things, but it sounds like he left a lot behind. Maybe he'll come back at the end of the season once he's healed up some, to see the show. He could've left her a note, at least, or his number. Even if she felt things cool between them last night, she still secretly harbored hopes for breakfast. Maybe he didn't care as much as he seemed to. The whole thing strikes Sarah as extremely strange and not exactly within character.

No point in being upset. Sarah learned a long time ago that she can't control what other people do, especially stubborn men. She stares out at the parking lot for a moment, trying to remember which car is missing, before giving up and heading to the buffet. Bridget's cinnamon rolls are indeed insanely good, and last night's dinner seems like it happened days ago.

The rabbits—it's unsettling, a tragedy.

What happened to Reid—also unsettling, almost a tragedy.

What happened to Bernie—well, it seemed natural enough, but the timing was terrible. Maybe it's a tragedy to the people who actually liked him, but not to Sarah.

She can't change any of those things.

But something very strange is happening here, a series of bizarre events that don't make much sense and that don't seem related . . . except by the identical cut nails that keep showing up. The same nails from the old hotel.

The same nails from Emily Engle's coffin.

As Sarah eats, her determination builds. She knows what she has to do.

Once she's finished breakfast and has cleaned up, she heads back to her cottage and yet again dresses in all black. She checks that her phone is fully charged and her flashlight still works and slips a few extra batteries in her pocket just in case. She thinks about going to find Ingrid, but she doesn't know how to explain her sudden interest in being back in the hotel—or why she's going exactly where she plans to go once she's within. Plus, she doesn't want to spend hours holding a flashlight at just the right angle over a stained drain while Ingrid takes dozens of photos. It'll be easier and quicker, alone.

The path to the hotel is familiar now, although she keeps an eye out for George. She scoots over the fallen tree like it's nothing, trails her fingertips over a statue of a nymph, smiles as sparrows erupt from the fountain, where they'd been drinking. It's a calm day, and she notices patches of bright-white mushrooms and the last purple beautyberries clinging to a fading bush. There's peace to be had here in the forest, a sort of private silence wrapped around the waterfall's roar. Sunbeams slant in through the trees, and Sarah can imagine what it would've felt like to recline in one of the falling-down lounge chairs in the shade, breathing in the fresh mountain air.

She slithers under the door and stands in the lobby and it's welcome and familiar.

Except—something is different.

Someone is playing piano.

Or trying to. The piano is fighting back, off-key and clunky.

She knows this song.

It's the one Lucas was playing yesterday, the one that feels like a mad dash around an out-of-control merry-go-round.

Lucas—he wasn't at breakfast. He must be here.

Before, she's always gone down the hallway to the left, but this time she takes the hallway to the right. She steps carefully, aware that although the floor seems steady in most places, it has clearly fallen through in that one sunroom. Much like the ladies who once stayed here, Sarah must tiptoe through an invisible minefield to avoid ending up in the basement.

"Lucas?" she calls, but there's no answer.

She uses her flashlight to navigate the carpeted hallway, wishing she could rip all the plywood out of the windows and let the sunlight stream in as it was meant to. This place . . . it wants to breathe. She opens the first door that she finds, but it leads to a large coat closet still crowded with moth-eaten garments. As she pads down the long corridor, the piano grows louder and more frantic. Two double doors are thrown open, but it's dark as sin inside.

She shines her flashlight into that open mouth of a doorway, revealing a restaurant filled with elegant tables and curly wood chairs left in place as if the diners recently stood en masse and calmly exited. There are plates and glasses and silverware on the tables, all in disarray. Once-white napkins drape over chairs and plates like deflated infant ghosts. Chandeliers hang down, their crystals dirty and swagged in cobwebs.

The music is louder here, echoing off the walls.

Sarah shines her flashlight around the back of the room. The beam dances over a bar still fully stocked with glass bottles of cloudy spirits and hanging racks of dust-coated cocktail glasses. Finally it lands on the piano, an old baby grand, gleaming black as if recently polished.

The open top of the piano perfectly blocks the person playing it, and although she knows it has to be Lucas, *it has to be,* still her mind tells her it's not. It's a ghost, a ghoul, a girl in a white dress, some ancient bartender in a striped vest with sleeve garters and a face sloughing off like wet meat. The keys pound, off-key and odd, and she sidles around until she can finally see the figure calling forth the old, skin-crawlingly jovial song.

It's Lucas, thank God—*of course it is, who else could it be*—hunched over just like he was yesterday in his proper studio, his sweaty black hair flopped over his face. The sound is manic, mad, galloping, and it draws to a thunderous close. He takes a ragged breath, sits up straight, and then curls right back over and slams his fingers onto the keys.

"Lucas?" she calls.

He doesn't respond. Doesn't even pause.

The song goes on, too fast, slightly off, the piano jangling like a child's broken toy.

Sarah hurries across the room, winding around tables with their chairs left just so, except for a few that have toppled as if their diners left too quickly to notice their carelessness. She realizes that before she showed up, Lucas was playing in absolute darkness. He doesn't have a flashlight, doesn't even have his phone out. She knows musicians can play with their eyes shut, but the whole thing strikes her as beyond creepy.

"Lucas!" she barks, loud, shining the flashlight directly on him from across the piano.

He looks up, and his eyes are soft black pools, their pupils completely blown. He doesn't seem to see her, doesn't even stop playing for a single heartbeat. Sweat has soaked through his T-shirt, beads on the fine hairs over his lip. After a moment of staring out into the darkness, seeing nothing, he refocuses on the keyboard, slamming his fingers against the keys with increasingly senseless violence.

Sarah goes around the piano, needing both for the cacophonous noise to stop and for Lucas to be conscious again, because wherever his mind is—it's not here.

"Lucas, stop!" she says from behind him, right near his ear. "I think you're asleep!"

Lucas does not stop. Whatever nightmare has him in a stranglehold won't give him up.

Oh, how Sarah wishes Reid were here right now instead of . . . wherever he's gone.

Bracing herself for a bad reaction, she wraps her arms around the boy from the back, securing his lanky arms to his sides. The music stops for a blessed moment as she drags him back, but as soon as his fingers leave the keys, he makes a desperate, animal moan and lunges forward as if it's painful to not be playing.

She redoubles her effort, wrenching him forcefully away, and the poor kid loses his balance and topples off the old piano stool. He lands awkwardly on the ground, blindly feeling around as he whimpers, and she slams down the fallboard and, for good measure, sits on it.

As she shines her flashlight on him, Lucas struggles unseeing, finding the stool and feeling his way up it to sit. The boy's fingers reach out for the piano like some colorless, sightless creature at the bottom of the sea tenderly feeling along the sand for sustenance. When he finds the fallboard down, the keys hidden, he tries to pry it up, making the sort of mindless, bestial grunts and whimpers a dog makes while dreaming.

"Lucas!" Sarah shouts, reaching for his face with her hands. "Snap out of it!"

His hands close over hers, and she realizes in that moment her mistake.

Yes, he's young, but he's still bigger than her, still stronger. His fingers pry her hands from his face and shove her out of the way, sending her sprawling on the floor. It's not cruelly meant; it's almost impersonal, an animal scrambling to safety. There is no carpet here, only hard wooden boards, and she catches herself painfully on her hands, the dull thud reverberating up her arms as her flashlight and phone skitter away.

Ignoring her, Lucas clambers back up to the piano stool and sits, wrenching back the fallboard and slamming his fingers down on the tooth-colored keys in that now familiar first chord. Sarah wishes there was some electrical plug she could pull, some breaker switch that could leave them in silence, but this is an analog world, and as long as the piano is functional, the boy will apparently keep trying to play it.

Well—maybe there *is* something she can do.

Collecting her phone and flashlight, she crawls back to her feet and looks into the open top of the piano, examining the ancient, dusty wires. Shining her light in with one hand, she picks up one of the dainty old chairs with her other hand and slams it into the open piano with all her might. It's a clumsy, awkward strike, but it's the best she can do without plunging them both into darkness again. The delicate chair breaks apart in her hand, pieces of it flying away to skitter on the floor. She can't quite see what's happened within, but the piano sounds even worse than before. Some of the keys don't work now. The chair—and time—have done their work.

Lucas whimpers like he's in pain.

"Why won't it play?" he asks in the high, dreamy voice of a small boy.

"It's broken," she says softly, sweetly, like a caring mother might, not that she would know. "Let's get you back to your studio, and you can play your own piano."

"This one was so pretty, though," he says, running a hand along the keys. "It wants to be played so badly. It misses the music."

"Maybe another time." Sarah takes his hand and pulls him away, and he stands up from the stool and allows her to draw him along, reluctant and heavy as a sleepy toddler. She notices that he's barefoot, his feet muddy.

Hand in hand, she tugs Lucas out of the restaurant, down the long hallway, and over to the broken door.

"You'll have to crawl through here," she warns him. "Be careful."

Lucas obediently crawls through the hole, murmuring, "I like the other door better."

"What other door?" she asks.

He's outside now, and she tucks the flashlight and phone in her hoodie pocket and hurries to join him. When she stands, the boy is looking around him as if he's completely confused.

"Where are we?" he asks in his normal voice. Then seeing her, "Sarah?"

"We're at the old hotel. You were inside, playing the piano."

"That's— No. I was in my cabin, asleep. I was having the weirdest dream . . ."

He trails off.

"What was your dream about?"

Lucas faces her, his pupils tiny again as the sun shines on his sweaty mop of hair. "A girl. She told me to come inside. She was in a white dress." He frowns. "She said someone had to fiddle while Rome burned."

32

"She said what?" Sarah asks, because that line doesn't make any sense.

But Lucas has already turned to the fallen log and is heading away from the building at a fast clip slowed only by his bare feet, closer to normal than he is to the dream. "I don't know what's up, but this place freaks me out. Did I miss breakfast?"

Sarah trots behind him as he moves at a boyish lope. "There's enough time to grab a plate to go. How long were you in there?"

He glances back at her, sweeps a hand through his hair. "In where?"

"The old hotel?"

A headshake, as if he's trying to dislodge a fly. "That place is creepy."

"How'd you end up in there? What door did you use?"

The look he gives her suggests she is old and stupid. "Sorry, but I have no idea what you're talking about."

She tries a few more times, but Lucas has no memory of being in the old hotel, and it's as if even thinking about it causes his thoughts to slide away, water off a duck's back. When December House is in view, he says, "See you later!" and gallops off to grab breakfast while he still can, keeping to the grass so the gravel won't hurt his bare feet.

Sarah stops to watch him, baffled by this interaction. Can he really not remember going into the hotel? Is it like a dream to him, a vague remembrance that makes no sense upon waking? At least Sarah's dreams of the hotel are just dreams, even if they muddle real life and some strange fantasy of the past; she always wakes up in her own bed. And what door did he use to get in? Because if there's a better way than crawling through a dark hole over broken glass, she'd like to know. She still needs to get back inside. Hearing the piano and getting Lucas out distracted her from her original quest.

She's just thinking about turning around to go back when she sees Gail watching her from the front porch of December House, arms crossed.

Today is not a good day to get into trouble.

She waves and heads for her studio.

Gail does not wave back.

It's still unsettling to find the pottery studio door closed and the lights off. Bernie was such a big, loud presence that she's surprised his ghost hasn't stuck around to torment her. Are there modern polter- geists, Sarah wonders, or are they all disappointed Victorian children? Are there ghosts from the 1990s changing the radio to boy band songs or knocking Pop-Tarts off shelves? Are there 1950s housewives mess- ing with the oven temperature and making vacuums short-circuit? Where are the modern horror stories about ghost children in Bratz pajamas playing phantom Nintendo Switches?

She snorts as she lifts the plastic off her first run of pots, back be- fore the chamber pot idea struck her. This place is getting to her. Old coffins, new corpses, sleepwalking teenagers, glass where no glass should be.

This studio, at least, is empty of Bernie now. His absence feels al- most luscious. Someone, probably George, has swept up the remains of his broken sculptures, leaving the room as if Bernie was never even here. Sarah no longer has to worry about him throwing a mug at her.

That evidence of his temper was swept away with the rest of the clay shards. She is starting over fresh.

The first round of pots are all leather-hard, so she lays out her loops and ribs and needle tool and settles in to trim. She loves this part of pottery, when the hard work is done and she is merely perfecting the form, making small decisions that result in pleasing rewards. As she finishes each piece, she stamps it with her mark—she didn't throw that away but kept it in her jewelry box so Kyle wouldn't notice—and places it on the bisque shelf in the kiln room. These pieces don't really fit in with her overall statement for this body of work, but then again, she did have the idea of kintsugi. Perhaps she'll fire them, glaze them, fire them again, and then carefully break them so that she can piece them back together with gold.

She might need different supplies for that, but she has no idea how to research what to buy, much less purchase whatever she requires. There are drawbacks to being so far away from civilization, after all. For now, she's just going to follow her instincts.

The morning stretches out long and languid, and she opens a new bag of clay and wedges several balls, going gently at first in case more glass or nails appear.

Which—

She reaches into the pocket of her pottery apron and pulls out the first nail she encountered. It looks so innocent on her palm, old and humble, flaking a little. Odd to think it came from a coffin. She wishes she still had all the other nails to compare it with—Bernie's nail and Reid's nail and Ingrid's nail and the nail from the rabbit hutch. But Bernie's nail is likely in an evidence locker, Gail has the nail from Reid's pottery mishap, and Ingrid will likely hold on to hers forever, possibly turning it into a piece of jewelry. Sarah needs to speak with her again, but not enough to go out looking for her.

She wonders what it is about these nails, that they keep finding their way into people's hands.

Then again, this place is held together with nails, and after all this time, it's only natural that it would begin to fall apart.

With her music on and the door open to let in birdsong, Sarah focuses on creating the most delicate teacup she can with the clay she's brought. She wishes she had porcelain, but when she was ordering her supplies weeks ago, she didn't know what she was going to do yet. That's another problem with being out here in the mountains—art requires options, but she's stuck with what she has. Yes, well, art also forces flexibility. Every little decision informs the final product. The journey determines the destination. Such philosophy does not make her miss next-day shipping any less.

By the time the lunch bell rings, she has eleven nearly identical teacups lined up on her boards and loosely covered with plastic. It's lovely, having the studio all to herself with plenty of room to stretch out and no reason to make herself smaller to accommodate someone else. She keeps forgetting that that's one of the reasons she came here in the first place—because she needed space to rediscover herself. She'd expected long, languorous swaths of time, sleepy afternoons and morning hikes. There was no way to anticipate coffins and corpses and drama. None of that was supposed to happen. This was to be a place of rest and recuperation after years under Kyle's oppressive regime.

In this moment, it strikes her that . . . well, Emily Engle came here for rest and recuperation, too. All those women in Dr. Calloway's ledger made the arduous journey by carriage up here to the mountains and paid exorbitant fees to stroll the grounds and take the waters and be fed patent medicines on silver spoons. Like those women, she came here to relax and better herself.

Like those women, she has been forced to watch in slow motion as things go sideways.

At lunch, the mood is subdued. Lucas isn't there. Ingrid grabs a plate and zips right back outside before Sarah can stop her, but the others are flagging. Antoinette's fingertips are all stained ink black, and her lipstick is so dark it nearly matches. She sits with Gertrude Rose, dead-eyed, listening to a monologue about mourning dresses and the use of corpse hair in Victorian jewelry. This tracks, as Gertrude Rose has changed out of her filmy white day gown and into an elaborate black confection that buttons tightly up under her sagging chin. She is, Sarah realizes, mourning the dead rabbits.

That, too, tracks.

Kim walks in late and pauses like a seventh grader in the cafeteria, eyes bouncing from Sarah to Antoinette and Gertrude Rose. With an obvious sigh, she flounces over to sit with Sarah.

"Pretty quiet today, huh?" she says.

Sarah nods as she chews her falafel but has nothing to add; the statement is accurate, and there's a tension between them still, even with Reid gone.

"So how's the pottery going?" Kim tries again with the dogged persistence of the aggressively extroverted.

"Slowly but surely. I think I finally figured out my theme."

"Oh, cool!"

Sarah hates it when people say this as a segue into what they really want to say, which is exactly what Kim does.

"So what happened to Reid? Is he really just gone?"

Sarah swallows her food and sips her water. "You don't know?"

Kim shakes her head. "Nope. One day we were sharing a bottle of wine and laughing, and the next day, poof!" She leans in. "Looked like you two might be getting close, though."

With a sigh, Sarah realizes that she and Kim will never pass the Bechdel test.

"He asked me to show him how to throw a pot, but when he sat down with his first ball of clay, it was full of glass and shredded his hands."

Finally, a real reaction out of Kim: shock.

"Glass? In the clay? But how—?"

"I think we'd all like to know that." Sarah watches Kim's face carefully as she says, "It was stained glass from your studio, actually. Very weird."

Kim absolutely goggles. Sarah can see lipstick clinging to the corners of her mouth. "From my studio? Was someone in there? I know the lock doesn't work, but I thought we were all going to respect one another, you know?"

Sarah shrugs. "No idea. It was a new bag of clay, and I'd just wedged it, so neither of us could figure out how it could've happened. His hands wouldn't stop bleeding, so Gail took him somewhere to get stitched up. He couldn't make art after that, so Gail said he just went home."

"Poor baby. That's so sad." Kim huffs a sigh and shakes her head. "Only cute guy here, and he had to leave. I sure would like to know who's been rooting through my studio, though. I guess it would be easy enough to grab some glass out of my scrap bins. I haven't missed any cut pieces, though. That, I would notice." She pops a cherry tomato in her mouth. "Who do you think did it?"

"I don't think it was possible for anyone to do it. We were right there. The clay was on the table. We would've noticed if someone came in. It makes no sense." Sarah focuses on her food for a moment, glancing up at Kim to see where the other woman's mind goes next. Because Sarah knows where her mind is going, and she needs to know if it makes sense to anyone else.

"So, what? You think it was ghosts or something?" Kim's laugh is high-pitched and nervous. "Oh, honey. Just because you dug up a coffin doesn't mean we need to call the Ghostbusters. There's always an explanation."

As Sarah hates the implication here, she says, "I briefly wondered if it was you."

Kim draws back like she's been slapped. "Me? Why the hell would I do something like that?"

"You seemed a bit jealous that Reid and I were spending time together. And it was your glass . . ." Sarah trails off, glad to have everything out on the table at last.

But Kim just stands and slings her big bag over her shoulder, gathering up her plate and water glass. "Screw you! I wasn't jealous. You two were embarrassing yourselves. And no one in their right mind would put glass in clay. Maybe you did it for attention and to—to frame me! So you could have him all to yourself." Her voice rises with every word.

Gertrude Rose and Antoinette are listening in now, as is Bridget, who's putting a basket of cookies at the end of the buffet.

"I told you it didn't make sense," Sarah says, a little louder. "And for the record, I don't think it was you, I just wondered."

Kim shakes her head and storms out the door without another word, slamming it behind her. Sarah slumps a little, pulled down by the bone-deep despair she feels whenever she's failed to adequately navigate through a social situation. Kim hates her now, she knows that much. There was a girl like Kim in her program back in college, and they never got along. Olivia. They had to share a shelf, and one of Olivia's vases got dented, and after that Sarah was treated to huffy sighs and eye rolls galore. When Sarah attempted to talk it out, Olivia threatened to have her kicked out of school for harassment. Sarah has seen this called "main character energy," and she finds it exhausting.

It shouldn't be that hard to get along. It's almost as if her time with Kyle molded her into a creature only fit to be with him, as she sometimes feels like an entirely different species that can't quite communicate with any subtlety. It's like she's forgotten how to act naturally, and every choice is a pantomime of being a person.

"Well, that was dramatic," Gertrude Rose says dramatically before launching back into her monologue.

Sarah finishes up and heads back to her studio to get her flashlight, which she luckily remembered to remove from her hoodie pocket before going to lunch. Once she's certain Gail can't see her even if she's on the lookout, she veers off into the forest, again making a beeline for the old hotel. She's losing her fear of it now, warming to it. When she crawls under the door and stands in the lobby, it feels less like an abandoned, dying building that might collapse at any time and more like a hotel she's stayed in before, a place where she's comfortable. Down the hall, down the stairs, creeping down the long white tunnel, she finally lands in Dr. December's office. Amid the age and damp, she can still smell some manly odor—a mix of tobacco and bourbon, maybe— living on in his books and effects, left scattered as if he'd just gotten up to use the restroom and never returned.

She sits at his desk, surprised by the squeak of the ancient chair.

The ledger, so like the one in her own cottage, is spread out before her, and she turns the pages until she finds the final entries. Dr. December's handwriting is less tidy than Dr. Calloway's, rushed and loopy with the letters leaning together like drunks at a bar. Each page has a date, and then a list of patients and brief descriptions of his thoughts. She shines her phone light down onto the curling ivory paper.

> *Miss Theresa Montgomery, 17. Sapphic inclinations, masturbation. Treated with cold hose, leather mitts. Rude behavior. Restrain at nightfall. Suggested father marry her off posthaste to a gentleman in the country.*

> *Mrs. Dorothea Payne, 26. Melancholic after stillborn child. Attempted self-harm. Prescribed laudanum and a calming tincture. Conferred with husband; another pregnancy would do wonders. She claims she would rather die.*

Sarah's heart wrenches, thinking about these poor women whose deep pains were seen as mere annoyances to the men in their lives. She flips forward to the later entries, searching for Emily Engle.

There. Her admittance notes.

> *Emily Engle, 19. Hysteria, marital troubles, general fever of the spirits. Refused husband's bed and hit him with crockery, requiring stitches. Calloway suggests rest and sunshine, but the chit needs to learn her place. Solitary confinement and restraints combined with the hose to start. Won't stop crying.*

The second entry is even worse.

> *Emily Engle, 19. Mrs. Engle has grown more agitated under our care, suggesting deeper problems than origi-*

nally suspected. Mania, insanity, possible schizophrenia. Undue rage. Too fond of the word no. One of the orderlies entered her room for his own needs, and she nearly took out his eye with a nail she'd concealed in her sleeve. The orderly has been reprimanded, and Mrs. Engle has lost the privilege of her embroidery and any other pastime requiring sharp implements. We shall explore more intense therapies. She is an excellent candidate for Burckhardt's novel psychosurgical procedure.

But the third entry shows a marked and, to Sarah, suspicious change.

Emily Engle, 20. Mrs. Engle has undergone a transformation, thanks to our therapies. An absolute success. She is biddable and sweet again. The medicines and leeches have calmed her significantly. She is being allowed to walk outside in the gardens today, which will be her ultimate test of self-control. I shall speak with her husband tonight in the smoking room after dinner and recommend release into his care, although he will wish to keep her on the antimony for quite some time to calm her general hysteria. Perhaps she will settle when she's matured and with child. Such a pretty girl; a shame she requires such a firm hand.

As she flips back a few pages and reads each entry, Sarah can tell that Dr. December saw all his patients as childlike nuisances requiring either punishment or numbing drugs. Looking around his office, it's obvious that this man was a doctor, that he was intelligent and powerful, that he was well read, that he continued his studies and took an interest in new technologies. But perhaps his main interests were in improving his own health and pains rather than offering his patients that same kindness. There are no books on pregnancy, childbirth, women's troubles. Perhaps Dr. December had the proper training and background, but his position here in the cellar appears to be less about helping and more about . . . silencing.

These women weren't put down here to heal.

They were put here to rot.

Just like Kyle, these men wanted their wives and daughters quiet and calm and obedient. They wanted to call the shots. They didn't want to be inconvenienced by such paltry things as noises or frowns or *feelings*. They wanted well-run homes, cheerful helpmates, stolid broodmares, silent mistresses, and obedient daughters.

With the flashlight in her mouth and aiming down, Sarah takes several pictures, including one of Emily Engle's last entry. It's tricky, getting her phone to focus until the text in the image is clear.

She can't stop reading the final lines.

> *Such a pretty girl; a shame she requires such a firm hand.*

Holding the ledger in both hands, Sarah stands and flings it across the room. It slams into the bookshelf and tumbles to the ground like a bird struck by a car.

As if in answer, somewhere down the hall, she hears the distinctive sound of a door slamming shut.

33

Full-on panic sets in, and Sarah scrambles under the desk. Once there, she realizes she left her phone flashlight up top, shining on the ceiling. She holds her breath, begging her heart to stop beating like a machine gun while she listens to see if perhaps the noise was just an old building settling or if someone else is down here. If it's George or Gail, she's in trouble. If it's Lucas, she has to stop him before he hurts himself. He must've been sleep-walking earlier, and there are too many holes in the floor for a kid to be wandering around alone and senseless. Especially if he's still shoe-less.

Footsteps are coming up the hall toward her. Slow, measured, care-ful, echoing down the cold white tunnel. These are not bare feet, she thinks; these are not the stark, curled-bone toes of the girl in the cof-fin, not some squelchy, ghostly monster.

They're shoes.

And they're not immediately outside the door, so Sarah pops out, grabs the phone, tucks herself back into the tiny cubicle of space, and flicks off the flashlight. Hard to believe she shared this same tiny cube of air with Ingrid, the last time she was here; it's barely big enough for one person, much less two.

The steps get nearer and nearer, gently tapping, and stop outside the office door. Sarah focuses every cell in her body on being quiet, on not moving, on barely breathing. She's getting a little light-headed, but she can't get caught. If only she had another chunk of Ingrid's pill, whatever it was. If only she didn't feel like she was having a panic attack again. She starts counting breaths, but it's harder alone.

After a long pause, the steps enter the office and move around to the bookshelves. A soft scraping noise suggests someone has picked up the ledger Sarah threw.

Stupid, stupid, stupid.

Kyle always told Sarah that her temper was one of her worst features, that she made bad mistakes because of it and it would hold her back from the things she wants in life, but . . . did he ever really see her temper? She used to get mad, but she never acted on it. She's beginning to think it's just one more thing he gaslit her about, and that really her fury has only come out again now that she's free of him.

"That's not where you go," the voice says, and Sarah exhales in relief.

It's just Ingrid.

"Yeah, I threw it," she says, gratified to hear Ingrid gasp and stumble back as she crawls out from under the desk. Her feet are numb from being all contorted, and she shakes them gently one by one as Ingrid glares at her in the ambient glow of her flashlight.

"I am going to expire." Ingrid huffs a sigh as she holds the thrown ledger. "I am going to have a heart attack, and it will be your fault, and that will be your third run-in with a corpse here, and they will kick you out. Three strikes, no thank you, good day, sir."

"You're the one who snuck up on me," Sarah shoots back. "I was just down here innocently throwing ledgers at the wall when you slammed a door and scared me to death."

"And I was innocently taking photos of a padded cell when I heard

someone throw a ledger against the wall and had to assume polter-
geists were hard at work and tiptoed over to try and catch a pic."

Sarah's head snaps up from where she's been idly digging through
the paperwork on the old desk. "Wait. How did you know it wasn't
George?"

"I heard Gail tell Bridget that he went into town to take care of his
mom."

"Is his mom . . . the Cryptkeeper?"

"Yes. Definitely. Because he is a thousand years old. Anyway, since
he's the only person who ever bothers to visit this place, I figured I had
the all-clear." She puts the ledger on the desk where it belongs, and
her black-painted nails tap on the moldering green cover. "Looks like
I was wrong. So what are you investigating?"

Sarah nudges her aside and flips through the ledger to the final
entries. "So the girl in the coffin was Emily Engle. She was a guest of
the hotel for her honeymoon and did the whole Change of Air thing.
Her husband tried to rape her, and she understandably freaked out
and smashed a chamber pot against his head so he needed stitches,
and they sent her down here, where a different doctor was basically
running an insane asylum for rich women who didn't behave."

Ingrid's eyes go big. "No shit?"

"Just look." Sarah runs a finger down the line of the ledger. "Hysteria, mania, schizophrenia, melancholia, sexual aberration, refusal to
submit to her father. These women weren't at a spa. They were locked
in cells. They were restrained and given drugs and blasted with cold
hoses. Maybe the story back home was that they were being treated
like treasured racehorses, but they were really being treated like . . .
like lab rats. You were right. This is very much a medical facility that
did sneaky shit." She pauses, realizing something, then flips past several pages to make sure. "And every single name in this ledger is female."

"That is fucking disgusting." Ingrid shines her flashlight on the
ledger, shaking her head. "Hold this." She shoves the flashlight in Sarah's hand, then adjusts it to shine exactly where she wants it. Sarah's

arm is already getting tired as Ingrid holds up her Leica and takes several pictures. When she's satisfied, she lets the camera dangle from the strap around her neck and takes back the flashlight. "This is going to be one hell of an exit show. As long as Gail doesn't find out what I've been up to and kick me out first, that is. I found the hydrotherapy room."

"And?"

Ingrid heads out of the office as if Sarah has already agreed to follow her. And of course Sarah follows her, because she's seen what she needs to see and doesn't particularly enjoy being alone in an abandoned asylum. Ingrid leads her down the hallway she hasn't seen yet, and it's just another dark tunnel with mold-streaked walls, something right out of a horror movie. The first set of double doors has a plaque that reads HYDROTHERAPY, and Ingrid goes inside and shines her flashlight around on . . . well, a torture chamber. Maybe they have posh baths upstairs and carved pools outside flowing with mountain springwater, but this room is a rusting sepulcher of pain. The walls are white, stained with bumpy blooms of algae, with odd metal light fixtures hanging seemingly at random from the ceiling. There are big metal tubs with doors that close over the top so that the patient's head would be the only thing visible. There's a row of white tables shaped like gurneys that are draped with ghostlike sheets. There's a white-tiled corner with a drain in the floor and a steampunk-looking hose coiled on a hook. Pipes crisscross the ceiling like something out of the boiler room in a slasher flick. All the metal is rusted, the white tiles grimed over and outlined with blackened grout. Somewhere, impossibly, a showerhead drips.

"Shit," Sarah says, a chill running up her spine.

"Shit is right. They didn't even have electricity back then, so this whole place had to be lit by gas. No sunlight, no fluorescents. Just a tiled underground room that could go pitch dark at any moment."

"I don't like this place," Sarah says. The hydrotherapy room fills her with foreboding, with a sinking sensation that makes her want to run right back into the office and hide under the desk. "Can we leave?"

Pain permeates the air, heavy as mist. Horrible things happened here. It's as if someone has just finished screaming. It's as if the orderlies might come back at any moment.

No one could see this room and think these women were being pampered.

"Yeah, this place wasn't meant to be liked." Ingrid inclines her head toward the double doors. "But I found a better way out than the hole in the lobby door, at least. Come on."

Sarah feels a thousand times better the moment she's back in the hall, which is saying a lot, because the hall is a place stolen from nightmares. They continue into the darkness, passing door after door, and Sarah can't help thinking about the noises that would've echoed down the corridor, long ago, women moaning and screaming, begging for help, crying alone in the night. She can't imagine what it must've been like for pretty, pampered Emily Engle, marrying well and going on a whirlwind honeymoon with her handsome banker husband, only to end up barefoot on the cold tiled floor in her chemise, experiencing real pain and fear for the first time in her life.

The orderly who attacked her deserved whatever he got, Sarah thinks. He was "reprimanded"; she was assaulted by someone with power when she was utterly defenseless.

Nothing and nowhere was safe for that poor girl.

And she was even more vulnerable once they drugged her to keep her quiet and calm. Who knows what happened to her, once laudanum was involved? The orderly most likely got his revenge, because who was going to stop him? A hand over the drugged girl's mouth, restraints on her wrists, and he could do whatever he wanted.

It makes Sarah sick.

Beyond sick.

And now she wants to know how a living girl came to be in that coffin, because even if her sanity might've been questioned when convenient to wealthy men, rich girls didn't just disappear back then.

They reach a staircase, the mirror of the one on the other hall. "It's safe," Ingrid says. "Sturdy. They sure knew how to build 'em."

"What's down the hall?" Sarah shines her flashlight down the corridor and sees only more doors, seemingly extending forever in the darkness.

"A rec room and cafeteria, I guess? Tables and chairs and a small kitchen. I bet the girls down here didn't get the same chow as the ones upstairs who behaved."

The steps wind upward in the opposite direction of the other stairwell, and Sarah is momentarily discomfited, as if she's entered a mirror world. They emerge on familiar carpet, but there's an acrid odor here that she doesn't recall from the other identical hallway.

"What's that smell?" she asks.

"Dunno. I was a little focused on getting to the gory bits downstairs, so I haven't fully investigated up here."

Nose twitching, Sarah moves ahead of Ingrid, who stops in front of a door.

"There's a way out here," she says. "A back door to a storage room. No crawling over glass. Vast improvement."

But Sarah shakes her head and keeps on. "I need to know what that smell is. It's so . . . familiar. It's going to bother me."

Ingrid pauses a moment before following her, swinging her flashlight up ahead. "Why not? Maybe it'll be something cool."

They pass a few more doors, and the smell is getting stronger. Sarah recognizes it now. It's fire—or the ancient remains of fire. Strange, that she didn't see any evidence from the outside of the building . . . but then again, the outside walls are thick stone, and she's mostly been on the other side of the hotel, the one closer to her cottage.

And then she's standing in front of a partially open door. She shines her flashlight in, pushing back the blackened wood to reveal what's left of a room—a study, maybe. She can see the old bones of bookcases, the skeletal fragments of club chairs and sofas struggling to rise from the black swamp of ashes. What was once perhaps a pool table lies in two pieces, its legs sticking out stiffly like charred animal bones. The curtains have burned away, the windows boarded over from the outside. Sarah walks to a powdery black wall, knowing the ashes will ruin her jeans, and touches the remains of what was once a portrait, its subject now reduced to empty eye sockets and curled canvas.

"Somebody wasn't careful in the smoking room," Ingrid says as she frames a photo of the destroyed bookshelf.

Sarah gasps as she makes the connection.

If this is the smoking room, this is where Dr. December was going to speak with Mr. Engle about his wayward wife. She knows gentlemen of that time period met alone in rooms like this to enjoy brandy and cigars and billiards, purposefully hiding away from the womenfolk who might spoil their fun. Here, they could speak freely, swear, have conversations ranging from ribald to erudite. She can almost see them, two men in nicely tied cravats, settled back in leather club chairs, cigars in one hand and expensive tipple in the other as they blithely determined the future of a woman causing them both distress due to her refusal to fit into the pretty little box they'd built for her.

Sarah takes another step, and something rolls under her foot. She trips and drops her flashlight, falling hard on her hands and knees, elbow deep in ancient shifting ash. Sensing her distress, Ingrid sweeps her flashlight over the ground. There, almost close enough to kiss, is a charred human skull.

34

Perhaps in another life, Sarah would scream and crawl away, but in this life, she has seen too much and can only marvel at the elegant lines of bone, the chiaroscuro brought to life by the quivering flashlight in Ingrid's hand.

"Holy shit," Ingrid crows. "You found another corpse. You're like a drug dog for dead people!"

Sarah sighs and sits back on her knees. Her jeans are already ruined, her hands coated in silvery ash and charcoal smudges. She dusts the powdery gray away from the skull, revealing a spine, arms, ribs. There is no hair on this one, no daintily aging white dress. Everything that touched it has burned away.

"Shouldn't it be, I don't know. Black? Or gray?" she asks Ingrid, assuming someone so comfortable with death might know a bit more about it.

"When human bone burns for long enough, it changes color and ends up white. Almost like ceramic. So maybe you would know more, since you're the potter." Ingrid squats beside her, her camera clicking as she focuses in on the skull's orbital bone.

When Ingrid points her lens at a gracefully swooping arm bone, Sarah reaches out and touches the brow of the skull, wondering if perhaps it's Bertram Engle or Dr. Warren December. She is certain now that if she were to shuffle through the room, she would find at least another skeleton if not more. Although she isn't sure how she knows it, she would bet anything that the two men conspiring about Emily Engle's fate died in this room. In this fire.

"So do we tell Gail?" Sarah asks.

Ingrid looks at her like she's an idiot. "And admit we were in here, thereby getting us both sent home early? Absolutely not. These people have been dead for a century. Us finding them is not some earth-shattering discovery. And I'm guessing that Gail already knows. It's her land. We know she and George have been in here. The weird thing is that . . . they haven't done anything about it."

But Sarah can already see the pieces falling into place. "If anyone found out what was in here, this place would be swarming with authorities and historians, and they'd figure out that it wasn't the luxurious resort Gail describes on the website. They'd know it was an asylum. They'd tear the whole property apart. It would be on the news. Tranquil Falls would be gone, and the whole business would be dragged through the dirt. I mean, who wants to go to an artists' retreat where women were once tortured to death?"

Ingrid nods as she looks around, shining her flashlight over the blackened bookshelves. "Okay, but why not . . . I don't know. Clean it up? Destroy the evidence? Have a big bonfire for all the books and ledgers, bury the skeletons. And then no one would know all the bad stuff."

Sarah stands and walks back to the remains of the oil painting. She's willing to bet it was a portrait of one of the doctors. "The main house—it's called December House. It was named for Dr. December. Gail grew up here, she owns the land. I bet she's related to him. She's proud of this place. As long as they keep everything boarded up and threaten everyone who goes anywhere near it, they're safe. I mean, they put up a fence with razor wire. It's not like anyone is randomly stumbling upon it. Until now, and the storm, and us. And Lucas."

"Lucas?"

"When I came back for my phone—thanks for leaving it behind, by the way—I heard someone playing the piano and found him in the restaurant. It was crazy—like he was sleepwalking. He was playing in the pitch dark, and I couldn't make him see me. I had to mess up the piano to make him stop."

Ingrid perks up at this news. "Why'd he do it? Did he say?"

Sarah shakes her head; they have their flashlights pointed slightly off so they can see each other as they talk. "He didn't even know he was doing it. Didn't know he was here. Didn't know why he would even be here. It's like he forgot, or was dreaming. He was barefoot. He looked drugged. As soon as he saw the cabins, he ran off for breakfast like it was totally normal."

Ingrid taps her chin with a finger. "Curiouser and curiouser." She looks up at Sarah, her glare piercing. "You know we have to tell the truth about this place, right? As our final project?"

Sarah has come to the same conclusion. "I'm making chamber pots and teacups. I could bisque-fire the clay and rub these ashes into the surface. And maybe I can roll out some slabs and copy down the entries from the ledger downstairs to make serving platters—because the women were just offered up."

"Or we could get Antoinette to copy the ledgers!" Ingrid says, jumping up and down excitedly in the ashes. "In her calligraphy. Maybe convince Gertrude Rose to add some embroidery to whatever dresses she's working on. And Kim could, I don't know, make ladies out of glass and then hit them with a hammer or something. We can all join together and turn our final show into a complete exposé. Women reaching back through time to tell other women they're seen, that they haven't been forgotten."

Something tickles Sarah's brain, and her jaw drops. "Remember the first night, when we found that installation in the woods? *The Forgotten Children*."

"If the women were restrained and the orderlies were men, I can guess where those children came from, and where they went," Ingrid finishes grimly.

"And there were pregnant mistresses who got sent to the cellar, and teen girls whose fathers said they were too promiscuous . . ."

Ingrid exhales low, like an angry dragon spewing smoke. "That operating room. An underground forced abortion clinic to get rid of inconvenient babies for the benefit of rich dudes. Of course. Because it just wasn't gross enough before."

"How did Gail let that installation stay?" Sarah wonders. "If she's trying so hard to hide what really happened here."

Ingrid tucks her Leica back in her bag and raises her chin, looking like the intrepid heroine of some movie that Sarah never saw because Kyle hated that kind of movie. "Let's go check it out. Maybe we can get the artist's name and go into a town with some internet and look her up. Maybe we can look up all this shit—the doctors, this girl you're so interested in. Maybe Gail can keep people complacent by not having any WiFi or bars up here, but the answers are still out there."

Sarah dusts the ash off her hands, eager to leave this room. It feels like a swamp, like there are things swimming around below knee level that she can't see and never wants to know about. Ingrid shows her the easy way out, an unlocked door through a storage hall off the restaurant that's full of old chairs and wooden crates filled with glasses and plates. The moment Sarah is back outside, she blinks up at the sun, wishing she could unsee the skull, the ash, the lines in the ledger. But she can't; it's inside her now. It's festering. It's part of her. Only the art can help her expunge it, expel it, expose it. She's eager to get back to the studio, the muse finally forcing her hand.

"I need to change real quick," she says, gesturing at her pants, which are so crusted with ashes that little flecks sift down as she moves.

"Yeah, if Gail sees that, we're toast. But then let's go talk to the others," Ingrid agrees. She has managed to avoid the worst of the ashes, although her Docs are a little silvery.

They stop at Sarah's cottage, and Ingrid pulls out her Leica and creeps around back, ostensibly to snap some images of the gravestone and its sad little fence. Sarah swiftly changes into new leggings, tee, and hoodie, plus a pair of sneakers. She'll have to figure out laundry soon and wipe off her boots. She wasn't aware she'd need so many costume changes.

They walk up the gravel road, and when they both hear Lucas playing that same mad song in his studio, they share a glance but don't have to say out loud how weird it is that a teen boy would play something like that.

Sarah swerves closer to the buildings and stops at Gertrude Rose's studio, motioning Ingrid over to show her the seemingly endless scarf winding all over the floor. Gertrude Rose is rocking in a chair, her face blank and smooth as she knits furiously in her mourning dress and black bonnet. Sarah isn't quite sure from this distance, but the pendant on the older woman's neck looks an awful lot like a rusty old cut nail. Ingrid snaps a few pics, angling her camera just right to avoid the glare through the glass. Gertrude Rose doesn't notice that she's being watched, doesn't so much as blink.

"She looks busy." Ingrid sounds oddly unsure. "Maybe we can hit her up after dinner."

The blinds are all pulled in the windows of the glass studio, which doesn't really surprise Sarah, as Kim wasn't feeling particularly open when they last parted ways.

"We can get her later, too," Sarah says.

When they get to Antoinette's studio, the older woman is again bent over her desk with her pen, carefully dipping her nib in ink and writing on her light box before tossing the paper over her shoulder to let it sift to the ground like a feather swooping back and forth.

But—wait.

The script is bumpy and rough, not elegant like it once was, and the pen is far too short. Antoinette's long, elegant hand clutches something much smaller and rougher.

Something about the size of a nail.

"What is she writing?" Ingrid whispers.

When the paper lands, they can both see that it says NO over and over again in ink the color of old blood.

"Why is everybody acting so freaky?" Ingrid says as she changes film canisters. "That's my job."

Reid said it was just artists being artists, but he's wrong. It's something more.

The artists are acting like animals before a storm, tapped in to some strange signal.

Sarah feels it, and it seems like Ingrid does, too.

"On to the creepy babies, then," she says.

They head past December House, and Sarah halfway expects Gail to come running after them as if she has some uncanny sixth sense about people trespassing on her family property and planning to shut it down with art. But the door doesn't open, and Sarah considers what it must've been like, long ago, when the grand old Victorian acted as a boardinghouse for all the hospital workers—and Dr. December. The people who worked here accepted a job out in the middle of nowhere, far from their family and friends, given horse-and-buggy transport. They probably saw it as an excellent opportunity, the chance to earn real money and interact with the wealthy, a *Downton Abbey* type of thing.

There were so many people involved in running this place, so many people who learned about the dirty little secret of the cellar and just quietly locked their lips. So many people who took part in the pain meted out to the so-called patients, women who likely swore they were sane, they were reasonable, they were *fine,* that they didn't need the injections and the hoses and the restraints. So many people who knew that what was happening was wrong but just . . . went along with it. And some of them found that they liked that job better than whatever originally brought them here. And a few of them found that the restraints and drugs and gags offered their own rewards.

It's nauseating, and it's wrong, and Sarah wants those women to have justice, even though they're all long dead.

She and Ingrid enter the forest, and it takes them a while to find the deer path that leads to the art installation that made Lucas scream and piss himself their first night here. By the light of day, it's not all that startling. Sarah can see the faults in the glaze, can recognize how carefully the artist arranged the porcelain dolls and doll parts for maximum effect. But when they go to where she knows she saw the ceramic tombstone, it's gone.

"You remember the sign, right?" she asks Ingrid.

Ingrid shrugs. "Nope. I was more focused on the terrifying monster children."

"Wait." The memory surfaces as slowly as a bloated corpse in a lake. "Kim took pictures of it. It was like a headstone, right here." She scrabbles her fingers through the leaf litter and finds a plaque-shaped indentation in the dirt. "It's gone!"

"So let's go ask Kim," Ingrid says grimly.

They walk back toward the stained-glass studio and knock on the door. There is no answer, but they can hear the sound of glass breaking inside—not the crash of a window, but the steady, thoughtful crack of purposeful cuts. Sarah knocks again, harder, and calls, "Kim? You in there, honey?" When there's no response, she looks to Ingrid. "I bet she's got earbuds in."

Ingrid just shrugs as if other women are a foreign species beyond understanding. She turns the knob and busts right on in, despite Sarah's gasp of protest.

What they find inside is . . . well, less of a surprise than it should be, considering everything that's happened this week.

Kim sits on the ground, surrounded by hundreds of shards of glass—maybe thousands. They're in shades of pink, periwinkle, seafoam, colors that suggest someone likes succulents and crystals and the moon. Sarah was expecting to see the neat assembly line of sellable suncatchers that was here earlier, but this is utter chaos. The pieces of glass follow no rhyme or reason, they are merely thoughtless shards. Kim is cross-legged in their center, pliers in her hand, grasping a square sheet of glass.

"Kim?" Sarah shouts, but Kim doesn't respond. Which is odd, because she's not wearing earbuds or earphones, and there's no music playing.

Sarah gingerly steps toward Kim, shoving the glass shards out of the way with her toe as she goes so she won't crush anything that might be important. She learned long ago that when it comes to art, what appears as clutter to a neutral observer might be a carefully planned pattern to the creator. Kim doesn't respond, just keeps snapping off seemingly random bits of glass. Sarah puts a hand on her shoulder and says, loudly and clearly, "Kim, you okay?"

Kim's head swivels toward her, her pupils empty black chasms and her eyes unseeing. "I'd rather die," she says in a soft, calm voice. She drops the pliers, and before Sarah can react, she turns the sheet of glass toward her own wrist and slashes blindly.

35

"Kim!" Sarah cries, watching the red blood bloom from Kim's wrist, right by a tattoo of an infinity symbol with the word LOVE scripted into the lines.

But Kim doesn't react, doesn't even seem to notice what she's done; she transfers the glass to her other hand and calmly slashes her unblemished wrist, then drops the glass and falls back as if she's luxuriating on a feather bed instead of falling onto a ring of glass shards.

"What the hell is she doing?" Ingrid says, sounding young and uncertain for the first time.

"Trying to kill herself!" Sarah shouts. "Go get Gail! Call nine-one-one!"

Ingrid's eyes goggle at her like a goldfish before she nods and gallops off. Sarah rips her hoodie over her head and stares down at Kim, who's lying on her back with her arms spread-eagled like she's happily making snow angels. She grabs Kim's first arm and winds a hoodie sleeve around her wrist, tying it tightly. Kim doesn't fight her, doesn't protest. She just stares beatifically at the ceiling, euphorically calm. And silent, which is something Kim never is.

"Kim, snap out of it!" Sarah barks, but Kim does not snap out of it, and the blood is soaking through the black hoodie, so she wraps the other hoodie arm around Kim's second, still-bleeding wrist and ties it tight, too. It's not enough; it's not stopping the blood. Kim isn't help-ing, isn't holding the fabric over her cuts or doing anything useful. Much like Lucas at the piano, it's like she's not even there.

"Shit," Sarah murmurs. She stands, sneakers crunching and skid-ding on the glass shards, and runs to the sink, looking for the red first-aid kit that surely has to be present in every studio. She finally finds it under the cabinet and digs through frantically, finding only small, use-less bandages and antibiotic ointment, the usual sort of thing one might need if manipulating glass with their fingertips for hours. "Shit shit shit!" she grumbles.

There is no gauze, none of that helpful medical tape that sticks to itself. But her pottery studio isn't far away, so she stands over Kim and says, "Stay there and don't do anything stupid. I'll be back in a minute."

Sarah has never felt this kind of panic, never run like this, never feared that her heart might beat out of her chest. She's never lived through a real emergency. It's not like in dreams, where running is slow as molasses. She's at her studio in seconds, busts through the door, grabs the first-aid kit, and darts right back, leaving her studio door wide open. Kim hasn't moved, but the tied hoodie sleeves aren't doing much to stanch the flow of blood. All Sarah can think is that at least Kim cut across instead of straight up and down, because other-wise, none of this would matter.

"Kim?" she says, fairly certain Kim won't respond, because she hasn't so far, and nothing has changed.

She grabs the first arm Kim sliced and gently unwraps the black fabric, wincing at how deep the wound is. Blood pours out of it, and she can see a light rim of yellow fat where the skin parts. It makes her gorge rise, but she doesn't have time for feelings.

"Come on, Kim. Get up. Let's go wash this off."

But Kim just lies there, spread-eagle, her sightless eyes staring up at the ceiling like she's waiting for a shooting star. Sarah tugs on her arm, but Kim is heavy and still, her arm floppy.

"Fine," Sarah mutters.

She hurries to the sink and brings back a roll of paper towels with several wet from the faucet. With Kim's arm flat on the ground, Sarah gently wipes off the wound, hating how the blood just keeps coming, how the veins are just *right there*, fragile and vulnerable, so close to the surface. Kim doesn't flinch at the pain, but Sarah does. She dries off the wound, squeezes antibiotic ointment all over it, and tapes a piece of gauze over it, then turns to the other arm.

"What in the Sam hell?"

Gail is in the door with Ingrid now, staring down at the scene like a mom who's walked in on two kids having a pillow fight past bedtime.

"She cut herself with glass," Sarah says.

"Ingrid told me. Is it bad?"

"Yes, it's bad! She slit her wrists! Did you call nine-one-one?"

Sarah finishes taping the second arm and sits back, the glass shifting under her leggings. Her hands are bloody, and she realizes she should've put on gloves. Kim just lies there with her arms out, the blood already soaking through the gauze.

"We don't need to call nine-one-one for this," Gail says. She groans as she squats by Kim, frowning. "I'll just take her to the urgent care."

"I think nine-one-one is more appropriate—"

Gail's head snaps around toward her, something like hate in her eyes. "You don't know how things work this far into the mountains. It'll be faster if I just drive her. The hospital is always backed up, and they'll take an hour and charge her an arm and a leg. You think an artist in the midst of a divorce wants to get that hospital bill? Now help me get her up."

Sarah huffs a sigh and returns Gail's hateful glare. "She won't move."

"We'll make her move."

With Ingrid helping, the three women get Kim on her feet. Sarah is worried she'll trip or sway or just fall over like a dead tree, but she's pliable enough and happy to be led. When Gail accidentally grabs her wrist, Kim doesn't even wince, doesn't complain, doesn't show any sign of the pain such an injury must cause. Sarah and Ingrid are on either side of Kim as Gail leads her up the gravel drive, holding her hand like a lost child.

"Drunk again," Gail says as if disappointed. "Never gonna get her kids back if she won't lay off the wine."

"This isn't drunk," Sarah argues. "I've seen drunk. Her breath doesn't smell of liquor. There wasn't any in the studio. And she's not staggering and falling all over the place."

Gail doesn't turn around as she marches toward the parking lot. "And how much time have you spent with Kim, huh? You ever seen her polish off a bottle of wine all by herself at dinner, or were you too busy shacking up with Reid? That made her drink more, you know. And she has plenty of pills. Anxiety meds and sleeping pills and alcohol don't mix."

"How do you know she has pills?" Sarah asks.

Gail's shoulders hunch up. "I see things. People tell me things. If you run a program like this, you find out a lot of secrets, whether you want to or not."

"If this was pills and booze, she would be acting drunk," Ingrid says. "Staggering, shouting, puking. Or she would be unconscious. You can't walk in a straight line on that shit."

Gail glances back at her, annoyed. "Okay, then, smarty-pants. What do you think it is? If it's not drink or drugs or drink *and* drugs, then what?"

Ingrid looks to Sarah, troubled—which is not at all like Ingrid. "I don't know, but it's not cool. Maybe a psychotic break or something?"

"Then urgent care can help with that, too. Come on, Kim. Let's get you in the car." Gail pulls her keys from the capacious pocket of her overalls and unlocks her minivan, and Sarah notices that there are dozens of keys on the ring, all colors and shapes. This stands to reason—Gail would need keys to all the cabins and studios—but that would only be twenty keys or so, and this is a lot more than twenty keys. Kim waits patiently as Gail opens the car door and then allows them to contort her into the passenger seat, pliant as a sun-warm Barbie doll.

"What should we do?" Sarah asks.

Gail buckles Kim in and slams the door before heading for the driver's side. "Go make art. That's why you're here, isn't it? And if you're too shaken to be creative, go for a hike. The waterfall will calm you down. My dad used to send me out there when I talked back." She gets in, slams her own door, and turns on the car, then rolls down the window. "But stay out of Kim's studio. Nobody needs you two playing Nancy Drew."

Sarah and Ingrid stand back as Gail pulls out and rumbles down the gravel drive.

"I kinda want to play Nancy Drew," Ingrid says.

As they stand in the parking lot, Sarah looks at each car in turn. "Do you know what kind of car Reid drove? Which car is missing now?"

"Do I look like the kind of person that cares about cars?" Ingrid shoots back. "My car is named Morticia." She points to a black Prius covered in bumper stickers. "But I can guess at what's left. The catering van is Bridget. The massive Arcadia Momwagon is Kim's. The dinosaur belongs to Gertrude Rose."

It's a beige Cadillac older than either of them. "The plate says GERTIE, so yeah," Sarah agrees.

"The other Prius is either yours— No? Okay, it's Antoinette's, then. The older Civic is probably Lucas." Ingrid walks toward the white Honda and peeks inside. "Yep. Mostly fast-food wrappers and sheet music. Which means you're the peppy SUV." Sarah nods. "So the truck is either Bernie, or maybe an extra car for Gail?"

They walk toward the beat-up old Chevy. It's got a distinct odor that makes Sarah stop in her tracks and Ingrid surge ahead to look in the bed.

"Didn't you say you found some dead animals?" Ingrid asks with a weird smile.

"A dead possum in my original cabin and a dead snake on my doorstep. Why?"

Ingrid steps onto the truck bumper, hops into the bed, and holds up a shovel covered with—

"The rest of the dead possum. So either Bernie really was an absolute asshole, or Gail and George wanted me in the cottage, depending on whose truck it is."

"Oh, what a tangled web . . ." Ingrid throws the shovel back down in the truck bed.

But Sarah's mind is running a mile a minute. "It must've been Bernie, because all Gail had to do was hand me a key to the cottage in the first place. It's not like I would've known better. And she was seriously annoyed at having to put me there."

"And I told you Bernie liked Cardinal Cabin, remember? He left an angry note on Gail's desk."

Sarah shudders. "So he was trying to get me out of his favorite cabin, but he destroyed the mattress. Ugh. It melted into the bed."

"He was probably too stupid to know how that sort of thing works. Probably never had to change his own sheets before. I guess it backfired on him."

And now it all comes together.

"And then the snake—he was trying to get me to leave. He wanted the studio for himself just like I did. He was trying to scare me away."

Ingrid hops down from the truck and bounces over. "Looks like you got the last laugh there, right?"

Sarah looks toward December House; she doesn't want to think about how Bernie looked like he was literally scared to death. "Do you think George is back yet?"

"Nope. He told Bridget he would be back after dinner and to save him a plate. So we have plenty of time to play Nancy Drew."

Ingrid grins, but Sarah is too upset to feel any thrill. They take off for Kim's glass studio. The door is still open, blood dotting the floor in delicate constellations smeared by Gail's sensible clogs. Ingrid whips out her Leica and zooms in on the fallen piece of glass Kim used to cut herself, lying alone in the center of the greater glass circle. Sarah is uncomfortably aware that it's the exact same color as some of the glass she and Reid found in the clay.

"Is this all she's gotten done?" Ingrid asks, nimbly standing and daintily stepping around the concentric rings of glass.

The pieces, although sometimes clearly cut in uniform shapes and outlined with bright copper, mostly appear haphazard. Several unfinished pieces have been soldered together in increasingly chaotic ways that look less like plants and more like explosions. Sarah remembers that first night, when a tipsy Kim expounded at length about the pieces she would be making to sell on Etsy, a boutique array of suncatchers she could sell alongside the essential oils gathering dust in her closet. There is no sign that she's made even one finished suncatcher, just hundreds or possibly thousands of component parts and some monstrous clumps. Here and there, if Sarah looks closely, she can see a perfect teardrop or moon or crystal facet, but for the most part, it's as if Kim just sat here with sheets of glass and snipped them into increasingly smaller chunks without really paying attention. When she looked in before, it seemed like there was a system, but that system has broken down.

"Found a notebook!" Ingrid calls, holding up a salmon-pink journal with GOOD VIBES ONLY printed in rose-gold foil.

She opens the book at the beginning and starts flipping through the pages, and Sarah grimaces as she hurries over. Yes, she wants to know what on Earth has been going through Kim's mind, but she is also very much against invasions of privacy. Kyle always insisted that healthy relationships had no secrets, which is why she never had a lock on her phone and he somehow always knew when she was about to start her period. She didn't dare keep a journal, because he had an uncanny way of stumbling across everything she attempted to hide. As things went south, she began to suspect that it wasn't uncanny so much as he was nosy and hid it well, but she's still not the kind of person who would willingly go through someone else's journal if it wasn't an absolute emergency.

But . . . well, a notebook in an art studio isn't really a journal. It should hold plans for art pieces, inspiration, that sort of thing. And this notebook was just sitting on the table by a Yeti cup with a tea string and a bouquet of gel pens, so it's not like it was hidden.

"Oh, shit," Ingrid says.

"You are saying that way too much lately."

As Sarah joins her, Ingrid flips back to the early pages. "Perfectly reasonable," she says. "Plans for her line. The Celestial. The Succulent. The Saguaro. The Manifestation. The Transformation. I mean, barf, but reasonable." She flips through to the latest pages. "And here's where things get dark."

She hands Sarah the book, and Sarah starts over at the beginning. Kim has bubbly handwriting and a good eye. She has a drawing of each piece, a breakdown of the different elements, and numbers for glass colors. Then there are some pages for future ideas, for places to sell her pieces, for logos, for booth design. These pages are normal, thoughtful, stained here or there with a splatter of coffee or tea. Then the drawings go from careful to . . . shaky. The logic disappears. There's a drawing of the old hotel, one of December House, one of the cottage Sarah has been staying in. There's one of the waterfall, but it's not peaceful, it's made of dark-gray slashes, at one point tearing through the page. Words appear.

No.

Help me.

He said it wouldn't hurt.

Obey.

Flowers.

I can't move.

He lied.

He promised.

I'm sane.

I hate it here.

It's wretched.

It will only hurt for a moment.

I'd rather die.

This is not Kim's bubbly handwriting but cramped, spidery script.

"Creepy, right?" Ingrid says. "This has got to be some kind of psychotic break."

But Sarah has seen these words before, and Ingrid has, too.

Many of them were stitched into the hems of the dead girl's clothes.

And more recently, Sarah is fairly certain she's seen them in Antoinette's careful cursive, lying all over the floor.

The same message, over and over again.

The worst message, though, is the last one.

It says only *He's coming for you.*

36

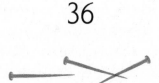

The glass studio feels cold all of a sudden, and Sarah wants very much to be anywhere else.

"Seem familiar?" Sarah asks.

"The photos," Ingrid says quietly, confirming Sarah's panic. "Did Kim see the coffin, too?"

"Kim and Antoinette must have. The same words keep popping up in their art." All the hairs on Sarah's arms are sticking straight up.

"I had a dream . . ." Ingrid begins before doing a full-body shudder. "Or maybe it wasn't a dream." For once, the spooky girl actually looks spooked. "I was in a room with rose wallpaper and a pink bed, and I was carrying a basin of hot water that was splashing out, scalding my wrists, and this woman was on her hands and knees, sweaty, pregnant as shit, screaming. She kept saying, 'Not again.'" She looks up at Sarah, her eyes shifty. "Does that . . . mean anything to you?"

This dream is different from Sarah's dreams, but she knows of a small room with rose wallpaper and a pretty pink bed, and it's between the office and the nursery in her own cottage's upstairs hall.

"Maybe, but let's get out of here before somebody sees us and tattles to Gail," Sarah says. They can deal with dreams about the dead after they've dealt with the living. The moment the journal is out of her hands and back where Ingrid found it, she feels immeasurably better, but not good enough to stick around.

Ingrid agreeably heads for the door, and once Sarah is outside and feeling the sun on her face, she can finally draw a full breath.

"Oh, God." Against her better judgment, Sarah hurries back inside. She snatches her blood-soaked hoodie off the floor and brushes a few pieces of glass off it. As they fall to the ground, she sees a familiar sight: another cut nail nestled among the remaining rainbow of shards. Rushing back out the door, she can't help muttering, "Oh, fuck this place."

"You got a souvenir!" Ingrid says.

"Yes, a pint of my crazy frenemy's blood. I'll be at the washing machine, I guess." Sarah looks down. "And my shirt and leggings, too. I don't even know how to get blood out of clothes."

Ingrid snorts. "I do."

Sarah raises an eyebrow. "Play with blood a lot, do you?"

That actually makes Ingrid laugh. "No, I have a really heavy period. But thanks for asking. Go get your laundry and something to change into and meet me around back at December House."

The hoodie is wet and heavy in her hand, and it smells like cold pennies, and this is not how Sarah thought an artist residency would go. She knows that Ingrid will abandon her if she takes too long, so she hurries back to her cottage, hating how her white T-shirt looks like it's been soaked in watermelon juice. When she unlocks the front door, she freezes.

Something is wrong.

Someone has been here.

She can feel it in her bones, and she is on high alert.

Dropping the sweatshirt on the front step, she grabs her backpack from just inside the door and pulls out her pepper spray, holding it out like she's about to face off with a bear.

"Hello?" she calls.

There is no answer, no squeak of the creaky floors. Leaving the door open, she flips on the lights and sidles around the room. There aren't really many places to hide, as the furniture is all that old, spindly, delicate sort of stuff instead of today's heavier monster sofas. There's simply no way to remain unseen under a divan.

As she tiptoes around, checking behind the bathroom door and whipping open the closet, she listens for scuffling, or maybe even the sound of footsteps upstairs. That dark, unwelcome, forgotten realm is exactly the sort of place someone might hide, and there is no way in hell she's going up there looking for them.

Instead, once she's satisfied that there's no one downstairs, she pushes the bookshelf back in place so it's flush against the wall.

If someone is up there, they're going to be up there for a while—or they're going to knock over the whole damn thing and expose their existence.

The pepper spray is still tight in her fist as she checks under the bed and—

Realizes that the bed is made.

She didn't make the bed this morning.

She never makes the bed, because Kyle always insisted she make the bed, and she fucking hated making the bed.

And on the foot of the bed is a neat stack of towels and washcloths.

She smacks her forehead with the hand not holding the pepper spray.

Because . . . of course.

Every week, Bridget is supposed to come in and provide basic hotel service.

And apparently, despite the fact that she feels like she's been here for months, something like a week has indeed passed.

Feeling like a paranoid freak, Sarah stashes her pepper spray back in her bag and takes a deep breath. She doesn't see anything else changed, other than noticing that her used towels have been removed from the floor of the bathroom. Her dirty clothes pile is untouched, and the books around the bookshelf appear unmolested. If Gail had been in here, Sarah would most likely be getting an earful for messing with the shelf, but Bridget is not a stickler for Gail's rules.

Sarah changes quickly into a fresh pair of jeans and a T-shirt. With Reid gone, she doesn't really care how she looks, and with what she's seen lately, she just . . . well . . . what even matters here anymore? She's dug up a corpse, been in an abandoned asylum, tripped on a human femur. It puts everything into a surreal perspective that isn't improved when she picks her hoodie up off the floor and it leaves a bloodstain behind on the old wood boards.

In a different life, she would put her stained clothes into a Target bag and carry them up to the big house, but in this life, she is living in a cottage with no kitchen and no way to contain blood-soaked clothes. She bundles them up with her ashy jeans from this morning on the outside, as they're the least stained of the lot, and locks the door on her way out.

As she crunches up the gravel drive, she feels a profound sense of displacement. Lucas is playing that same song, unceasing, one of the piano keys clearly messed up. The song ends; he immediately starts over again. Does no one else hear it? Does no one else recognize how nuts it is that even the most musically gifted teen boy would feel the need to play this same old song for hours on end? She hates it now, whatever it is. Luckily, when she leaves this place, she'll likely never have to hear it again, unless it's the song played by some creepy-ass music box in a horror movie, which would be totally appropriate.

She passes by Gertrude Rose's cabin, the rabbit cage open and sadly empty. She wonders if someone buried the rabbits, or if maybe poor George had to scrape them into another black garbage bag and stuff that into a garbage can and—well, how does trash service even work when you're this deep in the mountains? It's a shame, that pet animals should have such a violent, gory end. With all the Kim business, the rabbits seem suddenly insignificant. It's as if they never even existed and Sarah just dreamed the midnight screaming.

The curtains are drawn on the printing studio, but light shines around the edges, suggesting Antoinette is still in there, hard at work. Sarah wonders what she would see, if she could peek inside. Is the floor covered in snow drifts of creamy paper now, as thick and impenetrable as the ash in the smoking room at the hotel? Is Antoinette's hand cramping as she writes out nonsense with nail and ink and feverishly tosses it away? Has her friend Gertrude Rose even noticed that the calligrapher is hell-bent on what seems to be an unfruitful task?

It's like there's something in the air. Something messing with everyone. A gas leak or a group hallucination. Even Sarah feels it, like she's attuned to a different frequency, hearing voices on the edge of her consciousness, whispers in the pounding of the waterfall. Maybe Bridget put magic mushrooms in their breakfast frittata. It has to be something. Because what's happening here is far from normal.

There were eight artists, and now there are five.

How many more will leave under suspicious, improbable circumstances?

It doesn't matter.

Sarah has nowhere else to go.

No home, no money, no friends, just this place.

She is stuck here, just like Emily Engle. Just like all the women who ended up in the cellar.

She reaches into her pocket and is surprised to find a nail. Holding it up to the light, it has a friendly sort of familiarity to it. She doesn't know where it came from. This is not the nail from her apron, or from Bernie's fist, or from Reid's clay, or from Kim's sunburst of shards. It makes no sense.

But things have to make sense. Life is just a series of events that unfold in a certain order. What's happened here—it can be explained.

Finding the girl in the coffin was just pure dumb luck. This place has been settled for nearly two centuries. There are probably graves everywhere.

Bernie—he was an old, drunk smoker, and he was angry with her and ripe for a widow-maker.

Reid—well, if you accept that Kim has gone crazy, then it's possible she put glass in the clay to keep him away from Sarah. It was her stained glass, after all. And her behavior today proves that she's unstable.

Kim likes attention and can be very dramatic. To wait for witnesses, say something crazy, and then cut herself in the least dangerous way—it's possible. And yet . . . if someone put a pen in Sarah's hand and told her to write the story of Kim self-harming, she couldn't do it. This is a woman who will do anything for her children, who is fighting her ex-husband, against all odds, with every weapon in her arsenal in order to keep her children safe. She would not hurt herself if it would risk her kids. She would not willingly give that bastard any ammunition to use against her.

Yes, Kim has obviously been suffering. Her life has recently fallen apart.

And yet . . . she's a fighter.

Some people live out loud in order to hide the hurt inside, and sometimes those people make a brash decision to end the pain. But Kim?

No. Sarah doesn't see it.

Something else is happening here.

Not that she can explain it. Any of it.

Sarah reaches December House and pauses at the door to the café. Ingrid told her to go around back, to the walk-out basement under the old boardinghouse. The last time she was back there was to borrow a shovel, and she does remember seeing some ancient white machines. Gail isn't the kind of person who wants her guests traipsing in and out of the private parts of her life, so she probably has her own nicer washer and dryer upstairs somewhere.

She walks around back and finds Ingrid waiting for her by the basement door, scrolling through her phone with a frown.

"Did you find a bar?" Sarah says.

Ingrid looks up. "No bars. Photos. I haven't spent as much time editing as I should. I guess I wasn't expecting this place to be so batshit crazy."

Sarah looks down at her bundle of clothes. "Tell me about it."

Ingrid holds open the screen door and shows Sarah the ancient washers. "I don't see any enzymatic cleaner, but you start with cold water and try to rinse all the blood out, then rub with bar soap or peroxide. Then, ideally, you'd pretreat, but something tells me Gail doesn't plan for massive bloodshed." She digs around in a musty cabinet and comes up with a brown bottle of peroxide that's got to be eighty years old. "So have fun."

"You're leaving?"

"You expect me to stand here and watch you scrub your shirt?"

Sarah turns on the faucet and watches pink water run off her hoodie into the stained plastic sink, which is clearly not original to the structure and looks like it was added in the 1980s. "I could just use the company, I guess. Life without internet feels pretty lonely."

Ingrid considers it, lips twitching, then pulls a MacBook Pro out of her bag and sits in a rusty lawn chair. As she futzes with her photos, Sarah scrubs and scrubs and looks around the basement, giving it more attention than she did when fetching the shovel, back before things started to spiral. The walls are stacked stone, similar to the hotel. They've been painted sky blue, which makes it feel a lot less like a dungeon, but it's still got that cold, slightly wet feeling that makes it impossible to forget that they're underground. In addition to the screen door, there are two garage doors and a variety of machinery even more ancient than George. Some of it looks like it might even be original to the property, rusty rakes and shovels and wheelbarrows and a wicked pair of clippers. The only lights are bulbs hanging from their cords. Unpainted wood steps lead upstairs, and Sarah is curious about the parts of December House that are kept private . . . but not enough to go up there.

She'll go into an abandoned asylum, she'll sneak into someone's art studio, she'll reveal an ancient door and creep into the closed-off second floor of her cottage, but there's no way she's invading Gail's privacy. Knowing her luck lately, she'd immediately run into Bridget and have to have a very uncomfortable conversation that would involve getting yelled at. So she just stands here, back aching, and scrubs.

It's hard to tell when all of the blood—or even some of the blood—

is out of a black hoodie, but the water is running clear. Sarah tosses the sodden mass into the sturdy-looking washer and starts in on her white tee.

"Bleach," Ingrid says, not looking up, pointing to an industrial shelf with an aged bleach bottle nestled comfortably between ant killer and borax.

By the time Sarah is done scrubbing, her hands are pruney and raw and she wishes she could just throw all this shit away and buy replacements, but most of her stuff is in a PODS container that she won't see for another month, and money would be an issue even if she could just bop on into a Target and find something that fits. She adds detergent and starts the washer, and Ingrid snaps her laptop shut and stands.

"The dinner bell needs to ring right now," Ingrid says.

And as if it's as scared of her as everyone else, it does indeed ring.

But Sarah sees something beyond Ingrid's long, black skirt and platform boots that catches her eye—something shiny and white, half hidden behind an old box in a cobweb-covered corner. She walks over and picks it up.

It's the missing gravestone plaque from the creepy doll installation.

"Oh, dope!" Ingrid says, snapping a pic with her phone. "Now we've got her name. I'm totally looking this chick up when we get back to civilization. She can vibe."

Sarah takes a pic with her own phone, grateful that finally, her memory is being rewarded. The plaque really did exist. It has weight, it's real. The way things have been going lately, she no longer trusts her own mind, especially out in the woods at night.

She turns the plaque over, hoping for more information, but all she finds is the canvas-imprinted back of the slab, coated in dark, loamy dirt. "Why do you think Gail moved it?"

Ingrid looks up, her eyes clever and burning under their heavy black liner. "Because Gail is hiding something."

"Then why was it out there in the first place?"

Ingrid takes the plaque from her and slides it right back where it was. "Because something changed. Now come on. I'm starving."

They walk around to the front of the building, the first ones in the café door. There's no sign of Gail or Kim, but why would there be? Kim's wounds are not the sort of thing that can be fixed with a *Star Wars* Band-Aid. Something like that should probably go to the emergency room and involve a psychologist, but this is neither Sarah's circus nor her monkeys. When she downloaded the application packet there were lines about insurance and next of kin, so Gail must know how to handle this sort of thing.

Sarah still remembers how she felt, filling out that form, realizing that with Kyle firmly behind her and her mother on her shit list, she didn't know whose name to put as her emergency contact. It was painful, realizing how many friends she'd lost, thanks to Kyle. She didn't even know how to get in touch with most of the people she'd once depended on. Typing her mother's name on that line felt like defeat, but Sarah is young and healthy and not a flailing idiot, and she's a potter, not a chain-saw sculptor, so she didn't anticipate needing any emergency medical care.

So far, the odds of needing those services actually seem pretty high. Uncomfortably, improbably, insanely high.

The food is out on the buffet, although Bridget is nowhere to be seen. They fill their plates, and Sarah is forced to reckon with the fact that she's getting really goddamn sick of salmon patties. Ingrid sits beside her, which feels like a minor win for Sarah, but they both watch the door nervously as they poke at their salads. Sarah is waiting to hear about Kim, even though she knows it's unlikely there will be news tonight. She did the best she could to stop the bleeding, but it's the kind of wound that demands professional attention, and fast.

Sarah realizes with a sudden shock of clarity that there's a definite possibility that Kim could die, especially if it took too long to get real help. Those wounds were deep, and Gail said it was at least half an hour into town. Kim could bleed out, go into shock, have an undiagnosed heart problem. Or maybe she really was ODing on booze and pills, or has some weird kind of brain tumor driving her strange behavior. There are infinite things that could be wrong, infinite ways for the poor woman to suffer. The female body is a carnival fun house that isn't particularly fun.

Until Gail returns, there's no way to know.

Gertrude Rose and Antoinette wander in to dinner together, looking a little lost. They fill their plates and sit at their usual table, but they're oddly silent. Gertrude Rose is generally lecturing about some part of history that offends or annoys her, and Antoinette, when piqued, has harsh words for various calligraphers no one has ever heard of and thoughts on slam poets who think they have talent. And of course whenever there's something to gossip about, their heads bow together over the table like chickens fighting over a corncob. But tonight they don't speak at all, eating methodically, staring off into space.

It . . . kind of reminds Sarah of Kim's blank expression.

And Lucas, when he was in the hotel.

"That's odd, right?" Sarah asks Ingrid, jerking her head toward the other table. "They're quiet."

Ingrid watches as she chews on a cucumber slice. "Very odd." She swallows and clears her throat. "Hey, Gertie! How's the scarf?"

Gertrude Rose's head turns toward them, her stare blank. "Idle hands are the devil's tools," she says, her voice calm in a way that makes Sarah weirdly uncomfortable.

"She sounds like Kim did. Totally stoned."

Sarah looks up at Ingrid, nodding, hating how right she is.

"Antoinette, how's your project going?" Ingrid asks.

Now Antoinette's head swivels toward them, her eyes unblinking behind her huge glasses. Slowly, slowly she smiles, revealing ink-blackened teeth.

For a long moment, Gertrude Rose and Antoinette stare at them, then Antoinette's lips snap closed and their heads swing right back around.

"Are we in the Twilight Zone?" Ingrid whispers. It's meant to sound like a joke, but even Ingrid can't ignore how unhinged everyone is acting. "What's up with her teeth? I know sometimes you have to lick the nib to get the ink flowing, but that's too much black even for me."

Sarah isn't hungry anymore. "Have you seen Lucas today?"

"I heard him playing that weird-ass old-timey song when I walked by."

"He should be here eating. Don't kids his age eat constantly?"

Ingrid chews, looking like an emo Veronica Mars hearing about a hot new case. "Let's go find him."

They dump their trays, and Ingrid picks up an apple and a cookie and stuffs them in her bag. As they leave, Gertrude Rose and Antoinette don't even register their existence. It's like watching two robots pretend to eat. Sarah shakes it off as they head outside.

The music studio is the obvious first stop but it's empty, the door wide open. Then they head for Lucas's cabin, the Hobbit house. The door is closed but the curtains are all open, and he doesn't appear to be inside. They check every window, but all they can see is the expected messy detritus of an unsupervised teen. Normally, this would feel invasive, poking around someone's home, but Sarah feels a mounting sense of worry.

With Reid gone, no one's really keeping track of the boy, and his behavior is erratic and strange. Tranquil Falls is out in the middle of nowhere, with no fences and no boundaries, and Lucas could be anywhere.

They look in every studio, check in all the places someone might conceivably be hanging out. They head back up to December House to see if maybe Gail has returned with news of Kim, but her car is still gone. They go around back, and the basement lights won't turn on, and Ingrid holds her flashlight so Sarah can move her bleach-smelling clothes over to the ancient dryer, which thumps disturbingly like there's a human head rolling around in it. As the sun sets, they have to give up.

Lucas is nowhere to be found.

"I don't want to say it . . ." Sarah begins.

"But you think he's in the hotel again," Ingrid finishes.

Sarah can only nod.

"And let me guess—you're scared to go there at night."

Sarah's cheeks go red with shame, to think that she's too scared to go somewhere when a vulnerable teen boy needs her help. But after what she's seen—*what Emily's seen*—she can't explain that feeling to Ingrid. She can't make her understand what it's like, how the women's screams echoed back and forth down the dark, empty halls like mad coyotes, desperate for any kind of connection.

"No biggie. I'll go. And you can keep an eye out for Gail, stop her if it looks like she or George are headed that way. Deal?"

Sarah shifts back and forth; even in comfortable sneakers, her feet hurt after all this walking. "Aren't you worried? Being in there alone in the dark?"

Ingrid's smile is impish, cocky, proud. "This is what I do. This is my art. This place—I feel like it wants to be seen. It wants to be known." She holds up her camera. "So that's how I show it respect. And Lucas—that kid needs all the help he can get. Don't worry. I won't bite him."

"Are you sure?"

Ingrid turns and walks down the gravel lane. "I do this all the time," she calls over her shoulder. "In far more dangerous places. Go get some sleep." She glances back briefly. "No offense, but you look like shit."

And with that, Ingrid disappears into the night.

37

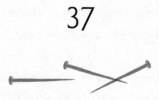

Sitting alone at the firepit, Sarah is both exhausted and anxious. She's had yet another day that somehow feels like an
entire week. When she got here, she found a fire already burning, and she tries to focus on her reading app even though it
feels like a thousand eyes are crawling over her back. She is alert for
headlights or the crunch of tires but Gail's minivan does not return,
nor does Ingrid skip out of the darkness with Lucas in tow. George's
car—an ancient Subaru—is back in the lot, which maybe explains the
fire, but she doesn't see him, and she grabbed her dried laundry hours
ago. She can barely tell the hoodie was recently covered in blood, but
the white tee, now mostly pink, is a lost cause.

She yawns so hard she see stars and checks the time. It's past two.
All the lights are out at December House. It's unlikely Gail and Kim
are coming back tonight, and if she waits any longer for Ingrid and
Lucas, she'll fall asleep right here and probably get eaten by a bear.

That's it. She'll check Ingrid's studio and cabin and then go to her
cottage. Knowing Ingrid, she's probably in the darkroom or some-

thing, obsessed with whatever she found in the basement of the old hotel. She probably sent Lucas on his way and just had to get to work. Or maybe something happened in the hotel—maybe she fell through a hole in the floor or got stuck in a stairwell. Sarah shivers and starts walking. She suddenly realizes that she doesn't remember what she's been doing for the last few hours. Just . . . staring at the fire? Maybe? She feels the echo of a smile on her lips, but it doesn't feel like her smile.

The woods are still and quiet as she hurries along the gravel path. Owls call back and forth and the leaves rustle nervously. She walks faster, then jogs, then runs, shoulders hunched against the clutch of claws that never comes. She knocks on Ingrid's door, but there's no answer. She opens the door to the photography studio, but all the lights are out and the darkroom is empty. Lucas isn't in his studio or cabin. As far as she can tell, she's the only person awake in the entire world.

Except maybe in the hotel, and she's absolutely not going there at night.

Back in her cottage, she paces, her mind catastrophizing a thousand different ways. She just came here to make pots and get away from her ex, goddammit, so why have things gotten so complicated? She has to go trim the chamber pots in the studio tomorrow or it'll be too late. Clay only has a certain window before it's too dry to work with, a lost cause, no longer pliable and open to the muse. She has to concentrate on her art—*the entire reason for coming here*—and not on the bizarre things happening to the other artists. Head down, butt in chair. It's not like anything she can do would make a difference.

Hell, maybe her just staying out of things will help. Everyone who's gotten hurt so far has done so in her orbit.

Tomorrow, Ingrid and Lucas will be back, and Gail will be bossy again, and everything will be one step closer to normal.

It has to be.

She knows Reid and Kim both used sleeping pills while they were here, and she wishes like hell that she had some of her own. She's both wired and tired to the bone. She was so cocky on her way out to these mountains, so certain that she would become one with nature and sleep like a log.

Ha.

She can't even stop her hands from shaking.

Maybe she's been having a panic attack all day. It's hard to tell when it doesn't ever really stop.

She checks the door, checks the replaced but still denuded bookshelf, paces some more. Something is off, and she doesn't know what—something more than a missing teenage musician and a cocky goth photographer and a determined stained-glass artist who inexplicably attempted suicide. She's missing something, and she doesn't know what. If only the constant pounding of the waterfall would stop, maybe things would make sense again.

She crawls into bed, but the air is too still, the fresh sheets too scratchy, the forest sounds too sly. She's straining to hear a boy's bare feet in the leaf litter or size 5 Docs stomping on her porch. Sarah is not a person who takes drugs, but she would take anything now if it would bring on some sort of pleasant oblivion. Her brain and heart are overloaded. No wonder she's not focusing on art. There's been no time to reflect or absorb. It's just been tragedy after tragedy with no rest. Only a couple of days ago, she was flirting with Reid and contemplating a relationship, or at least messing around, and now he's gone, possibly because of her. She hates that it feels like she's lost the thing she looked forward to the most every morning, hates that a man can give her a feeling and then take it away. She just wants to think about art and work on rebuilding herself so that she doesn't need a man to make her feel anything at all.

The silence is unbearably loud, the night untenably dark. The waterfall hisses softly in the background, a constant reminder that the hotel is always watching. She pulls up a book on her phone and starts reading, but the words barely make sense and she remembers nothing and has to reread every paragraph. She has to stay awake, has to wait up for Ingrid and Lucas. They should be back by now. Unless something happened, or Lucas wasn't there, or Ingrid forgot. She can't go to sleep, she has to stay up, she—

Falls asleep.

When she opens her eyes, everything is pitch-black. But it smells all wrong—not like an old cottage, but a mix of cold stone and antiseptic with a hint of mellowed urine. She reaches for the bedside table, but it's not there. There's a creak, and a seam of brightness shines in from beyond. A light turns on overhead, but not the instant glow of modern technology. It's the gradual brightening of gas being turned on, warm and warbling in the darkness.

She's in the cell again.

38

This is a dream.

The door opens all the way, and a female nurse bustles in, plump and motherly, built like a hen in a neat gray dress with a white apron and cap.

"Been a good girl lately," the nurse croons. "Doctor says you might take a turn about the garden with me this evening, if you like. It'll be good for you, to get some air."

"What lovely news," she says, but it's as if she's reciting someone else's lines.

The voice is not her voice, the lips not her lips. She sits up and notes the scratchy white sheet, the woolen blanket. She's in a white chemise. As her eyes focus on smaller, paler hands than hers, she notes the looping curves of letters in the stitching along the hems at her wrists.

Help me.

It hurts oh how it hurts.

She shoves her hands back under the covers, knowing that if anyone might notice this secret rebellion, it would be this particular nurse.
She sees everything.

Or almost everything.

"Get up now, lazybones. It's time for breakfast and your nice medicines."

The nurse stands, hands clasped, smiling, as Sarah—or Emily—or
both—stands and runs her fingers through her tangled blond hair.

"Let's fuss with that later, yes? Proper nutrition is tantamount to
healing, that's what Dr. Calloway always says!"

Emily has to stop herself from sneering when she hears that name.
Dr. Calloway was supposed to help her, but he sent her here instead.
Maybe he doesn't know what happens downstairs, but she has to assume he does. Perhaps he knows and looks the other way. Surely he
knows it is wrong. Emily has talked to the other women here, and although a few of them are very insane, most of them are baffled that
they are being treated as prisoners when they came to the resort as
valued guests.

Dorothea, a posh and haughty thing, was pampered like a prized
mare until her baby was stillborn. When she cried and cried and refused to return to her husband's bed to settle the question of an heir,
he brought her here supposedly to recover in style and comfort. She
tried to slash her wrists with the glass of her own hand mirror, and her
formerly loving husband sent her downstairs and left. There is neither
style nor comfort in her little white cell.

Theresa is such a dreamy young girl, but she fell in love with the
scullery maid instead of the governor's son. When she refused again
and again to marry the lad, her father sent away the maid and brought
Theresa here to learn her manners.

Nicolette was mistress to a wealthy politician but made the mistake of getting pregnant and not getting rid of it. When she demanded the babe's father pay her for upkeep, he agreeably brought
them both here so they could have an intimate family vacation. Instead the babe disappeared, and Nicolette ended up in the basement,

so angry that she spends most of her time screaming in French and tearing things apart.

None of these women are lunatics; they are merely a nuisance to powerful men.

Their wants, desires, needs—their *feelings*—are simply too inconvenient.

And that cannot be borne.

Emily has asked to see her husband, has promised to be meek and sweet and agreeable, but Bertram has made it clear he doesn't wish to see his wife again until she's completely cured of her "hysterics."

Ha. Once she's learned her lesson, more like.

And she has. Oh, she has.

The hose hurts so much. Emily had heard of hydrotherapy, of course. She'd been told it involved lounging in various pleasant pools or being wrapped in cool sheets. But the hose water hits her like a thousand screaming bees, and like the waterfall outside, it just won't stop. The medicines they give her make her dizzy and nauseated, and the food down here isn't half as good as what's served upstairs. The guests get steaks while the lunatics get rubbery stew clearly made from last week's leftovers.

The nurse—Dr. December's widowed cousin, Mrs. Mayhew—takes Emily by the hand and leads her down the long hallway to the cafeteria. She collects her porridge and sighs sadly over how much better it would taste with a little honey. They allow her weak tea, at least, even if there's no sugar. She asked for some, on the first day she behaved well enough to visit the cafeteria, and the cook laughed at her and said, "You won't be spoiled down here, missy! If you want sugar, you'd better learn not to cause the problems that got you sent away."

It was shocking. Raised in a large house in downtown Atlanta, Emily had never been spoken to so disrespectfully by a servant. Her jaw dropped, but she wisely kept silent. Perhaps Bertram will never think so, but she is a clever girl, and she will learn to play by this new set of rules if it will return her to her earlier status and comfort.

"Thank you," she merely said, and it wounded her pride, how the cook puffed up to hear her deference.

For the first couple of days, she hissed and spat and fought like a cat, but it did not go well for her. She swiftly learned that what is expected of her down here is the same, apparently, as upstairs: agreeableness, silence, stillness, and no trouble. She isn't to talk back, to question, to argue, to defend, to try to escape. She must surrender completely. It took her a while to understand it, but once she'd nearly put out that orderly's eye with a nail she found, Dr. December made his expectations clear. Sure, she lost her little scissors and needles, just in case she tried that stunt again with something sharper . . . but she'd already hidden a few needles, just in case. Since that night, the orderlies have not attempted to touch her in that private way, and therefore she is glad for her newfound ferocity, even if she must take pains to cover it up, smother it with the sugar sweetness they desire.

If they want meek and biddable, she will be meek and biddable. And patient.

The dream, in the way of dreams, flashes forward. Gone is the porridge, the dimly lit room full of listless women in stained gowns at long tables nibbling food most of them wouldn't foist on their least favorite scullery maid. Now Emily stands in her room—her cell—brushing her hair with something that looks like it has recently been used on a horse. She has no pins, no hat, no ribbons. All she can do is braid her hair and tie the end with a bit of thread bitten off with her sharp little teeth. She has no mirror, because mirrors are glass, and desperate women given access to sharp bits of glass often do desperate things—Dorothea taught her that. She started with a mirror but finally succeeded with the lenses of her spectacles, calmly stating that she would rather die than give birth to another dead child.

Now that she has learned to hate him, Emily is glad that her husband wasn't able to . . . well, put her in that position, for all that he tried. As long as she's been in the cellar, she's done her best to look unattractive to avoid all such male attention, but now she must rekindle her former beauty with what few supplies she's been given.

Someone has brought down her simplest overdress, and it hangs on her frame like a faded flag. She's lost a bit of weight in her days here—perhaps it's been already a week? Maybe two? Or is it six? Dr. December's medicines make everything so strange, and there are no clocks, no sunshine, no moon. The food is wretched, and she spends most of her time pacing just to have something to do.

The door opens, and there the nurse stands in her gray dress and white apron and smart white cap. "Oh, we can do better than that," she croons. She bustles over—because she always bustles—and moves about Emily's body, trying to adjust her dress and failing, because all of Emily's clothes are custom-tailored and don't account for what a few weeks of crying and near starvation have done to her.

Her greatest hope is that Bertram might see her and remember his own declarations of love and realize his mistake and immediately have her brought back upstairs. Her next greatest hope is that she might not be seen by anyone she knows, because her looks are not currently up to her own standards, and she doesn't know how to answer any questions she might be asked. She is fairly certain the garden is a bit separate, thanks to artfully grown hedges, so she might not encounter anyone at all.

The nurse takes her hand again and leads her out into the hall. "Now, listen up, love, because here's the rules, and if you break one, you won't be out again for quite some time. Understand?"

"Yes, miss," Emily murmurs.

"You stay with me, holding my hand. You be calm and polite. You go where I says to go. You don't make a peep. Got it?"

"Yes, miss."

The nurse pulls Emily's hand into the crook of her elbow like she's a gentleman escorting a lady to a ball. Emily allows it, as this looks a bit more believable than them holding hands like happy children. As the nurse walks her down the hall, Emily hears crying, shouting, a soft banging that can only be someone's skull hitting the door over and over again. They take the stairs up, and Emily is struck with the sad memory of her last moments surrounded by plush carpets and chandeliers, what it felt like, being drugged in the lobby and waking up in a hell she hadn't even known existed.

She'd heard people raving about Tranquil Falls back home, about the glorious views, the fresh mountain air, the bright mist of the waterfall; now that she thinks about it, it was always the men who sang its praises at her father's parties and dinner table. When her fiancé told her they would honeymoon here, she felt so mature and sophisticated.

"It'll set an excellent precedent," her father had said approvingly.

She still remembers walking to the hotel restaurant that first glorious day, passing a woman in a nurse's apron scurrying through the door to the stairs. When she expressed surprise that there was another floor below the lobby, Bertram patted her hand and told her every great hotel had a basement for storage.

She didn't realize, then, that it stored wayward wives.

How much has changed since that faraway day.

The bright hallway upstairs is a revelation now. Emily feels like some small creature that lives at the bottom of a well and is only just now realizing that there's a whole other world filled with sunshine. The scent of baking floats on the air, warring with the perfume of lilies. The windows are open to let in soft breezes purring up from the valley. Outside, she sees a fine carriage rolling up the drive and wishes she could tell the girl sitting beside her man that she'd best hold her tongue and make herself pliable if she wants to stay in a room with a window and flowers. She feels her shoulders release, her spine relaxing, her teeth unclenching. She has been a tight little knot, and now she loosens, just the tiniest bit.

They pass much nicer doors than the ones downstairs, and Emily hears the self-important rumble of men's voices. She'd like to peek in, but she dare not. The nurse doesn't give her a chance, ferrying her forward as steadily as a horse pulling a cart. At the end of the hall, they step outside into the kitchen gardens. Two other nurses are here with their charges, arms firmly entwined. No one speaks as they walk slowly among the herbs and flowers and trees. After a week—a month? Or more?—of darkness and stench, Emily takes big breaths all the way down to her belly, which no longer presses against her stays. It is good, to be outside.

The only bad part is that she knows she'll be sent back downstairs by dusk.

If only she might find Bertram and explain to him how good she is, what a fine wife she'll be.

She won't ever tell him how his touch makes her skin crawl, how she hates the stench of his heavy, bovine body, the curl of his mustache with its rancid wax. She will lie there and take it, as her mother commanded her to, and she will smile as she bleeds and thank him and bear his children, anything to never be in the cellar again, to never feel the touch of cold water spraying her body like a million hateful needles.

She will despise every moment with him, but then again, he'll be gone most of the day with work and the club, and once she's swollen with child he'll likely leave her alone—that's what Dr. Calloway's wife, Elizabeth, told her, when Bertram struck her. She hasn't seen that kind woman again, for all that she's looked. Perhaps she has a sweet little babe in arms and is being doted on, somewhere in the airy rooms upstairs. Surely a doctor's wife receives only the best treatment.

They walk behind the resort among the carefully trimmed bushes and beds of ferns. The waterfall is louder here, and if she cocks her head just right, it's almost as if she can hear words in it, harsh whispers, warnings just on the edge of understanding. They promenade by tall windows open wide, their curtains billowing in the breeze, and that's when it happens.

Between two hedges she sees him—Bertram, her Bertram, sitting on a rich leather chair and talking to—

Dr. December and Dr. Calloway.

She slows to listen, but the nurse tugs her away, intent on continuing their healthful perambulation. It takes everything Emily has not to plant her feet and stubbornly refuse to budge, but she knows that her every movement now is watched and noted and reported to the doctor. Any misstep could end up with Bertram gone back home alone, leaving her here forever.

If she could only get into that room and plead her case, surely she could make Bertram understand.

A shriek breaks the silence, and Emily looks up to see that one of the other patients, an older woman named Lucy, is screaming and swatting at her head. Everyone stops to stare as her nurse urges her to calm down while she is clearly being attacked by bees, although whether they're imaginary or real is anyone's guess.

Emily's nurse drags her to a bench and sits her down. "You stay right here, missy, and I'll make sure you get honey in your porridge."

The moment her nurse steps away, Emily knows what she has to do. Hitching up her skirts, she scurries through the break in the hedges and toward the open windows and climbs into the room. All five of the men within look up in surprise. The air is full of their pipe smoke mixed with the roaring fire in the chimney, the room warm for the season but cozy in that way men like things, stuffy and smelling of leather and port.

"Emily?" Bertram stands, gazing at her in shock. "What is the meaning of this?"

"I was out for a walk and I simply had to speak to you," she says, feeling bold but feigning shyness. "I'm doing ever so well in treatment, and I have made a full recovery and am ready to resume my wifely duties."

The two young men playing billiards snicker, and Emily wonders if she's said something wrong.

"My dear, we cannot allow patients to make their own reports," Dr. December says sadly, rising to grasp her arm more firmly than she'd like. "These things take time. I was going to recommend you return home, but now that you have interrupted us here, no doubt abandoning your nurse, it's clear that you need to stay with us a little while longer, so that your treatments might take full effect. I do believe it's for the best."

Emily lets out a little gasp, almost a sob. "Please, no." She turns to

Bertram, looks into his eyes, tries to put all her pain and fear into her gaze, hoping he might understand her as he once claimed to understand her on their Sunday carriage rides in the park. "It hurts, my husband. What they do—"

"Emily, you're embarrassing me," Bertram says, turning away stiffly and shaking his head. "The doctor will know best. It's just another symptom of your illness, behaving this way."

"Dr. Calloway . . ." Emily reaches for the kind doctor's hand and looks into his soft brown eyes. He seems sick, maybe a bit sad, but he was kind to her, when she was still upstairs. "Sir, surely you can see that these cures have done me good. Why, I'm as sane as I ever was. I would so enjoy taking the waters again, enjoying your Change of Air. And your wife was so kind—"

Dr. Calloway releases her hand forcefully and looks down, his eyes red. "Do not speak of such things, madam."

"You see, child, you are not fit for society now," Dr. December chides her. "Your husband is correct. This is an illness, and like any illness, it needs time and care. A few more months, perhaps?" He looks to Bertram.

"I can be good!" she says, voice strangled. "I can be anything you want! Just please don't—"

Dr. December, now holding her hand firmly in both of his, turns to the open windows. "Now, where is your nurse, my dear? Because I know I told her to take special care of you . . ."

Emily wrenches her hand out of his, runs to the window, and throws it shut, locking it firmly.

"What in the hell?" Bertram roars.

"I'll show you hell," she answers.

39

Sarah wakes up and lunges to sitting, drenched in sweat. The dream wasn't finished, and she feels as if someone has stopped a movie in the middle of the climax, as if she's going to miss the best part of the story.

But what woke her?

She doesn't hear anything, doesn't sense anything amiss—other than the usual utter disquiet that's dogged her almost every moment since she arrived. She gets up and turns on all the lights, checking under the bed and in the closets and looking for feet under the curtains like she did in middle school after watching too many horror movies while staying home alone.

There is nothing there that shouldn't be there, but it still feels like something is wrong.

She checks the time on her phone and realizes it's nearly dawn. Since she knows she won't be able to get back to sleep, she takes a quick bath and puts on her freshly laundered black hoodie that now smells like lavender instead of blood. Backpack over her shoulder and protein bar in hand, she walks toward Lucas's cabin.

She doesn't think he's there, but she needs to make sure before she does something she's going to regret.

Lucas's Hobbit hole is exactly as it was last night, the curtains open and the lights on and no boy visible within. His studio is empty, the lights out and no sign that he ever returned to it. Ingrid doesn't answer when Sarah knocks on all her doors and windows, and the photography studio has been likewise abandoned. While she's nearby and the world is washed indigo and not yet bright and busy, Sarah checks Kim's cabin, too, but there's no way to tell if Kim came back. The fairytale castle has no lights on, no sign that Kim ever existed. There's always a possibility that Gail had to take her to the real hospital for more than what a rural urgent care center could provide, and it's also possible they kept her for a psych eval.

Keeping to the trees, Sarah heads for the old hotel. The pine straw is soft under her boots, her path a straight line. The sky is the color of blueberry guts, almost a greenish gray, heavy with clouds. It's funny, how much her perception of this place has changed since she first drove around the moldering fountain out front and imagined she felt some kinship with the happy, smiling women painted on the plywood covering the windows. The hopeful blond girl—maybe that was Emily. The thoughtful old woman could've been her nurse. The dark-haired lady with the baby might've been Mrs. Calloway in a better world.

Maybe some of the women who came here were happy, but most of them did not end up that way. At least one of them ended up dead.

There's caution tape around the tree that fell over the fence, but caution tape never stopped anyone. Sarah scales the trunk, lands in the garden, and heads for the storage door Ingrid showed her. It opens without a fuss, and she sighs in relief to realize that she doesn't have to crawl over glass anymore.

The moment the door is open, she hears the sound she both dreaded and hoped for:

Lucas is here, and he is again playing that godforsaken baby grand piano.

She swings her flashlight back and forth, hurrying down the hallway, through the lobby, and toward the restaurant. The music gets louder as she approaches but it sounds even worse than it did last time. Nearly every note now is flat or just a thump, and the overall effect makes her think of a broken robot sadly short-circuiting. The intensity and speed never falter, and the moment the song is over, there's room for one big breath before the keys crash down again.

"Lucas?" Sarah calls from the open doorway.

She finds him with the beam of her flashlight, and the boy . . . looks like a ghost.

His T-shirt is soaked with sweat and clinging to his shoulders, his hair is madly gleaming, his eyebrows are drawn fiercely down. His face is aimed right at the keys and filled with an otherworldly passion, almost a rage. She walks to him, and he doesn't react, doesn't even look up.

As she gets closer, she sees that he's likely been playing this way in a pitch-dark room all night. When she shines her flashlight on the piano's keys, they're smeared with blood.

His fingertips are raw and bleeding.

"Lucas!" she barks, louder now, but the boy doesn't react.

She grabs his arm to pull him away, but it's like trying to bend a steel girder. The tension in his body is worrisome, unnerving—even worse than before. She pulls harder, and he yanks his arm back, not missing a note. Ah, but this time Sarah came prepared. Bernie left behind his old, rusted toolbox in the pottery studio, which held a rugged pair of tin snips. She's brought them along in case this happened— dreading that this had happened.

She sets the bag down, exchanges the huge flashlight for her phone's flashlight, and pulls out the heavy tool that—*ha ha*—once belonged to a tool. Up on tiptoes, phone in her mouth, she leans over the propped-open piano cover and snips a wad of strings right in the middle where he's concentrating his playing. The metal strings snap, a sharp and surprising noise that makes her flinch and cover her eyes. Lucas doesn't stop playing, but the keys she cut don't play anymore— there's just a soft thunk from bloodied fingertips on old ivory. Again and again she reaches in to snip the strings, holding her face away so she can't get cut by the violently snapping steel. Her fingers ache, her knuckles are bruised, but she keeps on until not a single string is left, until the piano can only make muffled thumps.

For a moment, Lucas plays harder, his face a mask of anger and confusion. Then his fingers slow on the keys until he stops and shakes his head.

"Sarah?"

He's looking up at her like that same lost little boy.

"Hey, Lucas," she says softly, once the phone is out of her mouth.

"What's happening? Why do my— Oh, shit! My fingers!" He holds up his hands in the light of her flashlight and winces. "What the fuck?"

"Sleepwalking, I guess," she says. "Want to go back to your cabin? It's almost time for breakfast. I think you missed dinner."

He stands, unsteady on bare feet. "Yeah, I— Ow. I dunno what happened. I'm starving. Everything hurts. Where are we?"

She leads him out of the room, keeping close in case he should stumble. With all the stray nails, splinters, and bits of broken glass here, she worries for his feet. She turns on her big flashlight, too, shining it at the ground at their feet while shining her phone flashlight down the hall.

"This is the old hotel," she tells him. "Second time you've sleep-walked here. I guess you just really like that piano, huh?"

He's inspecting his hands, making and releasing fists. Sarah can't imagine how much it must hurt, to play the piano for twelve hours straight.

"I guess," is all he says, but not like he actually believes it.

"Have you seen Ingrid?" she asks him.

"Why would Ingrid be here?"

Inside, she's screaming, but outwardly, she just says, "Don't worry about it. Let's get you back to your cabin."

They pass by the lobby and Sarah opens the door to the storage room, and—

There's someone standing there.

It's Gail, holding her own flashlight, looking both pissed and smug.

"Well, what have we here?" she says.

"I was looking for Lucas and heard him playing the piano," Sarah says. "I think he's been sleepwalking."

"I think so, too." Gail steps up, putting an arm around Lucas's shoulders and herding him out the door. "George!" she calls from just outside. "Come take this boy up to the house for breakfast. Let him use the phone to call his mom to come get him."

"What? No!" Lucas says, wrenching himself away from Gail.

She grabs his arm firmly. "The only rule here is that you don't trespass in the old hotel, and that's exactly what you're doing. Which means you're out. I guess you can just pack up your car if you don't want to see your mom, but I want you out today, understand?"

Lucas is in crisis, panicking, muttering, "But I—but—I didn't mean—I was asleep!"

"Trespassing is trespassing, honey," Gail says sadly. "It's not safe in here. So go on. I'm sure you'll find something else to do with yourself. And George'll help you with your hands. Looks like you got hurt, whatever you were doing."

Lucas looks to Sarah, desperate. "I didn't mean to!" is all he can say.

"Gail, come on," Sarah says, feeling more like an adult than she ever has before as she tries to protect this poor, confused kid. "It's not his fault if he's sleepwalking. If you're that serious about keeping people out, maybe get the fence fixed or put up cameras or just make sure all the doors stay shut. You can't blame a kid for what he does when he's asleep."

The weak light filtering in through the open door does not do Gail any favors; she looks stern and sleepless in her fuchsia sweater and glass bead necklaces, her left eye twitching. "I most certainly can blame him for something I caught him doing. You all signed the same form. If you didn't read it, or if you chose not to abide by it, the consequence is still the same."

"Come on, kid," George says, crooking a finger at Lucas like Santa trying to get a crying kid in his lap. "Let's go get you some breakfast. Biscuits and gravy this morning."

Lucas's eyes plead with Sarah, as if she has any power at all, and she nods and takes a step toward the door, knowing Gail will yell at her whenever she wants to, anyway. "Yeah, okay, let's all just go. We'll figure something out."

Gail steps in front of her, blocking her path. "Not you. We need to talk."

"But—" Lucas starts, looking like his last friend is abandoning him.

Sarah gives him a pitying look and shakes her head. "It's okay. Go on. I'll be there soon. Save me a biscuit."

Lucas lets George tow him away, stepping gingerly out into the morning on bleeding feet. The door shuts, and it's just Sarah and Gail in the narrow storage room, ghoulishly lit by their flashlights.

"Sarah, why are you at the center of every problem I've had this season?" Gail asks.

Sarah huffs a sad chuckle. "I wish I knew. I came here to forget my old life and start over, and everything just went to shit. Can we talk outside, maybe? This place gives me the creeps."

"Then why the hell do you keep coming here?"

Sarah's breath catches, and she's certain she looks guilty. "I don't know what you mean."

Because there are no cameras, right?

Gail walks past her and opens the door to the hallway. She stands there, waiting. Sarah doesn't move.

"What are you doing?" Sarah asks her.

"I'm waiting for you to show me what it is about this place that's got you so riled up. You think I haven't been in here a thousand times? I grew up on this land. I played hide-and-seek in here with my cousins. So please, show me what it is that's so interesting that you're willing to break my trust and the legal agreement you signed and get yourself kicked out of here when I know damn well you have nowhere else to go."

Sarah takes a deep breath, almost glad she got caught. Maybe Ingrid wanted to wait until the final exhibition to reveal what she learned at Tranquil Falls, but Ingrid isn't having increasingly disturbing dreams about one of the patients who died here—well, okay, it sounds like she had one dream about Elizabeth Calloway. Still, Sarah feels like she's the one with the connection to Emily Engle, the only one who can speak for the dead. Maybe saying it out loud, telling Gail what she knows, will help her make sense of everything, put all the puzzle pieces together.

"Well, first—is Kim okay?" she asks.

"They had to transfer her to a bigger hospital. I stayed with her all night to make sure she was settled in. I didn't leave until her sister arrived. They think she's going to be okay, but she's going to need a lot of counseling."

That's one relief, at least. "Thank goodness. Have you seen Ingrid?" Sarah asks next.

Gail rubs a hand over her face. "God almighty, is she trespassing, too? I swear, we've been running retreats here for fifty years and we've never had this many assholes."

"She's not an asshole," Sarah says, jaw grinding. "She just cares about the truth."

"And here I thought she just cared about photography. Her car's gone, so I guess she got what she needed. Now, again, tell me why you keep coming in here."

Sarah takes a deep breath, glad Ingrid is somewhere safe but annoyed that she left without saying anything. Maybe she went to find some internet, or maybe she just got the hell out because things got too weird. It doesn't matter. Sarah has nothing to lose and is ready to lay it all on the line. "The girl in the coffin was a guest here," she says carefully. "And then she was a patient."

Gail is silent, digesting this. Sarah goes on.

"There were messages sewn into her dress, 'help me,' 'it hurts,' 'he lied,' that sort of thing. Her husband tried to rape her, and she hit him with their chamber pot and cut up his head. And he had her sent downstairs. But it wasn't a spa, it was an asylum. They used the hose on her, drugged her, restrained her. Horrible things. I know the upstairs was a resort, but the cellar . . ." She takes a deep breath. "It was a place where rich men sent their women who wouldn't behave, to get rid of them. To let doctors experiment on them."

She waits for Gail to protest, to cuss at her, to send her home.

But Gail just says, "Show me whatever it is you found that makes you think that. I need to know."

Sarah nods and heads for the stairwell. Gail follows, their two flashlights making the shadows bounce and merge. Together in the stairwell, Sarah is overcome with Gail's perfume, that same stuffy lavender, a little too much. They step into the white-tiled hallway, and Sarah leads Gail to Dr. December's office. The door, oddly, is open. Sarah is certain she closed it, the last time she was here. Maybe Ingrid came back to take more photos.

The ledger is still on the desk, closed—also not as she left it. Sarah opens it up and flicks to the last entries.

"See? Emily Engle. She was the girl in the coffin. And these other women—she knew them. None of them were insane. These are bullshit diagnoses. Hysteria, mania, rebellion, whatever the hell 'moral insanity' and 'fever of the spirits' are. Just excuses to keep them down here. The doctor hurt them. He wanted to make them more . . . more pliant. More biddable. It's what their husbands and fathers wanted, too."

Gail runs a finger down the ledger, huffs a sigh.

"Anything else?"

So Sarah shows her the hydrotherapy room, and Gail shines her flashlight around and grimly takes it in. "We know the resort did hydrotherapy." Gail doesn't believe her, or maybe she's in denial, and it's maddening. "It was a cutting-edge program. People loved it."

"That's a fucking hose, Gail. Rich women don't get pelted with icy water from fire hoses for fun."

"They do if the girl next door did it and bragged about it."

"Okay, fine. I can show you the operating theater. Or Emily's cell."

At that, Gail suddenly seems interested. "Cell? Do you mean room?"

"Yeah, it's not a room. Rooms have windows and curtains and dressers. Believe me—it's a cell."

She leads Gail to Emily's cell and digs around in her backpack for the key. It turns in the lock and the door swings open on the sad little bed, the plain white chamber pot.

"See? A cell."

As she's turning to see if this, finally, has Gail's attention, Gail shoves her into the cell and slams the door.

40

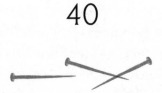

Sarah throws herself at the door, yanking at the knob, realizing she's an absolute idiot. She left the key in the lock.

The lock, which is outside the door, because this is a cell.

Not that the key works on this side, anyway.

"Gail, what the hell? Let me out!"

"No."

Sarah slams her fist against the door, but it hurts. The wood is real, and it's thick, and it's made to keep whoever's inside, inside. "Why are you doing this?" she shouts.

"Because this is my land, and I'm not about to lose my family's legacy just because you got nosy. I know what happened here. I've known since I was a kid. Dr. December was my great-great-grandfather. When he died, his family took control because Dr. Calloway didn't have any heirs after the fire. And we've held on to it ever since."

Sarah puts her forehead against the cold wood, feeling the chill of the place seep into her bones. It's very different, being in this room when the door is shut. It's too small, the walls closing in, the black

mold spots giving everything a feeling of sinking, of seeping, of struggling down into the earth.

"I don't care, Gail. I won't tell anyone. Ever. I'll sign whatever you
want. Just let me out. I've learned my lesson, okay?"

Gail barks a laugh. "Ha! So you're telling me you're good at keeping
agreements? That your signature means a goddamn thing? Then why
are you in here? It was the only rule!"

"So you're just going to leave me in here to die?" Sarah shouts.

There's a beat of silence, and she wonders if Gail is gone.

"As far as I'm concerned, you did this to yourself," Gail finally says.
"There are 'No Trespassing' signs, caution tape. But you came here
anyway. Old doors can't be trusted. You got yourself locked in."

"Someone will come looking for me."

Another beat, then a chuckle. "Oh, really? Who? Because I read
your sob story. You don't have anyone. You have an abusive ex you're
hiding from and a mom with dementia and nobody and nothing else.
Nowhere else to go to. Maybe when you don't show up to your new
apartment in a few weeks, they'll come looking for you, but by then
your car will be in a ravine off the side of the mountain and I'll tell
them you left early and didn't tell me why or where you were going."

Sarah's breath is coming in pants now, her voice husky as she says,
"You're insane."

Gail's voice is farther away as she abandons Sarah to her fate.

"Yeah, well, I guess I'm in the right place."

41

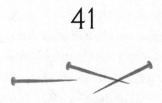

Sarah does all the things that she would consider stupid if she saw someone doing them in a movie. She pounds on the door with her fists, kicks the door until her toes are numb, screams at the door, and dissolves into ugly, racking sobs while sliding down with her back against the door. The flashlight is on the ground, pointed up, and she realizes that she has to ration light. She didn't bring extra batteries, and there's no way to charge her phone. The only light is the light that she brought with her, and it can't last forever.

She paces until she knows every square inch of the cell. She does a few push-ups and sit-ups but not enough to feel sore, because she might need her muscles for—something. Maybe there's some way to break down the door. Or pick the lock.

Wait.

In her dream, Emily admitted that she'd hidden some of her needles in this room. If the dreams are really real, then maybe they're still here. If nothing else, it's something to do. She puts her phone in power-saving mode and adjusts the flashlight until there's just enough light. Creeping around the room, she hunts for some secret place where a girl might've hidden her embroidery needles, the only remaining vestige of herself, her only outlet for artistic expression, 150 years ago.

After nearly two hours of searching, she finds three rusted needles squirreled away in a small chink in the stone wall under the bed. She pokes two of the needles into the lock, holding the flashlight in her mouth, but has no idea what she's doing. This is what it looks like on TV when people pick locks, but she knows absolutely nothing about locks, not today's locks and not the locks of the 1800s. Whatever she's doing, it's not working. She can't feel what's going on inside the mechanism, and no matter how she angles her flashlight, it doesn't help. There is no satisfying click. There is only desperate, sweaty squabbling around without purchase or meaning.

"Fuck!" she screams, barely stopping herself from throwing the needles across the room and probably losing them forever even though . . . well, it looks like forever is going to be a very short time, unless Gail has a change of heart. And it's not like she has anything else to do but look for tiny needles in a tiny cell in a huge hotel in the middle of the mountains.

She begins to understand that even the sanest person cannot hold on to their sanity for very long in a cell.

"Hello?" someone shouts from far away.

This time she almost drops the needles, but she clutches them at the last minute, pricking her finger. She'll have to update her tetanus shot, if she gets out in time. If she doesn't get out, it's comforting to know that she'll die of dehydration long before the lockjaw can set in.

"Hello?" she calls back.

"Oh, fuck. Sarah?"

"Yes! Ingrid?"

"Obviously. Let me out of here!"

Sarah's heart sinks right through the ground and into the granite of the mountain.

"You're in a cell, too?"

"Oh, shit. Shit. Yes. Yes. We're both in cells. Because of course we are. How'd Gail get you?"

They're both shouting at the top of their lungs. Ingrid sounds like she's farther down the hallway.

"I was showing her evidence," Sarah starts.

"Yeah, me, too. She wanted me to prove that the keys worked. Great villain reveal, right?"

"If you have a sick and twisted perspective, sure."

"I thought she was just an old stick-in-the-mud boomer biddy with nothing better to do than skulk around and shout at people, but really she's the great-great-granddaughter of a sociopath who retained a lot of her ancestor's worst qualities." Ingrid's voice is getting scratchy. She probably went through a screaming phase when she realized she was trapped here, too.

Just a few minutes ago, Sarah would've given anything to know that she wasn't alone, but apparently being on the pitch-dark path to a long, slow death makes Ingrid annoyingly talky, and it's exhausting because it takes so much energy to shout through the door. Her throat already hurts—and there's no hope of more water.

"True" is all she can say.

A moment passes in the utter silence that can only be achieved underground in a forgotten place with thick walls.

"So what do you have with you? Let's MacGyver this shit."

Sarah takes a deep breath and digs through her bag. "Two protein bars, half a bottle of water, the key to room 312 upstairs, a pen, a notebook, my phone, a charger, a hairbrush, pepper spray, lip balm, hand cream, three needles, and an old nail. Nothing that's gonna get us out. What about you?"

"Three granola bars, an apple, a bag of Sour Patch Kids, no water because I didn't expect to be trapped, a laptop that gets no signal, a phone that gets no signal, a camera, three rolls of film, and all the same girly shit you have that cannot be turned into a coconut bomb." A thump suggests she's thrown her bag against the door in resignation. "We're fucked."

They lapse into an uncomfortable silence because there is no way to be comfortable when you've been left in an abandoned asylum to die. If not for her phone's clock, Sarah would have no idea what time it is, what day it is. The minutes tick by with agonizing slowness. The darkness is impenetrable, and her head gets swimmy. She lies down on the cot, but it's somehow even less comfortable than it would've been when Emily lay here. It's crunchy and damp and smells of mildew, and when she feels the wetness soaking into her jeans, she stands up and lies on the ground instead.

No air moves. There are no sounds. She can't tell the difference between her eyes open and closed. Things begin to go funny.

She must go to sleep because she is suddenly very, very awake.

And she isn't Sarah anymore.

She's Emily again.

She's back in the smoking room, right where her last dream left off. She's just locked the window behind her, and the nurse is banging on the wood frame with her meaty fist, shouting threats.

Threats don't matter anymore. They can't take away her honey or her pillow or promise ten more minutes with the hose just to get her to pretend to behave.

She is past hope.

She only wants revenge now.

Shrugging out of her overdress, Emily takes great joy in hearing the men gasp at her white chemise. She thrusts her dress into the fire, and it instantly writhes with flames.

Bertram stands and says, "Emily, you stop that right now!"

Like she's a naughty dog or a spooked horse.

Like she's a child.

But Emily does not stop. Ignoring the burning pain threatening her hands, she darts to the curtains and whacks them with her dress, setting them afire. The dress—and she hated it, it was an odd olive color that didn't quite suit her—is a torch now, and everything it touches answers with leaping orange flame that's been waiting forever to bloom. The rugs, the horsehair couch cushions, the flocked wallpaper, the gold-stamped books, the felt of the billiard table. No one can get close to her as she swings her flaming dress. The younger men try to beat out the various fires with their coats, and Dr. December faces off with her as Dr. Calloway frantically tugs on a bell cord that must ring an alarm somewhere in the cellar.

"You're a very sick girl," Dr. December begins soothingly, adjusting his pince-nez, and Emily snatches up the glass decanter of brandy with her other hand and slams it into his face. It bursts, drenching him with brown liquid. While he's sputtering and wiping the brandy and blood from his eyes, she touches the burning dress to his face like a painter adding dabs of gold with a favorite brush, and he catches fire as easily as a match.

It's a beautiful sight, and while she's slightly mesmerized by watching her torturer run around screaming, Bertram grabs her from behind, arms clasped around her shoulders, shouting, "That's quite enough, you deranged lunatic!"

In response, Emily flicks the dress over her shoulder and onto his head and back and laughs as he sputters and beats at his hair. It must be all the wax he uses that makes it burn so hard and fast. Her dress has found his breeches, and now he's on fire at both ends. He looks like a daffodil made of flame, more handsome than she's ever seen him as he burns, and she runs for the doors in her chemise, no longer caring about all the rules that once gave her life order.

She stops for a heartbeat of a moment and looks back. The boys are trying to save the billiard table, Bertram is beating at his mustache while his lower half crackles merrily, and Dr. December is on the ground, fully engulfed in flames as Dr. Calloway tries to smother him with a jacket. She tosses the burning overdress onto the fancy Persian rug and slips out the double doors, closing them behind her, pleased to note that every wall within is on fire, the flames already blackening the ceiling. Grabbing a tieback from the hallway curtains, she wraps it again and again around the door handles and tightly ties them shut with several knots. Her hands are red and charred, but she doesn't care, doesn't even feel it. A fist beats on the other side of the door, but there's a baby grand piano playing loudly somewhere down the hall, the Infernal Galop jauntily covering the sounds of a dying man help-lessly hitting a door.

Clad only in her chemise, which is miraculously untouched by the flames, Emily swans down the hallway as if she were still a celebrated upstairs guest, chin high and steps lively, the daughter and wife of important men. She follows the music to the restaurant and enters, just one in a madding crowd. It's some sort of party, and she heads straight for the buffet table filled with all the delights she's recently been denied. She stuffs herself with cakes and little sandwiches, swigs punch and lets the sweet liquid run down her chin. The cool cup soothes her burned palms. With such a press of bodies, no one seems to notice her . . . until they do.

"You there," an old woman in expensively beribboned bombazine says, tapping a silver-tipped cane at her slippered feet. "Who are you?"

Emily curtsies as her governess taught her. "Mrs. Emily Vandiver Engle, ma'am."

"Where is your dress? Young women these days. You can't just run around like that. It is scandalous."

Emily feels her grin tugging too wide, revealing too many teeth. "Oh, I've done far more scandalous things."

Dropping another curtsy, she turns on her heel and disappears into the crowd. Perhaps she should feel shame, to be exposed out in the open and called out by the sort of wealthy widow her parents would likely expect her to impress, or at least respect. She winds her way toward the dance floor, ducks under a man's upheld arm, and joins the country dance. She knows the complicated steps to this one, of course; she knows them all. So what if no one's invited her? She's already mar-ried, and what a terrible choice that was. If a girl wants to dance alone, maybe she should just dance alone instead of waiting to be asked by some horrid disappointment of a man.

Even if her steps are correct and graceful, she makes one too many for the count, and it throws off the other dancers. They finally notice her, staring at her as if she's a dog walking on its hind legs. Her smile is a terrifying thing now, she knows, broad as a tiger's grin, full of just as many teeth. Women gasp and men take a step back. It's a delicious feeling, this power, and when a matron surges forward, frowning, Emily growls at her like the mad beast they believe her to be.

"Who is this person?" the woman bugles in stentorian tones. "Someone call the hotel security. This is an outrage."

"Don't shout too loud or they'll send you downstairs, too," Emily tells her. "I was once as fine as you, and look where it got me."

"Well, I never!" the woman all but shouts, and a cadaverously thin man steps up to Emily and firmly takes hold of her elbow.

"Hmm, let's escort you out, my dear, and, hmm, hope you'll find your way back where you belong," he mutters, propelling her through the crowd.

But again, Emily has had enough. She wrenches her arm out of his grasp.

"I belong here!" she cries, spit flinging against the old man's face. "I'm one of you!"

His jaw drops, revealing teeth the color of molasses. "My goodness! You brazen little harpy!"

When he tries to grab her again, she ducks into the crowd and heads toward the door. Perhaps she isn't fit for current society at the moment, but if she can just get up to her room and access her wardrobe and coiffure, no one will be able to see that she is secretly . . .

No, not insane.

She is *not* insane.

She is *sane,* and they are trying to make her into a lunatic.

She is secretly something else entirely, something without a name.

But she can pass among them, a wolf in sheep's clothing, if it will keep her upstairs, where things hurt less.

She is nearly to the restaurant door, and most people are ignoring the old man's cries, choosing instead to drink and shout and dance, the piano's pounding gallop providing the cover she needs to slip out without being noticed. She's almost there—

"Fire!" a porter shouts. "Fire! Get out! Get out while you still can!"

The crowd becomes a stampede, but no one knows which way to go. Tiny Emily is tossed about like a ship on an angry sea. She's closest to the door that leads to the hallway, but she's the only one in this room who knows that the hallway is where the fire will be, if it's managed to escape the smoking room—*ha ha! It really is smoking!*—and spread. She can smell it now, the acrid black clouds drifting in, rolling along the ceiling like fog on a winter morning.

She spins and aims for the French doors that lead to the back patio and gardens. Perhaps the nurse is out there looking for her still, but she'll keep her head down in the crush of escapees and find a way to avoid her pursuer. Now that she wants something, she's quite certain nothing can stop her.

No one notices her state of undress in their blind desire to get outside. Hands push against her back, shoulders bump into hers, formal shoes tread upon her slippers, but none of it hurts as much as the hose. None of it hurts as much as what Bertram did to her on their first nights here. She'll take the impersonal thumps and bumps of a thousand terrified partygoers before she'll willingly submit to the tortures she discovered upstairs in the guest room or downstairs in the cellar.

She pops out the French doors, and the crowd is a party again. Thinking themselves safe, people spread out in the garden, follow the path toward the waterfall, sit on the stone walls and artistically placed boulders and iron benches, anything to get away from the perceived danger within. On the other side of the building, smoke pours out of a shattered window, and it fills Emily with an animal joy to know that the barbecued pork she smells isn't really pork.

Furtively glancing around, she realizes that she's again invisible. It's dark now, dusk falling to night, and there are no lights. She turns and walks toward the forest.

"You! Stop right there!"

She glances back and sees two orderlies headed toward her. The one not holding the noose is the one who attacked her in the cellar, the one whose eye she very nearly poked out with a nail, and he's grinning. An animal again, she runs, but not fast enough. It's like a dream, where she's caught in syrup, too slow, too maddeningly slow, and she hears his footsteps, his heavy breathing, feels the air change as he leaps to tackle her. The impact hits her hard, throwing her forward.

It is dark.

She doesn't see the boulder.

She doesn't see anything anymore.

42

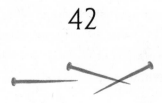

Sarah rises from darkness to darkness, asleep to awake, then to now. She felt Emily's head strike the stone, the weight on her small body as a man twice her size drove her into the boulder. At the end of the dream, she rose up again, as she did in the hotel room that horrible night, to look down on the body of Emily Engle as if floating overhead. This time, the body didn't move. Its chest barely rose and fell with each breath. The orderly dusted himself off and picked her up, carrying her like a bag of oats over his shoulder and down into the cellar, back to her small white cell. Back to room 115.

The fire was contained by then, but it had done its work.

The next morning, as the upstairs guests left hurriedly in their carriages, the widowed Mrs. Emily Engle was placed in a rough pine box.

She wasn't bathed and beautified and put in her nicest dress like a lady. She wasn't mourned. Her husband was dead and gone, her parents far away. The orderlies didn't know what else to do with her. Their founding doctors were dead, after all. Mrs. Mayhew said the girl would never wake up, that they might as well put her in the ground where she belonged before her family came around asking questions.

The comptroller ran off with the remaining cash. When there was no one there to pay their wages on payday and no guests left to serve, all the hotel workers decided to leave. Not only was there no pay, but it wouldn't do their reputations any good, should the truth get out about the basement. They took anything of value, including the parrots. The hotel became a ghost town.

Except for the women in their cells in the basement.

No one came for them.

Behind their locked doors, in the darkness, forgotten, they screamed and howled and beat their fists against the stone until one by one they went silent. Until they became the ghosts.

But Dr. December's family still lived in the big house—his wife and six children and his cousin, Mrs. Mayhew. Since Dr. Calloway left no heirs, his wife, Elizabeth, having died in childbirth a few weeks previously, the December widow settled into the property like a hermit crab choosing its shell to raise her children and protect what she could of her land and her husband's legacy.

Reporters came, but there was no story. Everyone listed as missing was said to have died in the fire. No one knew how it had started, and Mrs. Mayhew said not a word about what she'd seen. An accident, a tragedy, a sad end to a great experiment. Investors tried to buy the hotel off Mrs. December, but she refused. There was no way to hide what had happened in the cellar, and she wouldn't let her husband's Grand Works be discredited. Amazingly, a man who could do such horrific, painful, cruel things to the women in his care had been kind and loving and loyal to his wife. Funny, how some people can compartmentalize their monstrous behavior—or perhaps they are simply capable of fooling the people they profess to love.

In the dream, where she seems to just know these things like the omniscient narrator in a book, Sarah watches as the dirt is shoveled over the coffin she uncovered just last week. She sees the orderlies walk away like they haven't a care in the world, dusting their hands off as if they've done excellent work.

That's where the dream ends.

And she is grateful, because in these dreams, she's lived Emily Engle's life, felt her fear and pain, experienced her trauma and worn her skin and looked out through her eyes. Sarah does not want to feel what it's like to wake up in a coffin with a headache, hungry and alone and confused, and feel that wood against her burned palms and torn fingernails. It is almost a relief, waking up in her own life.

Until she remembers that she's in her own coffin, of a sort.

"Ingrid?" she calls out.

"What?"

"Just making sure you're still there."

A pause. "You screamed in your sleep."

"Yeah, well . . . it was a pretty shitty dream. Any progress on getting out?"

She hears Ingrid kick the door. "No. If I had a spoon, I'd start tunneling, but there's just . . . nothing. They put the hinges on the outside, you know? And I don't know anything about locks. And the door's sturdy as fuck. This is . . . kind of the perfect prison."

Sarah sighs, her neck aching and her shoulder numb from sleeping on it. "It was built that way on purpose. I know why the hotel closed, by the way."

"Oh?"

"One of the patients started that fire in the smoking room. On purpose. It killed both of the doctors who ran the place."

"How'd you figure that out?"

Sarah puts her head in her hands. Even after everything that's happened, she's not ready to say it out loud because . . .

It'll make her sound insane.

"Long story" is all she says.

"I mean, I think we've got time . . ."

Sarah stands and paces.

She'll tell this story, then, even if it destroys her throat, because someone else needs to know.

The story deserves to be heard.

"So you remember when I, uh, found the coffin?"

"Pretty hard to forget that," Ingrid admits.

"Well, that night, I started to dream about the girl who died. As if I *was* her. Emily. It's as if I . . ." She's never had to say it out loud before. "Like I woke up her ghost."

The laughter that follows this statement makes Sarah's mouth go watery, makes her heart bang like a shoe in a clothes dryer, makes ice trickle down her spine.

Because she knows that laugh, and it isn't Ingrid.

43

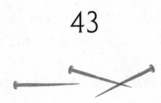

Sarah would know that mocking chuckle anywhere. She drove all the way across the country to escape it.

Kyle.

"How'd you find me?" she asks, voice low and deadly.

"I put a tracker on your car when you started acting distant," Kyle says matter-of-factly, near enough to the door that Sarah takes a step back. "Took me a while to figure out where you were, once I lost the signal. No bars out here, but I guess you know that. Probably did that on purpose, huh? But I'm smarter than you. I found you. I had to figure out if there was someone else, or if you were getting crazy ideas."

"I was realizing that you're abusive, and that I needed to leave."

"Like I said, crazy ideas. Did you really think you could break up with me and just run away? That I wouldn't find you? A relationship is two people. One person doesn't get to make a decision like that without input from their partner." The key turns in the lock, and Sarah lunges for her backpack and paws through it on her knees, trying to find the pepper spray. Of all the terrible things she imagined in this cell, being attacked in the present day wasn't one of them, and she is not prepared.

"Sarah?" Ingrid calls. "Sarah, who is that? What's going on?"

Sarah's hand closes around the spray, and—

No. It's the sunblock stick. Fuck.

The door is open, and Sarah can feel the difference in the air, the relief of open space and the cloying possibility of escape. She turns, her body crawling like an animal for the hallway, but Kyle is blocking her path. He shines a flashlight down on her, blinding her, and she shoves past his legs, almost to the door. There's something there, holding it open, so close—

He barks a laugh, grabs her by the hair, and throws her back into the cell, where she skids across the floor. Her scalp burns, but she doesn't have time to worry about lost hair, because Kyle is coming after her, his flashlight the only thing visible. There is no escape, and yet she rolls away, backing herself under the cot like a child hiding from a monster, the ancient chamber pot pressing painfully into her back.

"Come on, sweetheart. Do you really think that's going to work? We're all alone here. Don't be ridiculous."

He bends over and shines the flashlight directly into her eyes, making her flinch away with pain. His fingers close around her wrist, and he yanks her out from under the narrow cot with strength she didn't know he had.

"Get on the bed," he says with a chilling sort of calm.

Sarah is well aware that her body has frozen up. She can't fight, she can't flee, she can only obey. She doesn't know why she's so terrified of this man she once thought she loved, why her body is betraying her, holding her still, certain that he's going to do something horrible to her, but she climbs up on the bed and sits, shoulders hunched, knees pinned together tightly, making herself as small as possible.

"What do you want?" she asks.

Ignoring the question, he leaves her there and goes back to the door. He checks that the door is firmly held open, then brings in a bag and sets it down. Sarah can't see what's holding the door open, thanks to the darkness, but she has faith that Kyle is careful and that it's sturdy, and that this cell is no longer a death sentence. She'll leave with him, if he'll take her. She'll leave here and find some other way to escape him for good, once she's gotten Ingrid out and they've exposed this rotting hellhole for what it is.

She can be patient.

She can be good.

"What I want is for my girlfriend to behave," Kyle says. "Running away from your problems is childish. Let's talk it out. Why'd you leave, Sarah?"

He shines the light in her eyes, and when she holds up a hand to block it, he snatches her hand and cuffs her to the bed, so quick that she realizes he must've practiced this move. She gasps and yanks at the metal, but it only clanks and makes the bed jostle. When she tries to stand, he shoves her back down with a hand against her chest.

She's never been touched like that, and yet there's something so familiar about it that she racks her brain for a memory that will make sense of it.

Before now, Kyle was never rough with her, never physical. Cruel, yes, but polite and infinitely patient. A gentleman.

Wasn't he?

"Why are you doing this?" she asks, a variation on a theme he won't answer.

He reaches into his bag, pulls out a bottle of water, and opens it. "Your voice is raspy," he says. "This place is probably riddled with black mold." He swings the flashlight around at the black-stippled walls.

Sarah takes the bottle and drinks hungrily. He's right; she's been trying to ignore her thirst, but her mouth was dry, her throat sore, her body crying out for moisture.

"Slow down there." He takes the bottle from her easily, since she only has one mobile hand. "You'll make yourself sick. You've been down here for over twenty-four hours."

That's startling information, and Sarah reaches for her phone before realizing she has no idea where it is. It was on the bed while she was asleep, but who knows where it is now?

"Sarah?" Ingrid calls again. "Who is that?"

"I'm her boyfriend," Kyle shouts back. "Now shut up."

"Her shitty ex, you mean?" Ingrid yells, angry. "The one she came here to escape?"

"Ingrid, don't," Sarah warns. *Don't make him mad,* she means. "It's okay."

And it will be, because it has to be, because whatever Kyle is doing, whatever made him throw her and push her, he's still going to let her out of the cell, and that's all that matters, that's as far as she can plan.

Like Emily, she can behave. She can pretend. She can be good.

But . . . what's he doing now?

Just watching her.

Like he's waiting for something.

"What?" she says, blinking furiously. The room is going swimmy. It feels like she did two shots of tequila in a row, but the water tasted normal—maybe slightly salty, now that she licks her lips. "Did . . . what did you put in the water?"

He caresses her face, and God help her, she leans into his cupped palm. It feels so good to be touched.

"Does it matter?"

He leans in to kiss her, and she opens her mouth gladly, eagerly. When she tries to raise her hand to touch him, she can't, and she tugs on it but gives it little thought. He helps her to lie back on her bed, and she settles in, luxuriating in the feeling of softness, enjoying the way his hands run up and down her body, awakening every nerve. He removes her boots and socks and massages her feet deliciously, and someone is shouting her name, but it doesn't really matter.

"He's hurting you," a voice says, and something about it is shocking, because she didn't say it, and Kyle didn't say it, and Ingrid didn't say it.

Sarah's eyes open, and there's a light in front of the door.

Not a flashlight or a phone light.

It's a cool bluish white, misty and shimmering.

It almost resembles a girl.

A glowing girl with long blond hair in a white chemise.

Sarah blinks as she stares at the form. Kyle is unzipping her pants now, a light clipped to the bed and shining down, almost like an operating table, and something about this scenario briefly bothers Sarah, although to be honest, nothing really bothers her now, not the crackling mattress under her bare bottom as Kyle begins to pull off her jeans and not the hazy, transparent girl in the doorway walking toward her without a sound.

"He's hurting you, isn't he?" the girl repeats in a voice Sarah has only heard in her dreams.

"Emily?" she says wonderingly.

"Shh," Kyle says, standing before her. "I know a good way to keep you quiet."

Something in Sarah's heart curls up and dies at those words, at the sound of a zipper, and she's felt this before but isn't sure why, and as she looks past Kyle she sees the ghostly girl pick something up and hold it overhead.

She's seen this, too.

A white chamber pot, far less ornate than the one upstairs.

The girl swings it, hard, and it slams into Kyle's head and makes the most glorious noise in the world. But this chamber pot is not ceramic; it doesn't shatter. It's metal, because who could trust a lunatic with something that might become sharp shards?

Sarah laughs, because this is oddly funny, watching Kyle stumble and fall forward with his jeans gathered around his ankles and her own old urine soaking into his hair. He's kneeling before the bed, and she turns to him and laughs, and Ingrid shouts something that's all blurry, because everything is blurry.

"Sarah—" Kyle mumbles, and then she looks down and sees that the chamber pot is in her own hand, and as Kyle reaches for her, his face screwed up with confusion and rage, she gleefully slams the chamber pot directly into his face with every ounce of strength she has, right in his lying mouth.

"It will only hurt for a moment," she tells him.

The hit reverberates up her arm in the most delicious way, not like hitting the sweet spot of a bat, all bouncy and full of potential, but the hard, compact smack of an effective bunt. There's a pleasing crunch, and he grimble-gromble-grumbles with his mouth until teeth fall out like pennies from a slot machine. Blood drips down, and still he reaches for her, and this time she aims for his forehead, right where he keeps all his stupid, supposedly superior doctor brains.

Another satisfying thunk.

"Thunk," Sarah says. "Thunk, thunk, thunk."

"Sarah?" someone calls.

"Shh, I'm thunking," she says, giggling. "Right, Emily?"

When she looks up, the ghost girl is gone. There is no misty shape, no ectoplasm, no bright orbs, no neon-yellow glow-in-the-dark footprints like she remembers from *Scooby-Doo* ghosts. Only a light clipped to an old bed, and a man lying very still on the floor in a pool of blood and piss.

"Sarah, are you hurt?" the voice calls again. She knows that voice. "Did he hit you?"

"Ingles! Igor! Anchor!" she shouts back. She's getting so sleepy. "You're not very nice, you know," she says, then yawns at how exhausting all this yelling is.

"That's what keeps me alive," Ingrid calls back. "Did you kill that guy?"

Sarah burps and snuggles back onto the bed. "Emily did."

And then she's asleep.

44

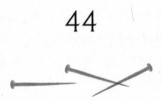

When Sarah opens her eyes, she's on the floor of a hotel room shower, naked and soaked, beside a rancid pile of puke. The lights are on, which would seem like the simplest thing in the world, except now it's a revelation, a veritable miracle. She never wants to be in a pitch-black room again.

"You puking?"

The door opens, and there's Ingrid in a black tank top and Venom pajama pants, her face noticeably different without the black circles drawn around her eyes. She's not looking directly at Sarah—because Sarah is naked. She pulls down a towel and huddles under it.

"I puked," Sarah croaks. "Where are we?"

Ingrid fills one of the water glasses at the sink, and Sarah vaguely remembers reading a story in a magazine a long time ago about how you're not supposed to drink out of hotel glasses because they're wiped down with toilet cleaner, but she's so thirsty that she doesn't care. She gulps the water, and a memory briefly surfaces of someone telling her not to drink too fast, but Ingrid doesn't say anything, so she drains the glass and hands it back to Ingrid, who refills it without being a bitch.

"We're in a hotel off the interstate. What do you remember?"

Sarah thinks hard, but it's like fishing in an empty pond, dipping a net in only for water to run out the holes. "Nothing. Gail locked me in the cell, and then . . ."

She's missing time. It's happened before. Kyle always said she couldn't handle her drink. But there's no way she was drinking in a cell in an abandoned asylum.

"A bright light. A thunk. The forest? A fence. It's . . ." She shakes her head as if trying to dislodge her thoughts. "Nothing. I don't even remember throwing up."

Ingrid hands her the glass of water and a hand towel before sinking to sit on the floor just outside the shower. "Your ex showed up. He let himself into your cell, handcuffed you to the bed, and tried to rape you. And then you beat him to death with a metal chamber pot full of your own piss. You were laughing the whole time. It was . . ."

"Insane?"

"Very metal. That fucker deserved it."

Sarah doesn't remember any of this, and yet somehow it doesn't surprise her at all.

"And then what?"

Ingrid leans back, her head thunking against the doorjamb in an uncomfortably familiar way. "Then things got quiet, like you were asleep. I started shouting at you, because I didn't know who'd killed who, you know? And then I heard my door unlock. It swung open, and I hurried outside, and . . ." She pauses and takes a shuddering breath.

"And?" Sarah prompts.

"I saw a ghost."

Like many of tonight's revelations, this is oddly not surprising.

"It was the girl from the coffin, I think. Same long blond hair, same white dress. She walked down the hallway and disappeared up the stairs, and then she was gone."

Tears spring to Sarah's eyes. "She just wanted to go back upstairs, where she belonged," she says softly.

"You saw her, too?"

Sarah racks her brain, but she can't come up with any images. "I think so, but . . . it's like I lost a bunch of time."

Ingrid points at the puke. "Pretty sure he roofied you. When I left my cell and went into yours, you were handcuffed to the bed, and there was a half-drunk bottle of water sitting there. Went through his bag and found some extremely sick shit, including pills. It's all in the other room. Blacking out and losing time are the major symptoms. And then throwing up, a headache, being achy. Has he ever done that before?"

The world shifts, and something clicks in Sarah's head, like when a Magic Eye poster finally reveals its image. All those times Kyle told her she'd drunk too much and blacked out, even though she'd only had two or three drinks. All those times she had stomach problems that no doctor could explain. The headaches the next day, the burst blood vessels around her eyes from throwing up, the aches deep in her bones.

They ran those tests at his hospital. *He* ran those tests.

They never found anything.

They weren't looking for drugs.

He made sure of that.

Kyle is—was—an anesthesiologist. He knew more about drugging people than anyone.

Jesus, what else did he do to her?

Her body shivers as if just now recognizing it has been violated.

He almost violated her again last night.

Or—

"Did he—was I—" she asks, looking down.

"It sounded like he was going to rape you, and your pants were mostly off, but then you killed him."

The memory slithers up, the chamber pot rising in the hands of a ghost . . .

"I think Emily did most of the work," Sarah says softly. "I can't explain it, but I think it was her. I was in her dreams. Maybe she was in mine, too."

Ingrid rubs her eyes like this is too fucked up, even for her. "Well, I'm glad you and your ghost buddy killed that asshole."

Sarah realizes she hasn't seen the rest of the hotel room, doesn't know what else has been happening. "Where is he?"

A grim grin. "I just closed the cell and left him there. Kinda wish I could see Gail's face when she opens the door in two weeks expecting to find your corpse. I took his bag and all your shit and got you uncuffed, and you were stupid and silly and acting real drunk, but you could walk. You were chattering the whole time, talking my ear off. You told me the whole Emily story. Her husband deserved what he got, too. I realized we couldn't go back to our cabins, so I used dipshit's iPhone to find his MacBook, which was in his car, hidden on some dirt road a mile away. You and me spent like an hour walking through the woods, and I kept having to tell you to stop shouting about ghosts and trying to like, hold my elbow like I was Dapper Dan. His keys were in his bag, so we just drove right on off. He even had some kind of superpowered GPS. We stopped at a Walmart for pajamas and undies and toothbrushes, and I found the nearest hotel and checked us in. You said you needed a shower, and here you are."

Sarah nods, impressed, then immediately lurches toward the drain and throws up again. When she's done, she rearranges her towel and says, "And we stopped for fast food, apparently."

Ingrid finally chuckles. "Yeah, on your insistence. You wanted a milkshake and fries, and now you're being punished for your gluttony."

After wiping her mouth with the hand towel, Sarah sips the water. "No. Punishment would imply I did something to deserve getting roofied, and I absolutely did not deserve that. I guess he's been doing that to me all along, then saying I was sick or I drank too much. What is it with shitty men and gaslighting?" She clears her aching throat. "Poor Emily."

"Well, look at it this way. She got revenge for both of you. That's pretty badass."

"Speaking of ass . . ."

"You probably want to get decent. And waffle stomp the rest of your dinner down that drain, because it fucking reeks."

Sarah gives Ingrid the finger guns, and Ingrid leaves, and it's funny, how Sarah used to think Ingrid was mean and prickly but now it's like they finally speak the same language.

Once she's followed Ingrid's suggestion, Sarah finishes her shower and puts on her new Hanes undies and Halloween pajamas and settles into the queen bed farthest from the hotel room door. She doesn't like doors just now, and she really doesn't like total darkness. Ingrid must feel the same, as she puts the TV on a cartoon channel and leaves it on all night, filling the room with light and color and sound, the opposite of what they experienced in those awful hours in the asylum. Sarah sleeps hard, thankfully without dreams, and when she wakes up, the sun is shining through the not-fully-closed curtains. When she goes to look out, she sees beautiful green mountains rising against the duck-egg sky, and she doesn't know where she is, but she's glad to be here.

Sarah has nowhere to go for a few weeks yet, and Tranquil Falls is out of the question. Her pots will never get fired, her belongings have likely been tossed in a bonfire, Gail and George have probably already destroyed her car, and there's no way to find out how Lucas, Antoinette, and Gertrude Rose are faring. She hopes that Emily's ghost can finally go to rest, and that the other artists are free of their . . .

Hauntings?

It doesn't seem like a possession, but something strange infected them in those last days, drawing them tangentially into a madness that wasn't their own. She feels bad for them, but she feels worse for herself. She barely escaped alive. They, hopefully, are back to working on their art, eating Bridget's food, and remaining blissfully unaware that they're living on the grounds of a place soaked in tragedy.

Sarah also thinks she knows now why Bridget is so angry. If she grew up on that land, then maybe she knows what happened there. And maybe, like Sarah and Ingrid, it's not something she thinks she can live with. But Gail hasn't given her a choice, and so she's stuck there, forced to live side by side with a legacy of pain, making cinnamon rolls to feed artists innocently pursuing their dreams a few steps away from a mass grave.

Ingrid has a place in Asheville, so they're going to drive toward North Carolina and plot their next move while listening to true-crime podcasts. Since Ingrid doesn't trust anyone, it turns out she has all of her photos backed up to the cloud, and she already scanned and uploaded everything from her Leica. Every photo of Emily's corpse and her embroidered dress, every photo of the damning entries in Dr. December's ledger, every photo of the hotel's rooms both upstairs and downstairs is securely stored in a place where Gail can never access it.

As it turns out, she never told Sarah, but Ingrid was having periods when she lost time and woke up with her camera in her hands and a full roll of film that turned out to be different shots of the same boulder. When Sarah tells her why that boulder was important, Ingrid just nods like this makes sense.

"I kept imagining a blood spot on it," she says softly. "But I couldn't find it."

When she was in December House, she also took a picture of Gail's roster, which means she has everyone's full name and contact information, but of course there's no signal in the valley to make them reachable.

"Should we call Lucas's mom?" Sarah asks. "Tell her he might be ... hurt?"

A snort. "No way. We're not gonna narc on that kid, even if he's dead."

"We've got to do something. We can't just leave him there. What if he's locked in a cell?"

Ingrid rolls her eyes but picks up Kyle's phone. Using a fake accent, she calls Gail's landline and asks to speak to Lucas. When he answers five minutes later, his voice trembles.

"Mom?"

"No. Not Mom. A friend who had to leave abruptly. Don't say my name. Cough once if you know who I am."

After a moment, he gives a raspy cough.

"Good. Are you okay?"

He pauses, clears his throat. "Yeah, I'm fine. Just working on a new song."

"It's not that whack-ass carousel song, is it?"

"I mean, I don't know what song you're talking about, but no. A classical piece on violin inspired by, uh, some really interesting photos someone showed me recently."

"Good. Stay the hell away from the piano. Wait. Didn't Gail kick you out?"

Another pause. "I guess she changed her mind. I, uh . . ."

"Cried a lot?"

"Yeah."

"Look. She might seem nice, but don't trust Gail, okay? Don't go to the old hotel. In fact, if you can, you should probably just leave. It's not safe."

An exhale of frustration. "No, I'm doing good. Don't worry."

"All good here," Gail says nearby, loudly and sweetly, as if trying to calm a worried mother. "He's doing great!"

"Seriously, don't trust her," Ingrid says. "Bye."

She hangs up, and Sarah is so relieved she could cry, if she had any tears left.

"Do you really think he'll be okay?" she asks.

"Why not? If Emily got her revenge, maybe she's done making everyone crazy."

And Sarah hates feeling like he's unsafe, but isn't that the whole point? Just because she sees Lucas as younger and more vulnerable doesn't mean she can decide to take away his freedom.

When she calls Reid and Kim, on the other hand, both of their phones go straight to voicemail.

"Do you think they're in the cellar?" she asks.

Ingrid's lips, for once not painted black, are a flat line. "Maybe. Or maybe she sent their cars careening off the mountain. Or maybe Kim really is in the hospital. Or maybe Reid can't answer the phone because his hands are too sore. You know things are messed up if there's a fifty-fifty chance they're rotting in an underground asylum cell or have too many boo-boos to pick up the phone."

"Then we have to get the police out there, fast."

Ingrid gives her a doubtful stare.

"Right," Sarah says, frowning. "The local police are idiots. Then we have to write the story ourselves, and we have to do it now. Today."

"I've got the pictures ready, and you have all the pieces of the puzzle . . ."

"Then I guess I write, you drive."

Maybe pottery was supposed to be Sarah's art, but she can say what she needs to say in words, too. Ingrid thinks they can get the story in a local paper, maybe even eventually get a book deal out of it. It's up to Sarah to tell the tale with proper drama while also doing justice to the women who suffered. Once they've put together their masterpiece, there'll be nothing Gail can do to stop the world from learning the truth about Tranquil Falls.

They stop at another Walmart somewhere in North Carolina, and Sarah uses Kyle's cash to buy a journal and a set of pens. This story feels too personal to type away on Ingrid's laptop, even if Sarah's pen shakes while they speed up and down the mountains. Her handwriting isn't as nice as the script stitched into Emily's hems, but her words are just as damning.

"There was once a woman named Emily Engle," she writes. "And she was very, very sane."

AUTHOR'S NOTE

In August 2019, I had one of the worst nights of my life ... even though I don't remember it.

My husband and I went to dinner at one of our favorite fine dining restaurants in Tampa Bay, Florida. I ordered a lemon drop and the scallops. We lingered at the table, enjoying the ocean view. When I ordered a second drink, a blueberry smash, the bartender, a woman in her twenties, came to the table to explain that she didn't have the right ingredients but would be happy to make a drink just for me. I told her I liked herbal, floral, fruity, tart, sweet drinks, and the drink that was delivered was delicious and included macerated strawberries and gin. After that, things got weird.

I don't remember ordering a third drink, because I never order a third drink. But I did, apparently—a chocolate martini. I don't remember stopping at the restroom on the way out and nearly forgetting my purse. I don't remember chatting energetically with my husband on the way home and commandeering his phone so I could introduce him to a new band. I don't remember thanking my mom for watching the kids or tiptoeing upstairs to kiss their sleeping faces or kissing my husband. I apparently did all these things and seemed like I was in the best mood ever. I wasn't slurring or stumbling. I was happy, funny, laughing.

And then I woke up at four A.M. and threw up in the bathroom sink. I don't remember that, either. And considering it was strawberries and scallops, that should've been pretty memorable.

I don't actually have any memories between the custom strawberry drink and waking up on the shower floor at nine in the morning, huddled under a towel, surrounded by puke. I'd vomited so hard and so many times that I'd burst all the blood vessels in and around my eyes.

I thought it was food poisoning.

I called the restaurant and asked them to check the dates on their scallops. The man I spoke to was brisk and rude, utterly lacking any compassion, and informed me that there was no chance I had gotten sick at their establishment.

Let me say, on behalf of past me: Fuck that guy.

I felt hollowed out, empty, in shock. My stomach was a wreck. My head was cloudy. I couldn't stop shaking. I couldn't stop crying. But it wasn't a hangover—I felt traumatized.

So I went to the doctor, and she told me that my symptoms suggested I'd been roofied, probably with GHB.

Even worse, she said that this sort of thing happens all the time— and that it can kill you. When I asked her why someone would drug a person like me—a woman in her forties, a wife clearly out with her husband at an expensive restaurant—she shrugged and said, "Sociopaths."

I was horrified, of course. The only way someone could've drugged me was by slipping something in my drink before it arrived at the table. Was it the bartender? Was my drink meant for someone else? Had I inadvertently used some nomenclature that meant I wanted to party, like that time in college I advertised my room for rent to a "laidback" person, not knowing it was code for "stoner"?

The scariest thing about this experience is that no one recognized that I had been drugged. That whole time that I was acting pleasantly tipsy and warmly effusive . . . is a black hole for me. It terrifies me to think what might've happened if I hadn't been with my trusted partner of seventeen years, if I'd been walking home from dinner at a ComiCon or otherwise out in the world with low inhibitions, acting unusually happy and friendly, with loving feelings toward everyone.

That experience heavily contributed to Sarah's journey in this story.

As I worked through what had happened to me, I was disgusted at how one tainted drink turned me into an object, into someone who had very little control over their own freedom. Under the influence of whatever was in my system that night, I was abnormally pliable, outgoing, affectionate, and passive. I would've been the perfect victim for all sorts of violence, which I would've then forgotten.

The thing about those lost memories is that they never come back. For many people who are roofied under the worst of circumstances, the only witness is the perpetrator of violence. But in this story, Sarah and Emily become each other's witnesses, and in a way, they help each other restore their stolen freedoms.

I still feel shame around this incident even though I did nothing wrong. I am a survivor of rape and childhood domestic abuse, and I thought I was so smart and so tough that this sort of thing could never happen to me.

I was wrong.

I hope this never happens to you, but if it does, please know that you are not alone. Please go to the hospital the moment you realize that something is not right. I was in real danger, and I had no idea. By the time I realized what was wrong, the drug was out of my system, and there was no evidence to prove it had happened. Whoever did this to me got away scot-free, and the manager at that restaurant *aggressively* did not care. Needless to say, we never went back.

I'm lucky that it wasn't worse. I'm lucky that I was in a safe place. I hate to think of the people who were not so lucky. This is a weird club to be in—a club that we rarely discuss in public because it feels like we did something wrong. But I'm here, and I didn't deserve it, and if it happened to you, you didn't deserve it, either. Like Sarah discovers, we are part of a sorority of survivors, and there is strength in our combined howls of indignation.

I am here, we must continue to remind each other.

I am here, and they didn't kill me.

I am still here.

ABOUT THE AUTHOR

DELILAH S. DAWSON is the author of the *New York Times* bestseller *Star Wars: Phasma*, as well as *Bloom, Guillotine, The Violence, Star Wars Inquisitor: Rise of the Red Blade, Star Wars Galaxy's Edge: Black Spire, Mine, Camp Scare*, the Hit series, the Blud series, the creator-owned comics *Ladycastle, Sparrowhawk*, and *Star Pig*, and the Shadow series (written as Lila Bowen). With Kevin Hearne, she co-writes the Tales of Pell series. She lives in Georgia with her family.

whimsydark.com
Bluesky: @delilahsdawson.bsky.social
Threads: @delilahsdawson
Instagram: @delilahsdawson

ABOUT THE TYPE

This book was set in Caslon, a typeface first designed in 1722 by William Caslon (1692–1766). Its widespread use by most English printers in the early eighteenth century soon supplanted the Dutch typefaces that had formerly prevailed. The roman is considered a "workhorse" typeface due to its pleasant, open appearance, while the italic is exceedingly decorative.